The Battles of
Jericho

The Battles of
Jericho

by Hugh Pentecost

Introduction by S.T. Karnick

Crippen & Landru Publishers
Norfolk, Virginia
2008

Cover illustration by Gail Cross

Lost Classics design by Deborah Miller

Crippen & Landru logo by Eric D. Greene

Lost Classics logo by Eric D. Greene
adapted from a drawing by Ike Morgan, 1895

ISBN (clothbound edition: 978-1-932009-74-3
ISBN (trade softcover edition): 978-1-932009-75-0

FIRST EDITION

Printed in the United States of America on acid-free paper

Crippen & Landru Publishers
P.O. Box 9315
Norfolk, VA 23505
USA

Contents

Hugh Pentecost and the
John Jericho Stories

by S. T. Karnick

If asked to characterize the classic, the archetypal, mystery writer, one would do very well to point to the late American author Hugh Pentecost. Ellery Queen aptly described Pentecost as "one of our most professional 'pros'—a wily tactician and technician who unfailingly excels in playing 'the grandest game in the world'."

Pentecost, whose real name was Judson Pentecost Philips, was born in Northfield, Massachusetts, in 1903. He wrote more than a hundred mystery or suspense novels and story collections under his own name and his main pseudonym (the name of a great-uncle who had practiced law in New York City during the early years of the last century) and as Philip Owen. He was a founder of the Mystery Writers of America and was awarded the organization's Grand Master honor in 1973.

Pentecost served a valuable apprenticeship in the pulps in the 1930s. Strong story lines, colorful characters, lots of action, the ability to create suspense, and an essentially wholesome worldview were necessities for success in the pulps, and Pentecost assimilated those lessons well. In addition, writing for the pulps at the low per-word rate they paid meant a writer had to produce prodigious amounts of readable product in order to survive. The prolific and highly professional approach to writing Pentecost developed as a pulp writer is reminiscent of fellow pulp graduate Erle Stanley Gardner, author of the Perry Mason, Cool and Lam, and Doug Selby novels. Both writers were skilled at describing action and writing dialogue, and they were exceedingly brilliant at inventing series characters.

As with Gardner, Pentecost was intensely interested in the social implications of his stories, and was even more explicit about it. But where Gardner's greatest strength was in his brilliantly inventive plotting, Pentecost's was in his characterizations and settings. Pentecost's qualities as a writer are exemplified by the almost thirty short novels he wrote for *The American Magazine* during the 1940s and '50s, and many more for other such "slicks." In these tales, he would take an unusual location or occupation, stir in a mystifying murder and an interesting detective, and examine the suspects' lives for clues to who dun it. This allowed Pentecost to explore individual motives and social conditions while providing the reader with a compelling and meaningful story populated by interesting and unusual characters.

Among the settings for Pentecost's *American Magazine* novellas are a Madison Square Garden horse show (originally published in *Argosy*), a Navy ship in the Pacific, an airplane factory, a carnival, a quarry in rural Pennsylvania, a military school, a television studio in the earliest days of the medium, a cattle auction, a coal mine, and the stock car racing circuit. Pentecost's books and stories present a panoramic view of American life in the second half of the last century. At their best, they examine the way we lived then and draw real moral lessons from the events they depict.

After graduating from the pulps, Pentecost created several successful series detectives, including the sophisticated hotel manager Pierre Chambrun; quiet, unobtrusive psychiatrist-detective Dr. John Smith; New York police detective Lt. Pascal; elderly small-town lawyer Uncle George Crowder; suave, handsome public relations expert Julian Quist; *Newsday* columnist and investigative reporter Peter Styles; divorced private investigators Carole Trevor and Max Blythe; New York City homicide cop Inspector Luke Bradley; gambler Danny Coyle; and artist John Jericho.

Jericho was the protagonist of more than two dozen stories and six novels published between 1964 and 1987. Frederic Dannay, editor of *Ellery Queen's Mystery Magazine* and half of the Ellery Queen writing partnership, was a great admirer of the Jericho series, and after sales of the novels cooled and Pentecost stopped writing them after 1970, Dannay kept the series alive by publishing Jericho stories regularly in the magazine. One can easily see why Dannay liked them so much: their combination of interesting settings, skillful puzzles, social concerns, and earnest melodrama matched Dannay's own approach to his Ellery Queen narratives co-written (mostly) with Manfred Lee.

The last five Jericho novels are narrated by the artist's sidekick, novelist Arthur "Hally" Hallam, whom he met during the Korean War, but the short stories are told in the third person from Jericho's point of view. John Jericho actually first appeared during the 1930s in a series of pulp adventures about the Park Avenue Hunt Club, in *Detective Fiction Weekly* (recently collected in two folio volumes by Battered Silicon Dispatch Box Press). Like Edgar Wallace's *The Four Just Men*, the Hunt Club defended the downtrodden from exploitation by powerful and unscrupulous forces. After a very successful run in the pulps, Pentecost put the group to rest when he moved on to the more lucrative slick magazines, but he revived Jericho (or at least his name) as the central character of a series of his own.

Jericho is an artist, a painter, but not a prissy aesthete, pseudo-revolutionary, or mocking pop artist, types that were so common at the time. He is a tough Korean War veteran who has seen much violence and horror. He is not an adventurer, however, but a crusader. As in his Park Avenue Hunt Club incarnation, his great concern is for the downtrodden and exploited, and he cannot resist a call for help. And he is a formidable adversary. Not only is he physically powerful and fearless, he is intelligent and perceptive, with an artist's eye for detail. In "Jericho and the Deadly Errand" (1972), Pentecost writes, "Jericho's artist's eyes picked up details that might have escaped others. A slight bulge in the other man's waistline spelled gun. Cop, Jericho thought."

As the author describes him in "Jericho and the Deadly Errand," the artist-crusader is "eye-catching: six-feet-four-inches tall, two-hundred-and-forty pounds of solid muscle, with flaming red hair and a flaming red beard." In "Jericho and the Studio Murders" (1975) and other stories he is described as resembling a Viking warrior. "Jericho and the Painting Clue" (1965) characterizes him as looking "like some ancient Viking hero, like a mythological god." In this story and others, he is said to be six-feet-six-inches tall. (Pentecost could not make up his mind about Jericho's height, but the two-hundred-and-forty pounds remained constant.) He has very pale blue eyes that can make him look somewhat distant and enigmatic.

His art is equally distinctive, reflecting his strong social conscience. In "Jericho and the Studio Murders" the narrator notes, "During a longshoremen's strike some years ago Jericho had done drawings and paintings of the violence." In "Jericho and the Silent Witnesses" (1965), he is engaged to paint a mural for a special exhibit at the World's Fair, in which he hopes to capture the meaning of the "war on poverty" President Lyndon Johnson had declared at the time.

In that story, Jericho describes his intentions as a painter as follows: "That's what I hunt for all over the world. ... The Truth. To be summed up some day in a final statement that will make all of us proud or ashamed, but in either case make us Men. Somehow in color, in design, in the emotional impact of the truth stated in visual terms, I hope to move people more than they can be by words, which can always be twisted around to mean two different things. There are no clever semantic tricks in my paintings." His paintings, Pentecost writes, display "enormous vitality." They also show a good deal of anger against social injustice, and as a result they sometimes cause controversy and result in critical dismissal.

Jericho, however, doesn't care what the critics think; he is entirely devoted to his cause. As a result of this single-mindedness, he is a bachelor, and his relationships with women are many and varied—and nearly impossible for the reader to work out chronologically. He has a strong sense of chivalry, however, and in "Jericho and the À Go-Go Clue" (1966) he muses, "These days the meaningless violence against young women in the city seemed to be a part of each morning's news—part of a dark anarchy that seemed to have taken hold of a new generation." He will turn away a woman who is attracted to him if he thinks the situation isn't right.

His work has brought him a good deal of success in spite of—or perhaps in part because of—the controversy his paintings generate. In "Jericho and the À Go-Go Clue," Pentecost writes, "Jericho's paintings were worth a great deal of money," and the artist drives a red Ferrari and never lacks for money. In the search for appropriate subjects, Jericho is a wanderer who lives in many places. In "Jericho and the À Go-Go Clue," Pentecost writes, "Wherever there was violence you were apt to find Jericho—in the Congo, in Algiers, in Vietnam, in New York's Harlem, on the campus at Berkeley."

His home base, however, is in crime- and drug-ridden Greenwich Village. "He walked the streets at any time of day or night without any fear of muggers. He was too formidable a figure to invite violence," Pentecost writes in "Jericho and the Studio Murders" (1975). In "Jericho and the Painting Clue," the artist fights off a physical attack with deadly power:

> There was a stab of flame from the gun, and Jericho felt a searing pain in his left arm. But there was no chance for the little man to fire a second time. Jericho was on him. He broke the little man's gun arm over his knee like a piece of kindling. Then he swung his right fist in a powerful backhand blow. It caught the little man on the jaw and he went spinning away like a top. He screamed as he somersaulted backward down the iron stairs.

Jericho is in his forties and starting to slow down physically, but he was a former commando in the Korean War, and his intellect, insight, and strength of character remain as formidable as ever. Thus the stage is often set for a confrontation between the energy of youth and the wisdom of age. The twentieth century was the Age of Consumerism in the United States, and awareness of that truth was one of Pentecost's strengths as a writer. He regularly used changing fashions, and individuals' reactions to them, as a means of characterization. In the first Jericho story, "Jericho and the Skiing Clue," Pentecost uses his protagonist's skiing style, outmoded corduroy jacket and baggy wool pants, use of a tobacco pipe, and conversation with a stylish young female fashion designer to stamp Jericho as both old-fashioned and aware of the importance of change.

The stories frequently take place among the wealthy and powerful, but these persons' privileged status cannot protect them from the encroachments of the immense social upheavals of the times. As social mores broke down rapidly during the 1950s, '60s, and '70s, crime transformed from an aberration to be seen on a case-by-case basis, into an immense social problem. Crime fiction reflected this change in attitude, and for many authors that meant increasing interest in the psychological and social factors seen as causing criminal behavior— and sometimes excusing it. Pentecost, however, stayed with the classical approach; in his narratives the emphasis is always on the individual's choice to commit the crime and their personal responsibility for the consequences.

This makes for an interesting tension in his writings, which is clearly visible in the Jericho tales, as the protagonist's highly traditional moral sense and thirst for individual justice clash with the chaotic, disturbed activities of the other characters. Philips once said he tried "to write stores that fit into the current climate," and he regularly includes current-events material as background in the Jericho stories. "Jericho and the Deadly Errand," for example, includes references to big-city machine politics, corruption in the U.S. military, the high cost of political campaigns, radical revolutionaries, marital infidelity, a car bomb, and more. Corruption of politicians, police, and business people is a common theme in the stories.

This violent and disorderly social environment is also evident in Pentecost's use of what we might call the Substitute Crime. In "Jericho and the Studio Murders," for example, the artist-detective has to solve a murder before it leads to an urban gang war. But might the motive of sexual jealousy be more important? In another tale, a person's intense devotion to another leads to murder, and to the revelation that the victim is in fact very different from the one the murderer originally intended. In yet another story, what appears to be a kidnaping for ransom may actually involve another motive. And in a very unusual Jericho case, the victim is actually the criminal, and all the suspects are victims.

Pentecost's concentration on characters' motives reveals much about the individuals involved and continually encourages us to judge the morality of their choices. That is what good detective stories do, and it is what makes Hugh Pentecost an exemplary mystery writer and one whose stories and novels are still well worth reading.

Jericho and the Skiing Clue

Every bone in John Jericho's six-foot-six, two-hundred-and-forty-pound body ached. Someone had pitched him a curve when Jericho was told that skiing, like swimming or horseback riding, was a sport you never forgot. You might remember techniques instinctively, but your muscles remembered absolutely nothing.

It was a pleasant kind of fatigue, however. Despite aching bones he had managed several of the more difficult upper trails at Darlbrook that afternoon, and as a climax he had negotiated what would be the official course for the New England downhill competitions the next day—in slow time, but none the less he had negotiated it.

He had been in for some surprises. He had learned his skiing fifteen years ago in the Swiss Alps. He had been trained in the Arlberg or French technique in which shoulder rotation was the key to all directional changes. That shoulder swing was a powerful movement that pulled your skis around through the snow. For a turn to the left you wound your shoulders back to the right and then swung them to the left; the force of that swing turned the skis to the left, with the tips pointing in the new direction and the backs of the skis following along like the caboose of a train. There was much up-and-down motion in the knees and hips to keep the weight off the back of the skis.

None of the youngsters on the Darlbrook slopes that day had used the Arlberg method. Everything today was the shortswing, the heel thrust, and the comma position. Shoulder rotation was out. The shoulders lagged behind, following after the skis had been set in a new direction. This new method of changing direction consisted of a subtle outward thrust of the heels, with shoulders twisted in the direction opposite to the turn. Instead of bending forward from the hips, these modern kids kept their bodies almost erect—upper body out over the skis, knees and hips curved toward the slope in the comma position.

It was a beautiful thing to watch, and it made Jericho feel like an old-fashioned bare-knuckles prizefighter pitted against the modern skills of a Sugar Ray Robinson in his prime.

Jericho was stretched out on the foam rubber cushion that covered a bench under the frost-coated picture window of Darlbrook Lodge's main lounge, overlooking the Vermont hills. He was full of fresh air, the need for sleep—and for another tall drink. In the center of the big room was a huge circular fireplace on which five-foot logs burned and sputtered. The fire produced almost the only light in the crowded room. Somewhere across the lounge a folksinger was bent over a sweet-sounding guitar. Everyone in the room listened with at least half an ear. There was a low chatter of conversation about the day's adventures and the competitions scheduled for the next two.

Jericho looked at his empty glass, decided to aim for the bar across the room, started to rise and instantly dropped back, moaning. At forty you should take things easier to start with. He lay still, his bright red beard pointing upward. A fresh cascade of laughter made him turn his head.

He had noticed the girl earlier, both with a man's eye and the eye of an artist. He had decided that what stretch pants did for a woman's figure explained why skiing had become the most popular sport since bundling. This one had dark red hair, and the icy pastels of her *apres*-ski costume blending into the warm tones of the fireplace embers set off a spectacular figure in spectacular fashion.

"What goes in it?" she asked, her cool fingers touching Jericho's hand as she took his glass.

"Bourbon and water," he said. "But don't go away."

She laughed again. "I'll be back, maestro."

He watched her thread her way across the room to the bar, moving in and out of the couples stretched on the fur rugs around the fireplace. He thought the shortswing technique was a part of her everyday manner of walking.

He sat up, subduing a groan, and realized he was out of key in more ways than his passé skiing technique. His worn corduroy jacket and loose fitting wool pants definitely stamped him Stone Age.

The pastel girl came back with his drink, properly dark in color. He was pleased when she sat down on the bench beside him.

"I'm Valerie Carter," she said. "People call me Val."

"I'm John Jericho," he said. "Nobody has ever called me Jack."

"Jack wouldn't go with the beard," she said, "although you couldn't have had that when you were a kid. Oh, I know all about you, John Jericho. About a month ago I saw an exhibition of your paintings at the Crankshaw Gallery in New York. And I saw you too. I read the story about you in the catalogue—commando in Korea, gentleman-adventurer who paints pictures between delivering right crosses to the jaw."

"Ouch!" Jericho said. "It's just that I'm so big. People are always coming to me and asking me to be on their side. I have an unfortunate impulse to take sides. So naturally I get into trouble."

"That's why I'm here," Valerie Carter said. There was a faint frown above the pert nose, and suddenly her dark blue eyes clouded.

"Not just a Good Samaritan? I could never have made the bar, you know."

"I'd like it if you laughed a little and pretended we were just having ordinary chit-chat," Val said. "We're being watched."

Jericho smiled without looking away from her. "And I was hoping you were here because I'm so handsome," he said. "The only reason anyone could have for watching us is green, boiling jealousy. I could feel it myself if you went away from me."

"That's only a small part of it," she said. "He's the crew-cut blond at the bar. Don't look at him now."

" 'Dear Miss Lonelyhearts'," Jericho murmured.

"He's going to die unless we can help him, John," Val said gravely.

"At least it's 'we' and not just me," Jericho said. "Come on, Val—nobody dies of a broken heart."

He had taken his black, curved-stem pipe out of his pocket and he managed to drop a package of matches on the floor. As he bent down to pick it up he glanced at the bar. The crew-cut blond gent was strikingly good-looking in profile—a Teutonic version of the Apollo of Belvedere—tall, broad-shouldered, lithe.

"He won't ask for help," Val said.

"He doesn't look as though he needed it," Jericho said. He began to fill his pipe from an old oilskin pouch.

"He's Carl Kramer," Val said. "German—West German. He's been in this country three years. He's going to be an American—if he lives. And he's my guy, John."

He grinned at her. "No hope for me?" he asked.

"No hope for you—or for me—unless we can help him," she said.

"When I look at you I'm all ears," Jericho said, holding a match to the bowl of his pipe. "But let's say I am listening, whatever else."

"If he knew I was talking about him he would come over, very cold and very hard, and take me away."

"He's not big enough," Jericho said.

"He's a lovely guy, John, who doesn't deserve to die." She drew a deep breath. "It's a very short story. Carl and his family were separated by the Berlin wall. Carl was on the right side—our side. He was part of a secret group trying to get East Berliners over and under the wall. He joined it with his own family in mind, and eventually he got them to safety. He kept on fighting with his friends, though. They'd helped him, so he had to go on helping them. He sent his mother and two sisters to America, but he stayed behind.

"One day he discovered that a new member of his organization was a traitor—a spy for the East Germans. I don't know exactly what happened—he won't talk about it. But—he killed the man. It must have been self-defense, because there was a trial and Carl was cleared. But he was no longer of any use to his organization. He was a marked man. So he joined his family over here. Part of his education had been in England. He speaks English better than you and I do. He's an aeronautics engineer, a brilliant one. He has a fine job at Sperry, and he thought all the black shadows of the past were behind him. He was—until a week ago—happily employed, with his family safe—and in love with me."

"He can't have fallen out of love," Jericho said.

She made an impatient gesture. "A week ago he got word from a friend in West Berlin. Someone connected with the man Carl had killed—or with the East German Intelligence—has come here to kill Carl."

"It's against the law," Jericho said gently. "So we turn the assassin over to the cops and that's that. Who is he?"

"That's the joker," Val said. "We don't know who he is. We don't know what he looks like. The only thing we know about him is that he is an expert skier, of Olympic calibre."

"So you both stay away from ski places."

"I'm a fashion designer," Val said. "Ski clothes are my business. I have to go to ski places. And skiing is Carl's sport. He's tops at it. But suppose we did stay away? It wouldn't really help. Actually, there's a better chance of spotting this man in a place like this than on Madison Avenue."

Jericho blew a cloud of smoke from his pipe. "Why won't your Carl accept help?"

"Because he feels it's hopeless. If this man doesn't get him there will be another—or another. And if an outsider helps, he too may be killed."

"But you're asking me to help. You don't think an outsider may also be killed?"

"I read the story about you in the catalogue," she said, looking up at him. "I thought you might help—just because what is going on is so *wrong*!"

He put a big hand out and covered her small cold one. "I'll help," he said. "But in turn I need help. I came here to paint—to paint people in motion. I don't know this ski crowd at all."

She smiled at him. "I saw you on Widows' Slope this afternoon. I thought you were going to break your neck. But you were really quite good in an old-fashioned sort of way."

"I'm as old as God," Jericho said, looking at her vivid youth thoughtfully. Men of forty did become involved with girls of twenty-two or -three—and quite successfully. Old-fashioned, indeed!

"I can write off a hundred and fifty of the two hundred people here at the lodge," Val said. "The other fifty?" She shrugged. "If we could trace them all down—but the man may be here, now, in this very room, watching Carl—and us. It could happen tonight. Or tomorrow on the slopes. There isn't time for a long, detailed investigation of people."

And then her voice changed to a little rueful wail. "Be my stern uncle! Be anything! But save me!"

"What's wrong?" he asked sharply.

"Coming toward us," she said. "A very nice, absolutely fatheaded young man who simply refuses to believe that I am a staid, engaged woman!"

The young man approaching them was of medium height with a pleasant, somewhat fatuous smile on his face. He had evidently just come in from outside because he was still wearing ski boots and a snow-streaked fur parka. He was carrying a tray with two martinis and a highball on it.

"The snow bunny to end all snow bunnies," Val said. "Notice the socks worn outside his stretch pants? That five-hundred-dollar Alaska-Arctic parka? Hundred-dollar boots? And I can tell you his Kneissl White Star skis cost him two hundred dollars. Somebody sold him the works! And he can't slide down the front lawn without getting tangled up in his skis and darn near breaking his neck. And because Carl has retired into his shell he's decided to make a play for me!"

"You could try being haughty," Jericho said.

"The trouble is I can hardly keep from laughing," she said. "He's really a very nice kid. But I'm not in the mood."

The young man arrived with his tray. "Hi, Val," he said. "Very dry ones for you and me." He handed one of the martinis to Val and grinned at Jericho. "I took the liberty of inquiring at the bar what you were drinking, sir. You looked a little too big for me to get rid of. I thought perhaps I could charm you into leaving me alone with my gal. My name's Pat McGrath."

Jericho knocked out his pipe in an ashtray and smiled. "I'm going to surprise you, Pat," he said. "I'll accept the drink and give you ten minutes alone with Val. Then I'll be back."

"No!" Val said.

"It's best," Jericho said, realizing that her "No!" was not a protest at being left alone with the amiable ski bunny. She had guessed what he was going to do.

He walked across the room to the bar and stood beside Carl Kramer. There was a tight, hard smile on the young German's lips.

"So she told you," he said.

"She told me," Jericho replied, putting his drink down on the bar.

"I don't want any help," Kramer said.

"Then you're a fool—if this is for real."

Kramer's laugh was short, mirthless. "It's for real, all right. But stay out of it, Mr. Jericho. There's no reason for you to get hurt."

"There's a hell of a good reason," Jericho said. "Now that I *do* know I wouldn't sleep well if I turned my back on you." He swung around so that he could look out over the shadowy room. "No suspicions?"

"Stay out of it, Mr. Jericho." Kramer brought his fist down on the bar. "Or, if you insist, stay in it only long enough to persuade Val to let me run my own risks. This is between me and this man, just as it was between me and—and the other—back in West Germany. There's no way you can help, nothing you can do—nothing, I tell you!"

"I'm not flattered," Jericho said.

"Do you think I enjoy seeing Val spend time with you, or with that grinning ape, McGrath?" Kramer said, his voice low and tense. "I want her to myself— now and for always. But there isn't going to be any always without terrible danger to her. It's quite possible the man I'm waiting for may try to attack me through her—or through my family, God help them. The best thing I can do is to stay out in the open—alone—and wait."

"Romantic, heroic, and nonsensical," Jericho said cheerfully. "Instead of waiting for him, I suggest we get to him first. Old military maxim, my friend: he who gets there 'fustest with the mostest' wins the war."

Carl Kramer was human. The screaming tensions under which he'd been living for a week seemed to give way in the company of the giant, red-bearded artist. Jericho's very size was reassuring. And Kramer knew that he was not a dilettante at action. The facts of Kramer's story tumbled out of him, as he stood there at the bar with Jericho.

The man Kramer had killed in Germany had been a white-haired boy in the East German Intelligence. Since his trial had brought Carl out in the open, no part of Germany was safe for Kramer any more. He had been carefully guarded until he left for New York.

He thought he would be relatively safe in the United States, and he had been for almost three years. Then word came from a friend in West Berlin: the avenger is coming.

The avenger's name was Hans Huber. He and the man killed by Kramer had been close friends and partners in the East German Intelligence Service. Huber was said to be their top man, cold, clever, and without conscience.

Kramer's friend had no physical description of Huber. He was, the friend had written, a man of many faces. He was also a brilliant linguist who could live in England, France, or anywhere else and pass as a native. Only one other scrap of information was added to this meager description: Huber was a superb skier. He had been the top German in the Olympic trials of 1960, but had withdrawn from the competition itself, probably for political reasons.

"This will be a perfect place for him to hide," Kramer said. "For the next two days fine skiers will be the rule here, not the exception." He took a deep drag on a cigarette. "I've gone over the entries in the competition with the committee. They all seem genuine enough—all have established reputations—and not one is unknown to the officials."

"So maybe he's not here," Jericho said.

"I can feel him in my bones," Kramer said grimly. "He's here. I can feel his eyes on me."

"Nerves," Jericho suggested.

"I don't have that kind of nerves, Mr. Jericho."

"All right, I'll buy it for the sake of discussion," Jericho said. "One thing we can count on. Your man doesn't want to be caught. He's a professional. He expects to do his job and get away with it. So it isn't going to happen here, in a crowd. He will wait until he can get at you alone. So it's simple—don't be alone."

"I want to get it over with," Kramer said, "one way or another."

Jericho looked around the fire-lit room. The people were almost like the faceless members of a costumed ballet—the stretch pants, the sweaters, the *apres*-ski boots, some of the girls in long pastel skirts. To the correct music they might all suddenly rise and dance, graceful, sinuous, lithe, with a curiously cool sexuality. The joyous sport of skiing, Jericho thought, might have remained forever the domain of a handful of enthusiasts if it hadn't been for the invention of women's stretch pants—and what they did for a woman's figure.

"We must arrange," Jericho said, "to have you alone, and yet not alone. I suggest that we plan very carefully where you will go tomorrow—out on the slopes. Some place away from the general activity. I will be there first, waiting and watching. If Huber hasn't guessed what we're up to he may make his move."

"No," Kramer said.

Jericho's bright blue eyes turned his way. "You're afraid?"

"I haven't the energy to be angry with you, Mr. Jericho," Kramer said. He nodded across the room toward Valerie Carter who was laughing at some clowning routine of the ski bunny. "I *am* afraid for her. If she's left unguarded, the attack may be against her. If Huber got control of her I would have to go anywhere, do anything, he ordered me to do. Huber knows that."

Jericho grinned. "She doesn't have to be alone," he said. "McGrath will stay with her, given the chance, even if he has to break a leg to keep up with her."

"Huber could twist him around his little finger," Kramer said contemptuously.

"All he has to be is a witness—Huber isn't going to do anything in front of a witness. Make sure that Val stays with the crowd or with McGrath."

"If anything happened to her—" Kramer's voice was a whisper because he had suddenly lost control of it.

It was a bright clear day, cloudless, the sky so blue it was painful to look up at it even through tinted goggles. Jericho, crouching in a little patch of pine growth on the top of the hill, stretched his aching muscles. A few yards away Carl Kramer, out in the open, maneuvered gracefully on his skis.

They were far away from the chair lifts and the T-bars and the ropetows that took tireless skiers to the top of the formal slopes. Out here there was only Kramer, and hundreds of acres of unmarked snow—three or four inches on top of a solid three-foot base.

Just below the pine growth was a sheer drop to the valley below—a half mile of what looked almost like concave face. On the other side were little dips into small hollows. Kramer, the expert, played about in this simple skiing area— waiting—making certain that he was constantly seen at the top of the hill. He moved near the pine growth, pushing hard on his poles. Without looking Jericho's way, he spoke clearly.

"Two hours," he said. "He didn't fall for it."

Jericho, who had been in his hiding place since daybreak, grimaced. "Let's give him a little more time."

Kramer started away toward one of the little slopes, pushing on his poles. Suddenly he stopped.

"Damn!" he said.

"What's wrong?" Jericho called to him.

"Val!" Kramer said. "She and that goon McGrath. I told her on no account to follow us."

"She loves you," Jericho said drily. "Get over that slope and out of sight."

Jericho changed his position so that he could watch the girl and McGrath struggling up the hill, following the clear trail of Kramer's skis. McGrath, tangled in poles and skis, falling every few steps, was laughing. Val, her face almost hidden by goggles and a knitted wool cap, was forced to wait for him, and she was obviously impatient.

"That puts an end to it," Kramer said. "Huber won't show with an army up here."

"*Get out of sight!*" Jericho thundered at him.

The big man bent down to check his bindings, and then he stood up and ski-walked out to the back of the pine growth. He pulled his goggles down over his eyes. There was a curiously set look to the mouth behind the red beard and mustache. Val and the struggling McGrath were about fifty yards below him. They had evidently not spotted Kramer before he ducked out of sight. McGrath had taken another spill and lay twisted in the snow, his skis at a grotesque angle; he was laughing weakly. Val had to go back to him, help untangle the hodge podge of skis and poles, and pull him to his feet.

"I'm sorry, Val, but I've had it," Jericho heard McGrath say.

Jericho bent forward, pushing with his poles, and when he came out around the pine growth he was moving fast. He headed straight for Val and McGrath, snowplowing to a stop as he reached them, and spraying them with the fine powdered snow.

"Avalanche!" he shouted at the top of his lungs.

Val and McGrath stared at him.

"Ski patrol warning everyone," Jericho said, panting. "I was deputized. You'd better get out of here, and fast." He pointed down the perilous half mile to the valley below. "If you can get to the pine woods at the bottom there, you'll be safe. For God's sake hurry, Val!"

She stared at McGrath. "What about him?"

"I'll take care of him," Jericho said. "You get going!"

She glanced up at the mountain top. The hot sun could have started the dreaded avalanche of snow and ice. It would come with the runaway speed of an express train.

"Good luck!" she shouted, and pushed off.

Jericho watched her slip away over the rim of the hill. He figuratively crossed his fingers. There were man-killing boulders and stumps on that dangerous descent. Then he turned to McGrath. The comic look had faded from the ski bunny's face, and there was a white, pinched look around his nose and mouth.

"I'll help you up into that pine growth," Jericho said. "You'll never make it down, Pat. If you're buried on that hillside we'll never find you. But that pine growth may protect you a little and I know where it is. Get your skis off. When the avalanche comes make constant swimming motions. It may help you keep near the top. And keep one pole free so that you can push it up. It'll give you some air and we'll be able to find you more easily when we come back for you. Hurry, man there's not a moment to lose!"

McGrath reached up and pulled his goggles down over his eyes. He smiled at Jericho, a wide white smile. "You're out of your mind," he said. "I'm getting out of here!"

McGrath gave a great, powerful push with his poles. Jericho watched him, the big man still as a statue. The bumbling beginner was gone, and the matchless skill of the expert had taken over.

Jericho saw a beautifully executed short-stem turn and then a wedeln, starting in a slow schuss into a series of hopping turns.

Jericho watched the man racing down the hill, varying the length of his traverses and the arc of his turns, controlling his speed, swinging past obstacles, picking the best terrain for each maneuver with the mastery of an expert.

Jericho heaved a deep sigh and started down the hill himself, slowly, snowplowing, following the track made by McGrath.

When he reached the bottom of the hill he saw Val, her goggles raised, staring open-mouthed at McGrath who was urging her to take cover in the woods.

Jericho reached them, jammed his poles into the snow, and bent to unfasten his bindings. He stepped out of his skis.

"We can't just stand here," McGrath said sharply. He looked up the hill, frowning. "Let's get into the woods!"

"No need," Jericho said.

"Ever see an avalanche?" McGrath shouted at him.

"There is no avalanche," Jericho said. "I invented it, Herr Huber."

The dark-tinted goggles of the man in the fur parka remained fixed steadily on Jericho. Except for the sharp intake of Val's breath there was no sound. Even the dark pine woods seemed to be listening.

"Man of many faces," Jericho said quietly. He leaned on one of his ski poles. His red beard was powdered with white snow. "That implies a master of disguise, Herr Huber. Your vacuous clowning fooled me until a few minutes ago. I watched you coming up the hill with Val. You fell and fell and fell again. Too many times, Herr Huber. I became aware of the instinctive grace of those falls. And then it occurred to me: 'How could an expert skier best hide himself?' By playing the fool, by being so obviously a rank beginner that he would be brushed off any suspect list from the start. The avalanche was a device to rip off your mask."

Jericho glanced at the girl. "What happened, Val? Did you tell him Carl's story and did he persuade you to come out here to look for him?"

She gave him a frozen nod. "Where is Carl?"

"Safe. He'll be turning up soon."

"I'm truly sorry about this," Huber said. A gloved hand came out of the pocket of his parka; it held a compact, black automatic. "I'm only interested in Kramer, but you two have got in the way."

The automatic wavered between Jericho and Val.

Jericho shifted his weight—a small movement. Then, suddenly, his ski pole, hurled like a javelin, buried its sharp point in Huber's throat.

The assassin screamed, and as he fell backward the gun went off, echoing upward. And then Jericho's two-hundred-and forty pounds landed on Huber, and the gun was ripped away and thrown into the soft snow. Huber lay still, moaning.

Jericho, sitting on the man's chest, glanced up the hill. "Take it easy, Val," he said. "The gun shot will bring him."

Coming down the hill in a beautiful series of wedelns of his own was Carl Kramer. The pastel girl hurried forward to meet him. Jericho wondered if there was any way to get that almost primitive eagerness into a painting. It would take genius.

Jericho and the Painting Clue

John Jericho, standing on the hillside a foot or two away from his easel, looked like a figure out of some other age and time. He was a tremendous man, six feet six, with a massive muscular body to match, his bright red hair and pointed red beard blowing in the wind. Against the high blue sky he looked like some ancient Viking hero, like a mythological god.

The view from where he stood took in a sweep of the Berkshire valley, brilliant in its fall foliage, with the town's church steeple and clock tower rising above scarlet maples. To his left, a few hundred feet down the hillside, was the old deserted brick factory which, they said, had once made guns for the Army of the Potomac.

Jericho, a black curve-stemmed pipe clenched between strong white teeth, scowled at the half-finished landscape on his easel. The enormous vitality that was characteristic of his work was somehow missing. He knew why. Sue Walker had got in the way of his work ten years ago, and she was in its way again.

Jericho had come to visit Sue at Fairleigh against his better judgment. He had known that she would get under his skin again and that it would be a long time before he could once more rid himself of his carefully buried hunger for her.

Their break-up ten years ago had been handled with a kind of dramatic reasonableness. He was a wanderer—a searcher for some kind of truth he couldn't find, a man who could only stay in one place long enough to record in oil what there was to see, to make what comment there was to make, and then move on. Sue, who laughed at the things he laughed at, who shared his bitter observations of a world which man made to flourish and then slowly destroyed, loved him as he loved her—with a passionate completeness that should have been perfect. But there was one flaw in an otherwise perfect relationship.

She was fabulously rich. She owned a vast estate in Fairleigh, a small island in the Caribbean, a duplex apartment in New York. Her life moved in a small circle, following the sun and the seasons from one place to the other. Her pleasures were expensive, luxurious. She could no more give up all she had and follow him around the world than he could settle down to being a well-kept, if beloved, poodle in her domain.

And so Sue and John had parted, and she had married George Walker who, two years before, had died of sclerosis of the liver. That particular poodle had lived on alcohol.

Three days ago Jericho had received a wire from Sue. I will never ask anything of you again. please come. He had wired back: impossible. And five hours later he had arrived. Of course, he should have known better.

There were four other guests at the Fairleigh estate. There was an attractive young couple named Conway. Ray Conway, a writer, had evidently been a project of Sue's—perhaps more than just a project at one time. But he was married now, and had a best-selling novel to his credit. There was Mike Farr, a dark Irishman in his mid-forties, lawyer and business manager of Sue's large fortune. And there was an amiable young man named Lucius Terrell.

Lucius Terrell was the reason Jericho had been summoned. He was to be Sue's new husband. God help him, Jericho thought when he saw him. Her energy and vitality would burn him up before he could escape.

"You could save him, John," Sue said in the first minute they were alone together after he had bluntly told her his thought. "You know there is no man in the world for me but you. And if there was any other woman for you, you'd have found her long ago."

For a futile moment they were suddenly in each other's arms, torn by the old hunger. Then he picked her up bodily and sat her in a chair. "Do we have to go through all the reasons why not once more?" he asked.

But Jericho didn't sleep that night. Around and around went the old arguments attempting to show how it could be. At six in the morning he was up, painting equipment under his arm, striding over the hills. Work was the only answer; work was more important than anything else.

Jericho was suddenly aware of the little Jeep bouncing cross-country, headed up the hill toward him. A young boy, unknown to Jericho, was at the wheel. He came to a skidding stop by the easel.

"Mr. Jericho?"

"Yes?"

"Mrs. Walker has been kidnaped, sir. Mr. Farr wants you to come at once."

"What are you talking about?"

"She went out driving in her sports car early this morning," the boy said. "She didn't come back for breakfast. A little while ago Mr. Farr got a phone call. Someone has her. They're demanding ransom."

Jericho vaulted into the Jeep beside the boy. "Let's go."

"Your painting things, sir."

"Later," Jericho said. "Get moving!"

"The instructions are simple enough," Farr said, his face white and set in grim lines. The Conways and Lucius Terrell were pale, motionless dolls. "No police. Draw two hundred thousand dollars in cash from the bank and wait for the next instructions."

"Two hundred thousand dollars!" Jericho exploded. "They must be out of their minds!"

"I can raise it," Farr said. "I have Sue's power-of-attorney. The question is, do we do it, or do we call in the police? I don't want to take the responsibility alone."

"Of course you do it," Terrell said in a shaken voice. "All that matters is getting her back."

"Jericho?" Farr asked.

Muscles bulged under Jericho's tweed jacket. He was in the grip of a kind of impotent fury. "How long will it take to get the money?"

"Couple of hours."

"You go that far," Jericho said. "They may be watching. Then when the next instructions come we'll decide."

Jericho needed to think, away from the frightened Conways and the helpless Terrell. Mike Farr had gone off to the bank, or wherever, to get the money. Jericho strode out across the country again. He would pick up his painting gear on the hillside.

Reason told him they should go to the police who would call in the F.B.I. Emotion told him they should pay the money. Sue could afford it. Why risk her life at the hands of some kind of twisted monster?

The conflicting ideas went back and forth, like a ball in a tennis game. The police would certainly be in it later no matter what they did. The kidnapers couldn't use Sue's flaming-red Ferrari to take her away—it would be too noticeable. They would have to abandon it, and sooner or later someone was bound to report it.

Jericho reached the point on the hillside where he had left his easel, with the canvas still on it. He bent down to pack his paint box and palette when his eyes rested for a moment on the picture he'd been painting when the word came. It was not quite the same as he had left it.

Someone, in his absence, had painted in a little patch of blue sky in the left-hand section of the picture, near the roofline of the old brick factory. The color had been already mixed on his palette. The new patch of sky was therefore right in color, but the amateurish brush work hit Jericho like a blow. It must be a piece of vandalism, he thought, the work of some mischievous kid.

Jericho glanced from the crude patch of blue sky to the factory at the foot of the hill. Slowly a deep frown creased his forehead. His artist's eye told him instantly that something was wrong. The factory was not precisely as it had been, but for a moment or two he couldn't tell what was different. A good painting is a matter of balance—a dark spot here balanced by a light spot there, a massive object there balanced by a bit of vigorous design or color here.

Then he saw what it was. A small thing. When he had been painting the factory, a steel boom for a block-and-tackle mechanism had protruded from the second-floor eaves. Now it was missing. The little patch of crudely painted sky had obliterated the boom from the picture. The vandal, he was suddenly sure, was no mischievous child.

Small hairs rose on the back of Jericho's neck. He had the sharp sensation of being watched. Was someone wondering if he'd noticed? He moved slowly, packing up his gear, not looking again at the factory. When he had it all together, he started down the hill, walking briskly until he reached the cover of the dark pine woods at the foot of the hill.

Instantly he put his gear on the ground and turned to look out through the protective brush at the factory. It had been deserted for years; it still looked deserted.

Jericho moved swiftly through the woods until he had circled back around the factory, where he saw a rear door hanging crookedly, on broken hinges.

Jericho darted across the open space to the door. The rusty hinges screeched as he opened the door and wedged his way inside.

"That you?" a voice called down from the second floor—a man's voice.

An old iron stairway led up to the second floor. Jericho reached it and bounded up. There was only a second in which to see what was there. Sue's bright-red Ferrari reposed placidly in the center of the floor. Sue was in one of the bucket seats, obviously tied there, a handkerchief knotted tightly at the back of her head acting as a gag.

And there was the man, small, dark, startled—but with an automatic aimed straight at Jericho as he came to the top step. It wasn't a moment for indecision. A shout of anger burst from Jericho, thundering in the open space, as he hurled his two hundred and forty pounds straight at the man with the gun.

There was a stab of flame from the gun, and Jericho felt a searing pain in his left arm. But there was no chance for the little man to fire a second time. Jericho was on him. He broke the little man's gun arm over his knee like a piece of kindling. Then he swung his right fist in a powerful backhand blow. It caught the little man on the jaw and he went spinning away like a top. He screamed as he somersaulted backward down the iron stairs.

Jericho was after him, pouncing on him almost as he hit the bottom. The little man lay still, his head twisted at a grotesque angle.

Jericho stood up, nursing his left arm with his right hand. A trickle of blood ran through his fingers. The little man, he knew, was dead of a broken neck.

He turned and hurried back up the stairs. His left hand was useless, but he slipped the gag off Sue's mouth before he began to work at the rope knots on her wrists and ankles. She was half laughing, half crying.

"John! John! My darling John," she kept saying.

"Stop yammering and tell me what happened," he said grimly.

She had gone out looking for him that morning and hadn't been able to find him. She'd finally parked, just to sit and think. The little man had come from nowhere, gun pressed at her throat. She'd been tied and gagged. He'd then driven the Ferrari straight across the fields to the factory. A crane had been fastened to the car—something evidently long planned—and had lifted it, with Sue inside, to the second floor of the factory. After that—just waiting.

"And dying slowly of terror, John."

They went out of the factory together, and he told her of the kidnap scheme. Out in the sunshine she helped him make a tourniquet for his arm with a strip torn out of her slip. They started to walk along the deserted back road toward home.

They'd gone less than a hundred yards when a car came toward them, traveling at a dangerous speed.

"It's Mike Farr!" Sue said.

She stepped into the center of the road, waving her arms. The car skidded to a stop. Farr got out, carrying a briefcase. His face was the color of ashes.

"My dear Sue, you're safe!" he said in a relieved voice.

"John found me," Sue said. "What are you doing out here, Mike?"

Farr patted the briefcase. "The ransom money," he said. "I got a phone call instructing me to bring it to the old factory." He looked at Jericho. "I didn't think it was wise to wait for you to return—Sue was in too much danger."

"They phoned you at Sue's house?" Jericho asked.

"No, my office. I went there after I'd raised the money. They must have been watching my movements."

"The first call you got," Jericho said. "I forgot to ask you. That came to your office, too?"

"Yes."

"No witnesses to either call?" Jericho's right hand closed tightly over Sue's wrist. "How did you know where to send the boy for me this morning?"

"Why—we guessed you were out painting."

"But you couldn't know I was at that exact spot because I didn't know where I was going myself. Sue looked for me and couldn't find me."

Farr moistened his lips. "The boy was just lucky enough to find you," he said. Jericho's hand tightened on Sue's wrist. "It won't work, Farr," he said. "Your little friend back there in the factory spilled the whole story after I did a little persuading on him."

"John!" Sue said.

"Quiet!" Jericho said sharply. His eyes blazed steadily at Farr, who seemed to have suddenly shriveled inside his clothes. "Your marriage to Terrell was going to be a disaster for friend Farr," he said to Sue. "There'd be an auditing of your accounts. How much is the shortage, Farr? Say, one hundred and seventy-five thousand? Your little friend had to have a piece of the action. Say, twenty-five thousand for him for risking the chair?"

Sweat ran down Farr's face. He looked quickly to the right and left. Jericho moved, and his right hand twisted Farr's arm in a painful lock.

"You pay off your accomplice," Jericho said, "and then replace the missing funds in Sue's account. She's out two hundred thousand, but it would seem to have been paid to the kidnaper."

"I'm sorry, Sue," Farr said. "I was desperate."

"Your little man made one mistake," Jericho said. "When I started to paint my picture, the boom was projecting from the factory, ready and waiting to pick up Sue's car when she was brought there. The steel boom was in my painting. After I was summoned back to the house, Sue and the car reached the abandoned factory, were lifted to the second floor, and the boom was withdrawn.

"Then your friend saw my easel. It worried him. He went over to see what I had painted and found the boom in my picture. He didn't want me or anyone else to remember that boom. So he painted it over with a little blue sky—he thought. What he didn't know was that I would instantly recognize any brush stroke that wasn't mine."

"He told you that?" Farr asked.

"He told me nothing," Jericho said. "He's dead." He let go Farr's arm. "I'll take charge of that briefcase," he said. "Suppose you now drive us to the State Police barracks."

Jericho and the Dying Clue

The screaming woke Jericho from a restless sleep. He had stretched out on the bed before midnight, his huge, muscular body covered only by a sheet. He had been troubled by a personal work problem, which, combined with the sultry threat of an electrical storm, had made the sleep that finally came fitful and unrelaxed.

At first, he thought the screaming was part of a nightmare. But, wide-awake, he knew it wasn't part of a bad dream. The screaming was real. It was high-pitched, hysterically rhythmic.

Jericho sat up, tugging at his bright red beard. A jagged streak of lighting seemed to spurt just outside the window, and the almost instant crack of thunder suggested that a tree in the front yard had been struck.

When he first heard it, Jericho thought the screaming had come from the boy. He had known twelve-year-olds who were terrified by thunderstorms. But when the screaming went on and on, he recognized the femaleness of it. Could it be the grim-faced Mrs. Rice? Or the sad daughter, Mrs. Powell, widowed mother of the boy David? Or the glamorous teen-aged girl who was the other house guest?

He put his money on the glamorous young girl, whose name was Joan Latham. She had exhibited a considerable talent for the dramatic during the evening. He had written her down as someone who was going to raise hell with a lot of men's lives before she was much older—if, indeed, she hadn't already begun to do so.

But the persistent intensity of the screaming suggested real terror, not a mere act.

Jericho heard voices in the hall outside his room. Between violent cracks of thunder one bit of dialogue came to him clearly.

"What is it, grandmother? What's wrong with Joan?" It was little David Powell.

Then the cold sharp voice of Mrs. Rice. "It's nothing, David. Go back to bed. Joan simply had a bad dream."

This was punctuated by another crack of thunder.

Bad dream my foot, Jericho thought. Miss Joan Latham, aged seventeen, already a full-blown woman who was sophisticatedly aware of her charms—very hip, indeed—was not one to be frightened by a bad dream.

Jericho switched on the bedside lamp, noticed it was only a little past one o'clock, and got up. He stood naked in the center of the room, listening. Then he pulled on a pair of trousers and reached for the sports shirt draped on the back of a chair. The screaming had stopped, but the voices, now farther down the hall, were still low, tense, excited.

Jericho's position in the house was unusual. He was there as a guest, yet he had never met any of the family until a few hours ago. He had accepted a commission to paint a portrait of the head of the house, Senator Willard Fulmer Rice. His fee was to be paid by James Latham whose enormous fortune was promoting Senator Rice's crusade for moral rearmament and government reform into a household word. Next stop, if all went according to plan—the White House.

Senator Rice's voice, heard on television and radio, was as instantly familiar as the late Franklin D. Roosevelt's. Rice was a powerful orator and a dramatic-looking figure. He was a big man, over six feet tall, with the shoulders of a blacksmith. His shock of white hair, his black beetling eyebrows, his square jaw and wide strong mouth, his dark eyes hot with the fires of enthusiasm and dedication to his cause, helped to make every movement, every inflection of his deep rich voice, arresting.

But John Jericho was puzzled by Willard Fulmer Rice. Profoundly puzzled. Unknown to the Senator, Jericho had gone to several huge public gatherings where Rice had worked his magic on cheering crowds. He had drawn a few preliminary sketches of Rice in action. These sketches were a kind of free association of pencil on paper, and the results were disturbing. Each of the sketches had a peculiarly sinister quality; a kind of irony; a mockery; a suggestion that Rice was laughing at the people who were so obviously inspired and uplifted by his words.

Jericho put this down to his own personal resistance to all types of highpowered salesmanship, even when it was related to so worthy a cause as reform. He decided that to rid himself of this off-beat reaction Rice he should spend a day or two with the Senator in the normal atmosphere of his home—before beginning actual work on the portrait.

The household consisted of Senator Rice, of his grim-faced, gray-haired wife, of their widowed daughter and her twelve-year-old son, David Powell. There was another guest, Joan Latham, teen-aged daughter of Rice's financial sponsor. Her constantly rippling daughter, her gay, flirtatious manner, seemed to light up an otherwise rather somber family setting.

Rice himself remained an impressive man. In his late fifties, he was a constantly boiling caldron of energy. He greeted Jericho with a handshake that would have been bone-crushing except for the fact that Jericho was twenty years younger and more than a match in physical size and strength.

The two men were a striking picture together—the white-haired spellbinder and the artist with his bright red hair and beard. That handshake was like the first hold in a struggle between two giants. In that moment Jericho had the same curious feeling he'd had about Rice at the public meetings. He felt a mocking challenge, as if the older man were daring the painter to find out the inner truth about him.

Jericho told himself he was never going to paint a portrait of this man that would satisfy his many thousands of adoring followers. That insistent quality of mockery, which Jericho could not dismiss, did not belong in a saint.

There was one set of good marks for the Senator, however. They came from what, for Jericho, was an unimpeachable source. Young David Powell idolized his grandfather. Jericho had arrived at the Rice home in his car about an hour earlier than he'd been expected. The family, with the exception of young David and the house servants, had been out somewhere. Jericho was welcomed with grave courtesy by young David.

The boy was immediately fascinated by two things—Jericho's red beard and his painting gear. Jericho had a gift for getting on with children. He treated them like adults, without any affection or condescension. David showed Jericho to his room and was instantly involved with the artist's unpacking, and particularly with his easel, canvases, and paints. He was eager at the prospect of being able to see his grandfather's portrait being painted from the very beginning. Without the boy realizing it, he was carefully pumped by the artist. Facts spilled out like marbles out of a sack.

The boy's father had been drowned in a sailing accident when young David was a baby. There was no memory whatever of his father. David had grown up in his grandfather's home, and the Senator himself had assumed the role of father. The boy clearly loved him, hero-worshipped him, and trusted him enough to walk into fire if the Senator had suggested it.

It's hard to fool a child, Jericho knew. The boy's adoration for the Senator was a powerful counterweight against Jericho's instinctive distrust, however deep that distrust was …

Jericho buttoned his sports shirt and stepped, barefoot, out into the hall.

There is something essentially comic about even so vivid a personality as Willard Rice when he is caught wearing an old-fashioned nightshirt. The Senator stood at the far end of the hall with his wife and daughter, his bare legs bony under the skirt of the nightshirt, his white hair ruffled. David, the boy, stood a few yards away, hunched against the wall.

Jericho closed his door sharply so that they'd be aware of his presence.

"You could have kept her away from the telephone until she calmed down," he heard Rice say.

Then, almost certainly, he heard two words from Mrs. Rice. "You skunk!" she said.

David obviously heard the two words and he turned and started down the hall toward Jericho. His eyes were wide with shock.

"She's a bad woman," he said to Jericho. "Grandfather could never in the world have done such thing. Not in the whole world!"

And then the boy ran past Jericho toward his own room.

Rice and his wife and daughter were now aware of Jericho's presence. Anne Powell—David's mother—seemed torn between the need to stay where she was and the need to be with her child. She decided in favor of the boy and hurried past Jericho, without even looking at him, to the boy's room.

Rice came down the hall toward Jericho. Mrs. Rice went into the room from which the screaming had come.

"Damned hysterical *women*," Rice said as he reached Jericho. His jowly face was wet with perspiration. "Sorry you were disturbed."

"What happened?" Jericho asked.

"I went into Joan's room to close the windows—it was raining in from that side," Rice said. "She was still awake. She's like a member of the family, you understand. She's staying here because her father has a houseful of business friends. I—I bent down to kiss her good night, as I've done ever since she was a child. She started to scream as though I'd tried to attack her!" He shook his head as if puzzled by the injustice. "Damned little idiot says I *did* try! A child like that! Now she's phoned her father and there'll be hell to pay."

A glare of light swept across the windows—the glare was not from the storm. Car lights.

"That'll be Jim Latham come to go battle for his precious daughter!" Rice said bitterly.

A servant evidently was ready to let the visitor in, because a few moments later a small man, his face white as a death mask, came bounding up the stairs.

"Where is she?" he asked, his voice shaking.

"The room at the end of the hall," Rice said. "But wait a minute, Jim—"

Latham ran down the hall to his daughter's room.

A dry pretense of a laugh rattled up from Rice's throat. "If I were a drinking man I'd need one now," he said, "badly. Jim'll listen to reason though, when he calms down."

James Latham was not prepared to listen to reason when he came out of his daughter's room. There was a small automatic in his hand, pointed shakily at the nightshirted Senator.

"I'm going to kill you for this, Willard," he said.

Jericho's reflexes were quick. He stepped toward the little man and brought the edge of his hand sharply down on Latham's wrist. The gun thudded on the carpeted floor.

"You'd better cool off, Mr. Latham," Jericho said softly.

Latham stared at Jericho, startled, rubbing his wrist. Something in the angry eyes suggested that he was marking Jericho down for later destruction. Then he turned and went back into his daughter's room.

"Sorry for interfering," Jericho said to Rice, "but he looked far enough off base to do something cockeyed."

The Senator nodded vaguely. Then he bent down and picked up the gun. He turned it round and round in his hands, thoughtfully. "Damn fool girl," he muttered. He started slowly down the stairs to where Jericho knew his private study was located.

A minute later, Latham came out of the bedroom with his daughter, his arm around her shoulders. She kept her head lowered so that Jericho got only a glimpse of her pale, tear-stained face. They went past him and down the stairs.

In less than a minute Jericho heard the front door slam, and then the suddenly raced engine of Latham's car.

Mrs. Rice came slowly out of the bedroom. There was a bitter smile on her gray face. "It would seem that we can now stop making plans for redecorating the White House," she said.

The storm continued persistently violent. It rolled down the valley and then came blasting its way back, the night streaked again and again with jagged lightning, the house shaken over and over by explosive bursts of thunder.

It was nearly an hour before Jericho could fall asleep again. When he woke again, at about 8:00, the storm was gone—as if it had never happened—and brilliant sunshine out of a cloudless blue sky filled his room.

Jericho got up, showered and dressed quickly, and went downstairs for breakfast. No one seemed to be about this early except a maid in the dining room—it had been a hard night for all of them. The maid took his order for juice, bacon and eggs, and toasted English muffins. Except for young David, no one else had come downstairs. The boy was outside somewhere, the maid said.

Jericho helped himself to coffee from a percolator on the sideboard, and when the maid brought his breakfast he began to eat with a sharp appetite. He was just finishing when, for the second time since his arrival, screams reverberated through the house.

He ran out into the hall where he saw the maid standing in the open door to Senator Rice's study. It was she who was doing the screaming this time.

Jericho moved quickly up behind her.

"I was going in to dust!" the maid managed to blurt out between screams. Jericho's fingers clamped her arm, trying to silence her. Over the top of her head he saw Senator Rice sprawled forward on his desk, his face resting in a pool of blood that had come from a round black hole in his forehead. There was no need to go closer to see that he was dead.

Jericho pulled the maid away from the door, closed and locked it pocketing the key. At that moment Mrs. Rice and Anne Powell came running down the stairs. Jericho had to break the news to them.

"It's a matter for the State Police," he said. "Would you like me to handle it for you, Mrs. Rice?"

"Please!" she said in a choked voice.

"Where's David?" Anne Powell asked. She turned and raced out the front door into the yard.

Mrs. Rice's cold hand rested on Jericho's wrist. "Do the police have to know about last night?" she asked.

Yes, the police had to know.

Senator Rice had been shot at very close range. There were powder burns around the wound in his forehead. It would easily have passed for a suicide except for the insurmountable fact that there was no gun in the room.

Jericho, unwillingly, was the primary subject of interrogation by Captain Blaine of the State Police. Mrs. Rice was in no condition to talk, and Anne Powell was upstairs with a heartbroken David, who had come back from an excursion into the woods just as the State Troopers arrived.

Jericho found himself forced to give an account of what had gone on earlier that night.

"There *was* a gun," he said in conclusion, "Latham's gun. The Senator picked it up after I'd knocked it out of Latham's hand. The last I saw of it he was carrying it with him into the study."

"It's not there now, or anywhere else in the house, for that matter," Blaine said. "You heard no shot in the night? The doctor says the Senator has been dead for about five hours. Killed not later than 4:00 a.m."

Jericho shook his head. "The thunderstorm," he reminded Blaine.

"You didn't hear anyone come back to the house?"

"You think Latham returned?" Jericho countered.

"He might have—it's not improbable. He comes back; the Senator lets him in and tries to explain things; the gun is lying on the desk in the study; Latham, still in a homicidal mood, grabs it and shoots him."

"You'd have a hard job proving it," Jericho said. "There'd be no tire tracks or footprints after all that rain. My bedroom is on the other side of the house. I wouldn't have seen car lights, and I didn't hear anything."

"If no one came in from outside," Blaine said, scowling, "then we have to consider the two women—his wife and daughter."

"Or me," Jericho said. "Or the servants." He heard the faint echo of Mrs. Rice's two words the night before. *"You skunk!"*

He reached in his jacket pocket for his black, curve-stemmed pipe. "Latham may have an ironclad alibi. He took his daughter home from here. He may have stayed with her. He has, I understand, a houseful of guests. It's just possible, if not likely, that he can completely clear himself."

But it developed that James Latham had no alibi. He had, he told Blaine, taken his daughter home, turned her over to his wife, gone back to his car, and driven around in the storm, trying to get a grip on himself, frankly reconsidering the possibility of killing the Senator. "That hypocritical four-flusher, putting his hands on Joan! If it hadn't been for this man," he said, pointing a shaking finger at Jericho, "I would have killed him on the spot. But I didn't—then or later."

"You did kill him! You came back and killed him!" a shrill voice cried from the doorway. They were in the dining room of the Senator's house, and David, his face wet with tears, was suddenly across the room, hurling himself on Latham, kicking, clawing. "He never touched Joan! She lied! She's a liar!"

Blaine pulled the child away from Latham and then Jericho put a strong arm around him. The boy's face buried itself against his coat. "She's a liar, a liar!" he sobbed again and again.

The small boy was rigid with grief and rage. Anne Powell ran across the room to her child and knelt beside him.

"Come, David. Come with me," she pleaded.

"Let him stay," Jericho said sharply. "He has a right to hear everything." It could be a trauma from which the boy might never recover, particularly if he imagined that secrets were being kept from him.

Captain Blaine had a very hot potato in his hand. The murder of Senator Rice would be a front page story all over the nation. By tomorrow the F.B.I. would be in on it, assuming the possibility that the murderer was a political enemy who had crossed state lines to reach his victim. The story of Rice's alleged attack on Joan Latham could wreck her life if it became a matter of public gossip.

Captain Blaine was confronted by one unassailable fact. No one had broken into the house. No one had let anyone into the house unless it had been Rice himself, and Rice could no longer tell them about it. So it had to be someone Rice had let in—or someone already in.

The boy raised his tear-streaked face to Jericho. "If Joan isn't lying, then it's what grandmother said. She had a bad dream. She imagined it. That's what grandfather told me. She imagined it."

Jericho ran his hand through the boy's dark hair. "When did he tell you that, David?"

"This morning. I mean, it was just about daylight. I wasn't able to sleep much. And I had to know, Mr. Jericho, *I had to know*. So I went to his bedroom and he wasn't there. So I came down to the study—and he told me. She just imagined it. Anybody who says it really happened is a liar." The boy turned his reddened eyes to James Latham.

Jericho stood very straight and still.

"Come with me, David!" Anne Powell pleaded.

The boy tried to turn to his mother, but Jericho's arm around his shoulder held him firmly.

Then the key question, the crucial question, popped into Jericho's mind.

"What did you do with the gun, boy?" Jericho asked gently.

"I took it to my—"

The boy stopped, his mouth open, his eyes dark with terror.

"You have some sort of secret hiding place, David?" Jericho asked. "A playhouse? A cave in the woods? When I was a kid it was a cave, with a secret hiding place in it. Is that where you took the gun? To your own secret hiding place?"

Captain Blaine started toward the boy but Jericho stopped him with a sharp gesture. "Is that it, David?"

Anne Powell was on her feet. She stared at Jericho with a cold fury in her eyes. "You can't try to blame it on David!" she cried. "What kind of a monster are you, Mr. Jericho? It would be nice to save father's reputation—and Mr. Latham's and Joan's and mother's—by blaming it on a child. No, I tell you! *No!*"

Jericho ignored her, looking down at David with deep sympathy in his eyes. "Was there a note, too, David?"

The boy seemed frozen, unable to speak.

Jericho drew a deep breath and looked up at Captain Blaine. "I think David will show us where the gun and the note are when he gets hold of himself," he said. He shifted his eyes to the white-faced mother. "I'm not trying to blame anything on David, Mrs. Powell—unless he can be blamed for loving a man who wasn't worth it."

There was a long shuddering sigh from Mrs. Rice.

"I'm sorry," Jericho said to her. "David didn't hear all our talk, you see. He didn't hear Captain Blaine say that the Senator had been dead for some five hours when the maid found him. That means David could never have talked to him at daylight. Given that slip, there are only two things we can think. I, for one, can't imagine David killing his grandfather; he adored him. The only other possibility is that he found him dead—a suicide. There was probably a note—the Senator would have left an explanation. But when the Senator and the note were found, it would be clear that he was guilty of Joan Latham's accusation. That David, young as he is, could not bear.

"And so he took away the gun and the note, leaving us with what looked like a murder, and hoping that he had kept his grandfather's reputation intact."

Jericho knelt down and faced the boy, his big hands on the boy's shoulders. "Loyalty is a fine thing, David. But not so fine or so important as truth. We can't live without truth, David. If we try, everything else becomes meaningless."

Jericho and the Silent Witnesses

A woman's scream, heard at two o'clock in the morning, will produce different results in different localities. In the plush areas of Park and Fifth Avenues, or in their expensive side streets, the scream would probably be ignored on the grounds that "it's none of my business." In the Times Square Subway station, or in Hell's Kitchen or the Waterfront areas, the scream could be a signal of violence to be avoided at the risk of one's own life and limbs.

In Jefferson Mews, in the heart of Greenwich Village, a woman's scream could be a part of Saturday night's music. Jefferson Mews had once been a group of stables built around an open court, where the rich kept their horses and elegant rigs. Eventually, with the arrival of the automobile and the passing of the horse car, the stables had been converted into apartments and studios, occupied by artists, writers, poets, and a collection of white-collar workers who found the surroundings "quaint." Greenwich Village today is no longer the home of great revolutionary talents in the arts. Beatniks and offbeat musicians hover there now, but real estate tycoons are gradually closing in. Modern apartment houses rise month by month above the remnants of old private houses.

Jefferson Mews remains intact, still housing writers and poets, artists and musicians, some really talented people and some outrageous fakes. A scream in the middle of the night in Jefferson Mews can have many innocent meanings— a wild party which will go on all week-end, a brawl between hopped-up women fighting over some cherished male. It could mean that Mike Guffanti was beating his wife again. Mike Guffanti, a former dockhand on the nearby Waterfront, was the landlord's handyman in Jefferson Mews. People would smile if they heard Bertha Guffanti screaming. They knew that Bertha Guffanti liked to be beaten—it was proof of Mike's manliness and her own attractiveness. She always sounded terrified, but actually her screams were a kind of savage love call.

But on the particular Saturday night—rather, Sunday morning—of this particular scream the Guffantis were already entwined in the miracle of a married love affair. They said later that they didn't even hear it.

But others heard it.

In one of the artist's studios in the Mews a man stood scowling at a blank canvas. Fluorescent lights turned the high-ceilinged room with its northern skylight into day. The artist was a huge man, six feet four, with massive shoulders and the tapering waist of a ballet dancer. He had fiery red hair and a red beard that jutted belligerently at the empty canvas. He was mixing paints on a palette with hamlike hands that moved with a concert pianist's dexterity. He heard the scream and it seemed to make him angry: it was an intrusion on his concentration.

Behind him, standing near the door of the studio, was a girl. She had high cheekbones, a pale white face, a bright scarlet mouth, hair that glittered in the artificial light like a blackbird's wing. Her dress was simple, with a deep V in front. She carried a small cheap-looking bag. She looked at a row of canvases stacked along the wall, brilliant in color, almost violent in their reflection of the artist's energy. The signature, in bold black letters, was clearly visible across the room.

Jericho.

The girl heard the scream too, and a nerve twitched high up on her ivory cheek.

"Where do I take off my clothes?" she asked.

"You don't," John Jericho said, scowling at his paints.

"I've never taken my clothes off to be painted," the girl said, "but I wouldn't mind doing it for you."

"I'd be flattered," Jericho said, without turning his head, "if I didn't know that in your profession taking off your clothes is an occupational technique."

"You don't have to talk dirty," the girl said. "You asked me to pose. I understood artists always wanted girls to pose in the nude. I am willing."

"And always at two o'clock in the morning?" Jericho turned and gave her a cheerful grin.

"I don't know much about artists," the girl said.

"Lucky you," Jericho said. "By the way, what's your name?"

"Lucinda Laverne," the girl said.

"The hell it is!" Jericho's laugh was like distant thunder.

"You're right," the girl said. "It's really Mabel Chernovsky. When I went into show business I took the name of Lucinda Laverne. It seemed easier to remember."

"But you're not in show business any more."

The girl lowered her dark eyes. "No."

Jericho put down his palette and brushes on a square wooden table beside the easel. "Let me take the mystery out of this—Mabel," he said. "I saw you standing on the street corner outside the Mews. I've been looking at this blank canvas all day and all night. You were suddenly the answer to a problem. Since I took it you were standing there waiting for business to come along I thought you might be willing to involve yourself in my business. As I told you, I'm willing to pay your usual fee for the time involved. I'm not interested in your beautiful white body. I just want you to stand over there on that platform, looking exactly the way you did when I saw you on the street corner, before you knew I was looking at you. I want to get that expression down in paint if I can. Do you know what you were thinking about just before you saw me?"

"I wish you'd call me Lucinda," the girl said. "It would sound nicer than Mabel—coming from you."

"It's a deal," Jericho said. "Now, what were you thinking about, Lucinda?"

The scarlet mouth drew down. "What a stinking world we live in," Lucinda said.

"But you were facing up to it," Jericho said, his eyes bright.

"What else is there to do?" Lucinda said, with a faint shrug of her shapely shoulders.

"It takes courage," Jericho said.

Out in the Mews the woman screamed again, this time with a piercing note of terror.

"I wish those jerks would do their brawling somewhere else," Jericho said impatiently.

Lucinda stood very still, listening. Her face had turned a shade paler.

"If I tell you what I'm after," Jericho said, "I may spoil it. But I think I must. You've heard all the talk about 'the war against poverty'?"

"Politics," the girl said, with unexpected bitterness.

"Right," Jericho said. He took a black, curved-stem pipe from the pocket of his corduroy jacket and began to fill it with a stringy black tobacco from an oilskin pouch. "The rich, the influential, the hopeful vote seekers—they all talk about it. But the poverty is here—all around us here in Jefferson Mews. I know. I've been painting in this studio for two months."

"You don't look as though this was the best you could afford," Lucinda said.

"I've been looking for a kind of truth," Jericho went on. "How can hundreds of thousands of people be persuaded that the 'war against poverty' is worth fighting? I'm supposed to do a mural for a special exhibit at the World's Fair. I've thought of it a thousand ways—the filth, the rats, the overcrowding, the degradation, the crushed human dignity. If people could see that, I kept telling myself, it would 'sell' the fight. Then, tonight, I saw you."

Lucinda looked at him, puzzled.

"You see, Lucinda, in theory I'm willing to fight rats. I'm willing to contribute to mops and brooms and carbolic acid; I'm willing to buy plants for flower boxes to make things look more cheerful. But I don't feel any passionate drive about it. What would make me fight with all my guts to do something real about this poverty? That's the answer I didn't find until tonight—when I saw you."

"I don't see what I—"

"Human courage in the face of it all!" Jericho said, his voice loud. "You stood there, your head up, your eyes clear, facing up to it."

"I'm just a prostitute," the girl said, her voice a whisper.

"I know, Lucinda. It takes courage to face the fact that you've been driven to that. I saw you, and I said to myself, 'If people could see that courage in the face of a thousand horrors they'd be much more likely to enlist in the fight than they would if they saw a realistic painting of a hungry rat eating from a garbage pail.' "

Out in the Mews the woman screamed for the third time. Now there were understandable words, wrenched out of an intolerable agony. "Please, please, please—*help!* In the name of God—*help!*"

Angrily Jericho walked over to the window. He leaned out to shout, to demand that the woman be silent.

Instead he froze.

Down below, at the end of the Mews, he saw her. She was down on her knees, bent backward so that her shoulders were against the sooty walls of a brick building. Standing over her was the shadowy figure of a man.

It was like walking into a darkened theater and seeing a play already on. Unbelievably there were other actors besides the woman and the man. There were people at windows, watching. Like Jericho.

The man's hand rose, and for a brief moment the blade of a knife glittered in the light of a street lamp some distance away. Then the knife came down, aimed at the woman's breast or stomach. Up and violently down again. Up and down. There was one final, wavering scream.

The people in the windows remained motionless. All but Jericho. He turned, and like a charging bull, swept out of the studio, clattering down a flight of stairs to the street level.

Behind him the girl Lucinda, who had seen nothing, turned and leaned against the wall. Her body shook with uncontrolled sobbing.

Jericho raced across the cobblestones of the Mews toward the dark corner. "Stop it!" he shouted at the top of his giant voice. "*Stop it!*"

Dozens of motionless people in the upper windows watched the red-bearded artist disappear into the shadows.

The man was gone. The woman had toppled over. One side of her face lay in a little puddle of stagnant water. Moments ago it had been a lovely face. A girl's face. She couldn't have been much over twenty.

There was a quantity of blood. You could smell it.

Jericho, his eyes becoming accustomed to the gloom, glanced quickly around him. No man. No sound of running footsteps. In the time it had taken Jericho to race down from his studio the man had vanished.

Jericho knelt beside the girl and lifted her face out of the dirty water. Her eyes were open, but they saw nothing. Jericho felt hot blood on his hands. He saw that she must have been stabbed at least twenty times. From the time of the first scream until now must have been an eternity for her.

Jericho's massive body shook with anger. If only he had gone to the window at the first scream—

He looked up and he saw them—faces blank with a kind of horror.

"I don't suppose any of you bothered to call the cops!" he shouted.

Faces withdrew, but no one answered.

From outside the Mews came the sounds of thinned-out traffic—the guttural roar of a night truck, the shrill whistle of the doorman outside a night club, the answering toot of a taxi horn, the vague medley of music from a dozen sources, including windows in the Mews.

Jericho, crouching on the cobblestones with the bloody body of the girl still cradled in his arms, glanced around at the now empty windows, and he was torn by a kind of fury.

"Somebody! Get down here!" he shouted. It could have been heard in the next block.

Then he heard someone and turned his head. It was the girl, Lucinda. She came up and stood beside him, her eyes round with disbelief, the back of her right hand pressed against her mouth.

"Stay with her while I get the cops," Jericho said. "She was murdered, and the killer can't be far away."

"No!" Lucinda said sharply. Then, "I called the police on your phone."

"Good girl," Jericho said, controlling his anger. "There were dozens of people watching—doing nothing! I never saw anything like it."

"If we'd looked when we first heard her—" Lucinda whispered.

"Yeah. Couple of drunks, I thought."

From outside the Mews came the sound of a police car siren.

Something in the girl's face made Jericho ask if she knew the woman.

Lucinda nodded slowly. "Mary Brady," she said. "Night club singer."

"She lives here in the Mews?"

"Yes."

People began to drift out of doorways, moving hesitantly toward the tragic tableau.

"They come *now!*" Jericho said, his voice harsh.

A police car swept in through the far entrance to the Mews. Two cops with drawn guns jumped out of the sharply braked car.

"Put her down," one of them said, pointing his gun steadily at Jericho's red-bearded face.

Jericho's teeth bared in a white, angry smile. "Better late than never," he said. "Put her down."

"Get something to cover her with," Jericho said, not moving.

"What happened here?" the second cop asked.

The people moved in closer. Their faces looked like frozen masks. A shrill woman's voice broke the silence. "She was stabbed three times!"

The second cop was kneeling beside Jericho. "More like three dozen times," he said. "My God, it's Mary Brady!"

"He stabbed her," the woman said, "and then he went away and came back and stabbed her again. He went away a second time and then came back and finished the job."

"I'm giving you ten seconds to put her down!" the first cop said to Jericho.

"Not him," the shrill woman said. "He came to help but he was too late. The other man ran away."

"You're the woman who turned in the alarm?" the second cop asked.

"Not me," the woman said.

"Dozens of them saw it," Jericho said, "but none of them turned in an alarm. My friend here, Miss Laverne, called you."

"You saw it?" the first cop asked Lucinda.

Lucinda shook her head. "Only when it was over—when Mr. Jericho ran out to help."

"You're Jericho?" the first cop asked.

"I'm Jericho."

"You with this Laverne dame when it happened?"

"Yes."

"She solicit you?" the cop asked.

"Listen, stupid," Jericho said, "this is a murder. You've got dozens of witnesses here. Stop worrying about other things. Do something about *this!*"

"Don't talk to me like that," the cop said.

A second woman pressed forward—a girl in a bright red housecoat. She had a patchwork quilt in her arms. "You can cover her with this," she said.

Jericho took the quilt and wrapped it gently around Mary Brady's body. Then he put her down on the cobblestones. He stood up, facing the cop, towering over him.

"I say it again," Jericho said. "You're stupid. While you stand here gabbling about 'soliciting,' the guy who did this is getting farther and farther away. Get a description of him and put out an alarm."

The cop's face was white but he lowered his gun, then slid it back in its holster. "You saw him?"

"He was a shadow in the dark," Jericho said. "But these people here, they all saw him close up."

A curious moaning sound from many people, like a soft wind, seemed to fill the Mews.

"You saw him make the three attacks on the woman?"

"I did not," Jericho said. "I heard her scream. I thought it was a drunken brawl. The third time I went to the window of my studio to yell down at them, to tell them to cut it out. I saw the final attack. But I was too late to catch him."

The cop glanced at Lucinda. "You two were too busy to pay any attention to the noise of the first two attacks?"

Jericho reached out and tapped the cop on the chest. "One more crack at Miss Laverne and you're going to be in the center of a riot!"

The two men stared at each other, and a slow grin moved Jericho's lips. Then the cop took a notebook out of his pocket.

"Let's start at the beginning," he said.

The police captain's name was Welch. He had been summoned from his home and he was wearing civilian clothes. He was a sandy, wiry man with a hard face and bright bird's eyes that moved quickly from person to person, from object to object, as if constantly searching for something. When they fixed on someone or something they were intense and penetrating.

Welch sat at his desk in the precinct station. Jericho stood across the desk, facing him. A green-shaded droplight illuminated Jericho like an actor in a spot. In a far corner of the room Lucinda Laverne sat on a straight-backed chair, her hands locked in her lap. This was the culmination of three hours of waiting.

"It says here you're an artist." Welch touched some reports on his desk.

"I am."

"Subletting a studio in Jefferson Mews?"

"Yes." Jericho's huge shoulders moved impatiently inside his clothes.

"How do I know you're an artist?" Welch asked. "Anyone can grow a beard and say he's an artist. The Village is full of 'em."

"Will my credentials help you find a murderer?" Jericho asked.

"Might."

Jericho reached forward before Welch could stop him, picked up a yellow pad from the desk, then took out a thick black pencil from his inner pocket. Quick, sharp lines were drawn on the pad. Then Jericho tossed it on the desk in front of Welch. The police captain stared at a brilliant, savage caricature of himself.

"Now, before you ask me a lot of questions of the kind your patrolman did," Jericho said steadily, "I was in my studio when Mary Brady first screamed. Miss Laverne was with me. She was there to pose for a mural I'm doing. Nothing else. I was preparing paints and canvas when we heard the first scream."

"You do your painting at two in the morning?"

"Often."

"You picked the Laverne woman up on the street?"

"I did. I saw something in her I wanted to paint. I asked her to model. She agreed. Period."

"You threatened a cop," Welch said.

"I called him stupid, if that's a threat."

"You handled him."

"I tapped him on the chest with this finger," Jericho said, pointing at the captain. "Instead of hunting for a killer who was still close by, your man chose to question Miss Laverne's behavior. There were dozens of witnesses. Your man didn't seem interested in them. I was burned up."

Welch pulled a surprise. "I've seen your painting of the Birmingham race riots in the Duckworth Gallery," he said. "It's good."

"It's very good," Jericho said, a faint smile twitching the corner of his mouth.

Welch leaned back in his swivel chair. "Were the police late in coming?" he asked.

"No—not after they were phoned. The incredible thing is that dozens of people watched it happen—three separate attacks—and nobody called."

"Public apathy is a disease of the times," Welch said.

"I just can't buy apathy as the answer," Jericho said. "Among three dozen people there has to be a spark of humanity somewhere."

"You didn't pay any attention to the first two screams," Welch said. "Account for that."

"God help me, I thought it was a drunken quarrel."

"None of your business?"

"I'm afraid that's how I felt."

Welch slapped his hand on the desk. "I have a couple of dozen descriptions of the killer here. Tall, short, thin, fat"

"He was only a shadow when I saw him," Jericho said.

Welch grimaced. "We questioned the witnesses. Their answers run something like this. 'I didn't want my husband to get involved,' one housewife said. 'We thought it was a lovers' quarrel.' 'I didn't want to get mixed up with the cops.' And so on and so on. Plus 'The cops never come on time anyway.' Well, we came as fast as we could after Miss Laverne turned in the alarm. Police procedures might be improved, but we can't get to trouble till we know about it. There are men who will jump into the river to rescue a drowning man. There are others who won't. They can't swim well enough; it's none of their business; a police launch will be along presently or ought to be."

" 'Let George do it'," Jericho said bitterly.

"Something like that. But there may be more reasonable explanations for what happened tonight."

"I'd like to hear them."

"You didn't know Mary Brady?"

"Never saw or heard of her until tonight—until it was too late," Jericho said.

"Folk singer," Welch said. "Current craze of the teen-age kids. Her records sell like hot cakes."

"*That* Mary Brady?"

"That one," Welch said. "She used to sing in the coffee shops and small cafes here in the village, getting nowhere, except for a small dedicated following. Pat Zander heard her somewhere, hired her for his club. He made her into a big name in the field. She rates along with Joan Baeza, Odetta, Leon Bibb, Bellafonte, and names like that. I suppose Zander got a commission. He also got the girl. No secret they were living together."

"So?"

"We're only a few blocks from the Waterfront here," Welch said. "This Patrick Zander runs a night spot, but we've been trying to nail him for a long time in connection with loan-sharking on the Waterfront. A million dollar sideline operated from inside his hat. In spite of the Waterfront Commission, the Harbor Police, the Customs boys, the waterfront is still a lawless jungle. I've handled dozens of murders that were obviously seen, but there's never a witness—there's never a witness to any criminal act on the Waterfront. Witnesses get their backs or their legs broken, their eyes put out; their children get run over by trucks. Mary Brady was Pat Zander's girl. Pat Zander is a waterfront king. People in Jefferson Mews might have been afraid to report what they thought was a waterfront feud."

"Not everyone is afraid," Jericho said.

"A pointless point," Welch said. "Tonight everyone was involved with fear— or apathy. You pays your money and you takes your choice. The result is the same—we have no clear description of the killer." Welch leaned forward. "There's a man outside wants to talk to you."

"Who?"

"Pat Zander. Mary Brady's boy friend. You're the only person in Jefferson Mews who made any effort at all to save his girl. He wants to know what you saw and heard, I guess."

"I can't help him," Jericho said.

"Afraid to bear witness all of a sudden?" Welch asked drily.

"Don't be silly. I can't describe the man. I was too late."

Welch picked up the phone on his desk. "Send in Pat Zander."

"Can I have a drink of water?" Lucinda asked unexpectedly, from the shadows.

"Help yourself at the cooler," Welch said.

Jericho went over to the cooler, filled a paper cup, and took it to Lucinda. She looked up at him, and there was fear in her eyes. Her lips moved. "Be careful," she whispered.

Pat Zander came into the office, slamming the door behind him. Inner violence was frighteningly near the surface. He was a big man, as big as Jericho. He was ash-blond. His face was white, with two dark burned-looking holes for eyes.

"You come up with something?" he asked Welch, his voice raw.

"Nothing. This is John Jericho, who got there too late," Welch said.

Zander turned, almost toe to toe with Jericho. He had on a white sharkskin suit and a pink shirt with a black knit tie. His clenched hands were calloused rocks.

"You son of a—" Zander said. "Fooling around with a two-bit call girl when you could have answered Mary's first cry for help."

Jericho's fist moved less than a foot to the point of Zander's jaw. The night club operator's head snapped back and he went crashing down against the wall of the office. He didn't move.

"If you don't need me any more," Jericho said quietly to Welch, "I think Miss Laverne and I will take a little fresh air."

Welch's face was a study in controlled satisfaction. "That's the first time anyone's laid a hand on Pat Zander in five years," he said. "It was overdue. I suggest the fresh air in the south of France might be a good place for a painter for quite a long spell. The Zanders of this world play for keeps, Mr. Jericho."

"Me too," Jericho said. He looked down at Zander. A little trickle of blood ran down the man's chin. "Where was he when his girl was screaming for help?"

"Working," Welch said. "Running his club. We picked him up there."

"Tell him he can find me in the Mews any time," Jericho said. "Come on, Lucinda."

At a garage about two blocks from the precinct house Jericho asked for his car. It was a Mercedes which he had been keeping there while he lived in the Mews. It was fire-engine red, with a custom-built body designed to store his painting paraphernalia on long trips. He held the door open for Lucinda when the car was brought out onto the street.

They had walked briskly from Captain Welch's office, Jericho's arm slipped casually through hers. They had spoken just two sentences on the way.

"You shouldn't have done it because Pat Zander won't forget," Lucinda said. "He's got an army to back him up."

"I had a ball," Jericho said.

The top of the Mercedes was down, and they drove through the dawn up the West Side highway, cutting off in the hundreds to Riverside Drive.

"Place up here we used to call Lookout Point," Jericho said. "Nice place to watch the day begin."

Eventually he pulled to a stop and they sat there, looking down at the Hudson River and at the New Jersey Palisades, coppery red as the sun rose. There was a little compartment between the two bucket seats. Jericho opened it, revealing a bottle of brandy and a bottle of Irish whiskey. He took out two little silver cups.

"I never drink before five o'clock," he said, grinning at Lucinda. "It is now ten minutes past five. Which?"

"The brandy," Lucinda said. "I—I still haven't stopped shaking."

"All the comforts of home," Jericho said, pouring brandy into one of the silver cups. "As a matter of fact it is home. I travel around in this until I decide to light somewhere for some project. I keep a room at the New York Athletic Club to store my clothes. Haven't slept there in five years." He poured Irish for himself and raised his cup. "Here's to the few vestiges of courage left in the world."

"Being reckless doesn't necessarily mean courage," Lucinda said.

Jericho gave her an interested glance. "You mean popping our blond friend back there? It's a habit of mine. I don't like to take it from anybody. I don't stop to think it over. Mr. Zander may be a little more careful with his mouth from now on."

"Was it worth having to spend the rest of your life looking over your shoulder for trouble?" Lucinda said. She sat hunched in the seat beside Jericho. "Zander runs that part of town."

"That's the way those people in the Mews felt," Jericho said. "Better to avoid trouble than to face it. Mary Brady is dead because of that attitude. Welch called it apathy. Just plain no guts, I say."

"Not everyone can bend iron bars like you, Mr. Jericho. How many of those people were physically equipped, do you think, to face a man with a knife?"

"They didn't have to face him," Jericho said. "All they had to do was pick up a telephone."

"And be identified as the one who called the cops."

"Was Welch right—is cop a dirty word?"

"The cops never did anything for me," Lucinda said. "Oh, they'll arrest me for being on the street. With Mary Brady lying dead at their feet they ask me if I was soliciting. They're real quick about laws of that kind. You think they'll even come close to the man who killed Mary Brady?"

"I will if they don't," Jericho said.

She turned her head to look at him, her eyes wide. "You must be some kind of a nut!" she said.

"Honey, I just got my feet wet," Jericho said. "I can't back out of the water now." He took a sip of his whiskey, then looked at her gravely. "I'm really not a nut, Lucinda. You don't know much about painting, do you?"

"Nothing, really."

"You paint because you're driven to it," Jericho said. "Good painters like good poets have something to say. It may be a big thing, it may be a small thing. The poet says it in language the prose writer can't use. The painter says it in a way that can't be expressed in words at all. Maybe a small thing like 'Nature Is Beautiful.' It may be a bigger thing like 'Fascism Is Evil.' Ever see Picasso's *Guernica* or reproductions of it?"

"No."

"I'll show it to you sometime." He emptied his silver cup and put it back in the compartment. "There are people who don't think I'm a good painter. Too literary, too intellectual, too concerned with a message. To hell with them. The answer is they can't bear the truth. Same way a lot of people can't bear to hear what Freud said about the human psyche.

"What happened tonight hit me right in the middle of where I live," Jericho went on, his voice harsh. "Maybe it began with human extermination in the Nazi gas chambers. How can a man be regarded as an animal, as a subpar, subnormal citizen simply because of his race, creed, or color? Is the struggle for a democratic world just an excuse we use to cover up a struggle for power? These are all fundamental questions leading up to the big one: What is the Truth, with a capital T, about man? What is the truth about all the senseless violence, the don't-care-ism, the apathy we saw tonight, the fear to recognize a stranger as your brother—or in the case of Mary Brady, as your sister?"

"That is what I hunt for all over the world, Lucinda. The Truth. To be summed up some day in a final statement that will make all of us proud or ashamed, but in either case make us Men. Somehow in color, in design, in the emotional impact of the truth stated in visual terms, I hope to move people more than they can be by words, which can always be twisted around to mean two different things. There are no clever semantic tricks in my paintings."

He laughed suddenly. "Forgive the lecture. What I really mean to say is this: it's possible to guess how the Christians felt about the lions in the Roman arenas; but if you really want the truth about how they felt you've got to get down there with the lions yourself. I'll never know the truth about tonight, Lucinda—about all those people who stood by and watched a woman die—unless I get down in the arena.

"One way to get there was to make clear to Patrick Zander that when he calls me a dirty name he has to smile. I grew up on that line—from *The Virginian*. Zander will probably come after me, but that's the only way I know of finding out the truth about him and his world and making an unmistakable statement about it."

"And that's important to you—making a statement?"

"It's my life," Jericho said. He grinned and reached in his pocket for his pipe. He'd filled it hours ago, just before he heard Mary Brady's final scream for help. At last he got to light it. "And the next most important thing, at this moment, is breakfast. I know a special place to get it."

The Mercedes headed downtown, turned east, and moved like a softly purring cat through Central Park. The special place to get breakfast was on Beekman Place—a modestly large, immaculately kept apartment house.

"You live here?" Lucinda asked, as Jericho opened the car door for her.

"I told you, I don't live anywhere," he said.

They went into the deserted lobby to a brass nameplate board with a house phone and buttons. Jericho found the name Fanning, put his finger on the button, and held it there. With his other hand he took the phone off the hook and held it to his ear. After a long time a woman's voice shouted into the phone so loudly that Jericho pulled it quickly away from his ear.

"Cut that out!" the woman's voice said.

Jericho took his finger off the button. "Lee, my sweet. Breakfast, please."

"It's only just past six in the morning, you big ape!"

"I know."

"*Sunday* morning!"

"I know. I have a friend with me."

"You stinker!" There was a long sigh. "All right. Bring him up."

"It's a 'she,' dear."

"Double stinker!" the voice said, and there was the click of the phone being hung up.

"She's delighted to see us," Jericho said to Lucinda.

"I know. I heard her," Lucinda said.

"Her way of being affectionate," Jericho said. "Come on."

They got into the self-service elevator and Jericho pressed the button for eleven. At the end of the corridor on eleven the door to Apartment 11F stood ajar. Jericho pushed it open and gestured to Lucinda to precede him.

The living room of 11F had a charming, lived-in quality. No decorator had planned it. The rug was Oriental and costly. There was a three-paneled, carved, Burmese screen with some sort of silk Chinese robe draped over one end of it. There was a Florentine desk, with a high-backed, delicately carved armchair behind it. There was a modern, deeply upholstered couch facing a fireplace. Nothing matched, but everything looked loved.

The east wall was all windows, looking down over the East River, and sunlight poured through them. Over the fireplace was a portrait of a golden-haired woman, painted in bold, almost passionate strokes. Jericho's signature was vivid in the lower right-hand corner. On the west wall, its colors seeming almost to burst out of the canvas, was a still life of chrysanthemums. On the north wall was a self-portrait of the artist, looking like a red-bearded Viking.

From somewhere down the hall came the sound of a briskly running shower.

"Make yourself at home," Jericho said to Lucinda. "I'll see about coffee." He barged off in the direction of what was obviously the kitchen. He clearly knew his way around 11F.

Lucinda sat down in one corner of the couch. Her hands lifted to her face, and they were unsteady. She was fighting the recurrence of earlier tears. Whether she heard the shower turned off or not she gave no sign of it. She seemed unaware of the sudden appearance of Lee Fanning in the doorway.

Lee was the golden girl of the painting. She was wearing a maroon satin housecoat and mules. Her generous mouth was a little too large, her nose a little too small to describe her as a classic beauty. But you would turn to look at her because of a kind of high-headed thoroughbredness—a special, individual charm.

"Hi," she said. "I'm Lee Fanning. You are the Stinker's friend."

"Lucinda Laverne."

"Welcome to our city," Lee said.

"Where the hell is the coffee?" Jericho bellowed from the kitchen.

"Coming, Master," Lee said. She winked at Lucinda and disappeared into the kitchen.

Jericho had the coffee made and was just plugging in the percolator. Lee noticed this without comment. She walked over to Jericho and was instantly taken into his arms. His kiss was tender, curiously gentle.

She pushed herself away from him but her hands still clung to his bulging shoulders. "This is a new one," she said. "Bringing your other women around at six in the morning."

"We've had a rather shocking experience, Miss Laverne and I," Jericho said.

"Do I get the first-aid kit?"

"You, my sweet, are the first-aid—you and breakfast."

"I don't care for the linkage."

"It's the best. What have you got to eat?"

"A steak for you. Juice and toast for Miss Laverne. She doesn't look your type, Jericho."

"Model," he said. "She could probably use an egg. We were witnesses to a brutal murder. The girl is somewhat shaken. Be nice."

"She's a medium-priced call girl. Right?"

"She's to be the symbol of courage for my poverty mural," Jericho said. "I punched a guy a while back for saying she was a two-bit call girl. Don't ire me, girl."

"I could smell Irish whiskey on your mustache, bub," Lee said "What's the girl drinking?"

"Brandy. Where's the steak? You take her a drink and talk to her nice-like, and I'll rustle food."

"Murder?" Lee said.

"That's the longest double take in history," Jericho said.

"I know your kind of elaboration," Lee said. "Murder, he says and means somebody stepped on a tulip bud in the park."

"Not this time," Jericho said, his voice hard. Briefly he outlined the events of the evening, through his encounter with Pat Zander at the precinct house. "So if Lucinda suddenly starts screaming it means it's just caught up with her."

"All those people watching!" Lee said, her eyes wide.

"Apathy, the police captain calls it. How apathetic would you be watching a woman being stabbed to death?"

"I could freeze," Lee said.

"That I could understand if not admire," Jericho said. "I think I'd like to get George over here."

"He won't like being called at this time of the morning."

"He'd sell his mother into slavery for a scoop. I have a kind of scoop for him," Jericho said.

Lee waved toward the kitchen extension. "You call him, not me," she said. "I'll get your lady friend a drink and hold her hand. Steak's in the fridge."

Lee disappeared into the living room. Jericho turned on the oven broiler, found the steak, doused it with salt and pepper. Then he went to the wall phone in the corner of the kitchen and dialed a number. After five or six rings a man answered.

"George? Jericho."

"God help me," the sleepy voice said.

"I've recently been an eyewitness to a murder," Jericho said. "The police have my story, but so far no member of the fourth estate. Want it?"

"If this is some kind of gag—"

"I gag you no gags at this time of day," Jericho said.

"Where are you?"

"Lee's."

"Oh." George sounded like a man with a large wound.

"If you get over here fast you can share a steak with me and talk to another witness as well. Girl type witness."

"So help me, Jericho, if this is—"

"See you," Jericho said cheerfully.

George Godfrey, byline reporter for the *Chronicle*, leaned back in his chair, having demolished one-third of the steak Jericho had cooked. Jericho was still working on his two-thirds. The girls sat in opposite corners of the couch, coffee cups on the low table in front of them. Godfrey lit a cigarette and refilled his coffee cup. He was a sharp contrast to Jericho—medium height, dark, very gentle.

"There's something you learn about news," he said. "Lightning *always* strikes twice—or more. A few weeks ago some kookie gent out in Queens shot his twelve-year-old daughter and then himself. The girl had some incurable disease. Next day another father in Brooklyn picked up the cue—shot his small son and himself. There was a third one in Harlem a few days later. Your apathetic witnesses aren't new, Jericho. A lady bartender was killed under similar circumstances more than a year ago. Thirty-eight apathetic witnesses, as I recall. Another girl, couple of months later, was attacked and beaten to death in full view of some forty silent observers. Now your Miss Brady. There's nothing new on earth."

"Wrong, and I'll debate it with you some other time," Jericho said, putting down his knife and fork. "The world we're living in is very new, and the people around us are new, and they act and react in new ways. But we use old words to describe their new actions. Apathy!"

He snorted and reached for his pipe. "Fear is at the core of our today, George— fear of the bomb, fear of poverty, fear of people who say the hell with the law. Fear makes most of us inhuman. Waterfront war, my police captain suggests.

Maybe. Better let someone die than get involved in some sort of family feud. That would be apathy. Incredible apathy. I think something else."

"What?" George Godfrey asked.

"I think it's more likely that every damned one of those people knew the killer and was specifically afraid of *him*." Jericho glanced at Lucinda. "Not everybody is afraid of a generalized danger. But specific, identifiable danger is something else. One of those witnesses in the Mews can be broken. When it is done, the others will all remember what they pretended not to know tonight. If they can be sure the killer and his friends will be dealt with, they'll talk."

"Can you assure them the killer will be dealt with?" George Godfrey asked.

"I'll do it with my own little hatchet if necessary," Jericho said. He was smiling, but his bright blue eyes were cold and humorless.

"That could just be talk," George said. "That's not your world down there."

"The hell it isn't," Jericho said. "The whole world is my world, chum."

"Pat Zander will find the killer, Mr. Jericho," Lucinda said. "He has ways and means of covering every rathole in the city. It was his girl. It's his problem."

"It's everybody's problem," Jericho said. "George should make it the problem of everybody in New York City through his paper. I'm damned if I'm going to be like those people in Jefferson Mews who saw everything and did nothing."

"What with punching a night club king and shoving cops around you haven't left yourself in the position to carry on a quiet investigation," George said.

"My dear George, I'm the noisy type," Jericho said. "While I thunder and threaten, you will do the quiet stuff. Why do you think I got you up so early in the morning? Somewhere in Jefferson Mews there must be someone whose guts aren't too rusty. Someone who'll talk."

"It's not going to be easy," George Godfrey said. "I'll make you a small bet that your Mews is jammed at this very moment with hundreds of hysterical teen-agers grieving over the passing of Mary Brady. They'll have trampled every possible clue to death."

"She was that popular?" Lee Fanning asked.

"The goddess of folk music," George said. "This isn't just a little back-alley horror. People all over the country are going to be focusing on Jefferson Mews."

"What can I do?" Lee asked.

"You stay out of it!" George said sharply.

"For the time being," Jericho said. He pushed back his chair and stood up. "Come, Lucinda, I'll drive you home. As for you, George, down in the Mews you and I don't know each other. Connected with me you'd be useless. If we have messages for each other we make contact through Lee. Right?"

Lee reached out a slim hand and rested it on Jericho's arm. "Take care," she said.

His cold blue eyes softened for an instant. "I haven't turned my back on anyone for years," he said.

The Mercedes moved westward and downtown, through the light Sunday morning traffic. Lucinda, in the bucket seat next to Jericho, was staring straight ahead. At a pause for a changing light she gave him a side glance.

"Strange setup back there," she said.

"Oh?"

"Mr. Godfrey's in love with Miss Fanning, Miss Fanning's in love with you, and you aren't in love with anyone."

"You're really asking me a question, aren't you?" Jericho said. "There are several questions people always ask me. Am I in love with Lee? The answer is, she's the nicest girl I know. Do I sleep with my beard inside or outside the covers? The answer is, outside. Why don't I stick to my painting instead of always looking for trouble? The answer is, you don't have to look for trouble in this world—it comes looking for you. The question should be whether you face it or whether you run. I face it, because, as I told you, I'm looking for some kind of Truth. This makes me bad husband material, to get back to your question." His expression became grave. "Will your having been with me tonight mean trouble for you?"

"Who could care?" she asked.

"Someone who may think we saw more than we've so far admitted," Jericho said.

"There's something you may not know about my business, Mr. Jericho," Lucinda said, an edge of bitterness to her voice. "We don't talk. We don't talk about anything we see or hear. If we do we're marked 'dangerous' and then we don't do any business."

"Talk to me about your 'business' some other time," Jericho said. "You don't belong in it."

"I did two years in the State penitentiary for shoplifting," the girl said. "I wanted a little hat with a black veil. In this world of do-gooders you still don't get a decent job after that. They don't let you."

"Talk to me when this is over," Jericho said. He stopped the car near the corner of Eighth Street and Greenwich Avenue. "I'm letting you out here, Lucinda. No point in having anyone see you come back into the neighborhood with me. You know where to reach me—at the Mews or through Lee Fanning." He took a wallet out of his pocket and extracted several bills. "Modeling fee," he said.

"I can't," Lucinda said. "I didn't earn it."

"You will," Jericho said. "I still want you for that mural. Call it an advance if you like."

She got out of the car, clutching the money. Standing on the curb, staring at him, she looked somehow small and helpless. The red-bearded giant in the car seemed reluctant to leave her.

"Something you haven't told me?" he asked. "Something that scares you?"

She shook her head, her lips a tight red slit.

"Don't lie to me, Lucinda!"

"I'm not."

Jericho drew a deep breath. "See you around."

The girl watched the Mercedes drift away across town. Then she opened her cheap little handbag and stuffed the bills into it. She searched the interior of the bag and found a dime. She walked a little way down the block to a sidewalk telephone where she closed herself in the booth and dialed a number.

It was nine o'clock when Jericho reached the entrance of Jefferson Mews. Ordinarily it was a quiet, almost lifeless time of the day. Now the street outside the Mews was crowded with cars, including police vehicles. Two uniformed cops stood at the entrance to the Mews. They stopped Jericho as he approached.

"You got business in there?" one of them asked.

"I live here," Jericho said.

"Where?"

"Second floor studio—Number 29."

"You're the guy who slugged Pat Zander, aren't you?" the second cop asked.

"You mean I'm famous?" Jericho grinned.

"Okay, go ahead," the first cop said.

The Mews was jammed with a curiously silent crowd. They faced a building at the far end where a hearse stood outside the door. They were, Jericho noticed, mostly teen-agers. A high-pitched, hysterical sob broke the silence. Mary Brady's army of admirers was here to pay their respects.

Jericho elbowed his way quickly toward the door of Number 29. He had the uncomfortable feeling someone might recognize him as the knight errant who had failed and that he might be mobbed. He got inside Number 29 and hurried up the dark stairway to the second floor.

Outside the door of the studio, rented from an artist who had wanted to spend some months in the country, he stopped. His huge shoulders seemed to hunch inside his corduroy jacket. The door stood two or three inches open. A small dangerous smile parted his bearded lips. He took a step forward and kicked the door wide open.

Reflected sunshine poured through the northern skylight. The blank canvas stood untouched on the easel. Jericho's paints and palette were exactly as he had left them. But canvases stacked along the wall had been moved, as though someone had looked through them.

A man sat in a dilapidated wicker armchair facing the door.

The man grinned at Jericho. "Figured you'd be coming back soon," he said. He was dark, broad-shouldered, with curly black hair. His nose was crooked. Jericho realized he had seen him around the Mews before.

"How did you get in here?" Jericho asked. He was balanced on the balls of his feet, his hamlike fists hanging loose but ready.

"Passkey," the man said. "I'm Mike Guffanti. Handyman for the landlord. When the ceiling falls in or someone drops through the floor to the apartment below, I fix it." His grin was white, almost pleasant.

"So the ceiling hasn't fallen in," Jericho said.

"My being here is friendly," Mike Guffanti said. "Say how do you paint that stuff? It's real good." He waved at the paintings stacked along the wall.

"Let's stick to the point," Jericho said.

Mike Guffanti chuckled. "I heard you knocked Pat Zander cold in the police station."

" 'Heard'?"

"One of the cops in the precinct house is a brother-in-law of Mrs. Markowitz who lives down the Mews. Like a fire it spread."

"Am I a hero or a villain?" Jericho asked.

"It all depends on where you sit," Guffanti said. His smile faded. "There are some like me who think you're some kind of a nut. Cops are still around, Mr. Jericho. You could take that fancy red car of yours, pack up your stuff, and get the hell out of here—unless Mary Brady's friends decided to take you apart … I'll help you if you want to load up now."

"I'm not going anywhere, Mike," Jericho said.

"It figured. But I thought I'd make the offer. Friendly, that's me. Call you John?"

"If you want to."

"You should learn to figure the angles, John."

"Such as?"

"People around here respect you for what you did this morning. You tried to help. You were late, but you tried. But there are certain kinds of reputations you can't upset. No one's ever hung one on Pat Zander and got away with it. He can't let it happen or someone else might try. They'll be holding a nice drunken wake for Mary starting this afternoon. Crowd's already gathering. The undertaker's brought the body back. She looks real good, they say. Fellow never cut her in the face. After Pat's received the mourners, he'll come looking for you."

"I'll be here."

Mike Guffanti shook his head. "You go and that'll be that. He'll be able to say you were scared and ran. That may be good enough for him. You'll know you weren't scared, and that should be good enough for you. Peace on earth."

"I'm staying here, Mike, until we find out who killed Mary Brady and why no one lifted a finger to help her. Zander should consider me an ally, not an enemy."

"He won't."

"Why didn't anyone help her?" Jericho asked.

Mike Guffanti shrugged, pulled a cigarette out of his shirt pocket, and lit it.

"Were you in the Mews when it happened, Mike?"

Mike's black eyes danced. "Yep."

"And you didn't do anything?"

"I had a previous engagement," Mike said. "I was making love to my wife. Special Saturday night-Sunday morning edition. We don't hear nothing under those conditions."

"I've heard about you, come to think of it," Jericho said. "You're the wife-beater."

"Yep. Bertha's got a black eye right now. Wears it like a medal. Different people treat each other different. Bertha and I, we understand each other. She wouldn't like it if I treated her like one of them Park Avenue dames."

"There were a hell of a lot of people who were awake and not making love at two o'clock this morning, Mike. Why didn't they call the cops?"

Mike's eyes narrowed. "You're just slumming down here, John. You don't know what it's really like."

"I want to know."

"That why you were spending time with Mabel Chernovsky?"

"She was modeling for me," Jericho said.

Mike flicked the ash from his cigarette. "Now I've heard everything," he said.

"That's the way it was," Jericho said evenly.

"Okay, I believe you. You're a nosy type guy, John. You ever nosed around the waterfront?"

"Not the way you mean. I've painted ships."

"I saw." Mike waved toward the stacked canvases. "They look great coming up the river. But that's not the story of docks, or shipping, or pilferage, or who's in the middle. Just a few blocks from here there's a whole new world, John—a different world. The Waterfront. In spite of all the cleanup talk this world is run by big-shot racketeers who get rich on narcotics and God-knows-what-else. One of the big wheels in that world is the moneylender who has a big share of the community by the short hair. Interest, compounded. Guy borrows a hundred bucks and pretty soon he's paid back four hundred and still owes the first hundred. And they keep on paying—or else.

"Pat Zander runs a night club, but one of his real businesses is loan-sharking. Longshoreman out of work comes to Zander's back room and borrows. If he doesn't pay off Pat sees to it his neck gets broke. Zander has got to make it clear he means business. Everybody hates him, but everybody's afraid of him. It might leak over into the Mews here. Lot of these artists and writers might need to borrow a buck and they all know about Pat. So when something happens to Pat Zander's girl it looks like it might be part of the waterfront world. Who wants to get his neck broken for butting in? Let Zander defend his own. Let Zander get even for his own. No point in getting caught in a meat chopper."

"If this happened in a waterfront district I might believe it," Jericho said. "But the Mews doesn't represent any one class or type of people, social or economic. They can't all be afraid of Zander. They can't all be indifferent."

"How do you explain it then?" Mike asked. "Obviously no one but you wanted to take a chance. Frankly, I'm glad I was occupied and didn't hear it. And if you're going to play detective nobody around here's going to help you. Too damned risky. The woods will be full of Zander's boys."

"Why have you bothered to warn me?" Jericho asked.

Mike's smile was wry. "Bertha wanted it."

"Your wife?"

"Yep. It was like this, see. Once Pat Zander pinched where he shouldn't in his club on Twelfth Street. She doesn't want him to have the satisfaction of being a big shot by knocking you over."

"I don't believe you," Jericho said.

"It's my story," Mike said. He got up from the wicker chair and stretched lazily. "Help I'll give you beforehand, John, but not after you mix Pat a second time. You see, like I'm the handyman for the landlord, I could help you pack your stuff and take off. But I don't step into the middle of no war after it starts."

Jericho walked over to the square table beside his easel. He took the lid off a blue tin of tobacco and began to fill his pipe. "There's just one way you can help me, Mike," he said.

"You can try naming it," Mike said.

"Let Zander know I'm back."

Mike grinned. "Not necessary," he said. "The minute you walked into the

Mews twenty people told him. Way to show their sympathy. See?" He started for the door.

"Mike!" Jericho's voice was sharp. "Don't use the passkey again. I like my privacy."

"Sure. No need to use it again, John. I've spoke my piece."

"If anyone wants to give a real description of the man who killed Mary Brady, I'll listen, Mike."

"Don't sit up nights waiting for it," Mike said. "I feel sorry for a guy who gets into trouble because he don't know the score. But once he knows the score and still sticks his neck out—" He shrugged and was gone.

The sun poured down on the crowd in the Mews. It was going to be a hot day. The hearse moved slowly through the reluctant crowd, away from the corner house. Mary Brady's body was now lying in state in her little apartment.

A woman came out of one of the buildings across the way carrying something covered by a dish towel. Food for the wake.

On the steps of the building next to the corner house a young man with a straggly beard stood up above the crowd, a guitar cradled in his arms. He began to sing. It was a hymn, done to rock-and-roll rhythm. *I Come to the Garden Alone.* After the first few words the crowd joined him, uncertain at first, then clear and loud. It had been one of Mary Brady's favorite songs.

The woman who had delivered the gift of food returned through the singing crowd toward her own house. A thin man in a dark suit stepped out of a doorway to intercept her.

"May I speak to you for a minute?" George Godfrey asked.

The woman looked around anxiously. "You a cop?" she asked.

"Would I ask you nicely if I was?" George said, smiling.

"Reporter?"

"Yes."

"What do you want?"

"They're holding a wake for Mary Brady today?" George asked.

"Yes," the woman said. "My name is Meloney. Mrs. Thomas Meloney. Spelled M-e-l-o-n-e-y. Most people spell it with an 'a' "

"I'll make sure of it," George said. He went through the motions of making a note on the back of an envelope. "Isn't it rushing things? A wake the same day she was killed."

"Don't they sound wonderful, singing like that? It's a free day for everyone," Mrs. Meloney said. "I just took in a bowl of potato salad."

"It's a strange story, Mrs. Meloney," George said. "How so many people watched it happen and nobody lifted a finger to help Mary Brady or even to pick up a telephone and call the police."

Again Mrs. Meloney took as anxious look around. "There was that artist guy—he tried, but too late."

"But that was at the very end, as I understand it," George said. "Almost half an hour after Mary Brady screamed the first time."

"He had a girl up there," Mrs. Meloney said.

"But there were thirty-forty other people, Mrs. Meloney. They didn't all have girls or fellows. Not one of them did anything."

"Screaming isn't unusual down here," Mrs. Meloney said.

"But they *watched it happening!*" George said. "They actually saw the man knifing Mary Brady."

"It was dark," Mrs. Meloney said. "You couldn't be sure what was happening."

"You saw it? You were one of the ones who saw it, Mrs. Meloney?"

A man's voice shouted from behind them. "Sally! Get the hell back in here where you belong!"

"Excuse me," Mrs. Meloney said, and was gone.

George Godfrey took a handkerchief out of his pocket and wiped his face. He had turned at the sound of the man's voice, but he'd seen no one.

Another woman carrying a cooking kettle headed for the Brady building. George started toward her. She glanced at him and hurried on. At the same moment a big man came out of the Brady building—a big blond man. He wore a white shirt, open at the neck, and a pair of white buckskin shoes. He came straight toward George, ignoring the singers.

"You want something, bud, you might as well get it from me," the man said to George. "I'm Pat Zander."

George looked him over slowly. Zander's angry eyes were bloodshot, and there was a strong smell of liquor about him.

"I'm Godfrey of *The Chronicle*," George said.

"You got 'reporter' written all over you," Zander said.

"May I express my sympathy," George said.

"What do you care?" Zander asked.

"I'm a human being. I'm sorry for the troubles of other human beings," George said.

"You want a story. You don't give a damn," Zander said. "These people are here to pay their respects. I don't want any reporters around, making a fancy story out of it."

"How do you account for the fact that nobody was willing to help your girl last night?" George asked.

Zander looked as though he was trying to decide whether it would be fun to break George's arm.

"I talked to reporters at the police station," Zander said. "People are people. Down here they're no different than anywhere else. I'd give my right eye if one of them had the guts to pick up the phone. They didn't. It could have saved Mary—but people are people."

"If it had been my girl," George said quietly, "I'd be taking those witnesses apart one by one."

"I'll handle it my own way," Zander said. "I know how to square things for Mary."

"What are you going to do about the guy who knocked you cold in the police station?"

Muscles bulged along Zander's jawbone. "That's a private fight." He turned and looked up at the skylight of Jericho's studio.

"There's going to be a lot about this in the papers," George said. "About how nobody would lift a finger to help a famous woman in desperate trouble—just let her die on the street. These people all knew her and none of them would act. Would you say they were your enemies, Zander?"

"I'd say it was time you took off," Zander said grimly.

"My job is to get an explanation of what happened," George said. "My paper isn't going to let the story die. The people of the city are going to want to know how it could have happened—how people could stand by callously and watch three separate attacks on Mary Brady. Maybe you take a poke at me, Zander, but there are a dozen other guys to follow up for me in case I can't go on with the job. It's not good enough to make some kind of one-word explanation for what happened, like 'fear' or 'apathy' or 'indifference.' There's a story behind the behavior of these people and it's my job to dig it out. You can help or not as you choose, but the story will be dug out."

George, watching the blond giant who faced him, drew some conclusions about him. Pat Zander wasn't just an impetuous powerhouse. There was a shrewd, calculating look in the bloodshot eyes.

"I'll level with you," Zander said.

George, an experienced reporter, braced himself for the runaround.

"You could say it's mostly my fault that things happened the way they did," Zander said. "We live tough down here and I'm one of the tough ones. I've scared people into keeping their noses out of my business. Time comes I need 'em to stick their noses in and they act the way I've learned 'em to act. They don't budge. They acted the way they've been warned they should act. It was tough it worked out that way for Mary—and for me."

"You figure someone tried to get at you by attacking your girl?"

"What else?" Zander said.

"It just doesn't smell like a revenge killing," George said. "I wasn't quick and clean and certain. He hacked at her, then went away hacked at her again, then went away again. Then he came back a third time! A fumbler, or maybe a guy who got his kicks out of making it long and agonizing. Not a killer for a mob. Not a knockoff and a quick getaway."

"And it'll take me just as long as finish him when I find him," Zander said. "Long and slow and rough!"

"You and Mary got along well?" George asked quietly.

"Ask around, if you don't think so," Zander said.

"I will," George said. "If she was cheating—"

"That'll do, bud!" Zander said. "Mary never looked at another guy."

Up in the studio in Number 29, Jericho stood by the north window looking down on the Mews. He had watched George talking to Mrs. Meloney and Zander. His black pipe, cold, was gripped between his strong white teeth, and his fiery red eyebrows were drawn together in a scowl.

There was something fascinating about the slowly enlarging crowd in the Mews pressing forward toward the house where Mary Brady had lived and now lay in her coffin, the ravages of death obscured by the undertaker's art. In the beginning the crowd had seemed to consist almost entirely of teen-agers. But now there were people of all ages.

The bearded guitar player still led them in song, the voices curiously moving as they sang the music that had made Mary Brady famous, and apparently much loved. The inevitable television cameras had appeared at the mouth of the Mews, and reporters, equipped with walkie-talkie devices, were scrounging around for interviews with anyone who would talk.

A knock at the studio door turned Jericho around. With a gesture of impatience he crossed to the door and slid back the bolt. Captain Welch stood outside.

"So you did come back," Welch said.

Jericho nodded.

"This isn't official," Welch said. "You don't have to ask me in."

"Help yourself. Box seat over there by the window."

Welch walked over to the window and stood looking down at the singers. "What do you make of it?" he asked.

"Festival of Death," Jericho said. "They're all having a great emotional binge over it."

"Liquor will presently be added," Welch said. "Once they open the doors for the viewing it will start to flow." He glanced at Jericho, towering beside him. "You recognize any of the faces you saw down there last night?"

Jericho shrugged. "I've been asking myself that," he said. "There was a woman, talking to a reporter. She took some food to the Brady house. She was the one who brought a quilt to cover the body with last night. There was another woman who did some talking to the cops, but I haven't seen her this morning. The rest—"

Jericho gave an angry tug at his beard. "If there's one thing I normally pride myself on it's my ability to observe detail—a kind of photographic memory for the visual. There were dozens of faces in the windows last night, staring down at that killer knifing the girl. And now I draw a blank! It's as though they all wore identical masks. I was concentrating on the girl, and peering into the shadows for some sign of the murderer. When I yanked myself back from that and looked around for the faces at the windows they were gone."

"Only four or five people have come forward," Welch said. "They all agree with you that there were thirty-five or forty witnesses. We've talked to every person with apartments facing on the Mews. Some of them say they came to their windows too late to help. Some insist they never went to their windows at all—we know they're lying. No specific description of the man. Most of them admit they recognized Mary Brady. She had dark hair which she wore shoulder length. Unusual, attention-getting. She'd bend over her guitar when she sang and that dark hair would hang down around her face. She'd make little gestures of brushing it back from her face between choruses."

"You've heard her perform?"

Welch nodded. "A phenomenon of the times. Operating in my precinct. It got to be a habit to drop in at Zander's club around midnight to hear her. Once you started to listen to her she got her hooks into you."

"That good?"

"Very good," Welch said. "You should pick up some of her records. I don't know how to describe it—a kind of purity."

"Purity!" Jericho sounded angry. "And living with Zander?"

"Loose phrase. Only a presumption," Welch said.

"You said so yourself."

"I shouldn't have said it," Welch murmured. "Zander doesn't usually hang around a girl for a year and not make it. So we assumed—" He shrugged. "She lived here in the Mews. He has an apartment over his club on Twelfth Street. He's handled her career. Manager. But she's never seen out with other men. Oh, they crowd around her in the club, but she never went anywhere with them. She didn't drink, didn't smoke. Those kids out there think of her as a kind of angel."

"You know so much about her," Jericho said. It was almost a question.

Welch gave him a quick, shy glance. "We've been on Zander's tail for a long time. I told you we suspect him of loan-sharking. 'Suspect' is a technicality in this case. We know, but no one will testify against him. A guy like Zander could be in on a dozen rackets. So we check out on everything about him. Mary Brady was one of the things 'about him.' But I kid you not, Jericho. She had a strong appeal when you saw her as often as I did. I wouldn't like this case to go in the 'Unsolved File'."

"I wouldn't like it either," Jericho said. He walked over to the window, scowling. "There have to be people down there who'll talk, people who felt about her the way you did."

"But they won't talk to me," Welch said.

"So you dropped by for a cup of coffee and a friendly chat," Jericho said. "Coffee in that electric percolator. Help yourself."

"No, thanks."

"So chat," Jericho said sharply.

"I gave you some advice," Welch said. "South of France, I suggested. So you're still here. Again I say South of France. Will you go?"

"Don't be a fool," Jericho said.

"People might talk to you if you stay in one piece long enough," Welch said. "If they see you're back. If they see you're not scared. I think maybe the wrong girl was killed for the jungle law of see-nothing, hear-nothing, tell-nothing to hold up this time."

Jericho looked down at the singing crowd. Their voices were louder. They seemed to be developing a kind of religious frenzy.

"It's my intention to pay my respects to the dead," he said.

Welch's eyes narrowed as he lit a cigarette. "You're going to the wake?"

"Seems to be a public affair. I'd like to say a small prayer for the girl and ask her forgiveness."

"Forgiveness?"

"For not listening to her cry for help until it was too late."

"You're a romantic," Welch said.

"You're an unusual policeman," Jericho said. "Of course I'm a romantic. Love affair with life, and a feud with death. That's me."

"I have the machinery to close in with," Welch said, "if I had two witnesses."

"Two?"

"That's the law."

"The law, the law, the law!"

"It protects everyone—the good and the bad," Welch said.

"If I get on the trail of this guy I won't wait for two witnesses to settle with him," Jericho said.

"Leave the settling to me," Welch said. "I don't want to have to tangle with you."

"I'll play the cards as they fall," Jericho said.

"You'll keep in touch?"

"Fair enough. When there's anything to tell, I'll tell you."

Welch gestured toward the window. "Zander won't welcome you down there."

"I'll welcome his lack of welcome," Jericho said.

"Miss Otis regrets
She's unable to dine tonight, Madam—"
The voices in the Mews rose in the slow rhythm of a dirge. The famous satirical ballad sung by those young voices had all the quality of a genuine hymn of grief.

Jericho, now wearing a dark-gray tweed suit and a black knit tie with his white shirt, edged into the outer fringe of the crowd, moving toward the house where Mary Brady's body lay. The first few yards, gently shouldering his way through the traffic jam of mourners, attracted only some irritated glances. Then a shrill voice broke out over the music.

"He's the one! He's the one who tried to help her!"

The singing broke off in mid-phrase. They swarmed around him like a rising sea, clutching at him, babbling questions.

"You must have seen the man?"

"Why didn't you go after him?"

"Did Mary speak to you?"

"What did she say? Didn't she name him?"

"Shut up! *Give him a chance to talk!*"

There was sudden silence. Young faces, twisted by sorrow, stared at him eagerly. Jericho glanced over their heads to the door of Mary Brady's house. A line that had started to move slowly in and out of the house had stopped, puzzled by the sudden end of the singing.

"I can't help you," Jericho said in a loud voice, "but there are people here who can."

"Who?"

"Tell us!"

"Listen to me!" Jericho thundered, and they were silent. "Thirty or forty people watched it happen. Some of them must have seen clearly. Some of them could probably tell you the man's name. Ask them! Insist on an answer. I saw only a shadow. I was too late. She never spoke to me. She was dead when I reached her."

A murmuring wail seemed to run over the crowd.

"I would like to pay my respects," Jericho said.

For the moment he was one of them. They opened a way and he walked toward the house, into the shade cast by the overhanging buildings. He stepped into the line that had started to inch forward again. A man in a black suit, obviously one of the undertaker's staff, stood at the door.

"We'd like to keep the line moving," he said in a somber voice. "If you are a personal friend there are refreshments being served in the garden at the rear."

Mary Brady's apartment was on the ground floor of the house. It had not been lavishly furnished, and now those furnishings had been moved from the living room to make space for the coffin, banked by white flowers, and a dozen or so folding chairs from the undertaker's. People in the line went to the chairs, sat for a moment with bowed heads, praying, then rose and walked slowly toward the coffin.

At the back of the room Jericho his eyes bright and hard, glanced quickly around, looking for Zander. There was no sign of him. From behind a closed door in the far corner which opened into the garden came the incongruous sound of muffled laughter.

Jericho had no formal religion. He slipped into one of the chairs and lowered his head. His lips moved.

"Wherever You are, and whoever You are, help her," he said softly.

Then he stood up and returned to the line, towering over a small woman who was in front of him. This little woman reached the coffin, knelt, kissed it, rose, and moved hurriedly on. Jericho, his muscles suddenly tense, was at the coffin, looking down.

The quality of this girl had escaped him in the early hours of the morning when he had held her in his arms, the last warmth of her blood staining his hands. The moment had been incredibly violent. Now he saw her, serene in death, her dark hair framing her face. Even in death there was something about her that explained the adoration of the young people outside. She must have aroused an impulse to protect her when she was alive. It was there now—a silent plea for help.

"I'm sorry, baby," Jericho heard himself say. "I was too damned concerned with my own piddling little project."

He took a quick look around the room, stepped out of the line, and opened the door to the garden. For a moment the quiet of the chamber of death was jarred by a man's high-pitched laugh, and then Jericho closed the door behind him and walked out into the sunlight.

Two long tables, covered with white cloths, were stretched from one wall of the small garden to the other; the tables were weighted down by dishes of food. There was a cold turkey, a ham, a roast of beef, and assorted salads and relishes. There were plates of sliced Italian bread and bowls of butter. These was a large supply of liquor in bottles and many glasses. An ice machine had supplied a mountain of cubes in a cast-iron pail.

The laughter came from a group of hard-looking men. Jericho labeled them "waterfront." Pat Zander, now wearing a dark suit with his white buckskin shoes, stood in the center. Jericho didn't hear the joke that had caused the laughter.

Separated from the men were a group of about a dozen young people who seemed to represent the crowd outside. Among them was a tall sad-faced Negro. He was the only one in the garden who seemed to notice Jericho's sudden appearance. He took the few steps that brought him face to face with the artist.

"You're Jericho," he said in a husky voice. "I'm Harry Baker. I play the piano in Zander's club. Mary was my friend. I wanted to thank you for trying."

"Too late, too little," Jericho said.

"You tried," Baker said. "That's more than anyone else can say. You crazy, man, coming here?"

"I don't think so."

"Pat and his friends have plans for you," Baker said. "I don't think they'll start anything here, so that gives you time to put distance between you and them, man."

"I'm not going anywhere, Mr. Baker, until the man who's responsible for Mary's death is identified and made to pay."

"It's your hide," Baker said with a little shrug. "Want I should get you a drink?"

"No, thanks. But you can answer some questions."

"You can ask them," Baker said.

"I didn't know her," Jericho said. "How did she fit with Zander?"

The grave, dark eyes stared steadily at Jericho. "Gratitude," Baker said. "Obligation. He made her famous. She felt she owed him."

"She loved him?"

"You got to make a definition of that word—love," Baker said.

"Was there any other man?"

"All of us," Baker said slowly. "All of us loved her. But not the way you mean. No other man."

"You think it could simply have been some psychopathic stranger?"

Baker lowered his eyes. "It'll say so in the papers," he said.

"But you don't think so?"

"Man, what I think couldn't matter to nobody."

"To me," Jericho said.

Baker hesitated. "She left the club early, like she had a date. Kept looking at her watch, then left early. Pat asked me if I knew where she was going. I told him I thought she was going home. What else could I tell him? She didn't confide in me. But I thought she had a date with someone."

"No idea who?"

"No, man. And maybe if I did I wouldn't tell you. I'm like those people out there early this morning. I don't want any involvement. No, man."

Jericho was about to ask another question when the comparative quiet of the garden was shattered by Zander's voice, loud and angry.

"Out! Out of here—now!"

Jericho spun around, thinking the words were directed to him—that Zander had only just spotted him. But Zander wasn't looking at him. He had moved out of his group of friends toward the door to the house. Standing just inside was Lucinda Laverne. She had backed away at the sound of Zander's voice so that she was leaning against the closed door, her face dead-white.

"We don't want anybody like you here pretending grief!" Zander said. "Get out!"

Jericho touched Baker's arm. "Talk to you later," he said.

"Easy, man," Baker whispered.

Jericho took several quick strides across the garden so that he stood beside the trembling girl.

"I was looking for you," she said.

Jericho gave her a reassuring pat on the shoulder. His bright blue eyes were fixed on Zander's face. "This is where I came in," Jericho said.

"Later!" Zander said. "You and I will have it out later." He didn't turn but he spoke to his friends behind him. "Take a good look at him, boys. This is the one."

"I'd like it now," Jericho said.

"I don't want that woman here," Zander said. "It soils the occasion. And you soil the occasion. Better advise her to go—and you go with her."

"Please!" Lucinda whispered.

Jericho ignored her. He took a step closer to Zander. "I don't like what comes out of your mouth," he said. "I think I'd like you to apologize to the lady."

"Lady!" Veins stood out on Zander's forehead, but for some reason he controlled what was obviously an overwhelming rage.

"Now," Jericho said softly. His body moved slightly, balanced on the balls of his feet.

Zander spun around, his hands clenched at his sides, shaking. "Just go away," he said. He seemed to be strangling. "Sorry I blew my top."

Jericho stared at him, puzzled. It seemed out of character for Zander so back down, especially surrounded by his strongarm friends. Lucinda was tugging at Jericho's sleeve.

"Please come," she said.

Jericho glanced at Baker. The solemn pianist's lips moved in what might have been a silent prayer. His eyes were lowered.

"I want to make it easy for you, Zander," Jericho said. "But play it your way. Any time, any place suits me."

Zander lowered his head, apparently fighting for control. He didn't speak. His group of friends stared at Jericho hungrily.

Jericho shrugged and turned to Lucinda. "Let's go," he said.

Lucinda's arm was cold as ice. Jericho opened the door to the inner room and they stepped through into the stillness where Mary Brady lay. Curious faces lifted to look at them, but the line of mourners kept moving slowly, steadily, past the dead girl.

Jericho and Lucinda edged out into the sunlight of the Mews. The singing had stopped and the crowd had thinned a little. Most of them had worked their way into the line that would pass through the house.

Lucinda almost ran, with Jericho striding alone beside her.

"I saw you go in," she said. "I was afraid of what might happen to you."

"I don't get it," Jericho said. "Why didn't something happen? The odds were all with him and his friends."

"Witnesses," Lucinda said. "I didn't know Harry Baker and those others were there, or I wouldn't have gone in. Zander won't indulge in any public violence. The police are too interested in him, too eager for an excuse to nail him. But now you've made it ten times worse for yourself. You forced him to back down in public."

"Good for his soul," Jericho said.

"For God's sake, it's no joke!" They had reached the mouth of the Mews. "Please, Mr. Jericho, drop this. Go away."

"It's just getting interesting," Jericho said, his eyes cold. "But what about you? Will he be saving up something for you, now?"

"I—I can take care of myself," she said in a low, frightened voice.

"I think not," Jericho said. "You get a few things together and take a taxi to Lee Fanning's place. I'll phone her you're coming. Stay there for a day or two till things straighten out."

"I couldn't do that. It's not fair to involve her."

"Who will know? Which is the point, Lucinda. You just disappear for a while. If you argue with me I'll have to take you there myself."

"I don't think I—"

Jericho's hand closed over her arm and he steered her back into the Mews. A man in a dark suit stood in one of the doorways.

"There's George Godfrey," Jericho said. "Don't look at him or pay any attention to him."

He led her to a spot directly in front of the doorway where George stood. He bent toward her as though he were talking to her, but his voice was raised so that George could hear him.

"Our Lucinda has stuck her neck out, George," Jericho said, smiling at Lucinda. "I want her to stay with Lee for a while. She argues. I want you to take her there, George."

"You saw Zander?"

"We both saw Zander," Jericho said. "Lucinda isn't safe. So do what I tell you. I'll phone Lee."

"What about you?" George asked.

Jericho chuckled. " *'I'm bidin' my time'* " he said. " *'Cause that's the kind of guy I'm.'* Now you be a good girl, Lucinda, and obey orders."

Standing by the window in his studio Jericho talked to Lee Fanning on the phone.

"George is bringing her," he said. "Knowing George, he'll make certain he isn't followed. Once the girl is with you, Lee, she's safe."

"Of course." Lee's voice was clear and steady.

"I wouldn't involve you in this if I could see any way she can be traced to you, Lee."

"I don't mind being involved." And when he didn't speak, "What about you?"

"I begin to smell fish," Jericho said. "A large, decaying fish. But I can't put it together yet. So I wait here in my box seat and watch."

"Is it worth it, Jericho?"

"My darling Lee, don't you know that's my trouble—I can't mind my own business."

"I know it only too well," Lee said, a note of bitterness in her voice.

The sun rose in the sky and it was hot in the Mews. The line of viewers still seemed endless, moving slowly in and out. Sitting at his window, chewing on the stem of his cold black pipe, Jericho kept watching the door of the Brady house. Neither Zander nor any of his personal friends had left the building.

Shortly after noon Harry Baker, the piano player, walked quickly out of the house, across the Mews, and out of sight. His was the only familiar face that Jericho saw in what seemed to be an endless vigil.

Soon after that the phone rang. It was Lee. George had arrived with Lucinda. George himself got on the wire and assured Jericho they hadn't been followed. He'd taken a long excursion around and through Central Park and changed cabs twice.

"The girl says they'll wait until they can get you alone," George said. "Do you have to be a hero?"

"I have to satisfy my curiosity," Jericho said. "You want to make like a reporter again?"

"Could be."

"Check on a man named Harry Baker who plays the piano at Zander's Twelfth Street Club. I think he'd like to talk, but he's afraid to. Maybe he has a record. You might find something that would loosen his tongue."

"I don't get it," George said. "What can he talk about unless he was there and saw something?"

"He hinted to me that Mary Brady had a date last night, that she went back to the Mews to meet someone. I think he may know who that someone was, but I don't think he'll tell unless we find a way to twist his arm."

"You think the Brady girl was killed by someone she had an appointment with in the Mews?"

Jericho hesitated. "Or someone who wanted to prevent her from keeping that appointment," he said.

"Okay, I'll get on to Baker," George said. "Not that I love you, but watch your step."

As the afternoon lengthened, the line of viewers continued to file in and out. Jericho made himself a pot of coffee and a sandwich and sat by the window, watching, waiting, watching.

A little after three his phone rang again. It was Captain Welch.

"Glad you're in," Welch said. "I have news."

"Good, I trust," Jericho said.

Welch's voice sounded odd. "I have my two witnesses," he said.

"To the killing!"

"Yes. Two people who have identified the Brady girl's murderer."

Jericho's breath eased out of him in a long sigh. "Who?"

"You," Welch said tonelessly.

"What?"

"You," Welch said. "A man and a woman, both living in the Mews, identify you positively. They saw you come back three times, stab the girl each time, and then come back again and pretend to help her."

"So!" Jericho said softly. "So it's come to that. The chips are down…"

"I'm calling you, unofficially, from a phone booth," Welch went on, "I'm leaving the precinct house in about five minutes with a couple of men to pick you up. I have to act on the information."

"Why are you telling me?"

"Because I think it's a fake," Welch said. "But they can make it stick. There'll be more witnesses who'll come forward. They'll wrap you up for the D.A. like a Christmas package."

"I have a witness to what I was doing and where I was when the screaming began."

"The Laverne girl?"

"Yes."

"Not the best of character witnesses. But hang onto her in case I find you."

"In case?"

"You damned fool, I'm calling to tell you to take a powder!" Welch said, suddenly angry. "If you stay out of sight we may still latch onto the right guy. I pick you up and the case'll be closed faster than you can say Jack the Ripper. Get going—you have no more than a fifteen-minute headstart."

Jericho put down the phone and stood very still for a moment, staring down at the long line of mourners in the Mews. Then he turned quickly away and went to his closet. He changed back into his loose fitting corduroy jacket, checking on his pipe, pouch, and wallet. As he slipped on the jacket, he stared, frowning, at the stack of canvases against the wall. He seemed reluctant to leave them.

But his decision was made, and he turned abruptly, stalked out into the hall, and locked the door behind him. He moved quickly and silently down the stairs.

Mike Guffanti, ex-prizefighter turned handyman, was lounging by the front door. There was something different about him. He wasn't smiling. His face had a kind of ash-gray look to it.

"Goin' out, John?" he asked.

"The heat is suddenly on," Jericho said. "Is there a back way out of here, Mike?"

Mike Guffanti moistened his lips. "No."

"Where does that door at the back of the hall lead?"

"Basement."

"And no way out of the basement?"

"No."

"You're lying, Mike," Jericho said quietly.

Mike Guffanti moved, casually, so that he stood between Jericho and the back door. "Have it your way," he said. "But if you go out you got to go out the front."

"You've changed sides. Right, Mike?" Jericho asked.

Mike's hands opened and closed at his sides. "Maybe," he said.

"I'm leaving by the back way, Mike," Jericho said. "Let's not have any trouble about."

The ex-prizefighter raised his hands awkwardly. "You'll have to go through me, John," he said.

Jericho's left shot out and caught Mike on the jaw. Mike led clumsily with his left and Jericho's right smashed against his mouth. Mike's knees turned to rubber and he sank down, a silly smile on his bruised lips. But he reached out and clung to Jericho. Jericho tried to wrench free.

"Make it look good, John," Mike whispered.

Jericho stared at him, his eyes wide. Mike was deliberately taking a beating. No former pro would have handled himself so badly.

"Hurry!" Mike whispered.

Jericho's right raked the grinning face, leaving a scarlet bruise across Mike's cheek. Mike went down and lay on his side, his eyes closed. Jericho stepped over him and opened the back door.

It led to an alley stacked with garbage cans. There was a high board fence opposite the door, obviously blocking off the gardens of houses in the next street. Jericho bounded toward it, jumped, grabbed the top of the fence, and pulled himself over. In a small ill-kept garden on the other side he hesitated, listening. There were no sounds from the Mews, no cries for help from Mike.

Jericho found an alley between buildings. He ran along it and out onto the street. By some miracle a taxi was just cruising by. Jericho flagged it and popped in.

"Times Square Subway Station," Jericho said, and slumped down in the back seat of the cab. After they had driven a few blocks he straightened up in the seat and looked out the rear window. Sunday traffic was moderate. There was no sign of anyone tailing them.

"Something wrong?" the driver asked.

Jericho glanced into the rear-view mirror. "Running out on my wife," he said.

The driver laughed. "She don't beat you, does she? You look pretty big for the average dame."

Jericho lowered his eyes to the man's license in its metal frame. "Sean Flannery. Well, Sean, I just don't want to be caught," Jericho said.

Shrewd Irish eyes glanced up at the mirror. "I'd say no one was tailing you, but you want me to give it the Houdini treatment?"

"Whatever that may be."

Brakes squealed and cab shot east off Fifth Avenue and raced the crosstown block to Park Avenue South, swung downtown, cut east the next block, then raced back to Fifth.

"Breath easy, Mister," the driver said as he slowed his pace and started north on Fifth again. "No one following."

On Thirty-ninth Street they headed west and then up Sixth to Forty-second and west again to Times Square. Jericho climbed out and paid off.

"Thanks for the joy ride," he said.

"You could be Irish with that beard," Sean Flannery said. "Only an Irishman can run from a dame with honor."

Jericho grinned at him and walked quickly to the subway entrance. He would not be forgotten by Sean Flannery if there was a public alarm for a big man with a red beard. For that reason he had not taken the cab to his destination.

He took a Queens train and got out at its first stop on the East Side. From there he strode toward Lee Fanning's apartment on Beekman Place. In the lobby of the apartment house Jericho gave Lee's buzzer the special ring that would identify him.

There was no answer.

Frowning, he walked to the self-service elevator and rode up to the eleventh floor. No one answered his ring at the door of 11F. He hesitated for a moment, then took a keyring from his pocket, selected a key, and unlocked the door. He went in, calling out Lee's name.

Still no answer.

The two girls weren't in the apartment. Everything seemed to be in order. The breakfast dishes had been washed. The coffee percolator, half full, unplugged, stood on the kitchen table.

Jericho went back into the living room. On a small table near the front door he saw one of Lee's handbags—the one he had given her for her last birthday. He opened it. Her keys were in it; her change purse, a compact and lipstick; a handkerchief; a memo book with a grocery list scrawled on its front page. If Lee had gone out, taking another bag, wouldn't she have at least transferred the keys and change purse to the bag she took with her?

Jericho hurried to the bedroom. No disorder, and no sign whatever that Lucinda Laverne had ever been there.

Jericho returned to the living room and checked the front door. It hadn't been left on the latch. Without her keys there would have been no way for Lee to get back in without rousing the janitor for the use of his passkey.

Jericho stood in the center of the room, his thick red eyebrows drawn together in a deep scowl.

The phone rang.

Jericho moved quickly, but hesitated when his big hand closed on the instrument. Then he picked it up and spoke in a muffled voice.

"J. J.'s Delicatessen," he said.

"*What?* What the hell's wrong there, John?" It was George Godfrey.

"No women," Jericho said.

"What do you mean?"

"Just that. No women. How did I get in? I don't like to jar your moral code, George, but I have a key."

"All hell's broken loose down here," George said. "They're looking for you. Cops, plus Zander's friendly little mob. They found the handyman you beat up. But where *are* the girls?"

"I had hoped you could tell me," Jericho said. "Lee left without her keys, her change purse, and other necessary female do-dads."

"Damn it, John, I never wanted Lee mixed up in this mess."

"You told me you were sure you weren't followed here when you brought Lucinda."

"I wasn't. You must have been followed this morning in that fire engine of yours."

"I wasn't," Jericho said.

"Maybe they just went out to a movie or something," George said, not hopefully. "I told them not to leave the apartment till we knew what the score was. But maybe they got restless."

"Without a key to get back in?" Jericho asked.

"You know women—they forget things."

"All right. Now we've played that game out, how do you really figure it?"

"We're both sure we weren't followed but one of us must be wrong," George said. "But where would they go? Or why would someone force them to go somewhere, John?"

"It's part of a frameup—of me," Jericho said. "The cops know it. I was warned by Welch, the precinct captain. The killer wants me off his back. I wish I knew what I had on him that makes me so dangerous."

"You'd better get out of there, John," George said. "Do I tell Welch what's happened—that the girls are gone?"

"You tell him," Jericho said. "But tell him you found it out on your own. Don't mention me. I don't want to burden him with facts he'll feel he has to act on."

"Will do."

"Did you get to talk to Harry Baker?"

"Haven't been able to locate him yet."

"Listen, George," Jericho said. "You haven't talked to me, you haven't heard from me, you don't know where I am. Clear?"

"I don't like it, John. I'm scared for the girls."

"Me too," Jericho said grimly. "I wasn't followed here, but there might have been someone stationed across the street, watching for me. Whatever we do we'll have to do it fast. Talk to Welch, then find Harry Baker. He's our one small lead."

Captain Welch's face was a rigid mask of fatigue. He'd been called out of bed shortly after two in the morning, after one hour's sleep, to deal with the murder of Mary Brady. It was now late in the afternoon. He needed a shave. His eyes were red and dry-looking, as if they burned. He listened to George Godfrey's story without comment.

"Let me get this straight," he said. "Jericho turned over the Laverne girl to you with instructions to deliver her to Miss Fanning for safekeeping. You took her there and you're sure you weren't followed."

"Right."

"Now they're gone, without word to you, and Miss Fanning left her bag, with keys and change purse, inside the locked flat?"

"Yes."

"How do you know?"

"Because—because the keys and purse are there!"

"So how did you get into the apartment, Mr. Godfrey, to know that the keys and purse are still there?"

"Well, I—"

"Suppose you and I stop playing games with each other," Welch said wearily. "That's where Jericho went when he skipped out of his studio earlier this afternoon. You've been in touch with him there."

"No!"

"All right, Mr. Godfrey. This office isn't bugged. What you say here is to me. But if you don't want to say it, at least let's understand that I know what you're talking about. Now, you imply that somebody—probably the man who killed Mary Brady—had the girls taken away from that apartment against their will. Why?"

"Maybe he thinks they know something," George said.

"Kidnaping is a serious crime," Welch said, "We can throw the whole book at someone for that. As I said before, suppose we stop playing games. Just what does Jericho know?"

"Nothing. I mean, he doesn't know what it is he's supposed to know."

Welch's mouth twisted in an exasperated grimace.

"My guess is that Jericho thinks Zander was involved in Mary Brady's murder," George said. "But he has no evidence, no proof."

"Zander? But Mary Brady was Zander's girl!" Welch said sharply.

"I know. John knows."

"And he still thinks Zander's involved?"

"That's my guess, Captain."

"Okay." Welch lit a cigarette, puffed hard, then looked as if the cigarette had no flavor. "You want me to look for the girls. We have to walk softly, Mr. Godfrey. If it is a kidnaping, what next?"

"I'm trying to locate a man who plays the piano at Zander's club. Name of Harry Baker."

Welch's eyes narrowed. "I know him. Lives in the neighborhood. Why do you want him?"

"John thinks he knows something."

Welch took another deep drag on his cigarette. "This begins to get real sticky, Mr. Godfrey," he said. "Harry Baker used to be one of the top jazz piano players in the country. He still is—but he's not professionally reliable. He's an addict."

"Heroin?"

Welch nodded. "We know it. We could pick him up. We have picked him up a couple of times. Two trips to Kentucky. As soon as he gets back the boys find him and start him off again. Behaves himself. No point in whipping him, and we know he won't reveal his source. None of them will. Mary Brady got him his job at Zander's club. He'd been working in some dive with her when Zander discovered her. Baker owed Mary. He liked her. He might want to help, but he won't, Mr. Godfrey. They'd cut off his supply. He couldn't stand that."

"I could try if I knew where to find him," George said.

"I'll get you his address," Welch said, picking up the phone on his desk. "We know where all the addicts in our precinct live."

He asked the desk sergeant for the address and wrote it down on a piece of paper. "Your friend Jericho's a romantic type guy, wouldn't you say? Damsels in distress appeal to him. Well, he's got a hatful of them right now."

"He's a lone wolf," George said. "Kind of crusader. He runs cock-eyed risks himself, and he expects other people to run cockeyed risks. I asked him to keep Lee Fanning out of this."

"She goes for crusades?"

George's mouth tightened. "She's in love with him," he said.

"You with her?"

"Yes, God help me," George said.

Welch pushed back his chair. "I'll put a flea in your ear, Mr. Godfrey," he said. "I told Jericho we've been trying to get the goods on Zander for a long time. We have a dossier on Zander as long as your arm—suspected activities, lists of friends and associates. My flea is this: on that list of friends and associates is the name of Mabel Chernovsky—Lucinda Laverne to you."

"But according to John, Zander blew his top at the sight of her—flew at her here in your office, flew at her later at the wake."

Welch shrugged. "All the same, she is or was connected with Zander."

"What are you trying to tell me?" George asked.

"Just that she may not be in as much trouble as your friend Miss Fanning," Welch said.

George Godfrey paused on the third-floor landing of a small apartment house on Jane Street. From up above came the sound of a piano, crisply played in jazz rhythm, with a solid left hand and a virtuoso right. *When The Saints Go Marching In*, with brilliant variations.

Harry Baker was at home, and evidently feeling no pain.

George climbed the top flight of stairs and knocked on the door of the apartment from which the music came. Nothing happened until he repeated the knock several times. The music ended in an impatient discord, then the door was yanked open and the Negro piano player looked out, bright-eyed and hostile.

One look was enough for George. Harry Baker had had a recent fix and was flying high.

"I'd like to talk to you, Harry," George said.

"Some other time, man."

"Now," George said. "It's important. About Mary Brady."

A spasmodic twitch lifted the corner of Harry Baker's mouth. "You hear me playing in there, man? That was Mary's favorite beat tune. I was hoping she could hear it somewhere." His eyes narrowed. "You a cop? I don't recognize you from these parts."

George hesitated. "I'm George Godfrey, a friend of John Jericho's," he said.

"He needs friends," Harry said. "I can't help you."

"Let me be the judge of that?"

"I saw him at the wake," Harry said. "He don't make sense, man. You don't mess around with Zander unless you hold all the cards, and then some."

"May I come in and talk to you a minute?"

A little shudder seemed to move inside Harry Baker's clothes. "I don't want any part of what's going on, man. Like I said, I can't help you."

"Maybe if you won't answer questions I'll know which are the important ones," George said.

"Sorry."

"I don't want to get rough with you, Harry, but I'll tell you how it is. The whole city is looking for John on a bum murder rap. He didn't kill Mary Brady, and you know it. While he's trying to save his own skin, his girl and that Laverne woman have been kidnaped. That's supposed to tell Jericho to lay off—or else. I'll tell you this, Harry: if anything happens to that girl—Jericho's girl—neither he nor I will let up as long as we live. The first thing I'd arrange would be to have your supply cut off—forever, man. Because, in spite of what you say, I think you *can* help."

"Supply?" Harry's voice was hollow.

"Let's stop talking in circles, Harry. You know exactly what I mean."

Harry stepped back from the door. "Come in," he said. "You play kind of rough yourself, man."

It was darkish in the apartment. The only windows in the place opened on a court which the sunshine of late afternoon had passed by. Music in manuscript was scattered on the upright piano and on the floor around it. The furniture belonged with a cheap rented room. Ashtrays were piled high with old butts. There was a glossy photograph of Louis Armstrong thumb-tacked to the wall, with an inscription to Harry Baker written across the bottom of it.

"You want a drink or a cup of coffee?" Harry asked.

"I want to talk," George said. Little beads of perspiration stood out on his high forehead. It was suffocatingly hot in the small room. Stale cigarette smoke almost choked him. "Could we get a little air in here?"

"Sure," Harry said. He opened a window onto a fire escape. "I don't know what you think I can tell you. I don't know nothing about your missing girls. I don't know nothing about who killed Mary. I was playing piano at the club when she died."

"But you saw her leave the club and you thought she went to meet someone."

"Jericho told you that?"

"Yes."

Harry sprawled himself out on a couch with broken springs, which creaked. He closed his eyes. "You never got on the stuff, did you, Mr. Godfrey?"

"No."

"If you were told, or you read about it or heard about it, you still couldn't know what it's like," he said. "They had me in Lexington, Kentucky, twice. And twice I kicked it because I had no choice. And twice I came back and couldn't wait until I made my contact again. I couldn't live a week without it, Mr. Godfrey. It could get so bad that I might kill a man to get it. It's got nothing to do with who I like, or what I believe in. *I just got to have it*, and I won't do anything at all that might make it tough for me to get. I'm sorry about Jericho. He tried to help Mary. I'm sorry about your girls. *But I can't help you!*"

The expression on George's tired face was peculiarly hard and unyielding. "I guess, Harry, when you find yourself in a squeeze you have to choose. You think helping me might result in a cutoff of your supply. Which means Zander has something to do with that supply. So, much as you'd like to help, you can't."

"That's it, man."

"Well, let me show you the other side of the squeeze, Harry. I'm a newspaperman. I can bring all kinds of pressures to bear. Captain Welch lets you alone because you're a small-time, hopeless user. But if he wanted to take you in, all he has to do is catch you with the stuff. He'll catch you, Harry, because if I have to have an army watching you I'll do it."

"Oh, man!" Harry moaned.

"If we fight this thing through to a win, Harry, then Zander will be out of business—with or without help from you. But if you don't help now I won't forget you, even if we win. So figure the odds. I think your best chance would be to play our side of the street, Harry."

"Oh, man!"

"There isn't much time to think about it, Harry. If anything happens to those girls we'll go through everybody even remotely connected with it like a dose of salts."

Harry opened frightened eyes. "You don't look like a man without a heart," he said.

"I've got a heart, but right now it isn't working for anyone who won't help take the heat off those girls."

The black eyelids closed again. "Tell me how it was," he said. "Tell me how they were taken."

"We don't know," George said. Briefly he outlined what he had done. He'd taken Lucinda to Lee's apartment. He was certain they hadn't been followed. He'd left Lucinda with Lee Fanning, with instructions that neither girl leave the apartment until they had word from him or Jericho that it was safe. No one had told them it was safe, and now they were gone, with Lee's handbag, containing her keys, still inside the apartment.

Harry Baker lay stretched out on the couch, his eyes closed. His lips quivered as he listened.

"Surely, if you weren't followed," he said, "you must see how the girls were found by whoever took them."

"I don't see," George said.

"Who knew where they were besides you, man?"

"Jericho."

"Then there's only one answer, man. Just one answer."

"What is it?"

"For God's sake, George, don't make me tell you. *Think!*"

George lit a cigarette, staring with narrowed eyes at the miserable man on the couch. He was about to speak when some movement at the window caught his attention. It took an effort for him not to speak. Crouched on the fire escape was the huge bearded figure of Jericho. A silencing finger was raised to his lips.

"If no one but you and Jericho knew where the girls were then there's only one answer, man," Harry said.

"I still don't get it," George said.

Harry's body writhed. "I can tell you some places you won't find them," he said. "You know they're not at the Fanning girl's apartment. You won't find them where Lucinda lives. You won't find them in Zander's apartment over the Twelfth Street Club. They're not here—you can see that for yourself. You might look where they're still holding the wake, but I doubt they're there. Isn't that enough, man? Won't that save you time looking?"

"How did Zander locate them? I want the answer, Harry."

Harry's breath came out of him in a long sigh. "You know why it's so tough to stop the flow of heroin into this country?" Harry asked.

"How did Zander locate the girls?" George demanded, pounding his fist on the arm of his chair.

Harry spoke in a dreamy voice, as if he hadn't heard George. "Most of it comes from Italy," he said. "Grown in the Middle East, processed in laboratories in Marseilles and other places, shipped to Italy where the big shots get rich smuggling it into this country. It's hard to stop 'em because you can bring in a million dollars worth stuffed in your ear! It gets here by ship. Maybe dropped overboard in a floating package, maybe carried onto the pier by a sailor or a steward, then passed to someone working on the dock and carried off in a lunch pail. Thousands and thousands of bucks' worth, man. It's split a lot of ways. To the grower, the laboratory technician, the shipper, the carrier, the receiver on the dock."

"Zander?"

"Someone with contacts on the docks," Harry said, shaking his head as though he were in pain. "The man on the dock passes it to the pusher who gets it to me—diluted, costly. So damned costly, man."

"I'll be interested in this lecture—with colored slides—some other time," George said, angry. "Time's running out, Harry. How did Zander locate the girls?"

"Listen to me, man, will you? *Listen!* The pusher's got it on me because I *need* it. The dock man has it on the pusher, and vice versa. The man on the ship has it on the dock man, and vice versa. The shipper has it on the ship man, and vice versa. And so on and so on, back to the Turkish farmer who grows the poppies. If any one of them gets in trouble and needs help from the others, he gets help. He's got to get help or the whole chain of operation is in danger. So—"

"So *what?*"

"A boat came in from Italy yesterday. It sails back tomorrow," Harry said.

"What are you trying to tell me?"

"Man, I'm trying to help you!" Harry cried out. "I am helping—but I can't name names."

George lifted his eyes to glance at the window.

Jericho was gone.

It was dark. The night watchman on Pier X was sitting in a little cubicle reading a paperback detective story. The dark tunnel of the pier, spotted along its length by a few raw electric light bulbs, was as still as a tomb. The dark sides of a passenger liner, the Contessa Dimarco, loomed up beyond the ceiling of the pier. Lights twinkled in a dozen or more portholes, but there was no sign of life on the ship's decks.

Outside the mouth of the pier a dark shadow crept closer and closer to the watchman's booth. A few trucks clattered along the avenue underneath the West Side highway.

The shadow reached the rear of the booth. The watchman put down his paperback and began to fill a pipe from a can of tobacco. The shadow was motionless. Then, his pipe going, the watchman went back to his reading.

Instantly the shadow, crouching low, moved directly in front of the booth and onto the pier, jumping noiselessly over the protecting chain, quick and graceful as a stalking jungle tiger.

The shadow moved in the darkness of the far side of the pier from the Contessa Dimarco. It paused by a stack of crates, obviously there to be loaded on the boat the next morning. Stuck in the side of one of the crates was a cargo hook.

The shadow raised a hand and twisted the hook loose. The shadow's other hand tested the murderously sharp point on the hook's curved end. Then it moved again until it was directly opposite the gangway leading up to the Contessa Dimarco's Deck A.

Here the pier was lighter. Anyone on deck could clearly see a person approaching the gangway. The shadow crouched in the darkness, watching. A ship's officer moved casually along the deck, past the gangway, then out of sight.

The shadow came out into the open—a red-bearded man, the cargo hook grasped in his left hand. He raced across the lighted open space and up the gangway. Just as he approached the top he was hailed by the ship's officer.

"What you want? You no can come on ship!"

They met at the top of the gangway. Jericho's right hand hit like a pile driver on the man's jaw. Down went the third officer of the Contessa Dimarco with Jericho on top of him. Seconds later the man was trussed up, his own handkerchief stuffed in his slack mouth. Jericho then dragged the unconscious body into the shadows and left it there.

In a cabin on Deck A a man and a woman sat at a table drinking champagne and eating tiny caviar sandwiches. The man was clearly one of the ship's stewards, out of uniform. The woman was Lucinda Laverne. A second bottle of champagne rested in an ice bucket on another table nearby.

The door of the cabin opened—and closed sharply. Lucinda and the steward turned to see Jericho leaning against the door, the cargo hook gripped in his right hand. He was smiling, but it wasn't a pleasant sight.

"Hello, Lucinda," he said.

She slumped down in her chair, terror in her eyes. The steward rose, belligerent.

"Whoever the hell you are, get out of here!" he said.

"You have thirty seconds in which to make up your mind to do exactly as I tell you," Jericho said to the steward. "Then a rip with this—" he made an uppercutting gesture with the hook—"and a tear—" the hook glittered in the cabin's light as he slashed down with it—"and after that I'll strangle every last breath out of your body and float you away in the river's garbage."

Lucinda moved—out of her chair and toward Jericho. "Oh, John, thank God you've come. I—"

He struck her, flat-handed, across the cheek; she spun around and went crashing against the table.

"I want you to take me to Miss Fanning," Jericho said.

The steward measured his chances and decided they were nil.

"Help her up," Jericho said, gesturing toward Lucinda.

The steward helped the girl to her feet.

"John, what's the matter with you? Why—"

"Fun's over," Jericho said. "I want Lee and I want her quick."

"They brought us here," Lucinda said, "God knows why. This man—this beast—was making a pass at me. I was playing for time. I—"

"Cut it out, Lucinda," Jericho said. "There's no way they could have found you—*unless you told them yourself.* What happened? Did you phone them while Lee was in the bathroom? Never mind. I'll get it out of you later, quietly and thoroughly. Now I want Lee."

The steward shrugged and led the way into the passage and to a cabin three doors away. He used a key to unlock the door. He went in, followed by Lucinda, with Jericho and his cargo hook right behind them.

Lee sat in an armchair in the middle of the cabin, her hands and feet tied, a piece of adhesive tape plastered over her mouth.

"Untie her," Jericho said.

The steward knelt to undo the ropes. Lee, her eyes wide, stared at Jericho. The steward rose and reached for the adhesive tape.

"I'll do that," Jericho said.

His hand touched Lee's cheek.

"It's going to hurt," he said.

He loosened an edge of the tape and then gave it a quick jerk. Instantly he bent down and kissed her very gently. "When I was a kid it was always 'kiss it and make it well'," he said.

Her hands were cold as she reached up and touched his face.

The steward made a sudden dash for the cabin door. Jericho spun around and reached out with the cargo hook. The sharp point tore into the man's shoulder. He screamed and went down on his knees.

"You two girls—into the passage," Jericho said.

The girls went out. Jericho eased the hook out of the moaning steward's shoulder. "March," he said. "After them."

In the passageway Lee Fanning closed her fingers on Jericho's wrist. "The girl's one of them, John."

"I know, darling," Jericho said, his eyes very bright. "It was when I figured that—and a couple of other things—that I knew where to look for you. But there's no time to talk. We've got to get out of here, and fast."

He tapped the moaning steward on his uninjured shoulder with the cargo hook. "You keep your trap shut or I'll really use this on you."

They made their way along the passage to the deck. Out in the night air Jericho moved quickly to the place where he'd left the deck officer tied up. The man was gone.

Far away, down the pier, they heard a shrill whistle, echoed by an answering whistle much closer. Jericho stood very still, muscles rippling along the line of his bearded jaw. Then he walked over and faced the steward.

"I'm sorry about this," he said, and knocked the man cold with one sledge-hammer punch to the jaw.

Then he reached out and closed his hand over Lucinda Laverne's wrist. "We may or may not get out of this alive," he said in a conversational tone. "I did a bum job tying up the deck officer and he's spread the alarm. But you, baby—" his bright eyes were fixed on Lucinda "—you and I are going to stick together like ham and eggs, because if anything happens to us it's going to happen to you first. From me—without love! Now, down the gangway, fast."

"No!" Lucinda said.

"Don't make me twist it off, baby."

"They won't let me off the pier," Lucinda said, her voice shaking. "I'll be the first one they'll go for, John—because I know too much. They'll never let me get away."

"After all the help you've given them, baby?"

"Because I know too much, I tell you!"

The whistle and its echo sounded again on the pier, closer this time. Jericho felt Lee's fingers grip his left arm. She was frightened.

"Back inside," Jericho said. "There has to be a way through to the deck on the other side."

They went back into the main saloon. There were still no signs of life on the ship itself, except the sudden sound of the ship's bells. From a wall rack Jericho took two life preservers. "Run!" he said.

They made for the other side of the ship and came out onto the deck. Jericho heard his breath come out in a long sigh of relief. The berth next to the Contessa Dimarco was empty. Silently he got the two girls into the life preservers. He stared down into the rippling black water.

"I can't see in the dark," he said, "but there are probably ladders down the pilings of the next pier to the water. You climb up on the rail, Lee, and I'm going to give you a push—well out from the ship. Make for the pilings. If we don't catch up with you, climb out and get away from here as fast as you can. But no noise. We want them searching the ship for a bit. Grab a taxi and get to Captain Welch at his precinct station, or turn yourself over to a cop, if you see one."

Lee nodded, her lips compressed. She climbed up onto the rail, clinging to one of the stanchions.

"No worse than a Coney Island roller coaster, darling," Jericho said. And he pushed her, hard.

The splash sounded small and far away.

"Now, baby, your turn," Jericho said to Lucinda.

"I can't swim!" she cried out.

"I go with you, baby," Jericho said. "You're my prize, my brass ring. I don't want anything to happen to you, you little double-crosser, until much later." He hoisted her onto the rail and climbed up beside her, still hanging on to her left wrist. "Now!" he said.

He projected them both out into the darkness and toward the water.

Lee Fanning, swimming strongly toward the adjoining pier, was almost certain she'd heard the impact of Jericho and Lucinda hitting the water behind her, but she didn't turn to look back. She reached the pilings of the pier and, in complete darkness, felt around until she found the ladder Jericho had said would be there. Clinging to it, she looked back for Jericho, just as a searchlight from the wheelhouse of the Contessa Dimarco swept the water.

Lee clung to the ladder, praying. She saw no sign of Jericho or Lucinda in the beam of light. The light swung Lee's way. She drew a deep breath and lowered herself below the surface of the water, holding her breath until she thought her lungs would burst, until she had to surface. The light had passed.

On the deck of the liner she heard excited voices. The light was suddenly extinguished. Either the men on the ship had decided they'd gone a different way, or they were already making for the next pier to greet them.

Still clinging to the ladder, Lee managed to unfasten the cumbersome life preserver. Then she climbed up toward the dark outlines of the pier. She reached the top level and quickly ran through the opening into the sanctuary of the pier itself. It was a great black tunnel. There were no lights here. Apparently no ship was docked on either side of this pier.

Dripping wet, her golden hair matted around her face, Lee raced for the street. There was confusion out there. She heard many voices raised in what sounded like commands. Then she heard shots.

At the mouth of the pier she hesitated. The watchman of this pier had left his booth and run out to the street. He stood with his back to Lee, watching what was going on.

Lee heard a little sob of relief come up out of her throat. Outside, the street was jammed with police cars. Ignoring the watchman, she ran straight out into the clear, her wet clothes clinging to her legs, as if they meant to hold her back. She shouted as she ran, and then two policemen, climbing out of a patrol car, their guns drawn, saw her.

"There are two others—back in the water," Lee cried, as she stumbled toward one of the cops.

And then, unbelievably, she heard a familiar voice calling her name. A moment later she was in the reassuring arms of George Godfrey, who kept saying her name over and over in a broken voice.

Captain Welch came into his office from the main section of the precinct station. Lee was there, wrapped in a warm coat, holding a towel with which she dried and fluffed out her blonde hair. George stood by her, protective, anxious. Someone had produced a pint of whiskey from which Lee had evidently had a stiff drink.

"Nothing," Welch said, his face grim. "They didn't come up onto either pier. We've got a police launch searching the river."

"Oh, my God," Lee whispered.

"You didn't hear any shots, Miss Fanning?"

Lee shook her head. "Not till I'd gotten onto the next pier and headed for the street. But the shots I heard came from the street."

"There were shots on the street," Welch said.

"John is a powerful swimmer," Lee said.

"But he had the girl to deal with," Welch said.

"Where do we stand?" George asked.

"In the middle of nowhere," Welch said. He sounded angry. "Let's go over it once more, Miss Fanning. You and the Laverne girl were in your apartment. Take it from there."

"Naturally I trusted her," Lee said. "John wanted her protected. She seemed exhausted. She hadn't had any sleep, she told me. I knew she'd been with John when the Brady girl was killed, and had been up all night until he brought her to my place for breakfast. I suggested she try to get some sleep, and I bedded her down in my room and left her there with the door shut.

"I puttered around the apartment. I had my hifi set playing some records. There was a knock at the door and I went to it." She shrugged. "I should have played it cautiously, but the whole thing hadn't really added up for me then. I just opened the door the way I would normally. I suppose it was about an hour after Lucinda had gone in to lie down."

"There were two men there?" Welch asked.

Lee nodded. "They barged into the place and one of them grabbed me. At that moment Lucinda came out of the bedroom. Then I knew. She'd phoned from the extension in the bedroom. She knew the men. One of them said 'Nice going,' or something like that. I was hustled out into the hall and to the elevator. A third man was waiting in the elevator. He'd turned off the juice so that no one else could use it. We went down. There was a car at the curb."

"You didn't get the license number?"

"I never got a chance to see it. We were driven straight to the pier—onto the pier itself. I didn't see any watchman."

"Conveniently having a quick beer across the street," Welch said. "We've talked to him. He admits he left his post, but he doesn't know anything." Welch made an angry growling sound. "Never any witnesses on the waterfront."

"The only person we saw on the boat was the steward. You'd have no difficulty identifying him. John wounded him in the shoulder with a cargo hook."

"But he hasn't been found," Welch said. "You could, obviously, identify the three men who took you to the pier. But it's a hundred to one you'll never lay eyes on them."

"Zander?" George asked.

"At his Twelfth Street Club all evening," Welch said, "in plain view of a hundred and fifty customers. The Zanders of this world are always thoroughly alibied when there's trouble. Indirectly, Harry Baker tipped you off to the ship and you tipped us, too late. But that's all you'll ever get out of Baker. He'd rather cut out his tongue than talk directly. His 'supply' depends on his silence."

"But Lucinda knows everything!" Lee said.

"She isn't going to do us much good if we find her and Jericho floating around in the North River, drowned corpses."

Lee raised a hand to her mouth.

"I don't say that's it. But that's the pattern. If they didn't get away that's how we'll find them." Welch paused to light a cigarette. "I'm going to give you a lot of pictures to look at, Miss Fanning. Mug shots. There's a chance you may recognize one or more of the three men who took you to the pier, or the steward. I'm not hopeful, but it's a routine we have to go through."

"And what do we do about John?" Lee asked.

"We wait and hope," Welch said.

"If he hadn't tried to handle it himself, if he'd only called you instead of trying to be a big shot," George said.

A thin smile flickered on Welch's lips. "I think I understand your resentment, Mr. Godfrey." He glanced at Lee. "But let me tell you something that as a policeman I shouldn't say. If he'd come to us the chances are pretty good they'd have been warned. When we arrived at the pier in force they had definitely been warned. The only safe witness is a dead witness. As a cop I shouldn't say it, but I don't think Miss Fanning would be here now if Jericho hadn't acted on his own. The minute we began to board that ship she'd have been silenced for keeps."

The evening at Pat Zander's Twelfth Street Club had been a strange one. It was, in effect, a continuation of the wake for Mary Brady. Early in the evening

Zander had made an announcement from the little platform where Harry Baker's piano stood.

"All of you know," he said to the assembled customers, "what a sad day this is for us. A great talent has been snatched away from us, brutally and without mercy. It had been my intention to close the club out of respect to Mary. But then it occurred to me there was one thing Mary would have liked. Not grief, not sorrow, not mourning. If she'd known it was coming she'd have liked to give a party for her friends. And so tonight is on Mary. No checks. Harry here will play some of the ballads and songs she loved so much and that you loved to hear her sing. She'd like you to have fun, I think, so don't be sad. It would please her to know that she could say 'thank you' to all of you in this way."

And so Harry, looking unnaturally bright and tense, played the piano, and eventually people began to sing. It never got raucous. Somehow the free drinks didn't lead to any excesses.

There was another odd thing about the evening. Zander never left the main room of the club. Ordinarily he spent the better part of the evening in his office, appearing only when he was needed. On this occasion he sat at a corner table alone, listening to the music, waiting—waiting for something.

Three times during the evening he received phone calls. He took the calls on the bar telephone in plain sight of the customers. He looked grim and taut as he listened, but he only spoke in monosyllables. Shortly before midnight he received a fourth and final call. It was lengthy, and as he listened, a knot of muscles moved along his jaw.

Shortly after that final call he signaled to Harry and mounted the music stand again.

"I hope you've all enjoyed yourself," he said to the crowd.

There was a ripple of applause.

"I'm going to close early now," he said. "As most of you know, the funeral will be tomorrow morning at ten." His voice broke. It would have been difficult to tell whether it was real or faked. "I want to spend the remaining time with— with Mary."

There was a moment of silence, and as Zander stepped down from the stand, Harry Baker began to play *When The Saints Go Marching In.* Ten minutes later the Twelfth Street Club was empty.

Zander left the club and walked the few blocks toward Jefferson Mews. Certainly he knew everything that had happened during the evening. Certainly he must have assumed that he was being watched. He looked neither to the right nor to the left. Far from being a time of mourning, the evening had been a solid alibi. Let them watch. He was clean.

The Mews was unnaturally quiet. The inevitable record players, radios, and TV sets were still. Ordinarily at midnight there were many lights in many windows. Tonight the residents of the Mews seemed to have retired early. Perhaps Zander was too preoccupied to notice this as he walked toward the house where Mary Brady lay in her coffin.

Zander was just a few yards from the door when a bulky figure moved out of the shadows.

"Hello, Zander," Jericho said in a sold, angry voice.

Zander stopped in his tracks. "So you got away." It was almost a whisper.

"Yes, friend, I got away," Jericho said.

"I ought to take care of you here and now," Zander said. "But it's out of my hands. The police are looking for you." His voice was suddenly loud. "You damn murderer!"

"That's right, Zander," Jericho said. "Turn up the volume. Because people are listening. Look around you, friend. Look up at the windows."

Zander's head jerked up. In the darkened windows of the Mews he saw faces—dozens of them.

"Don't worry," Jericho said. "No one will call the cops or give the alarm. You trained them, friend. You filled them with a nameless terror over the years, and they won't interfere. Just as they didn't interfere when you knifed Mary Brady to death."

"You're off your rocker!" Zander said, loud, with a kind of hollow defiance. He looked around at the windows. "Someone—call the cops!" he ordered.

The shadows in the windows remained motionless.

"You missed your calling, Zander," Jericho said. "You should have been an actor. My God, those cries of rage when a little street-walker entered on stage. A wonderful act, Zander, designed to let the world think you had no connection with Lucinda at all."

"Cheap, two-bit—"

"Hold it," Jericho said grimly. "I'm telling the story to your next-to-last audience, Zander. Your final audience may be a judge and a jury. I say 'may be' because it's just possible you won't live to face them."

"You crazy son of a—" Zander yelled. "Somebody call the cops!"

The shadows remained frozen in place.

"Mary Brady has been mourned today, and rightly," Jericho said. "She submitted to you, she was grateful to you, but when she found out the real truth about you she wouldn't let you go on. She came here last night to stop you—you and your go-between.

"Oh, Lucinda walked the streets all right. But not for the purpose most people thought. She was your delivery girl. She delivered the drugs you brought in off the docks. Mary Brady came here last night to watch the transaction, to get the final proof she needed. And you came after her and stopped her. Not quick and easy, because no one crosses you, Zander, and gets away with it quick and easy.

"And all these people watched, and all those people did nothing because they knew they would be next if they tried to involve you. Apathy, the papers called it. Not apathy, friend. It was cold, stark, gut-grinding terror. Well, ducky, now they're going to have a chance to watch again, and unless I'm wrong, they'll watch in silence. And even if they don't you've got no place to go. It's me or the cops, and either way you're finished."

"Where is Lucinda?" Zander asked, his voice hard.

"Where you won't find her," Jericho said. "All wrapped up and ready to deliver to the District Attorney. Ready to name names, dates, places. Right now it's between you and me, Zander. You had hands laid on my girl—filthy hands that worked for you. I'm afraid you may be able to talk your way out of that one in court. I don't suppose we'll find the men who did the job. You'd make sure of the safety of your own mob.

"But you've been careless about your own safety, Zander. You've been so careful about alibis. That figured. It also figured you wouldn't draw a gun and shoot me dead when I faced you here. You wouldn't be carrying a gun tonight, would you, ducky? There was just a chance Welch might pick you up. That was the first gamble I took in waiting for you here. If I'm wrong you'd better pull it now, because this is the moment of truth, ducky!"

For a moment the two men faced each other, motionless. Then Zander moved, quickly. He ripped off his coat, there was a clicking noise, and a beam of light reflected on a knife blade.

Jericho laughed. "Toys, yet," he said, and rushed in.

They said afterward that you could hear a shuddering breath of fear from those windows float over the Mews like a cold winter wind. They said there was no question in their minds what the outcome would be. Zander was invincible, Zander played by no rules; the red-bearded giant, showing a courage they all lacked, would be hacked to pieces by Zander's knife. Was foolhardy courage worthy of applause?

They said afterward that they looked around for Zander's friends. They were sure those friends would appear. Some watchers turned away from the windows—they couldn't bear their own cowardice. But then, when they heard the agonizing scream, they were forced back to see the end—the end of heroism, the end of decency.

What they saw was Zander down on his knees. They saw the knife lying on the ground a few feet away. They saw Zander's right arm hanging, obscenely crooked, helpless, at his side.

Those who had watched said that Jericho had moved like a ballet dancer inside the first slash of the knife, had caught the knife hand at the wrist, twisted it, and then broken it over his knee—like a man breaking a piece of kindling wood. They heard, they said, the splintering of bone. And then they all saw the red-bearded giant grab Zander by his shirt, pull him halfway to his feet, and smash a shattering blow to Zander's jaw that sent him sprawling and broken to the cobblestones.

No one timed it. It may have taken thirty seconds.

"The water was damned cold," Jericho said. He held a highball glass in his hand and the Irish whiskey in it was dark. He was scowling at the blank canvas on the easel in his studio in the Mews. Lee Fanning was pouring coffee for George Godfrey and Mike Guffanti, the janitor. Captain Welch had joined Jericho in a drink. "I'll have to get a new idea for this," Jericho said, turning away from the canvas. "That girl!"

"I've never cared for your taste in women—except me," Lee said.

Jericho seemed to wrench himself away from the blank canvas.

"When that searchlight came on I knew we weren't going to make the next pier," he said. "We had to submerge till the light passed, then we floated down the river and paddled our way to a pier about five or six blocks farther downtown. By the time we crawled up on a deserted pier we were damn near pooped out. But the lady was ready to talk. Oh, boy, was she ready!

"She'll make a statement, Welch. Last night she was standing on a street corner, waiting to deliver heroin, when she got word of trouble. Zander, on his way to the Mews, told her Mary Brady was about to spill the beans. Lucinda was about to take off when I came along—the big-hearted artist, seeing courage in her white face. Ha! What I took for courage was plain, white terror! So much for my remarkable gift for reading character in a face. She came with me because she knew that from my studio she'd probably see or hear what happened between Zander and Mary Brady."

Jericho took a deep swig of his drink. "Lucinda had to play along with me so she could warn Zander if we were getting close. In the end she knew we were, so she phoned from Lee's and the kidnaping followed."

"Well, to get back to that pier. The little lady spilled all. But she wasn't any good to you as a witness to the murder, Welch—she hadn't actually seen it. You needed a witness, so I decided to give you dozens of them—all those people in the Mews. If they could see Zander faced down and beaten, their fear of him would evaporate.

"I thought I had a friend here—Mike Guffanti." Jericho grinned at Mike, who winced as his battered face tried to smile back. "He was afraid too, but he had helped me get away from here ... Well the girl and I dried out as best we could, and a soggy ten dollar bill got us here in a taxi without any questions. Mike and his wife agreed to stand guard over the girl while I waited for a rendezvous with Zander. That's about it."

"You're right about the witnesses," Welch said. "About twenty of them have come forward naming Zander as the killer of Mary Brady." He looked at Jericho with a kind of wry admiration. "I'm glad I'm not your insurance agent, Jericho."

"One favor," Jericho said.

"I owe you more than one," Welch said.

"Go easy on Harry Baker. Poor devil, he's a lost soul. But without him we might never have found Lee—at least, not in time. I'd like to help him—money, doctors, whatever. And I'd like you to let him alone if you can."

"I can," Welch said.

Jericho nodded abstractedly. He turned back to the blank canvas. "I've got to have a new idea for this," he said. "Any of you got any ideas?"

Lee Fanning sighed.

Jericho and the Nuisance Clue

Mr. Jules Obermeyer played a very minor part in the drama of "the night of the nuisance." Jericho referred to him as the man who made a small piece of history in an age of indifference and don't-care-ism, an age when dozens of people watch murders and don't lift a finger to help the victims.

It was about a quarter of an hour before midnight when Jules Obermeyer went through a usual routine. Jules Obermeyer, a certified public accountant, did everything by routine. That night he stood by the open bedroom window of his fifteenth-floor apartment in a new building in New York's East Sixties, and he breathed. It was his nightly custom to take twenty carefully counted, deep inhalations of what is facetiously called "fresh air" in the city. Columns of figures danced before his eyes as he slowly inhaled and exhaled. Suddenly he stopped at the eleventh exhalation. His eyes widened. His tongue licked at dry lips.

Standing on a narrow ledge that ran around the fifteenth-floor level of the apartment house across the street was a woman. She stood with her back pressed against the wall of the building, her arms spread out like a drooping crucifix.

"Hey!" Jules Obermeyer shouted in a voice that couldn't have been heard eight feet away. "Hey, you!"

The woman stood motionless. It seemed to Jules Obermeyer that she was staring down at the street.

It was then that Jules Obermeyer carved his special little niche in history. Without hesitation he went to the phone and called the police. It seems impossible that no one else saw that transfixed woman, but it is a matter of official record that Jules Obermeyer's call was the only one the police received that night about the woman on the ledge.

Mickey Greenspan's Third Avenue saloon could never be considered one of New York's architectural landmarks. It had seen its first sunlight a few years back when the Third Avenue El was removed. It was being slowly squeezed out of existence by the great towers of stone and glass that grew up around it month by month. Progress was its mortal enemy. But Mickey's place waited for the wreckers' ball and chain with uncommon vigor and almost joyful defiance. It would go down laughing at what it considered the present day's inability to enjoy life.

For 30 years Mickey's place had been a headquarters for raucous and ribald wit. It was a place for drink and talk. Mickey had never allowed a television set to interfere with the spontaneous entertainment supplied by writers, artists, actors, famous sports figures and other celebrities who were the regular clientele. James Thurber had left his mark on the east wall. Otto Soglow's little king stared innocently, but with a subtly indicated passion, at a lush blonde nude on the north wall. Over the back bar a red-bearded giant pushed aside encroaching modern buildings with bulging biceps; it was a self-portrait of the artist, John Jericho.

On the "night of the nuisance" Jericho was sitting by himself at Mickey's bar, drinking a bourbon on the rocks, watching and listening with a relaxed feeling of well-being. Whenever he was in town, Jericho made the pilgrimage from his studio in Jefferson Mews to Mickey's place. He was bound to find some friends there, certain to get a couple of laughs out of the visit; there was always a good chance of sparkling conversation, an almost lost art these inarticulate days.

Jericho was one of Mickey Greenspan's favorites. There was a special flamboyance to the giant, red-bearded artist that seemed to belong to another and earlier time, yet suggested a kind of eternal youth. Mickey knew that the artist had to be about forty years old, but the six-foot-six two-hundred-and-forty pound body suggested some Viking warrior who had come down through the ages, unmarred by time.

Mickey, who would have had to stand on a chair to look levelly into Jericho's bright blue eyes, loved the big man for his gentleness and good humor under normal conditions, but he had been awed in the past when, on a few occasions, Jericho had been spurred into physical action in the little bar. Mickey envied big men and tended to dislike many of them because they were apt to be bullies. Jericho's instinct was to side with the underdog, to cast his lot with the short end of the bet. Mickey knew very little about art, except what had been scrawled on his walls by the famous and near famous; but he knew that Jericho rated high with the museum people.

On this "night of the nuisance" Jericho had chosen to stay at the bar, chatting idly with Mickey, rather than join a dozen or so friends and acquaintances in the drinking room at the rear of the establishment. The bar sitters were usually transients who came in for a quick one and a hello to Mickey, and moved on. The men in the drinking room were there for an evening's fun.

Jericho hadn't seen any particular favorites of his back there and had chosen to stay with Mickey. He had only just returned from Saigon where he'd done some sketches of the bloodletting. He felt disinclined to talk about it and he knew he'd be questioned in the back room. Mickey's genius as a bartending host was that he let you choose your own subject matter, or be silent if that was your pleasure.

Three empty bar stools separated Jericho from the dark, dapper little man who sat brooding over a pale drink in an old-fashioned glass. Two things caught Jericho's attention about this silent brooder. He kept checking his watch with the Swiss clock behind Mickey's bar as though the exact time was of enormous importance to him. And the pale drink was not liquor—it was ginger ale.

"Hit me again," the dark man would say to Mickey in a harsh voice, and Mickey would blandly pour him another soft drink.

The dark man was not much bigger than Mickey, but he suggested violence— explosive violence. Jericho, whose artist's gift for detailed observation seldom failed him, recognized the bulge under the dark, tailored jacket as a holstered gun.

"Your clock's a couple of minutes off," the dark little man said to Mickey.

"If you say so, Lou," Mickey said.

Jericho raised a red eyebrow. That Swiss clock was Mickey's pride and joy. He swore by it. He would normally argue about its accuracy.

The dark man turned black smoldering eyes on Jericho. "What time have you got?" he asked roughly.

Jericho smiled. "I go by Mickey's job up there," he said. "Set my watch by it when I came in."

Which wasn't so.

"I asked you what time it is," the dark man said angrily.

"Time for another drink," Jericho said, and pushed his glass toward Mickey.

A nerve twitched on Mickey's cheek as he refilled Jericho's glass. His voice was strident as he put the glass down in front of the artist.

"You asked me for Bill's telephone number," he said. "I'll write it down for you."

Mickey scribbled something on the back of a bar chit and handed it to Jericho. On it was written a name—*Luigi Marriotti*.

The dark man's lips were a thin menacing slit. "I'm waiting to get the time from you, buster," he said to Jericho.

Jericho's smile was lazy. "Christmas is a long way off, buster," he said.

"Big guys like you give me a pain in the neck," Marriotti growled. "You think your muscle is something, don't you?"

Luigi Marriotti's name was a synonym for violence. He was a notorious crime lord who somehow managed to stalk the city streets, untouched by the law.

"It's like the old days in the West," Jericho said amiably. "The fast gun was always a target to somebody ambitious to make a reputation of his own. Big guys like me are always being picked on by little punks like you."

Marriotti's right hand twitched at his side. He glanced at the clock behind the bar. It showed exactly ten minutes before midnight.

"You better finish your drink and get out of here before I take care of you," Marriotti said.

Jericho held up his glass and swished the liquor around on the ice cubes. "Please, mister," he said, his voice mocking, "pick on somebody your own size, will you?"

"You hide a pretty big mouth behind that red beard," Marriotti said.

"All the better to eat you with, Hood," Jericho said.

"Maybe I better tell you who I am," Marriotti said. A pulse beat at the side of his pale forehead.

"You don't need to tell me," Jericho said. "I know who you are, buster."

"Then you must know you're a big dumb ox for tangling with me," Marriotti said.

A curious silence had closed down over Mickey's place. The voices in the drinking room were suddenly quiet. A dozen men had left their tables and crowded in the archway to the bar, watching, listening intently.

"You're not drunk, Marriotti," Jericho said. "You've started this trouble with me deliberately. Care to tell me why you're making a nuisance of yourself?"

"I don't like guys who hide behind whiskers," Marriotti said.

Jericho gave Mickey, whose face was the color of ashes, a puzzled look. "It doesn't make sense," he said.

"Why don't you just take a walk around the block," Mickey said in a hoarse whisper. "I'll straighten things out with Lou here."

"Stay out of this, Mickey," Marriotti said hoarsely. "I'll show this wise guy he can't open his big mouth at me. I'll make sure he remembers this night."

"I too would like to make it memorable," Jericho said gently.

Marriotti was not the first man to be surprised by the speed with which Jericho could move. If the gangster meant to reach for his gun he was much too late. Jericho's big hands fastened like iron hooks on Marriotti's upper arms and the gangster was lifted like a small child into a sitting position on the bar.

Jericho then calmly reached for a large plastic ice bucket. He turned it upside down over Marriotti's head and jammed it down like an oversized derby hat. Ice cubes and cold water poured down over the neat black suit. There was a muffled cry of almost insane rage as Marriotti struggled to lift the bucket off his head.

Jericho grinned at the pale Mickey. "See you around," he said, and walked leisurely out of the bar and onto Third Avenue.

Jericho had always considered his physical strength as a special gift for which to be eternally thankful. He was not vain about it, or inclined to show off as the scene in Mickey's place might have suggested to the unknowing. But the accident of muscle and vitality had placed him, all his life, in the position of being asked for help. He had always given freely and generously to causes—especially lost causes—but it angered him to be used.

Marriotti, sober, had picked on him for a purpose. The gangster could have had nothing against Jericho personally—their paths had never crossed. Jericho's presence at Mickey's had been unannounced. If Jericho hadn't been there, Marriotti would probably have made a nuisance of himself with whoever else might have been sitting on a nearby stool. Why?

The whole thing smelled of "alibi" to Jericho. Marriotti had gone to great lengths to call attention to his presence in Mickey's at a certain time. Normally this business-man of crime would have remained in the shadow, but the carefully prepared alibi was a special technique employed by the Marriottis of this world. Jericho knew that if he waited until morning he'd probably read in the paper about a crime that Marriotti had planned and for which he would be suspected. But the scene in Mickey's place would now provide him with an ironclad alibi—Jericho would be that alibi.

Standing in a darkened doorway across the street from Mickey's place Jericho chewed on the stem of his black curve-stemmed pipe, wondering if there still might be some way to keep Marriotti from using him.

Back in Mickey's place Marriotti played a big scene—a scene of outraged dignity and open threats. He announced that Jericho was a walking dead man. Mickey, his pale face damp with sweat, tried to dry the gangster off, soothe him, help him to make himself presentable after his ice bath. All the time Mickey wondered how he could get to the telephone and warn Jericho to leave town until Marriotti's rage subsided—if ever.

Behind Mickey's bar a miniature Swiss yodeler popped out of the clock and yoo-hooed the hour of midnight. Marriotti checked with his wrist watch. His rage suddenly subsided. His threats were now uttered in a surprisingly conversational tone. He allowed himself to be led to the Men's Room by Mickey where he carefully combed his matted hair. He assured Mickey that he held nothing against him—only against the red-bearded artist who would pay for this night's insult to the great Marriotti.

After that the gangster walked briskly out of the bar where bedlam instantly broke loose. The customers were all convinced they'd been in on the prelude to a murder—Jericho's murder. Marriotti would never forgive the grotesquerie of that ice bucket.

There was a thin satisfied smile on Marriotti's lips as he hailed a taxi outside Mickey's place. He gave an address in the East Sixties. He didn't notice the second taxi which pulled away from the curb on the other side of the street.

Marriotti's taxi wasn't able to take him directly to the address he'd given the driver. The street was blocked off by the police. Marriotti showed no sign of irritation as he paid off the driver, walked away from the cab, and headed toward the crowd that blocked one end of a side street.

As he reached the edge of the crowd he spoke to a stranger at his elbow.

"Suicide?" he asked.

"Not yet," the stranger said.

It was then that Marriotti saw that all the faces in the crowd were turned upward. His own head went up and he seemed to freeze as he spotted the woman standing on the fifteenth-floor ledge of the building. His lips moved in some kind of soundless oath.

Then he began to elbow his way almost savagely through the crowd. As he reached the inner ring of people he could see the fire engines and police cars grouped in front of the building. A uniformed cop stopped him.

"End of the line," the cop said.

"You stupid moron, that's my wife up there!" Marriotti shouted.

Captain Whitfield of the local precinct station stood outside the door of Apartment 15G in the building where the woman stood on the ledge. With him was the building superintendent and a plainclothes detective. At a distance down the hall, held back by a uniformed patrolman, were other tenants of the building who were being urged to go back to their own apartments.

The geography of the situation had been made unpleasantly clear to Captain Whitfield by the building superintendent. Apartment 15G was at the end of the hall. The ledge on which the woman stood ran across the front of the building, but not around the corner. The only way to get to her on the ledge was from inside her own apartment. The superintendent had used keys to open the door of 15G, but a strong inner chain temporarily prevented their entering it. Whitfield had sent a man for a cutter to snap the chain.

The super didn't know the woman on the ledge. The apartment belonged to tenants who had gone away on vacation and lent the premises to a couple named Smith—Mr. and Mrs. George Smith. The super had never spoken to either of the Smiths.

The door of one of the two elevators down the hall opened and a small dark man, accompanied by a patrolman, hurried toward Whitfield.

"This is the woman's husband, Captain," the patrolman said. "George Smith."

A nerve twitched on Whitfield's suddenly darkened face. "Your name isn't Smith," he said. "I've seen a thousand mug shots of you, Marriotti."

"So Smith, Jones, Brown!" Marriotti shouted. "That's my wife out there. I can get her in. What are we standing here for?"

"She put the chain on the door," Whitfield said. "I've sent for a cutter. Why would your wife want to commit suicide, Marriotti?"

"How should I know? I was coming down the street and there she was. But I can get her in. She'll come back in for me."

"Let's hope so," Whitfield said. "Why are you calling yourself 'Smith'?"

"Because we'd get no peace from the other tenants—staring and prying—if they knew I was Lou Marriotti."

The second elevator door opened and another patrolman, accompanied by a giant of a man with a bright red beard, came hurrying toward 15G.

"This is the woman's husband, Captain," the second patrolman said. "He thinks he can get her in."

Marriotti spun around as if he'd been stung. "You!" he exploded.

"I never saw this man before," the superintendent said. "The first guy's her husband all right."

"Some crackpot! Get him out of here!" Whitfield ordered.

Jericho gave him an amiable smile. "My name is John Jericho," he said. "I had to get in here somehow. If you want to check on me call Lieutenant Pascal of Homicide." The bright blue eyes turned to Marriotti. "If you let him into the apartment, Captain, the woman will jump."

"You son of a—" Marriotti said. "Get out of here!"

"This isn't a suicide, Captain," Jericho said. "It's an attempted murder. If you let Marriotti near that woman she'll jump."

"Nobody can get near her till that chain is cut," Whitfield said. Something about the big man with the red beard disturbed him. He sounded quite calm and not at all like a crackpot.

A patrolman came along the hall with a heavy steel cutter that would snap the chain.

"A hundred to one there's someone else in the apartment," Jericho said. "He may try to come out shooting."

"This drunken jerk is out of his mind!" Marriotti said. "He attacked me in a saloon on Third Avenue not half an hour ago. Trying to make a big shot out of himself. He followed me here just to make trouble. Get him out of here, Captain."

The cutter snapped the chain.

"Don't let Marriotti near the woman," Jericho warned again. "And watch your step. There's someone else in the apartment."

Whitfield pushed the door open with Marriotti crowding behind him.

The living room of the apartment was a mess. Two chairs had been overturned. Someone had pulled at a cloth on the center table, overturning a lamp, ashtrays, and books. A brass candlestick lay almost at Whitfield's feet; there was a dark red stain on it.

"Lorraine!" Marriotti yelled, and started for the open window.

He didn't quite make it. Jericho reached out and caught him by the back of his coat collar. The gangster was yanked back and Jericho's huge fist ripped an uppercut to the jaw that snapped Marriotti's head back, cruelly. The crime lord crumpled to the floor.

"Okay, Jericho, you're under arrest," Whitfield said.

Jericho's smile was white and cold. "Not till I've had a look in the next room," he said.

Whitfield pulled his holstered gun. "Stand right where you are, Jericho."

"Don't shoot me in the back, Captain," Jericho said. "At least not till I show you what's in the bedroom."

He turned and walked calmly through the door at the far end of the room. Whitfield and the plainclothes man followed, both with drawn guns.

The bedroom was empty.

Jericho walked to the bedroom-closet door. "You'd better come out with your hands up," Jericho said. "There are two armed cops with me, friend. You haven't got a chance." There wasn't a sound. "Have it your own way," Jericho said. He pulled open the door, jumping aside as he did so.

Standing inside the closet, crowded against the hanging clothes of "Mr. and Mrs. Smith," was a man. His hands were raised. In his left hand was a bloody handkerchief. A little trickle of blood ran down his forehead.

Jericho turned to Whitfield. "Know him, Captain?"

Whitfield nodded grimly. "Rowdy Burke. Muscleman for Marriotti. Okay, Burke—out!"

"Figures," Jericho said. "Will you give me a chance at the woman, Captain? I think I know the right thing to say."

He didn't wait for an answer. He went to the open window in the living room and looked out. His first glance, downward, made his stomach flip. Then he turned his head to look at the woman. Her face was a gray-white, her eyes closed.

"It's all right, Lorraine," he said. "We've got both of them—Burke and Marriotti. The police have them. They can't hurt you any more."

The woman's eyelids fluttered. She was really no more than a girl, and under other circumstances her face would have been beautiful.

"I promise you, Lorraine, they can't hurt you," Jericho said. He reached around the window frame as far as he could, but he was still a couple of feet short of the girl. He turned to Whitfield. "Take hold of my belt," he said sharply. He stood on the sill with the Captain hooked firmly onto his belt. Now his hand was only inches from the girl.

"Just one step to your right, Lorraine, and I'll be able to hang on," Jericho said.

"I—I can't move," the girl whispered.

"Try! You've got to try!"

He could see the enormous effort she made. With her eyes still closed she inched toward him. Then fingers like ice touched his.

"Just a little farther," Jericho said.

Then his big hand closed like a vise over her wrist. "Easy does it," he said, "easy."

Then she was back in the room, sobbing wildly, clinging to the bearded stranger.

"Rowdy tried to throw me out the w-window," she cried. "I fought him—hit him with a candlestick. But—but I couldn't get out the door in time. My only chance was to get into the next apartment. I—I went out there, b-but I—I turned the wrong way. Then I couldn't move. I just c-couldn't move. He—he was afraid to come after me, but he knew that sooner or later I'd fall, or I'd come back to the window and he could—could push me out. Oh, my God, my God!"

Jericho drank hot coffee in the Captain's office at the precinct house.

"I still can't figure how you knew," Whitfield said. "How could you be sure Burke was in there?"

"Someone had to be," Jericho said. He reached in his pocket for his black curved-stem pipe and oil-skin pouch. "I'd had an encounter with Marriotti earlier tonight, just as he said." He described the incident at Mickey's place. "I figured he was setting up an alibi. I was hopping mad, Captain, so I decided to follow him and see what it was all about. I didn't like being a patsy for scum like Marriotti. When I saw the woman and heard Marriotti tell the cop on the street that she was his wife, everything clicked."

"I still don't get it," Whitfield said.

"You don't set up a careful alibi for a *suicide*, Captain," Jericho said. "How do you know exactly when it's going to happen? Prospective suicides don't tell you in advance. If they do they're pill takers or wrist slashers who want to be saved in time. Now, how could Marriotti know his wife was going to jump out a window at precisely the time he had covered himself with an alibi? He couldn't—

unless it was planned beforehand, and you don't plan someone's else's suicide—not the window-ledge kind.

"So it seemed clear to me, when I saw her up there, what Marriotti was up to. One of his boys was to do the job. She wasn't to be knifed or shot—that would result in questions. She was to be cold-bloodedly thrown out a fifteenth-story window. If she fought—if she was bruised—no one would ever know after she hit the pavement. Fortunately, you got the alarm before Burke could find a way to get her off that ledge while Marriotti was covering himself with an alibi."

"But how did you know Burke was still there?"

"The chain, of course," Jericho said. "He had to be there. He couldn't put the chain on *after* he left, and she certainly hadn't come in from the ledge and then gone out there a second time. Burke had to be there. The man who turned in the alarm made things happen too fast for Burke to get away. He had to finish the job or face Marriotti's wrath. But he had waited just too long and then he couldn't leave without being seen."

Jericho held a match to his pipe. "The motive will come out when the girl is better able to talk. Maybe he was interested in another girl—the Marriottis of this world take what they want. He didn't dare walk out on Lorraine—she probably knew too much. He had to get rid of her and at the same time keep her quiet forever. And he had to have an alibi because it was probably well known that the marriage was on the rocks. Any violence surrounding a Marriotti gets questioned. An alibi was essential."

"If you hadn't come when you did," Whitfield said, "we'd have let him go to the window and he'd have managed to scare her into jumping."

"That's what he was hoping," Jericho said. "And in the excitement Burke could easily have slipped away. What did you say was the name of the man who turned in the alarm?"

"Jules Obermeyer. Building across the street," Whitfield said.

"I'd like to buy him a drink," Jericho said. "We don't have too many responsible citizens around town these days."

Jericho and the Dead Clue

The rain beat against the windshield of the red Mercedes. The windshield wipers fought a losing battle against the torrent of water. The night was pitch-black except for an occasional jagged flash of lightning in the distance, which revealed the trees bent by the swirling wind. Jericho, his huge body crouched over the wheel, was straining to see the few yards ahead of the car which was all the vision of the narrow dirt road his headlights revealed. Damn the gas-station attendant who had told him this short cut would save him five miles in reaching the Foster estate! In places the road had been so encroached upon by brush it was almost impassable.

Fortunately the Mercedes was only creeping through the storm when Jericho saw the girl just eight or ten yards ahead of him. She was sitting in the middle of the road, cradling something in her lap. The brakes squealed as Jericho came to a stop a few feet in front of her.

She sat there, bent over the thing in her lap, apparently unaware of the cones of light that surrounded her. She was wearing some kind of open-necked blouse and slacks. Her hair was matted to her head.

Jericho swore. He had no raincoat or hat in the car. He sounded the horn. The girl didn't move. Jericho turned up the collar of his tweed jacket, opened the car door, and stepped out into the wild night. The rain slashed at him. He stepped over to the girl and bent down, water running off the tip of his red beard.

He touched the girl's shoulder. She didn't move. She was still bent down over the thing in her lap. Jericho saw that it was a large dog, a Golden Retriever he thought. A tongue lolled grotesquely out of the side of the dog's mouth.

The girl said something he couldn't hear over the rain and wind and the distant rumble of thunder.

"What?" he shouted at her.

She looked up at him. Her face was small, pert, tragedy-twisted. "I think he's dead," she said in a high thin voice.

"You can't sit here in the middle of the road," Jericho said.

"I—I can't lift him," the girl said.

"I'll help you."

"Can—can you make sure he's dead? I mean—if he isn't and moving him would be painful—"

Jericho squatted close to her and raised the dog's head. The side that had been in her lap was smashed in like a broken eggshell. Jericho sensed the sticky feel of blood in the palm of his hand.

"He's dead," he said.

"Please help," the girl said. Her mouth was drawn down at the corners. Jericho couldn't distinguish rain from tears. For a moment he thought she might be only twelve or thirteen. Then, as he bent closer to get his arms under the dog's body, he became aware of the smell of liquor on the girl's breath.

He lifted the heavy dog into his arms and carried it over to the side of the road. He started to put the body down. The girl was at his side, her slim shoulder touching him. He could feel her shaking.

"We can't leave him here," she said.

"Where?" Jericho shouted at her.

A flash of lightning revealed her small tortured face. He was angry, annoyed, soaked to the skin, but he felt pity for her. She waved vaguely down the road.

"My cabin is about a hundred yards in from the road," she said. "Could you— would you—?"

"I can't leave my car here," he said.

"There's a place to park just ahead—on the right-hand side," she said.

He couldn't be any wetter than he was. He put the dog's body down on the grass. "Show me," he said.

She knelt beside the dog, a hand on the shattered head. "It's just a few yards," she said.

Jericho went back to the car, muttering to himself. He got in and pulled ahead. He saw a little area cut out of the brush and a narrow path leading away into the darkness. He parked the car, got a flashlight out of the glove compartment, and went back to the girl.

"You light the way," he said.

She stood up and took the flash. Jericho lifted the dog again and followed. The girl's judgment of distance was faulty. He guessed it was closer to three hundred yards before they came into a clearing. He saw a feeble light burning in the window of some sort of shack.

The girl reached the door and opened it. She stood aside.

"You want him in the house?" he asked.

"Where else? This is where he lived," she said.

The light came from an old-fashioned kerosene lamp. The shack consisted of one large room. There was an iron sink in one corner with a pump-handle device that evidently produced water from a well. There was a kerosene stove, a double bed, a box spring on an iron frame, covered with a torn spread and some cushions. There were two overstuffed armchairs, a small table with a wooden kitchen chair pulled up to it. On the table was a jelly glass, an empty bourbon bottle, and one half full. Beside the bed was a new and modern-looking AM-FM radio, obviously battery operated. At the foot of the bed, on the floor, was a small mat covered with an old army blanket. The girl pointed to it.

"That's Igor's bed," she said. "Will you put him there, please."

Jericho put the dog down and stood up, flexing his aching arm muscles. The girl had gone to a bureau and came back with a bath towel which she handed to Jericho.

"Help you get a little dry," she said.

He took the towel and dried his thick red hair and his bearded face. The girl got a towel for herself. When she had dried her hair a little he saw that it was long and blonde. She went over to the stove and got a second jelly glass, then poured two large drinks of bourbon into the glasses.

"You don't want to get pneumonia," she said.

There was a strange elfin quality to her.

"You camping out here? Vacationing?" he asked.

"I live here," she said.

He took a long swallow of the bourbon and was grateful for its quick warmth.

"I'm sorry about your dog," he said.

Her lips quivered. "I—I just don't understand it," she said.

"It's pretty hard to see anything in this storm," he said. "If I hadn't been crawling I'd almost certainly have run you down."

"It's the first time Igor has ever left me since—since David went away," the girl said.

"David?"

"My David," the girl said. "He left me the shack, and he left me Igor. Igor has never gone twenty yards away from the shack before unless he went with me. But tonight, in this storm, he went all the way out to the road. I just don't understand it."

"So he wandered off. I'm sorry. You didn't see or hear a car?"

"You couldn't hear a motor in this storm, and you can't see lights on the road from here. Igor asked to go out. I thought he must have an upset stomach or something because he's afraid of thunderstorms. When—when he didn't bark to come in again, I finally went to look for him. I—I opened the door and I—I thought I heard him howling—far away. Of course, it could have been the wind. I ran down the path and finally, when I reached the road, I stumbled over him.

I—I think he was still alive then. But he died while I was trying to comfort him. Another slug?" She pointed to his glass.

"Thanks," he said.

She poured him a generous refill. "You're wondering about me," she said.

"Well, yes, I am."

"David brought me here," she said. "I mean it was the only place he could bring me to after his family cut him off."

"Cut him off?"

"They didn't approve of me," the girl said. There was a threat of underlying hysteria in the high voice, in the compulsive rapidity of her words. "I had been a hostess in a discotheque in Vegas. David was there on leave. We—we got together."

"And his family cut him off because of you?"

"That left us up the creek because of course David couldn't get a job—he was still in the Army. But he did own this shack, and there was Igor, and there was the Jaguar convertible which he turned into cash. David deeded over this place to me in spite of everything Milo could do, and he told me to wait here till he got back—which would be about a year—and he—"

"Back from Vietnam?"

"Only he isn't coming back," the girl said, her teeth chattering against the rim of the jelly glass as she swallowed her bourbon. "Missing in action. And Milo tells me there's no use waiting, and I should go somewhere, and if I should happen to be pregnant he will arrange for—"

"Milo. I'm on my way to visit a man named Milo Foster. Is he—?"

"David's father," the girl said.

"Were you married to David?"

The girl shook her head. "David thought it wouldn't be fair. He thought it might happen just the way it has happened. He'd turn up missing, or something, and I'd be tied to a ghost—that was the way he put it. But he gave me all he had. This shack his father gave him when he was a kid, and Igor. And the money from the Jaguar. And it's almost a year now."

She glanced down at the body of the dog. "Maybe it's the best way out for poor Igor. Because there isn't much money left and soon I might've had to turn Igor over to the SPCA. That would have killed him because David told him to stay with me and he did, every minute of every day and night—until tonight. If Igor had any time to think about it before he died, he must have thought God had struck him dead for disobeying David's orders."

"You loved David?"

"If he had asked me to lie down and let a truck run over me I would have.

Loved him?" Her voice rose. "He was the only decent thing that ever happened to me in my whole life—him and Igor. So I will wait here for him forever—or until the Army changes the word 'missing' to 'killed in action.' As long as there's a chance for him to come back. I'll be here when he comes. No matter what Milo does! No matter what!"

Jericho drew a deep breath. "My name is Jericho," he said. "John Jericho. I'm a painter."

Her eyes widened. "David was a painter, too," she said.

"I know."

"You've seen his work?" Her excitement was high.

"No. But Milo Foster is giving a new wing to a museum in David's name. That's why I'm on my way to see him. To arrange the details."

She seemed to freeze. "Does he know David is dead and hasn't told me?"

"I don't know."

Her hands reached up and touched the sodden lapels of his tweed jacket. "Will you find out? Will you please, please find out for me? Because if David is dead and Igor is dead—"

"What will you do?"

"I don't know," she said vaguely. "Go back to where I was—or maybe take a handful of sleeping pills. I don't know."

"What's your name? You haven't told me, you know."

"Angel Kelly," she said.

A flash of lightning revealed the Foster mansion. Jericho had the absurd notion that he was looking at the castle of the Wicked Witch in *The Wizard of Oz*— turrets, towers, battlements. Lights blazed in dozens of windows.

The violence of the storm had decreased by now, the lightning being of the "heat" variety. The wind had let up, but the rain was still heavy and steady. Jericho glanced at the clock on the dashboard of the Mercedes. It was just a few minutes past midnight.

As Jericho pulled up at the front of the house a man in a black slicker and black rainhat came running down a short, wide flight of stone steps carrying a bright-colored golf umbrella.

"Mr. Jericho?" A dark face peered through the side window of the car.

"Yes."

"Mr. Foster was very worried about you, sir," the man said. "He was about to alert the State Police. Your bags, sir?"

"In the trunk," Jericho said.

"If you'll give me the keys, sir, I'll get them. You take the umbrella."

Milo Foster was impressive. He couldn't quite match Jericho's six-feet-four-inches, but he was almost as broad and powerful-looking, even though he was ten years older. Curly white hair glittered in the bright lights of a huge entrance hall. Behind him on the stuccoed walls Jericho recognized a priceless Velasquez and a Chagall he had never known existed.

Foster's smile was white and wide, his handshake rock-hard. "My dear fellow, I'm relieved to see you," he said. His face clouded. "You're soaking wet, man. Tire trouble?"

"A small adventure, thanks to a filling-station man who assured me there was a short cut over the mountain."

"On a night like this? Idiot." He turned to the black-slickered man who appeared with Jericho's bags. "Take Mr. Jericho's bags to his room, Max. See that he has what he needs. I recommend a good solid whiskey or brandy, Jericho. Can I have some food ordered for you?"

"A drink would be fine," Jericho said. "And a hot shower."

He followed the slickered Max to the foot of a wide winding stairway—and was confronted by a vision. His painter's eye told him he was looking at one of the most beautiful women he had ever seen. She was dark, tanned by the sun, tall, lithe, with a magnificent figure that was not hidden by a bright scarlet floor-length housecoat.

"Miss Arabella Khalkis—Mr. John Jericho," Foster said.

The girl's smile was dazzling.

Miss Khalkis is—was—David's fiancée," Foster said. "Mr. Jericho will join us in the library when he's had a chance to get into some dry clothes, my dear."

"I look forward to that," Arabella Khalkis said. "I'm a great admirer of your painting, Mr. Jericho."

"I am instantly an admirer of yours, Miss Khalkis."

She looked pleased. Khalkis? It rang some sort of bell in Jericho's memory. One of the Greek industrial tycoons? If so, Arabella must be the heiress to a fabulous fortune. It would seem that drowned rat of a girl in that miserable shack in the woods, crooning over the body of a dead dog, could never have provided a moment's competition for Arabella Khalkis.

Max took Jericho to a high-ceilinged bedroom. Again there were paintings—a Benton, a Wyeth. Foster's interest in art was genuine, his taste impeccable. There was a fully stocked portable bar next to a giant fourposter. Max put the bags on a folding rack, then opened the door to a bathroom, revealing a black marble tub as large as a small swimming pool.

"Would you like to soak in the tub, sir, or would you prefer to use the shower?"

"The shower will be fine," Jericho said.

"Can I make you a drink, sir?"

Jericho glanced at the bar. "Bourbon on the rocks, please." Max, he saw, with his rainhat removed, was handsome in a way—dark, aquiline, only a thin scar running from the corner of one eye up into the coal-black hairline spoiling a kind of rugged perfection.

"You had trouble on the mountain, sir?"

"I ran into someone who had trouble," Jericho said.

The black eyes narrowed. "A girl, sir?"

Something warned Jericho. "A dog," he said. "Run over by someone in the storm."

"I see." Max drew a deep breath. "You'll find the library across the hall to the right when you come downstairs, sir."

"Thanks," Jericho said.

A steaming hot shower, dry clothes, and a stiff drink made a new man of Jericho. He found Foster and the beautiful Arabella in a book-lined library. There was another portable bar, and on a side table were a cold ham, cheeses, breads, crackers, olives, shrimps with a Russian-dressing dip. Arabella sat in a high-backed armchair next to a low-burning fire. The flickering flames cast mysterious light changes on her lovely face.

"Max tells me that you came on an injured dog on the mountain road," Foster said.

Jericho crossed to the bar and made himself a drink. He was aware of being watched closely. "A dead dog," he said. He poured bourbon on the rocks. "The girl is alive." He turned and looked at his host and Arabella. Foster's smile was gone. Arabella's expression was unchanged—a kind of mysterious inner amusement.

"I almost ran over the girl," Jericho said. "She was sitting in the middle of the road holding the dog in her arms."

"Too bad," Foster said. "The dog was a valuable dog, extremely well-bred."

"Unlike the girl," Arabella said, smiling into the fire.

A small muscle rippled along Jericho's jaw, under the red beard. "I found the girl refreshingly loyal," he said.

"So you met Miss Angel Kelly," Foster said.

"I met her."

"Most extraordinary and inexplicable situation," Foster said. "Would you believe it, Jericho, that the first night David met her he paid her for the time they spent together?"

"A common tramp," Arabella said.

"There's essentially no difference between the street girl who demands five dollars on the barrelhead," Jericho said, "and the society girl who insists on cocktails, caviar, and a visit to the Royal ballet before she says 'yes.' "

"Even five dollars would seem to be an exhorbitant price to pay for that scrawny little plucked chicken," Arabella Khalkis said.

"But loyalty can't be bought," Jericho said.

"Loyalty!" Foster exploded. "She's sitting there, waiting for the news that David is dead. She thinks then I will pay her to get out of my sight."

"Then why don't you tell her the boy is alive?" Jericho said, deadly quiet.

"If only we knew," Arabella said.

"Where have you got him hidden?" Jericho asked.

Foster's face had turned to stone. "What are you talking about?"

"The fact that you can't buy loyalty," Jericho said. "The girl has it. The dog had it. Is David here in the house now?"

"He's missing in action—in Vietnam," Foster said.

"Are you trying to convince me he's not here?"

"You're out of your mind, Jericho!"

"You can't buy loyalty, particularly from a dog," Jericho persisted. "That retriever had never gone twenty yards away from Angel Kelly until tonight. Whom would he leave her for?"

"Another dog," Arabella said.

"I think not. I think the dog left Angel Kelly to follow his master—David."

"*She* told you that? The girl told you she'd seen David?" Foster exchanged a quick glance with Arabella.

"She didn't see him," Jericho said. "I suspect he went to see her. Maybe, in view of your plans for him, he just meant to catch a glimpse of her without her knowing. Maybe you discovered he was missing, went after him, and got to him before he could reach the cabin. But the dog sensed his nearness."

Foster stood very straight and still. "You have come here as my guest, Mr. Jericho. We have tried to offer you every courtesy. You repay us with this lunacy. Arabella and I have both suffered too much from the tragedy of David's probable death to be subjected to this cruel and senseless melodrama. I must ask you to leave."

"I offer you an alternative," Jericho said. "Let me search the house for David. Otherwise I will have the proper authorities here with the proper warrants before you can whisk him away to some Greek island paradise—which I take is your plan."

The door to the library opened and the man called Max came in. He was wearing a dark suit with a black turtlenecked sweater. He had a machine pistol tucked under his arm. Jericho smiled at him.

"I see you are readier to believe I mean business, Max, than your employers are," he said.

"Why, Jericho? Why?" Foster cried out in a shaken voice.

"I'm an admirer of loyalty," Jericho said. "The dog and the girl are getting short-changed for theirs."

Arabella leaned her dark head back against the high-backed chair, still smiling. "Have you ever heard of Theofiledes Khalkis, Mr. Jericho? He is my father. He has money enough to buy anything he wants. He was even able to buy David's release from a Vietcong prison camp."

"Then why not a ticker-tape parade up Broadway? Escaped war hero! No, Miss Khalkis, David is a deserter and you and your father—and his father—are helping him to avoid the consequences."

"Have you no sympathy, no pity?" Foster cried. His rock-hard exterior was crumbling.

"Yes, I have sympathy for any man who wants to get out of a war," Jericho said. "I just might turn my back on his efforts to escape such a horror. But he said to the dog, 'Stay till I come back,' and he said to the girl, 'Stay till I come back,' and they both did exactly what he asked. And now he will slip away without their knowing—at least for a long time—that they have been discarded. I don't choose to turn my back on that, Foster. Quixotic? Perhaps, but that's the way it is."

"What is your price, Mr. Jericho?" Arabella asked. "Every man has his price."

"And your father can pay whatever it is?"

"Yes."

"Your father couldn't pay my price," Jericho said.

"What is it?"

"David Foster must go to that cabin in the woods. He must help the girl bury their dog. And then he must tell her that he no longer cares for her, that he chooses freedom and the glamorous Miss Khalkis. I think Angel Kelly might understand that—but she must be told by him. That is my price, Miss Khalkis."

"There is another alternative, Miss Khalkis," Max said quietly. He lifted the machine pistol. "Let me use this."

"Does your father also pay your gunman, Miss Khalkis?" Jericho asked.

Arabella rose and stood, straight and lovely, by her chair. "Everything in the world is paid for by someone who wants it badly enough, Mr. Jericho," she said. "I want David, and my father will pay anything required to get him for me. Your disappearance might cause a ripple or two, but no one in the world could trace it to this house or to us."

"Then you'd better get on with it," Jericho said, "because you can't count on any promise I might make you under pressure." He had gauged the distance between himself and Max and he knew he could never cover even the few feet of Turkish rug and stay alive.

"I'll give you one last reasonable argument," Arabella said. "I admit that David had doubts. He didn't want to go away without explaining to that little tramp in the mountain cabin. We made it clear to him that if he saw her she could ruin his chances of getting away. He finally seemed to see the light, but when we had relaxed he took off for the mountain. Max went after him, but it proved to be unnecessary. David got to the shack, peered through the window at her, and knew that he had been dreaming a false dream. He came away without letting her know he'd been there. He had made his choice."

"Then he was a damn fool," Jericho said. "Maybe Angel Kelly is better off. Any man who would choose to be a pet poodle on a Greek island instead of a real man living with a real woman deserves someone like you, Miss Khalkis."

"You are being a foolish, old-world knight in shining armor, Mr. Jericho. Why on earth should you give up your life for that stupid slut?"

"Because I would have to live with myself if I let you have your way," Jericho said.

Arabella turned with a weary shrug of her lovely shoulders. "Take him away, Max. Do what has to be done," she said.

"No!" Foster cried out. "Not murder. There has to be some other way."

"Max!" Arabella said.

"Come on, buster," Max said to Jericho, the machine pistol aimed at Jericho's heart.

"You're going to have to do it here, Max, right on the Turkish rug. I want Foster and Miss Khalkis to live with the picture of it for the rest of their lives."

Arabella turned again, her eyes blazing. "If it must be that way, so be it. Max!"

Okay, Jericho thought, his muscles tensing, I can at least die rushing him.

There was a sharp knock at the library door. It opened and a maid in a black and white uniform came into the room.

"I'm sorry to interrupt, Mr. Foster," she said, "but Mr. David said I should give you this immediately." She crossed to Foster and handed him a folded piece of paper. She seemed not to see Max or the machine pistol. Then she turned, and hurried out of the room.

Foster unfolded the paper. A nerve twitched high up on his cheek. A great physical weariness seemed about to overcome him. He steadied himself with a hand on the back of a chair. His voice was low and hoarse as he read aloud.

" 'Father: I have been listening, and Jericho has made it clear to me what a heel I've been. I have betrayed the only two people who really love me. Poor Igor! He followed me home after my cowardice and Max ran him down. Igor's presence here would have been a giveaway, wouldn't it? And Max would have killed Angel if she had seen me! Well, it's too late now, Father. I've gone back to the mountain and I'm going to turn myself in. If I have to pay for Angel and her loyalty with a piece of my life in jail it will be worth it … David.' "

"Idiot!" Arabella said.

"Surely you wouldn't want an idiot for a husband, would you, Miss Khalkis?" Jericho said. He was smiling.

"Get out!" Arabella said.

"Thanks," Jericho said. He glanced at Foster. "I think you can start being proud of your boy." He moved toward the door. Max had turned his head toward Arabella, expecting some last-minute change of heart. Jericho's move was deadly. He ripped the machine pistol out of Max's hands. His right fist struck with sledge-hammer force to the man's jaw, hurtling him back against the wall where he slid down and lay still.

"That, friend, is for the dog," Jericho said, and walked out of the room without looking back.

Jericho and the Two Ways to Die

The place probably had a name, Jericho thought, like Lookout Point or High View or something equally imaginative. The road wound around the side of the mountain, with vertical cliffs on one side and a drop into space on the other. From this particular point there was an incredibly beautiful view of a wide valley below: farming country with fenced-in fields that made it look like a non-symmetrical checkerboard; cattle looking like tiny toys in the distance and grazing languidly. And color! Autumn glory was at its peak, gold and red and russet brown and the dark green of pines and fir trees.

Jericho had discovered this spot a few days ago and his painter's eye had been caught and held. He'd taken a room in a motel in the nearby town of Plainville and come here each of the last three days with his easel and painting gear.

The town fathers of Plainville had obviously been aware of all this magnificence. The two-lane road had been widened so that visitors in cars could pull out to the very edge of the drop, guarded by a steel-cable fence, park, and take in God's handiwork at their leisure. Jericho had chosen a spot above the road, above the lookout point, to do his painting. He had found a place to pull his red Mercedes off the road, had scrambled up the bank with his equipment, and set himself up for the day. Unless someone was searching for his car or craning his neck to look straight up, his presence would remain unknown.

He was sitting with his back propped against a huge boulder, filling a black curve-stemmed pipe from an oilskin pouch, when he first saw the small sports car with the girl at the wheel. She was driving up from the town, hugging the inside of the road. The car's top was down and he was attracted by the bright blonde hair of the driver that blew around her face, wondering idly if the color was real or if it came out of a bottle. While he watched, the girl stopped the car directly below him and got out. A very short skirt and very nice legs, he thought, and an exquisite figure. She was wearing a pair of amber-tinted granny glasses.

She walked across the road to the lookout area, reached the steel cable of the fence, and instead of looking out at the view she leaned forward and looked down. Some people are fascinated by dizzying heights. She stood there for a full minute, gazing down. Then she came back to the car, got in, and started the motor. She started, faster than was good for the motor or tires, swung the wheel to the left, and aimed directly at the spot where she'd been standing.

Jericho pushed himself up on his haunches and his mouth opened to shout when she came to a sudden skidding stop, the front bumper of the sports car hard against the steel-cable fence.

"Idiot!" Jericho said out loud, standing up.

The girl got out of the car and went to the fence—staring down again. Slowly she came back and got into the car. She backed across the road, almost in her own tracks, and stopped where she had first parked. Then she started up again, with a spray of gravel from the rear tires, and once more headed straight for the fence. And once again she stopped, just in time.

Jericho went sliding down the bank, braking with his heels. He reached the car and stood gripping the door on the passenger's side, towering over the girl. He was a giant of a man, standing six feet four and weighing about two-hundred-and-forty, all muscle. He had flaming red hair and a buccaneer's red beard and mustache.

"There are two ways to die," he said in a conversational tone. "One is to give up and kill yourself; the other is to go down fighting whatever it is that has you up a tree." He smiled. "The second way, there's a chance you won't have to die at all."

The eyes behind the granny glasses were wide, frightened. He couldn't tell their color—they were shielded by the amber lenses. The mouth was wide, drawn down at the corners. The face was classic: high cheekbones, straight nose, eyes set nicely apart. She would have been beautiful if something like terror hadn't contorted the features. Her hands gripped the wheel of the car so tightly her knuckles were white knobs.

"Oh, God!" she said in a strangled whisper.

Jericho opened the car door and got in beside her. "This isn't a very heavy car," he said. "I don't know if you could plow through that steel cable or not." He took his pipe out of his pocket and held his lighter to it. "Care to talk about it?"

Her head was turned away toward her target at the lookout point. "You're John Jericho, the artist, aren't you?"

"How did you know?"

"Plainville is a small town. You're a celebrity. Word gets around." Her voice was low and husky. She was fighting for control.

"And you are Miss—?"

"Mrs. Virgil Clarke," she said. She turned to him. "You've heard of my husband?"

He looked at her ringless fingers. "Famous trial lawyer," he said. "You live in Plainville?"

"We have a home here, an apartment in New York, an island in the West Indies."

"Nobody can say that crime does not pay," Jericho said. Fragments of memory were falling into place. Virgil Clarke was endlessly in the headlines. His Lincolnesque face was as familiar as a movie star's. He was the Clarence Darrow of the 1970s, the hero of people with lost causes. He must be, Jericho thought, sixty years old, at least twice the age of the girl who sat gripping the wheel of the sports car.

Memory again: a girl charged with murder; a brilliant defense; an acquittal; a headline romance and marriage. It was the first marriage for the noted lawyer; the bride was a widow, accused and acquitted of having murdered her husband.

"You've remembered," she said.

He nodded, his strong white teeth clamped on the stem of his pipe. "Care to tell me why?" he asked.

"Why?"

"Why you were contemplating a plunge into oblivion?"

She looked at him, forcing a smile. "You thought I meant to—?"

"Didn't you?"

"I—I'm not a very good driver," she said. "I wanted to turn around. I couldn't seem to figure out how to—how to do it."

"Have it your way," Jericho said. "It's really none of my business." He opened the car door, swung his long legs out, and stood looking down at her. "At least you've had a chance to think about it twice." His smile was mirthless. "Pull back, cut your wheels right, back up some more, then head for—wherever you're headed for, Mrs. Clarke."

About a hundred yards from Jericho's motel, down the main street of Plainville, was a delightful small country inn. Jericho had tried to get a room there when he decided to stay over but the inn was full. He had discovered, however, that they had an excellent kitchen.

He dined there the evening of the day he encountered the girl at Lookout Point. He had a dry martini, a shrimp cocktail, a very good brook trout helped along by a small white wine, a delicious mixed green salad. He was debating a homemade lemon meringue pie when the boy from the motel came to his table.

"Mrs. Clarke left a note for you, sir," he said. "I knew you were having dinner here."

Jericho opened the pale-blue envelope.

"Dear Mr. Jericho:

I tried to reach you on the phone without any luck. We are having an open house party tonight and my husband and I would be delighted to have you join us and our guests at any time after eight o'clock.
Janice Clarke.

P.S. I hope you won't mind being lionized. Incidentally, anyone can tell you where we live."

People who behave strangely and without explanation were irresistible to Jericho. He went back to the motel, changed into slacks, a blue blazer, and a yellow turtlenecked sweater-shirt. At about 8:30 he drove through the big stone gates that guarded the entrance to the Clarke estate. In the moonlight he saw the old Colonial house ideally situated on a hillside, with its magnificent lawns, shrubbery, and gardens. The house was brilliantly lighted and as he came close he saw this was not a small party. There were more than thirty cars parked along the side of the wide circular driveway.

The sound of music and laughter drifted toward Jericho as he approached the front door. The music was loud—rock rhythm. He was admitted by a uniformed maid and found himself in an enormous living room which seemed to occupy most of the ground floor of the house. All the furniture had been pushed to the sides of the room and the floor space was crowded with jumping, gyrating couples. The music came from a bearded trio in a far corner—two electric guitars and drums. There was a bar, loaded with every conceivable kind of liquor. There were two bartenders in scarlet shirts and leather vests. The dancing couples wore all sorts of mod dress.

Jericho, looking around for his hostess, spotted his host standing at the far end of the room, his back to a blazing fire in a huge fieldstone fireplace. Virgil Clarke was unmistakable, tall, angular, with a lock of hair drooping over his broad forehead. He looked wildly out of place in this gathering in his dark business suit, button-down white shirt, and black knitted tie. His attention was focused on his wife who was dancing with a long-haired, not unhandsome young fellow wearing a batik shirt that hung loose outside his trousers. Virgil Clarke's face looked carved out of rock. What he was seeing obviously gave him no pleasure.

Watching the dancers, Jericho thought how things had changed in the last twenty years. When you danced, back then, the music was soft and you held your girl close. Now the music was deafening and the couples danced apart from each other, not touching, each performing a kind of individual war dance.

Jericho's attention was diverted by a luscious blonde girl, not more than twenty, he thought. She was wearing a startling peek-a-boo dress that revealed almost everything of her gloriously suntanned young body.

"Jericho!" There was delight in the young voice and she was instantly clinging to his arm. "Jan is a genius! How did she manage to get you here? I'm Dana Williams, by the way. My father owns two of your paintings."

"Bless your father. And Mrs. Clarke didn't have to be a genius to get me here. She invited me and I came."

"We've been trying to guess how to meet you for the last three days without barging up and brazenly thrusting ourselves on you. How did Jan manage it?"

"She brazenly thrust herself at me," Jericho said, "which is the best and quickest way."

"Does she know you're here? She'll be wild when she sees I've glommed onto you first. Oh, there she is, dancing with Roger."

"Who is Roger?"

"Roger Newfield. He's one of the young lawyers who works in Virgil's office. You'd better have a drink. You're way behind everyone here."

They fought their way around the edge of the dancing throng to the bar. So far Janice hadn't noticed him. She was totally concentrated on the young man opposite whom her body twisted and turned.

Jericho ordered a Jack Daniels on the rocks and Dana a vodka martini. Watching the dancers again, Jericho found himself puzzled. They were all young. There seemed no one here even approaching Virgil Clarke's generation. Jericho suspected that he, at forty, came closest to his host in years. It was odd, he thought, that in the home of a famous man there seemed to be no other famous people, no sycophants, no hangers-on, no yes-men. Clarke, moving away from the fireplace as Jericho watched, seemed out of place in his own home.

"Shall we dance, Jericho?" Dana asked, smiling at him over the rim of her glass.

"It reveals my antiquity," he said, "but I don't—can't—do this modern stuff."

"You want to hold me close we can go out on the terrace," the girl said.

"To dance?"

"No, silly, to hold me close. I like older men, Jericho. Ask and ye shall receive."

"You ought to have your backside paddled," Jericho said.

"Oh, please! I'd love that!"

Before he could reply to that gambit Jericho felt a hand on his arm. He turned to face the uniformed maid.

"Mr. Clarke hopes you will join him in his study for a moment, sir," she said.

"A summons from the All Highest," Dana said. "Maybe he wants to buy a painting, maestro. I'll be waiting on the terrace. You be thinking about what you want to ask me to do."

"I'll be thinking," Jericho said, thinking about a number of ungallant suggestions. He liked to make his own passes.

The maid led him away from the bedlam of the dancers and down a short corridor to an oak door. She knocked and a deep voice invited them in. Virgil Clarke was standing by a far window and looking out over the moonlit lawn.

"Mr. Jericho," he said, as he turned. "Thank you, Millicent."

The maid left, closing the door behind her. The jumping rock rhythms were suddenly silenced. Jericho realized that this room was soundproofed. "Good evening, sir," he said.

At close quarters Clarke was even more impressive. The deep lines at the corners of his mouth were lines of character. The mouth was firm and uncompromising without suggesting vanity or inflexibility. The eyes were deep and dark and somehow tragic, as if he couldn't shake the memory of a thousand violences. Fighting against violence had been his lifework.

"We've never met, Mr. Jericho, but I have been an admirer of yours for some years."

Jericho had noticed the absence of any art in the house. "I hadn't thought of you as being interested in painting, sir."

"I'm not," Clarke said. "Never had a chance to develop a taste for it. I've never seen one of your paintings to know it. I've admired you since the trial of the Faxon brothers."

Jericho frowned. A good part of his own life had been devoted to traveling to the scenes of violence and trying to put on canvas his outrage at man's inhumanity to man. The Faxon brothers had murdered two civil-rights demonstrators. Jericho had been a witness for the prosecution.

"I don't recall your being connected with the case, sir," he said.

"I wasn't, except as a spectator," Clarke said. "I was interested in the defense counsel. I thought of asking him to become a partner in my firm. You broke his back in that case. You stood up under a damn good cross-examination and you broke his back."

"I told the truth."

"You convinced the jury it was the truth."

"It was. Did you hire your man?"

"I did not," Clarke said. "He committed the cardinal sin of getting to admire you while trying to break you down. I would have beaten you, I think, because I wouldn't have allowed myself that luxury. But as a spectator I admired you. There is a good honest man, I told myself. Honest and strong."

"A nice compliment," Jericho said, wondering.

Clarke gestured toward a comfortable armchair. "Can I get you a drink? I noticed you were drinking Jack Daniels out there." He had noticed from across the room. "I'll join you in fruit juice, if you don't mind. I have hours of work ahead of me tonight."

"Lucky your study is sound-proofed," Jericho said, smiling. "Thanks. Jack Daniels on the rocks would be fine."

Clarke went to a small sideboard, made Jericho's drink, and poured himself some cranberry juice. He handed Jericho his glass and said, "Why, if I may seem to be impertinent, are you here?"

"Because I was asked," Jericho said.

"What I would like," Clarke said, "is that you, without asking for any explanation, leave this room, go out to your car, and return to your lodgings."

"If you, my host, ask me to leave I will," Jericho said, "but I damn well want to know why. I'm entitled to that, I think."

"I am not your host," Clarke said. "Janice evidently invited you here."

"She did."

"Then go," Clarke said, his voice raised. "You have been asked here to be used. Janice never does anything without a purpose. If you imagine it is your maleness that's attracted her, forget it. Her tastes lie in areas which I suspect would bore you. She has some other reason. I would dislike seeing you used, Mr. Jericho."

"That's a rather extraordinary thing for you to say to a stranger about your wife," Jericho said.

"If you were to say that in front of Janice or that little tramp Dana, you would promptly be labeled a square," Clarke said. His face looked haggard, and there was a kind of frightening bitterness in his voice. Jericho felt acute embarrassment. The man was revealing some kind of deep unhealed wound without hinting how it had been inflicted. Perhaps it was just age, the inexorable process of growing old surrounded by a desirable young wife and her young friends.

But there had been Lookout Point and Janice Clarke's tentative exercise in suicide.

"Perhaps I should tell you how I came to meet your wife, Mr. Clarke," Jericho said. So he told the lawyer about Lookout Point and the little car and the frightened girl and the preparations to die which he had been lucky enough to forestall.

Clarke listened attentively, and when Jericho finished, the lawyer said, "I saved her once and I have been laughed at ever since—betrayed and laughed at. And now, if you don't leave, you will be betrayed and laughed at too. You have already sprouted donkey's ears, Jericho. You have been deliberately made to feel that you were Sir Galahad saving the desperate princess. The next step will be some grotesque practical joke that will have them all laughing at you."

"Why?" Jericho asked.

"It is their prime pleasure," Clarke said.

"Why me?" Jericho asked.

"Because you are a famous man. Because you are a crusader for decency and fairplay—causes that seem antiquated to them. Because you are over thirty and your generation must be discredited. Because it will delight them to show you up as a romantic square, to show you up publicly."

Jericho looked at his pipe which rested, cold, in the palm of his hand. "Your wife must be reaching that thirty deadline," he said.

"Which is why she will go to any lengths to show that she is still part of that young world—go to any outrageous lengths, I tell you!"

Jericho looked at the haggard face. "Why do you put up with it?"

"I was once Sir Galahad," Clarke said. "I defended her against a murder charge. I set her free. I was bewitched by her youth, her helplessness, and I wanted to protect her forever. I persuaded her to marry me. And then—then I was laughed at because I couldn't begin to satisfy her needs. Everyone out there knows that, in her terms, I am an inadequate lover. I have no taste for orgies, which makes me a square."

"Why haven't you walked out on her? Your values are sound and you know it. You are miserable, so why do you put up with it?"

"Because there is a bigger joke," Clarke said. "I defended her in court because I believed in her innocence."

Jericho drew a deep breath. "Are you telling me—?"

"That she was guilty," Clarke said, grinding out the words. "I, the Great Defender, was suckered into believing in her innocence. I married her. I showered her with luxuries. I was fooled, blinded."

"But if that's so, she must be ready to do anything you ask. She can't risk your displeasure."

"Double jeopardy," the lawyer said. "There is no new evidence. She can't be tried again. I can bear to be laughed at for my personal inadequacies but there is one area where I can't face public laughter."

"Your legal reputation?"

"It's all I have," Clarke said.

The study door burst open and Janice Clarke swept into the room. "Jericho!" she cried out. "I've been looking for you everywhere! How selfish of you to keep our celebrity to yourself, Virgil." She appropriated Jericho, her arm linked in his. "It's my turn now."

Jericho glanced at the lawyer. Virgil Clarke had turned away. He had revealed himself and issued his warning. Now it appeared he couldn't bear to confront his wife.

Jericho was led out into the hall and instantly assailed by the cacophony of the rock group and the shouting, laughing dancers.

"Take me for a ride in your car," Janice Clarke said. "I need to get away from this for a bit." She looked up at him with a wan smile. "It's been something of a day."

Either Clarke was a vicious liar or this girl deserved an Oscar for her acting talent, Jericho thought. He had a deep instinct for the fake, the phony, but the instinct was blurred at the moment. Someone had lied to him, he knew—either the lawyer in his study tonight or the girl with her performance at Lookout Point this afternoon.

They walked across the lawn to where the red Mercedes was parked. She was hanging onto his arm as though terrified of being separated from him. He helped her into the car and walked around to the other side.

"Where to?" he asked as he settled behind the wheel.

"Anywhere. Just away from here for a while."

"Won't your boy friend miss you?"

She looked up at him, her eyes wide. "Virgil's been talking to you! Who is alleged to be my boy friend tonight?"

"My own guess," Jericho said. "The young man you were dancing with when I came in."

"Roger Newfield?" She laughed, a harsh little sound. "Roger is a lawyer on Virgil's staff. He's one of the family. He worships Virgil, not me."

Jericho started the motor and drove the car slowly down the drive and out through the stone gates. He turned right for no particular reason. He wondered if this was part of the "practical joke" that Virgil Clarke had warned him about. Jericho wasn't afraid of laughter, so there was no reason for him to feel uneasy. Yet he did feel uneasy.

"You're too kind to ask me what you want to know," Janice said after a bit. "Oh?"

"About Lookout Point today. What could have—could have driven me to think—of—of what I was thinking."

Jericho felt the small hairs rising on the back of his neck. "I *was* wondering," he said, looking straight ahead into the cone of light from the car.

"Virgil saved my life, you know," she said, "I owed him everything. I loved him for what he had done for me. I was deeply moved and deliriously happy when he asked me to marry him. I would have married him even if I hadn't loved him. I owed him anything he asked."

"And he's given you a great deal—every luxury you could desire. But not love?"

"Have you never been astonished, Jericho, when the curtains are lifted and you can see inside the house? Virgil, so calm, so cool, so brilliant when he is onstage, turned out to be a sadistic monster in his private world. It is beyond endurance, and yet I owe him my life. Sometimes—and today was one of those times—it seemed I couldn't stand it any longer. If it hadn't been for you—"

Jericho's foot was on the brake. "I think we'd better go back," he said.

"Oh, not yet!" She glanced at her little diamond-studded wrist watch.

"Now," Jericho said, and swung the car in a U-turn.

"Oh, please, Jericho! Let me have a little time to get hold of myself."

The car leaped forward, back toward the stone gates. The girl glanced at her watch again.

"Please, Jericho, not just yet!" she cried out over the sound of the wind and the squealing tires.

They cornered through the gates and up the drive, past the parked cars to the front door. Jericho sprang out of the car and ran into the house, leaving the driveway blocked. He heard the girl call out behind him but he paid no attention. The rock band belted at him, and the almost hysterical laughter.

He ran along the passage to Virgil Clarke's study and put his shoulder to the door as if he expected it to be bolted. There was a splintering sound and he hurtled into the room.

Virgil Clarke was sitting at his desk, his eyes wide with astonishment. Standing beside him was Roger Newfield, the young lawyer in the mod clothes.

"What in the name of—"

Clarke was staring at the door bolt which hung ripped from its fastenings.

"I'm afraid the joke—a very grim joke—was to be on you, sir," Jericho said, rubbing his shoulder.

"Joke?"

"Death is a joke played on all of us, sooner or later," Jericho said. He moved slowly toward the desk, aware that Janice Clarke had come through the door behind him. She was standing there, her face a white mask, gripping the doorjamb to steady herself.

"Do you own a gun, Mr. Clarke?" Jericho asked.

"Why, yes, I do," Clarke said, bewildered.

"Where do you keep it?"

"Here. Here in my desk."

"May I see it?"

Clarke was not a man to take orders, but something of Jericho's violence had thrown him off balance. He opened the flat drawer of his desk and fumbled inside it. Then he looked up.

"It seems to be gone," he said. "I must have—misplaced it."

Jericho took a stride forward and was facing Roger Newfield. He held out his hand. Newfield stared at him, a nerve twitching high up on his cheek. Then Jericho stepped in and started to pat at Newfield's batik shirt. The young lawyer sidestepped and swung at Jericho.

Jericho's left hand blocked the punch and his right swung with crushing force at Newfield's jaw. The young man fell, his eyes rolling up into his head. Jericho bent down, searched the pockets, and came up with a small handgun. He dropped it on the desk.

"Is that yours, Mr. Clarke?" he asked.

The girl in the doorway screamed and ran to the fallen Newfield, crooning his name. "Roger! Roger!"

Clarke had picked up the gun. "It's mine," he said, in something close to a whisper.

"Suicide is the name of the game," Jericho said. "A fake suicide. Two fake suicides, in fact."

"I don't understand," Clarke said. His eyes were fixed on his wife, fondling the unconscious Newfield.

"You and the Williams girl both told me something I wasn't supposed to know," Jericho said, his voice hard. "You both implied that Mrs. Clarke was aware I was painting above the bank at Lookout Point. That meant the whole suicide gambit there was a fake, a setup. I was to stop her. I was to feel sorry for her. I would almost certainly be curious as to what had driven her to contemplate suicide, so I would accept her invitation to the party.

"You almost told me why, without knowing the reason yourself. I was to be the object of a practical joke, you said. But why me? Yes, I'm well known, but not to this crowd. What could she possibly do to me that would make me the butt of laughter? And then, when she asked me to take her away from here, I began to wonder. And when I suggested coming back she instantly looked at her watch. We hadn't, it seemed, been gone long enough. Long enough for what?"

"I don't follow you," Clarke said.

"Why the elaborate scheme to get me here? What could my presence here tonight possibly do for her? It suddenly hit me. I could provide her with an unbreakable alibi. Her friends might not be trustworthy. Her friends might be suspected of playing along with her, lying for her. But I, God help me, am a solid citizen with a reputation. If I testified she was with me it would hold fast."

"But why did she need an alibi?" Clarke asked.

"Because you were going to commit suicide, sir," Jericho said. "You were going to be found here, shot through the head with your own gun. The gun would be found in your hand with your fingerprints on it. But there was bound to be at least a faint suspicion. People close to you must know that your marriage isn't a happy one, and your wife was once charged with a murder. There are people who must still wonder if she was innocent of that crime or if it was your brilliance that set her free. They might ask if a woman who might have killed one husband might not have killed another. She didn't dare have that question asked. I could prevent it. I, the solid citizen, the stranger who had no past connections with her. I could have provided her with the perfect alibi if I hadn't insisted on coming home too soon."

Janice Clark looked up from where she was cradling Newfield in her arms. "It isn't possible for you to prove a word of this insane theory," she said. "Surely, Virgil, you can't believe—"

"It's not my job to prove it, Mrs. Clarke," Jericho said. "Your husband is the legal expert here. Maybe if he can stop feeling sorry for himself long enough, he'll know how to deal with you."

Jericho turned toward the door and then back again. "You were right, Mr. Clarke. I was asked here to be used. I trust my donkey's ears have disappeared."

He walked out into the night, the rock band hurting his ears. He was eager to get away, as far and as fast as he could.

Jericho and the Deadly Errand

It was a chance meeting with an old love, almost forgotten with the passage of years, that brought John Jericho face to face with a violent murder. Words spoken to him in the strictest confidence set him on a path totally different from the ones taken by the police and the District Attorney's staff. That he walked that path at all was due to a blazing anger that made it imperative for him, personally, to see to it that Justice was not blind.

What developed into a bloody horror began in the most pleasant of ways. It was a summer day in New York City, one of those rare blue-sky days without smog or unbearable humidity. The sky was cloudless. Jericho, walking uptown on Fifth Avenue, felt younger than he was and carefree. This was a coincidence because, unsuspecting, he was about to encounter his youth again. He found himself thinking of a day like this in Paris, ten years or more ago, when he had been sitting at an outdoor café with friends, drinking a particularly good wine, watching the world go by, and thinking how marvelous it was just to be alive. He had been a young artist in those days, just launching a career that was to make him world-famous. The future hadn't seemed too important that day in Paris—just the present, the joy of being alive and doing what he wanted to do, of being mildly in love.

Remembering that, Jericho now paused at a crossing and looking east saw a sign outside a building: *WILLARD'S BACK YARD*. This was an expensive little restaurant he could afford to patronize in these days of success, and in the summer months there was a charming outdoor garden, shaded by awnings and potted trees. It would be pleasant to sit there and drink a glass of wine and remember Paris. So he turned east and went into Willard's.

Coincidences are the enemies of fiction writers, but life is full of them. Willard's was filling up for luncheon, but Willard, an old friend, found Jericho a table in the garden. People turned to look at him as he was led to his place. He was eye-catching: six-feet-four-inches tall, two-hundred-and-forty pounds of solid muscle, with flaming red hair and a blazing red beard.

He sat down, ordered a split of champagne, filled and lit a black curve-stemmed pipe, and leaned back to watch the world go by, just as he had years ago in Paris.

A woman was led to a table a few yards away from Jericho and he looked at her, enjoying her as he always enjoyed looking at beautiful women. She was, he guessed, in her very early thirties, expensively dressed, with an unusual personal electricity. There was something familiar about her, he thought—the familiar charm of a woman of taste and experience, without a veneer of toughness. This kind was rare—familiar but rare.

The woman looked at him, her dark violet eyes widening. "Johnny?" she said. It was a question.

She was no stranger. The absurd thing was that he had been thinking about her as he walked up Fifth Avenue, thinking of her as she had been ten or more years ago, thinking of her as she had been in Paris when he was mildly in love with her.

"Fay!"

He went over to her table and her small cool hands were in his.

"The beard," she said. "I wasn't sure for a moment."

He had been a smooth-faced young man in Paris. "May I join you? Are you expecting someone?"

"Please. No," she said.

He beckoned to the waiter to bring his wine.

"It's wild," she said. "I came in here because I was thinking of you and the old days."

"ESP," he said. "That's exactly what happened to me."

"Oh, Johnny!"

He ordered a stinger for her. Her taste couldn't have changed. Nothing had changed. He said something to that effect.

"I wear a size twelve dress today," she said. "It was an eight back in those days. That much has changed."

She had been a model in those Paris times. She had also been a member of a young group of Revolutionaries bent on destroying the establishment in general and General de Gaulle in particular. Jericho had thought of them as crack-brained and lovable, particularly Fay. She had posed for him and they had made love and she had forgotten about the Revolution. There had been no anxieties, no guilts, no regrets when they came to the inevitable parting.

"Of course I've kept track of you, Johnny. You're famous now. I've gone to all your exhibitions, including your one-man show at the Mullins Gallery last month."

"You're living in New York?" he asked.

"Yes."

"And you never tried to get in touch with me? I'm in the phone book."

"So am I. You've forgotten, Johnny, that it was you who walked out. You would have to do the getting in touch—if you wanted to."

"I was young and stupid," he said. "I always thought of you as still being back in that other world, taking pot shots at General de Gaulle."

She laughed. "We were pretty crazy kids, weren't we? No, I came back here right after we broke up. I am a respectable secretary now, for a man in the brokerage business. You may have heard of him. He's in the news these days. Lloyd Parker."

"He's running for the United States Senate. That your man?"

She nodded. A tiny frown edged lines in her forehead. "A fine man," she said. "A good warm idealistic man."

Her man? Jericho wondered. Something in her voice—

"I don't have very good luck with men, Johnny," she said, reading his mind. She'd been like that in the old days. "First it was you who mattered. You walked out. Then there was—is—Lloyd Parker. I am his efficient, loyal, ever-ready office machine. He couldn't get along without me—in the office. Out of the office he is married to a beautiful, exotic, fabulously rich gal. Crandall Steel— she was Ellen Crandall. I am the classic figure of the secretary hopelessly in love with her boss, preferring to work with him every day and not have him rather than drop him and find someone who might want me as a woman."

"There are probably a hundred such someones," Jericho said.

She seemed not to hear that. "I was thinking of you when I came in here, Johnny, because I need help."

"Oh?"

"I need advice from someone who understands how complex people are, who wouldn't make judgments by hard and fast rules. I thought that of all the people I'd ever known you never prejudged, never insisted that all people follow black-and-white formulas." She tried a smile. "I thought that if I could only get advice from you—and presto, here you are."

"Try me, before I make improper advances," he said, answering her smile.

Her frown returned and stayed fixed. "Lloyd is running against a man named Molloy—Mike Molloy to his friends. Molloy is a machine politician, supported by the big-city moguls, the hard-hats, the labor bosses. Perhaps not a bad man, Johnny, but not a man of Lloyd's caliber, not a potential statesman, not in any way an idealist. Lloyd could be Presidential material in the future. Molloy belongs to other men. Lloyd belongs to himself and his country."

"He can have my vote."

"Lloyd is about forty-five. He has always had a little money. His family was Plymouth Rock-Mayflower stuff. I say 'a little money' in comparison to his wife's fortune. He was graduated from Harvard in the late forties, having missed the War. He knew that sooner or later he would be faced with the Army, and he didn't know what he wanted to do, really. A college friend persuaded him to put some money into a business, one of the first computer-dating services. Lloyd had nothing to do with the operation of the business; he was just a part owner. Someone blew the whistle on them. Lloyd's partner was using information they gathered to blackmail clients. He was indicted, convicted, and sent to prison. Lloyd was cleared."

"So?"

"After that came the Army in Korea. One day Lloyd's top sergeant asked him to mail a package for him. On the way to the post office Lloyd was stopped by M.P.s and it was discovered that the package contained about thirty thousand dollars in cash. The sergeant, it turned out, had been stealing the P.X. blind. There was a court-martial. The sergeant went to Leavenworth. Lloyd was cleared. He had simply been an innocent messenger boy."

"But not lucky with his friends or connections," Jericho said.

"Neither of these things was a great scandal at the time," Fay said. "They've been long forgotten. But suddenly they've reappeared in Wardell Lewis' political column. Lewis is supporting Molloy. Someone has fed him these two old stories, along with some malicious gossip about a love affair which Lloyd is supposed to have broken off in order to marry the Crandall money."

"A love affair with you, Fay?"

"No," she said sharply. "There is some truth in it, though. He did have an affair with a girl, he did break it off, he did marry Ellen Crandall five years ago. Lewis is using all this and I've been trying to find out who's been feeding Lewis this information."

"Any luck? The partner, the sergeant, the dropped girl?"

Fay shook her head. She looked at Jericho, her eyes wide. "Ellen, Lloyd's wife, is having an affair with Wardell Lewis."

"Wow!" Jericho said.

"Of course Lloyd has no knowledge of it," Fay said. "That's what creates my problem. He loves his wife deeply. If he learns the truth, I think it will destroy him. What do I do? Do I go to Lloyd and wreck his life with the truth? Do I go to her and Lewis and threaten them with exposure? They would laugh at me. Exposure, beyond what it might do to Lloyd personally, would ruin his political future. A cuckolded candidate for the Senate becomes a national joke." Fay brought her closed fist down on the table. "What do I do, Johnny?"

"Have another stinger," he said, wondering just what she should do. She obviously was in love with the man.

Jericho didn't come up with an immediate answer for Fay Martin. Parker, his wife, and Wardell Lewis were not real people to him. They were X, Y, and Z in a problem. Fay was real, very real. She had set out to help a man she loved and she could only help him, it developed, by hurting him terribly. It mattered to her whether or not Lloyd Parker won an election; but it mattered even more that he not be hurt.

The only thing that occurred to Jericho was that there might be a way to silence Wardell Lewis without using Ellen Parker's adultery as the weapon. Lewis' kind of muckraking journalism suggested the kind of man who might well have skeletons in his own closet. Jericho had friends. He would, he promised Fay, put something in motion.

Would she have dinner with him? That was impossible. She had to go to a public debate that was being held up in Westchester between Parker and Molloy. She would, however, join him for lunch again tomorrow. By then he might have dug up something that could be used as leverage against Lewis. A newspaperman and a friend in the District Attorney's office would nose around for Jericho. But Jericho promised he would not tell either of them about the triangle.

The next morning Jericho woke early as usual. He was in his apartment on Jefferson Mews in Greenwich Village. When he came out of the shower he switched on the radio to hear the eight o'clock news. What he heard turned him to stone.

Fay Martin was dead.

The facts, put together from the radio account and from the morning papers, were as follows: the debate between Lloyd Parker and Mike Molloy was to be held in the auditorium of the Community Center Building in White Hills. Parker and his wife had driven out there in his Cadillac and left the car, locked, in the parking area. Shortly before the debate was to begin, Parker's secretary, Fay Martin, had come out to the parking area and asked the attendant where the Parker Cadillac had been left. She identified herself and showed the man keys. Parker, she said, had left something he needed in the Cadillac's glove compartment.

The attendant pointed out where the car was and watched her go to it. She unlocked the door, got in, and leaned forward to open the glove compartment. An explosion blew the car and Fay to bits, started a raging fire, and severely damaged a half dozen other cars parked nearby.

The debate was never held. Some odd facts were turned up by the police. Parker, in a state of shock, denied that he had sent Fay to the car to get anything for him. She had, he told police, come to White Hills in her own car to make sure everything was in order for the debate. He hadn't sent her out to his car for anything. There wasn't anything he needed. Furthermore, he insisted that she didn't have a set of keys for the car, which he had locked himself. There was only one set of keys, his own, and he had them in his pocket. There was no other set! Why Fay had gone to the car and where she had got a set of keys were completely inexplicable to Parker.

The police were certain the bomb had been planted in the glove compartment and rigged so that when the compartment door was opened, the bomb would go off. The bomb had obviously been meant to kill Parker, the police said, since he was the only person who drove the Cadillac and the only person who had keys to it.

Except that there must have been a second set of keys.

Mrs. Ellen Parker confirmed her husband's statement. There was no second set of keys that she knew of. She had her own car—she never drove her husband's Cadillac.

Public outrage was high. People were sick of bombings and assassinations. A political analyst expressed the opinion that Parker, who had been running behind Molloy in the polls, would now be an odds-on favorite to win the election. Sympathy would push him into the lead. The Molloy forces would be high on the suspect list. Innocent as it might be, the Molloy machine had been put behind the eight-ball.

Jericho, his muscles aching from tension, didn't give a damn about the election.

Fay was dead—loyal, dedicated Fay, in love with a man who had passed her by for ten years, and for whom she had been murdered.

Someone must have handed Fay a set of keys, probably saying they were Parker's. "He wants you to get an envelope he left in the glove compartment of his car." Of course she had gone, cheerfully. She would have done anything in the world for Parker without question. Whoever gave her the keys, not Parker's, had to know what would happen when the glove compartment door was opened. The bomb hadn't been meant for Parker, not ever.

Fay was dead, and it had been meant that she should die.

Do you set an elaborate and dangerous trap to kill a girl simply because she has found out about a case of adultery? What did Ellen Parker have to lose if her affair with Lewis became public? She had all the money in the world; she was tired of her husband.

What did Lewis have to lose? His man-about-town reputation would only be enhanced by the news that Ellen Parker was his latest conquest. This was 1972, not 1872. Infidelity was no longer a "curiosity." Fay had wanted to keep Parker from learning the truth about his wife. To kill her to keep her silent made no sense, not when she would have kept silent under any circumstances.

But she had known something, or had done something, that called for violence—something, Jericho concluded, that she hadn't mentioned to him during their brief reunion.

The police, Jericho learned from his friend in the D.A.'s office, were still working on the theory that the bomb had been meant for Parker. Experts had put together small pieces. The bomb had evidently been a simple device—sticks of dynamite tied together, set off by a Fourth of July cap and triggered when the glove compartment door was opened. The killer didn't have to be an explosives expert.

There was simply no way to guess who had sent Fay on her deadly errand. She had died with that information unrevealed. The unexplained set of keys to the car was a puzzle. Parker, under persistent questioning, remembered that when he'd bought the Cadillac a year ago there had been a duplicate set of keys. He'd put them "in a safe place" and now hadn't the faintest recollection where that had been. Ellen Parker denied all knowledge of them. Fay might have known, but Fay was dead. The dead kept their secrets and the living would lie to suit their own purposes.

Jericho, convinced that the bomb had not been meant for Parker, was inclined to bypass the Molloy forces. Parker, dead by violence, could do nothing but harm them. Parker's forces could run Mickey Mouse and win. Molloy could only be involved if Fay had discovered something criminal about him and had kept it to herself long enough for Molloy's men to rig her death. But it didn't make sense. If she was a danger to Molloy he would have struck swiftly and less obviously, and would have made sure that it didn't appear to have been aimed at Parker.

Yesterday had been a blue-sky day, a day for reunions, a day to remember a carefree time, a day to promise help. Today the skies were dark and the rain, wind-swept, was swirling in the gutters. It was too late for promises, but not too late to demand payment in full.

A man wearing a slicker and a brown rain hat stood in the foyer of a remodeled brownstone on the east side. He had a bright red beard and his eyes were pale blue, and cold as two newly minted dimes. He had stood there while half a dozen people left the building to go to work, and two or three tradesmen arrived to deliver orders. The building's custodian had approached him on the subject of loitering, and a crisp ten-dollar bill had changed hands.

At about eleven o'clock a taxi stopped outside the building. A woman got out and ran across the sidewalk to the sanctuary of the foyer. She was a tall, very beautiful, very chic blonde. She looked at Jericho with a kind of detached curiosity as she pressed one of the doorbells in the brass nameplate board. The ring was a signal—one short, one long, two shorts. The woman's picture had been in the paper that morning, so Jericho had no doubts about her. "The Beautiful Mrs. Lloyd Parker" had been the newspaper caption.

The front door made a clicking sound and Ellen Parker opened it. Jericho was directly behind her, then inside before the door could close in his face. She gave him a startled look and hurried up the stairway to the second floor. Jericho was behind her and he could sense her sudden panic. She almost ran along the second-floor hallway to the apartment in the rear. The door was opening and a man in a seersucker robe was smiling at her—and the man with the red beard was directly behind her.

There was a moment of confusion.

"Ward!" Ellen Parker cried out.

She was pushed hard from behind, then she and Wardell Lewis and Jericho all wound up inside the apartment. The door was closed and Jericho was leaning against it. Lewis, tall, with longish dark hair and a mod mustache, was naked under the seersucker robe. He looked around, obviously frightened, for a weapon.

"He followed me in," Ellen Parker said in a husky voice.

The world is full of black tales about the city and its violences. Women are attacked and robbed in the hallways of their apartment houses; drug addicts steal, even kill, for the price of a fix. It would come like this, they were thinking—unexpected, catching them totally unprepared.

Jericho took off his rain hat and shook the water out of it. He tossed it onto a chair near the door.

Lewis' eyes widened. He was the man-about-town, the gossip hunter, the man who knew everyone. "You're John Jericho, the painter!" he said.

"I'm John Jericho, friend of Fay Martin's," Jericho said. "We'll have a talk and I hope for your sake you'll answer questions."

"What do you mean by breaking in this way?" Lewis demanded.

"I wanted to catch you two together," Jericho said. "Fay told me about you. I wanted to make sure for myself. Now I'm going to get the truth about last night if I have to scrape you out of your shells."

Lewis walked over to a table in the center of the room and took a cigarette from a lacquered box. It was a cluttered room, every inch of the wall space covered with photographs of celebrated people in society, politics, and show business, all autographed to Wardell Lewis. Lewis held a table lighter to his cigarette with an unsteady hand.

"If you were a friend of Parker's secretary," he said, "I can understand why you're so steamed up. But so help me, I'm going to have you arrested for breaking and entering, and for threatening us with violence."

Jericho's pale eyes were fixed on the woman who was standing behind a chair, gripping it to support herself. He appeared not to have heard Lewis. Fay had been right—she was beautiful. What, he wondered, did she see in a creep like Lewis?

"Fay had found out about you and Lewis," Jericho said to her. "But she was willing to do anything to keep your husband from finding out that you were having an affair with this clown and feeding him information that could hurt your husband. You didn't need to kill Fay."

Ellen Parker's eyes were wide with fright. "That bomb wasn't meant for Fay, God help her," she said. "It was meant for me!"

"Keep still, Ellen," Lewis said. "This man is your enemy."

"What makes you think the bomb was meant for you, Mrs. Parker?" Jericho asked.

"Because I was meant to go to the car," she said. She looked as if her legs were about to fold under her. She clung to the chair.

"Take it slowly from the beginning," Jericho said. He told himself he had an ear for the truth. Lewis was the kind of man who'd grown up saying, "I didn't do it!"—but Ellen Parker was something else again. She was two-timing her husband, betraying his secrets, but she obviously believed what she had just said. She believed the bomb had been meant for her.

"It was at the White Hills Community Center, just before last night's debate was about to begin," Ellen Parker said. "I had left my seat to go to the powder room. When I came back there was an envelope on my seat. In it was a set of car keys and a scribbled note saying my husband wanted me to get an envelope he'd left in the glove compartment of his car. He was up on the speaker's stand on the stage. He smiled and waved at me. I waved back, indicating I'd do what he asked—waved back with the note."

"Was the note in your husband's handwriting?"

"No. I thought one of his staff had written it. I was just starting to edge my way out of the row of seats when Fay appeared. She asked me if anything was wrong, because they were just about to start. I told her Lloyd needed something from the car and she said she'd get it. I—I was glad not to have to go, so I gave her the keys and the note."

"Which were blown up in the car with her," Lewis said. "Ellen can't prove a word of what she's saying and he denied he asked anyone to get anything."

"He?"

"Parker, for God's sake. Who else? Of course he denies it—he meant to kill Ellen!"

"Why?"

"Because he'd found out about us, why else?"

"I don't dare go home," Ellen Parker said, her voice shaking. "The police were there all last night—to protect him. But once they're gone he may try again."

"The man's turned into a homicidal maniac," Lewis said. "Ellen and I are going to have to get protection from the police."

"Were you at the Community Center in White Hills last night, Lewis?" Jericho asked.

"Of course I was there," Lewis said. "I'm covering the campaign, as you know if you read the papers."

Jericho glanced at Ellen Parker. "And how you're covering the campaign!" he said. "A man who goes berserk and tries to kill his wife for an infidelity doesn't usually leave out the wife's lover. Well, maybe Parker's saving you for dessert."

"You think it's something to joke about?" Lewis said. "I've had about enough of this." He bent down and opened the drawer of the table behind which he was standing. His hand didn't get out of the drawer with the revolver—Jericho moved too fast. His left hand grabbed Lewis' right wrist and brought it down on the edge of the table. The gun fell noiselessly to the rug. Jericho's right hand swung to Lewis' jaw. The columnist's head snapped back and he collapsed on the rug without a sound.

Ellen Parker didn't move from her place behind the chair, still clutching it for support. Her eyes, wide with fear, were fixed on Jericho, as if she expected to be next. He was moving toward her and she obviously wanted to scream, but couldn't. He took her arm gently.

"There are things I need to know about your husband," he said. "Could we go somewhere else to talk—somewhere that smells less of treachery?"

She made no move to go to Lewis, but asked, "Is he hurt?"

"He will have a severe headache—I hope," Jericho said.

They sat together in a corner booth in a little restaurant a couple of blocks from Lewis' apartment. The rain had let up and they had walked there, Ellen Parker in a kind of trance. Jericho ordered coffee, with brandy to lace it. He leaned back in the booth, watching her, waiting for her to speak. There was something unexpectedly vulnerable about her. She wasn't the kind of woman he had expected.

"I've destroyed myself," she said finally, not looking at Jericho. "It's always been that way. I have always destroyed everything that has been good in my life."

"Your marriage?" he asked quietly.

"Since I was a little girl I've always been afraid that people only liked me because I was so rich. I never believed that any man really wanted me for myself. I always tested them and tested them until I drove them away. Then Lloyd Parker came into my life and for the first time I really believed I was loved and wanted for myself, that my money didn't have anything to do with how he felt about me. For the first time in my life I was happy, without doubts, without fears."

"What changed it?"

"This venture into politics," she said, drawing a deep breath. "You can't get elected dog catcher these days, Mr. Jericho, without spending a great deal of money. Lloyd asked me for a great deal of money and I gave it to him gladly, happily. Then, as soon as I did, he seemed to lose interest in me. Our love life came to an end. I told myself it was because he was working fourteen-eighteen hours a day. But the old doubts, the bitter certainty that it was only my money he wanted, took charge again. I guess I went a little crazy. I went out on the town looking for a man, any man, who'd find me attractive without knowing I was rich, rich, rich. It was Ward Lewis who picked me up and restored my ego."

"Lewis, who knew who you were from the first moment he laid eyes on you, knew you were rich, rich, rich, and who planned to use you to help the Molloy crowd."

"I wanted to hurt Lloyd," she said, her lips trembling. "I wanted revenge. And—and I hated myself."

"Good for you," Jericho said.

"Last night, when Lloyd told me that he knew about Ward and me, I—"

"He *knew*?" Jericho sat up straight.

"He told me while we were driving out to White Hills. There'd been an anonymous letter. He'd checked on me and found out it was true. I knew how much it hurt him and I was glad for a moment. But he was wonderful about it. He took the blame, admitted he'd neglected me, begged me to give him another chance. I almost began to believe in him again."

"Why do you suppose he told you he knew if he was planning to kill you?" Jericho asked.

She looked at him, her eyes wide. "So I'd know, at the last moment when the bomb went off, why I was dying."

"That makes him into some kind of monster," Jericho said.

Ellen Parker closed her eyes. "God help me," she said.

The receptionist in the brokerage offices of Sheftel & Parker was not cordial.

"I'm afraid Mr. Parker can't see you today, Mr. Jericho. If you've heard the news—"

"Give him this note," Jericho said. "I think he'll see me."

Jericho felt out of place in the paneled waiting room with its rich green-leather furnishings. His corduroy jacket and turtlenecked shirt were altogether too casual for this palace of wealth. There was another out-of-place man sitting in one of the big chairs across the room. Jericho's artist's eyes picked up details that might have escaped others. A slight bulge at the other man's waistline spelled gun. Cop, Jericho thought. The police weren't risking another attempt on Parker's life.

The receptionist, looking mildly surprised, reappeared. "Mr. Parker will see you," she said.

She led Jericho into an inner room. He was aware that the waiting man had risen and was following him. In the inner room another out-of-place man faced him. He showed a police shield.

"Mr. Parker doesn't know you, Mr. Jericho. Under the circumstances you'll understand why we must make sure you're not armed."

Jericho raised his arms languidly. The man behind tapped Jericho over. There was a moment of tension when he felt a bulge in the pocket of the corduroy coat. It turned out to be Jericho's pipe.

Lloyd Parker was about six feet tall, with soft, curly brown hair. He had a square jaw, and the crow's-feet at the corners of his brown eyes suggested a man of good humor. But those eyes were red-rimmed, probably from lack of sleep. He looked like a man fighting exhaustion. This had been Fay's kind of man, Jericho thought: gentle, undemanding, considerate. Most people would instinctively like Lloyd Parker under normal circumstances. Now he was undermined by tensions and anxiety. He stood in front of his big flat-topped desk, leaning against it.

"Your note, Mr. Jericho, tells me that you were a friend of Fay's, which is why I agreed to see you. It also says that you know where my wife is. Why should you think that would interest me?"

"Aren't you wondering if she's gone back to Wardell Lewis?"

A muscle rippled along Parker's jawline. "Just what, exactly, do you mean by that?"

"Oh, come, Mr. Parker, let's not waste time with games. I've just been talking to your wife. I knew about the affair from Fay."

"Fay? Fay knew?"

"Fay knew and was prepared to do anything to keep you from finding out about it. But you did find out."

Parker's face hardened. "What do you want of me, Mr. Jericho?"

"I want to ask you a question before I call in those cops out there and charge you with the murder of Fay Martin and the intention to murder your wife."

Parker's mouth dropped and he gasped for air like a landed fish. "You're out of your mind!" he whispered.

"I think not." Jericho's voice was matter-of-fact. "Your wife got your instructions to go to the car, where a bomb was waiting for her. By mischance Fay offered to do the errand for her. I said in my note that I know where your wife is. I do. She's not with Lewis, if that matters to you. But it must be obvious to you that she won't see you or go back home with you. She's afraid you might try again."

"This is sheer madness!" Parker said. "I don't want my wife dead. I love her. There's nothing in the world that matters to me without her. I had nothing to do with the bomb, I sent no message asking her to go to the car, I had just been pleading with her to give our marriage a second chance."

"When did you tell Fay she could stop looking for the person who was feeding Wardell Lewis with information about you?"

"Last night, just a little while before the debate was to begin. I told her the truth—that I'd found out Ellen was having an affair with Lewis, which explained his source of information."

"She wasn't shocked, Parker. She had told me earlier in the day about the affair. She was, as I told you, prepared to do anything to keep you from knowing."

"She told me that. I was grateful, but I explained to her that Ellen was all that mattered to me, that I'd do anything to get her back."

Jericho's eyes wandered toward a small bar in the corner of the office. "Do you mind if I pour myself a drink?"

"Yes, I mind!" Parker said. "Does Ellen really think I tried to kill her?"

"She's sure of it," Jericho said. He went over to the bar and poured himself a bourbon. He looked at Parker and raised his glass in a silent toast. "Maybe I can persuade her that she's wrong."

"But you just threatened to—"

"I know," Jericho said. "You have an extraordinary effect on women, Parker. One of them runs away from you and into the arms of a heel because she thinks you don't love her enough. Another gives up being a woman for ten years just to breathe the same air that you do. But I don't suppose Fay ever gave up hope that some day, somehow, you might be more than that to her."

"Poor Fay."

"Yes, poor Fay," Jericho said. "It could have been this way, Parker. When she found out about your wife's affair with Lewis she wanted to save you the hurt. Your wife's death might be a terrible blow to you, but having your male ego shattered would be even worse. I think she had already planned a way when she talked to me at lunch yesterday. Maybe she hoped I'd come up with a better answer, but unfortunately I didn't.

"So it was she, it was Fay who rigged the bomb in your car. Keys? There was a spare set which you'd put 'in a safe place' that you no longer could remember. Fay knew. Your secretary, Parker, your devoted, loving secretary knew. Your wife might not know your 'safe place,' or the size of your collar, or how you liked your eggs, but Fay knew; she knew everything there was to know about you and she cherished the knowledge."

"It doesn't make sense," Parker said, his voice shaken. "How would *she* know how to rig a bomb? Fay? Impossible!"

"Quite possible," Jericho said. "There's an odd fact I know about her that you'd have no reason to know. When I first met Fay in Paris ten or twelve years ago she was a model. I am a painter. She was also a member of a wild young revolutionary group that was constantly demonstrating, bombing, and burning. Their aim was to get rid of General de Gaulle. They were trained by experienced people. She would have the know-how to make a simple bomb.

"I met her, she modeled for me, we fell in love in a sort of way, and for a good many months she forgot about being a Mata Hari. When we parted she came back here and went to work for you. But she had the knowledge about explosives."

"And you say she meant to kill Ellen?"

"I think so. She would kill Ellen and at the same time improve your election prospects, because Molloy and his crowd would be suspected. She prepared the note that would send your wife out to the car and left it on her seat. It must have been after she'd done that you told her you knew. More important—more devastating to Fay—you made it clear that Ellen was still all that mattered to you. That there'd be no future for Fay even if Ellen died. If Ellen was the only one you wanted, poor defeated Fay would make certain you had her. She must have hurried to retrieve the note and the keys. But Ellen already had them."

"Good God."

Jericho looked at his empty glass. "So she volunteered to run the errand for Ellen."

"Knowing the bomb was in the car?"

"Maybe she thought she could deactivate it. Maybe, in that brief trip to the parking lot she decided to take it as a way out. Perhaps she thought she would be doing you a last service. The bomb would at least end Molloy's chances of defeating you in the election."

"Can you prove this?"

"Not one word of it," Jericho said. He turned back to the bar and poured himself another drink. "But I might persuade your wife that it's true. Care to come with me and help me try?"

Jericho Plays It Cool

John Jericho, the crusading artist, is not often to be found in his studio on Jefferson Mews in New York's Greenwich Village. He uses the studio largely as a storage place for paintings, materials, and clothes. Most of his time is spent traveling around the world painting, almost invariably scenes of violence, in a personal outcry against man's inhumanity to man.

Jericho is a huge man, standing almost six-feet-four-inches tall and weighing two-hundred-and-forty pounds, of solid bone and muscle. His hair and beard are a flaming red, and he reminds one of an old Viking warrior. His life has been devoted to exposing injustice and fighting for the little man in a world where power structures and special privileges ignore individual rights and freedoms.

This may explain how Jericho became involved in the death of Jimmy Kane. It was partly accidental because Jericho was spending a rare few days in the Jefferson Mews studio. If he had been away he would never have met the girl, and if he hadn't met her he would have read about Jimmy Kane's death, been distressed by it, and filed away his memories of Jimmy in the category of human tragedies. The suicide of a young man is sad, tragic, but there is nothing you can do about it after the fact.

Jimmy Kane had grown up in the Village area of the city, only a few blocks from Jefferson Mews. He had faced all the problems of poverty while trying to survive in a huge city. By the time he reached high school Jimmy had become a fine athlete, starring in football and basketball. His special talent, however, was boxing. Before he was twenty he had been taken on by a professional manager, had fought a dozen fights in the small-club circuit, and begun to gain a reputation by knocking out a few seasoned professionals on the fringe of the big time.

He was beginning to earn good money when Jake Slattery, the number one challenger for the heavyweight crown, inadvisedly agreed to fight Kane in what was advertised as a warm-up for Slattery prior to his fight with the champion. Jimmy cut Slattery to pieces and was suddenly a headline maker. The champion was reluctant to face this new challenger, using the excuse that Jimmy was still not well enough known to attract the big money of a Madison Square Garden fight and closed-circuit TV. Jimmy proceeded to rectify this situation by knocking out two other top-ranked contenders.

But the end to his big dream came about in a most unlikely fashion. Jimmy was working out with a sparring partner in a neighborhood gym when he slipped on a wet spot in the ring, fell, and struck his head against a ring post. The result was a skull fracture and partial paralysis. His fighting career was over—*snap*, just like that.

Jericho had had a brief contact with Jimmy while Kane was still on his way up. He had seen him fight, been fascinated by his physical perfection, his amazing reflexes. He had drawn some sketches and shown them to Jimmy in his dressing room. The young fighter had been pleased and flattered. He had come around to the Mews to look at some of Jericho's paintings. He was, Jericho thought, a bright, intelligent, warm-hearted young man.

Jericho was out of town when Jimmy had his accident. He read about it. The paralysis had eventually been cured, but Jimmy wasn't able to regain his sharp physical skills. His chance for the big money was gone. Somehow he got to taking drugs, ran the whole gamut of self-destruction, and wound up in Lexington, Kentucky, having served several jail sentences for possession of narcotics.

Basically, Jimmy Kane was a gutty guy. At Lexington he kicked the habit. He returned to New York and found a new aim in life—helping others in his own world who had fallen into the drug trap. He was loved and respected for a new reason by the people in his part of town.

The night before Jericho read of Kane's dramatic death, Jimmy had walked into the neighborhood police precinct house. He was known and respected there. He often turned up to ask about kids he was trying to help who might be in trouble with the cops. Patrolman Martin had been at the water cooler and had waved a hello to Jimmy. Sergeant Kohler was standing with his back to Jimmy, bending over a desk to fill out some forms. Suddenly Kohler felt his gun being wrenched out of its holster. He spun around to find himself facing Kane, the gun in Jimmy's hand. Before Kohler could act Jimmy lifted the gun and blew out his own brains.

The newspaper story Jericho read expressed the shock of the community. Jimmy's life story was told—the accident that had ended his career, the resulting deep depression, the drugs. But he had licked the drug habit. People thought he was happy at what he was doing. But evidently it had all been too much for him.

Jericho was sorry. He would find out when and where the funeral would be held and pay his respects to Jimmy. But before he could make those inquiries the girl came to Jefferson Mews.

Jericho answered the door and found himself facing an attractive blonde girl. She had the figure of a fashion model and she was dressed inexpensively but in style. He guessed she was looking for work, posing for him. Word seemed to get around whenever he was in town.

"Mr. Jericho?" she asked. It was a warm low voice.

"Yes." He was aware of a kind of dark tragedy in her blue eyes.

"You are—were—a friend of Jimmy Kane's?"

"Yes, I knew Jimmy. Rotten shame what happened. I read about it in the paper."

"May I come in and talk to you?"

"Of course."

She came in. She looked around at the brilliant paintings on the wall. He could have sworn she didn't see them. She took the chair he waved to and sat, gripping the arms so tightly her knuckles showed white.

"Jimmy talked about you," she said. "My name is Marilyn Sims, by the way. So I know you know about such things, Mr. Jericho."

"What things?"

"I don't believe Jimmy shot himself," the girl said.

Jericho felt his eyebrows go up. "My dear child, two men saw him do it," he said. "Two policemen."

"I don't believe he did it," the girl said.

Her lips trembled and her whole body was shaking. She was very close to hysteria, Jericho thought, so he played it cool. "I only know what I read in the paper," he said. "It seemed pretty clear that Jimmy shot himself in front of two reliable witnesses."

"I tell you I don't believe it!"

"Look," Jericho said, "would you like some coffee?" He didn't wait for an answer, but went over to the electric percolator on the sideboard and poured her a cup. "Sugar? Cream?"

She shook her head.

He turned to a large open bookcase that contained stacks of sketchbooks. He selected one and brought it back with the coffee.

"These might interest you," he said.

The book contained the series of sketches he'd made of Jimmy Kane. Some of them were the full figure—Jimmy in action. Some of them were just fragments—studies of his back, the muscles of his shoulders, a fighter's profile, chin tucked in against his chest.

"They're beautiful," she said after a moment, and her voice broke. She looked up at him, her eyes wide. "Would it shock you to know that just two hours before Jimmy is supposed to have shot himself he and I were making love together?"

"Why should it shock me?"

"We've been lovers for nearly six months, Mr. Jericho. For the last two months Jimmy has been pleading with me to marry him."

Jericho smiled. "Why not? It may be an old-fashioned idea, but quite a few people still believe in it."

"Because we both came up out of the bottom," the girl said. "Jimmy was on drugs, with several convictions against him. I—I have served time for shoplifting and—and other crimes. I have a brother who was on drugs. Jimmy helped him—it was through him I met Jimmy. He got me straightened out and we fell in love.

"Just two hours before he is supposed to have killed himself I had said 'Yes,' I would marry him. He was very high on happiness, Mr. Jericho, when he left me to go to work. He works—worked—in the drug rehabilitation center, you know. He had to see a couple of kids who were in trouble. We made a date for dinner to make plans for when and where we'd be married. There is no way, absolutely no way, he could have been plunged into such a state of despair that he would kill himself two hours after he left me."

"And yet he did it in front of two witnesses."

"Never!"

Her conviction was very real. She wasn't trying to sell herself something. She was as certain as anyone could be.

"What do you want me to do, Marilyn?" he asked.

"Find out what really happened!"

Slowly Jericho began to fill a charred black pipe from an oilskin pouch. "I can't even guess what happened, Marilyn. I can't imagine what toppled Jimmy from the pinnacle of happiness to suicidal despair. I don't know where to begin. I—"

"You don't believe me!" she said. "I know it couldn't have happened the way they tell it."

Jericho held his lighter to the pipe until he got it well going. "Nothing can bring Jimmy back," he said. "If I dig into this I may come up with answers that are more painful than the way it stands now. His reasons, his motives—"

"He didn't do it!" she said. She stood up, unsteadily. "If you don't believe that, you won't be able to help."

He put his big hand on her shoulder. He could feel her trembling. "I'll do what I can, Marilyn. But I can't promise anything."

Police Captain Swann, who commanded the local precinct, was a decent man. Jericho knew him. Once a few months back there had been some trouble with gang wars in the area. Jericho had involved himself and found Swann to be a tough cop but also a man with compassion for human problems.

"Long time no see," Swann said, when Jericho was admitted to his office.

"I'm out of town a lot, Captain."

"What can I do for you or is this just a social call?"

"I was distressed to hear what happened to Jimmy Kane," Jericho said. "He was a friend."

"Poor guy," Swann said. "It was something hard to believe, Mr. Jericho. He was in and out of here all the time, you know. He was doing a great job at this drug rehabilitation center. We tried to cooperate with him—let him know if we saw any of his kids where they oughtn't to be, or hanging around with the wrong people."

"The reason I'm asking about him," Jericho said, "is that I have reason to believe things were all going his way. He was a success at his job. He'd licked the habit himself. He was riding the top of the wave. Why would he do such a thing?"

Swann frowned. "Maybe I can help you there," he said. "There were some facts we decided not to give out to the press, and I think you'll understand why when I tell you."

So there was an answer, Jericho thought.

"Naturally, after it happened," Swann went on, "we searched the body. We found a couple of ounces of heroin on him, a needle, a tourniquet—the whole equipment. We put two and two together, Mr. Jericho. He was hooked again. After two years of private struggling he'd lost his biggest fight. He couldn't face it."

"You say you had a reason for not telling this to the press."

"It wouldn't do any good and it could do a lot of harm," Swann said. "Those kids he worked with. They loved him, trusted him, idolized him. If they knew he'd lost his own fight, a lot of them might throw in the towel."

Jericho drew a deep breath. "That answers a big question for me," he said. "Maybe it's just morbid curiosity, but I'd like to hear from the two men who saw it just how it happened. Possible?"

"Ordinarily they wouldn't be here this time of day," Swann said. "They're on the four o'clock shift. It was less than a half hour after they came on yesterday that it happened. They were pretty shaken up, both of them. I sent 'em home and told 'em to come back this morning to make out a full report. You want to talk to them I'll have them in."

The two cops were in civilian clothes. Sergeant Kohler was a gray-haired veteran with bright blue eyes. Patrolman Martin was young, eager-looking.

"It was the damnedest thing," Martin said. "We'd just come on duty. The sergeant and I were the only ones in the front room. The sergeant was at the desk, his back to the door, and I was over at the water cooler when Jimmy came in."

"He came in often," Kohler said, "just to chew the fat, rap about his kids, you know."

"I said, 'Hi, Jimmy,' " Martin said. "He said 'Hi!' and walked over toward the sergeant. There didn't seem anything odd about the way he looked or acted."

"I knew he was there because I heard Martin speak to him," Kohler said. "I was busy with the reports the off-duty officer had left me, so I didn't turn around."

"He walked right over to the sergeant," Martin said. "He reached out and pulled the sergeant's gun from its holster. I couldn't believe what I was seeing—except that I guess I thought Jimmy meant it as some kind of a gag."

"I felt the gun go and I spun around," Kohler said. "He'd taken a step or two back from me. I was about to yell at him like what the hell he was doing when he put the gun up to his temple and pulled the trigger."

"I just froze where I was," Martin said. "I couldn't believe what I was seeing."

"He went down, his brains spattered on the floor," Kohler said. "I just couldn't believe it at the time."

"At the time?"

"I told Mr. Jericho what we found on him," Swann said.

"Oh." Kohler looked relieved. "Well, that explains it, I guess. Too bad. He was a good Joe."

Jericho stood very still, a nerve twitching high up on his cheek. "Thanks," he said, in a flat voice. "Thanks for telling me."

Jericho spoke as gently as he could to the blonde girl.

"They found drugs on him, Marilyn—heroin, needle, the works."

She looked at Jericho steadily. They were in her small apartment on Jane Street. "So?" she said.

"He was evidently back on the stuff, Marilyn. Perhaps he was high on that as well as on happiness when he left you. When it wore off—" Jericho shrugged. "He knew he couldn't make it. He knew he'd destroy your life as well as his own."

"That, Mr. Jericho, is utter nonsense," the girl said. "Jimmy was clean for almost two years. I can swear to that."

"Then how do you account for what they found on him?"

"He took it from somebody else, from one of his kids. He just happened to have it on him when they killed him."

"When who killed him?"

"That's what I hoped you'd find out."

Jericho sighed. "What a wife you'd have made, Marilyn. A woman who believes in her man the way you do—"

"We should be able to find out about the stuff," Marilyn said. "The boys at the Center might know if he took it from one of the kids."

"Let's try," Jericho said. Something was bothering him, something was itching at him. He was, he realized, beginning to believe the impossible.

The Drug Rehabilitation Center was located in the basement of an old church. There were Ping-Pong tables, dart boards, and other games. It was like a club for boys. Marilyn was evidently well known to the boys. She had worked there with Jimmy in her free time. They crowded around her, shy of Jericho at first.

Here Marilyn had real allies. She was flooded by variations of the same question: "What really happened to Jimmy?" Mr. Jericho was helping to find out, she told them. One thing he needed to clear up. The police had found drugs and a needle and other equipment on Jimmy and they assumed he was back on the stuff.

"Oh, way out, man!"

"No way! Not Jimmy."

"Then where did he get the stuff he had on him?" Jericho asked.

"Took it from Teddy Washington," a boy said. "Teddy had it on him yesterday afternoon when Jimmy come in here. Jimmy took it off him."

"Teddy tell him where he got it?" Jericho asked.

"No way, man. You squeal on the pusher and the big shots who supply the pusher don't like it. They fix you good and that way they make it clear to everyone else. Jimmy wouldn't even ask Teddy because he'd know Teddy couldn't tell him."

Jericho nodded. He was beginning to believe, but there was still a small doubt. These kids would stand back of Jimmy, would lie for Jimmy. If Jimmy had slipped and was back on the stuff they'd deny it forever. But there was a way to make sure.

Jericho went to the pay phone in the far corner of the room, dropped in a dime, and called a number. The man he eventually got on the other end was Lieutenant Pascal of the Homicide Squad, an old friend.

"Not working these days, Lieutenant?" Jericho asked.

"There are so many murders these days, Johnny, I've thrown in my hand. I just sit here doing *The Times*' crossword puzzle."

"Is the puzzle too engrossing for you to do me a favor?"

"Name it."

"A fellow named Jimmy Kane committed suicide in a police station yesterday."

"I read about it. Friend of yours?"

"Friend of mine," Jericho said. "How tough would it be for you to get the Medical Examiner's report?"

"Like a phone call," Pascal said. "What do you want to know?"

"Was he on drugs? Were there signs of it in his system? Were there any recent needle marks on him?"

"You got another dime?" Pascal said. "It shouldn't take me longer than that. Hold on."

Jericho held on. The operator asked for another dime and he fed the machine. Then Pascal came back.

"Your boy was clean," he said. "Nothing in the blood. No needle marks. Some very old scars. He was on the stuff some years ago, you know. But clean right now."

Jericho frowned. "Wouldn't Captain Swann, who was in charge of the case, know that?"

"Not unless he had a reason to inquire," Pascal said. "It isn't in the report, Johnny. I found out by asking because you wanted to know. The M.E.'s report doesn't say what they don't find. Man died of a gunshot wound in the right temple, close enough to be a suicide. It doesn't say that your friend didn't have stomach trouble or didn't have diabetes or wasn't on drugs. It only reports what they did find."

"Thanks, Lieutenant."

"Hey, wait a minute. I have a normal amount of curiosity, you know."

"I may have work for you," Jericho said.

"How do you mean?"

"I think Jimmy Kane was murdered," Jericho said.

"But two cops saw what happened!"

"I know they did," Jericho said. "See you around."

He went back to Marilyn and the waiting boys. He smiled at the girl. "The Medical Examiner says Jimmy was clean—no drugs, no new needle marks."

"I didn't need him to tell me," Marilyn said.

Jericho looked around at the faces of the boys. "How many of you know Sergeant Kohler and Patrolman Martin at the precinct house by sight?"

Four hands went up.

"I'd like to ask a favor. Kohler and Martin are on the four o'clock shift, which means they get off at midnight. Could you guys watch them for me when they leave? They may go somewhere together, they may go separately. I want you to see where they go and phone me. Can do?"

"No sweat, man."

"So they'll go home," Marilyn said.

"Not when I get through with them," Jericho said.

Jericho had the capacity to turn to work when he wanted to shut out other problems. Most of the rest of that day and the early part of the evening he stood before the easel in his studio, painting. The case of Jimmy Kane was apparently erased from his consciousness. But at exactly 9:30 in the evening he put down his brushes, undressed, took a steaming hot shower, and then put on fresh clothes—dark-gray slacks, a black turtlenecked knit shirt, a tan corduroy jacket.

It was ten o'clock when he picked up the phone. He had taken his handkerchief out of his pocket and he held it, crumpled, over the mouthpiece of the phone as he dialed.

"I'd like to speak to Sergeant Kohler," he said, when there was an answer.

"Kohler here," Kohler said when he came on, brisk and efficient.

"I want to talk to you about Jimmy Kane," Jericho said.

"You better take the hot potato out of your mouth," Kohler said. "You're not coming over clear."

"Clear enough," Jericho said. "You see, Kohler, I know exactly what happened to Jimmy Kane. I figure it ought to be worth five thousand bucks to you and Martin for me to keep quiet about it."

Kohler's voice was suddenly tense. "What the hell are you talking about?"

"I'll give you till morning to get up the bread," Jericho said. "I'll call you again so we can figure out how you get it to me."

"Now listen, Mac, I don't know who you are or what you think you know, but I'll tell you one thing. I don't have—"

Jericho put down the receiver. He smoothed out his handkerchief and put it back in his pocket. He went about the business of making himself three eggs, toast, and coffee. After he'd finished eating he sat in a big armchair, a sketch pad in his lap, playing games with a pencil.

Time moved slowly. About fifteen minutes past midnight his phone rang.

"Mr. Jericho? About those two cops."

"Yes?"

"They went straight from the precinct house to Guardine's Bar and Grill. It's about two blocks from—"

"I know the place," Jericho said.

"Well, that's where they're at, Mr. Jericho."

"Thanks, son."

"No sweat, man."

"I'll see you around."

"Count on it, man."

Jericho turned out the studio lights and went out. He walked out of the Mews and turned south. Guardine's was only a short distance away. Guardine's was a steakhouse and bar, not frequented by high society but not cheap. At this time of night the dinner business was over. A few male customers were at the bar and some of the booths along the west wall were occupied by men and women.

In the farthest booth from the door Jericho spotted Kohler and Martin sitting with a sleekly groomed man who was talking to them earnestly. The two policemen were in civilian clothes. Jericho's mouth hardened, then he sauntered over to the booth. Martin and the sleek man were sitting together on one side of the table. The gray-haired Kohler was facing them.

Jericho stopped by the booth. "Hello, Sergeant," he said.

Kohler jerked his head around and forced a smile. "Hi, Mr. Jericho. This a watering place of yours?"

"I just dropped in," Jericho said. "Hello, Martin."

Martin nodded. "This is Bill Guardine who owns the joint," Martin said.

Guardine's dark eyes glittered. "Hi," he said.

"Ah, yes," Jericho said. "Guardine. Move over, Kohler, I'll buy a round of drinks."

"Look, Mr. Jericho," Kohler said, "we've got a little business to transact, so if we could have a rain check—?"

"I have a little business to transact, too," Jericho said, "and I imagine it's connected with yours. I decided not to wait till morning to work out the way you'll get the money to me." He moved in and sat down next to Kohler, facing Guardine.

Kohler moistened his lips. "You were the one who called me?"

"The hot potato was a handkerchief held over the mouthpiece," Jericho said. He smiled, a cold smile, at Guardine. "You going to put up the money for the boys, Guardine?"

"You blown your mind or something?" Guardine asked. His narrowed eyes moved out toward the bar, looking for someone or something.

"I don't think the price is too high," Jericho said. "You don't pay and my friends here, Kohler and Martin, will get the business. With the heat properly applied I suspect they'll talk, which means that in the end you and your pushers will get the business."

"What is it you think you know?" Guardine asked.

"I know how Jimmy Kane died and why," Jericho said. "Jimmy was a smart boy. He had something like his own police force—about three dozen desperate kids who would do anything in the world for him. I imagine he set a trap for you guys and he came to you with the evidence—heroin, needle, the rest of it. He'd found out you two noble bluecoats were protecting the pushers on the street. He faced you with it and you knew he had you cold. You, Kohler, and Martin, just happened to be alone and you did the one thing you could to save your miserable corrupt hides. You pulled your gun, Kohler, and you shot Jimmy in the head. All so smooth, so slick, and whatever Jimmy knew about you died with him."

"You're dreaming, Jericho," Kohler said. His face had gone a pasty white and he was sweating.

"I figured you weren't being paid off by the pushers on the street," Jericho said, "so I thought I'd find out who was the Big Man. So I phoned you and you led me here." He smiled at Guardine. "So you turn out to be the Big Man, Dad."

"And you expect to get paid off with nothing but a dream in your head?" Guardine asked.

"I'll let you in on a secret," Jericho said, smiling and smiling. "I really don't want the money. I just wanted to get led to you and it worked. I may not have evidence in my hands, but I can make enough noise so that honest men will find the evidence and pin it on you."

Guardine had been sitting with his hands in his lap. He moved slightly, then he spoke in a very low voice.

"Pointing at your belly button under the table, Jericho, is a gun with a silencer on it. I suggest we talk about this in my office."

"I like it here with witnesses around," Jericho said.

"Let me tell you something, wise guy," Guardine said. "There isn't a person in this place who will see anything that happens, and if they do see something they won't remember what it was. So start moving."

Jericho still smiled. "You don't give me much choice, do you, Big Man?"

Jericho suddenly moved. Under the table he kicked out savagely. There was the faint sound of a silenced shot and Kohler screamed. The bullet had shattered his kneecap. At the same moment Jericho stood up and the table went over against Guardine and Martin, pinning them in the booth.

Jericho reached out, grabbed Guardine by the collar, and yanked him out of the booth. His left hand came up against Guardine's jaw in a devastating uppercut so that the gangster sagged in Jericho's collar hold.

Jericho's bright eyes turned to Martin. "Don't reach for your gun, friend, unless you want me to break your neck."

Jericho spun Guardine around and flattened him against the wall. "No witnesses, you said, Guardine. I had a feeling that's the way it would be, so I brought my own. Take a look around."

Guardine turned his head and found himself faced by a semicircle of young faces, white, black, brown. In the center of the group was a lovely blonde girl. Beyond them Guardine saw customers and waiters hurrying out of his place.

"One of you kids call Captain Swann," Jericho said, "and maybe we better have an ambulance for our friend Kohler. He's hurting." He swung Guardine around and literally threw him into the booth with Martin and Kohler. He took a step or two toward the girl. "So we know, Marilyn," he said. "Unfortunately it isn't going to do Jimmy much good."

"But you finished his job for him and left him clean," the girl said. "Thank you for that, Mr. Jericho."

Jericho looked back at the three crumpled men in the booth. "My pleasure," he said.

Jericho and the Missing Boy

John Jericho saw the woman come out of the woods and start across the lawn toward his cottage, half running. She stumbled, as though she was close to exhaustion, a runner uncertain of reaching the final tape in a race.

For a moment Jericho's reaction was mixed. He had rented the cottage because he wanted privacy. There were moments in his life when he wanted to be shut away with his creative energies undisturbed. He was standing in front of a half-finished painting on an easel, a large canvas, with brilliant colors reflecting Jericho's enormous energy, and he didn't want any interruptions. The prospect of one made him angry.

He saw the woman fall to her knees, struggle up, and come on again. It was, he told himself, something more than an ordinary emergency. He put down his palette and brushes, took the black curved-stem pipe out of his mouth, slipped the pipe into the pocket of his corduroy jacket, and went out onto the terrace. He was a giant of a man, six-feet-four-inches tall, two-hundred-and-forty pounds of solid bone and muscle, with flaming red hair and beard.

The woman reached him, gasping for breath. She grabbed at his arms to hold herself up. "Thank God you're home," she said.

"What's wrong, Mrs. Redmond?" he asked.

He knew her, knew of her, only casually. She was his nearest neighbor, some five hundred yards as the crow might fly through the woods. She was the ex-wife of the famous film star, Anthony Redmond. She was living here in New England with her twelve-year-old son while her ex-husband cut a romantic swath in Hollywood, Europe, or wherever his career took him.

Laura Redmond was an attractive, dark, withdrawn woman. She suggested a special kind of female mystery, Jericho thought, that made her irresistibly interesting to men. At this moment, clinging to him, some sort of fear had ripped away her sophisticated exterior.

"It's Dicky," she said.

Dick was the twelve-year-old boy. One day, a week ago, he had fallen out of a tree at the edge of the woods. He had been spying on the red-bearded giant who had taken over the cottage. It was simple boyish curiosity about a neighbor who chose to stay hidden away from the community.

The boy had been badly jarred by the fall, and Jericho had taken him into the cottage, medicated a cut knee, produced a cold bottle of pop from the refrigerator, and made friends. Eventually he had driven Dick home in his red Mercedes and met Laura Redmond. He had found her pleasant, engaging.

Jericho had been tempted to follow up the meeting—she did things to his maleness. But he had turned his back on it because it would interfere with his concentrating on the six paintings he'd promised to produce for a new one-man show at the Mullins Gallery.

"Dick fall out of another tree?" he asked.

She shook her head and handed him a small piece of paper that she'd carried, crumpled, in her hand. There was a strange scrawled writing on it.

Your son has been kidnaped. You will prepare to pay $1,000,000 or the most you can afford. I will know if it is not enough. You will be told what to do next. Don't call the police or your son will be killed.

Jericho felt Laura Redmond's fingernails bite into his arm. He frowned at the note, a dark anger starting to simmer inside him. We live in a cock-eyed world— a world of skyjacking and bombing, of blackmailing by power groups that are, laughably, considered legal. We accept this as a part of the seamier side of living. Using helpless children to pry money out of people is the lowest of all these holdups.

"Take it easy," Jericho said. "You've called the police?"

She raised wide violet eyes to him, eyes filled with terror. "Of course not. It says—"

"I know what it says." Jericho scowled at the paper. "It always says not to call the police. It's a decision you have to make—if this is for real."

"What do you mean, if it's for real? Dicky's gone."

"Tell me about it."

"I went into town to shop," she said. "Dicky stayed at home, playing in the back yard. He's twelve. There's no reason not to leave him alone any more."

" 'Any more'?"

"There was a time when I thought Tony—my ex-husband—might try to take Dicky away from me. But he's lost interest in Dicky."

"So you left Dicky alone in the yard."

"He has a tent at the back of the house. He was playing there when I left."

Jericho gestured with the note. "Where did you find this?"

"When I came back from marketing, Dicky wasn't there. He always comes running—to welcome me back, to help with packages. So I called to him, without getting any answer. Then I went to his tent and found—found that note thumb-tacked to the tent pole where I couldn't miss it. I tried to call Mark Taylor, my lawyer, but he's out of town for the day. I didn't believe the note, I tried to tell myself it was some kind of joke. I don't have that kind of money."

"But your husband does."

"My ex-husband. Yes, Tony could raise that kind of money if he had to. If he wanted to." She was struggling to get control of herself. "Then I wondered if you might have seen Dicky—if possibly he'd come over here. He took a great liking to you, Mr. Jericho. I—"

"He hasn't been here," Jericho said.

Jericho drove Laura Redmond back to her house in his car. On the way he tried to put the facts of life in front of her. The F.B.I. were experts in kidnaping cases. It was his advice that she get in touch with them at once. There was no guarantee that Dick would be returned unharmed if she didn't. The boy's best chance was to have skilled professionals looking for him.

Anguished, she protested that she couldn't. She'd have to reach the boy's father first. If she made the wrong decision Tony would blame her.

"So reach him. I'll talk to him," Jericho said.

"God knows where he is," she cried out.

"He has an agent, doesn't he—someone who handles his affairs? The agent will know where to find him."

"I've left word for Mark to call," she said. She was desperate in her uncertainty.

"Your lawyer?" he asked, sensing that perhaps this lawyer was more to Laura than a legal adviser.

The Redmond house was an old remodeled Colonial on a side street of the village. There was a pleasant stretch of front lawn, a small well-cared-for flower garden, two old shade trees. Laura went directly into the house to try to reach her husband's agent on the telephone.

Jericho wandered around to the rear. There he saw the boy's small green canvas tent. He hesitated a moment. He didn't want to destroy any evidence of the kidnapers—footprints, for example. He walked down the edge of a flowerbed and then cut in, an indirect approach not likely to have been taken by anyone in a hurry.

He had to bend almost double to get into the tent. There was nothing much to see. Along one edge was a collection of wilted pine branches. It might have been the basis for a bed, he thought, but there were no blankets and no sleeping bag. There was a Sears catalogue on the ground beside the pine boughs, a Boy Scout hat hanging from a nail in the tent pole, and a detective-story magazine.

He heard a door slam in the house and he backed out of the tent. Laura was coming toward him from the house. She had been lucky. Anthony Redmond was filming in Hollywood. His agent would get to him as quickly as possible and she could expect a call.

"You can also expect a call from the kidnapers with instructions," Jericho said. "If you'd notify the F.B.I. now, they could bug your phone and trace the call."

"I can't," she said. "Not till I've talked to Tony." Tears were streaming down her face. "Oh, my God, what will they do to him?"

"They may take good care of him if you and your husband meet their demands," Jericho said reassuringly. "Tell me, were there any blankets on those pine boughs in the tent?"

"A sleeping bag," she said. "Isn't it there? I didn't notice."

"They evidently took it," Jericho said. He looked out to the woods in back of the house. The absence of the sleeping bag suggested the boy was being held somewhere outdoors, perhaps not too far away. Anger burned at the center of his gut. The boy might be close by, but an open search of the woods could result in violence.

"I don't know what I can do for you, Laura," he said. "If you won't call the F.B.I.—"

She reached out to him. "Please, please don't leave me," she said. "At least until Mark comes. Tony will be calling and there may be things to do. The kidnapers may get in touch. Please don't leave me."

"All right," he said. "You may not be giving Dick his best chance. But I'll stay."

They waited in the house for whatever might happen next. Doing nothing in crisis was almost more than Jericho could stand. She offered him some bourbon and he accepted. They sat in the living room, waiting for word from the kidnapers, waiting for Anthony Redmond's call, waiting for Mark Taylor to appear. From time to time Jericho wandered to a rear window and looked out at the woods. The house could be watched without their being aware of it.

Laura felt compelled to talk. It was the only way for her to stay sane. She talked about her husband, perhaps because his phone call was imminent. She had loved him, he had been her whole life. She had grown up in this village, had met him here when he was on location for a film. He had been romantic, glamorous, had swept her off her feet. Her friends, including Mark Taylor, her boy friend since high school, had warned her it would never work. Anthony Redmond belonged to another world, an unreal world. He would never tie himself down to one woman.

But the marriage, at the start, had been good beyond her dreams. Dicky had been born in the second year. Anthony had been so proud and had loved the baby with a passion. Dicky would tie them together forever, she thought.

When Dicky was less than a year old, Anthony had gone to Spain to make a film. It would only be for two months or so. Things started to fall apart then. There was a famous Italian actress, a great beauty. The gossip about her and Anthony was true; he admitted it when he came home. He begged for her forgiveness. Away from Laura the temptation had been too great.

She forgave him, but it was only the beginning of the end. It was never the same again. There'd been one woman after another. So she had sued for divorce and come back here to live with Dicky. It had been relatively amicable. No trouble over money. For a while he kept in touch with his small son, came to visit him. But finally the separation was total. It had been nearly two years since there'd been any contact with Redmond, except for the monthly check which came from his agent.

The phone rang.

It was Redmond calling from Hollywood. Laura told him what had happened. She read him the note. Jericho could hear the voice on the other end, shouting.

"Tony, please—" she pleaded. "I've been advised to call in the F.B.I.—a neighbor, the only person who knows. He's here now. Please, will you talk to him?" She held out the phone to Jericho.

Jericho took the phone. "Mr. Redmond? I'm John Jericho."

"I don't care who the hell you are," the familiar harsh voice said. "The new Bogart" they called him. "Put Laura back on."

"I've had some experience with crime, Redmond," Jericho said. "I think you people should call in the F.B.I. If you try to handle it yourselves you may not get the boy back."

"You listen, man," Redmond said. "They say no police, so that's the way we'll work it. So help me, if you try to muscle in, whoever you are—"

"I'm not going to muscle in."

"Good. I'm flying East. I'll have money the first thing the banks open in the morning in New York. Take me two hours after that to drive up there. Let's say eleven thirty tomorrow morning. If the kidnapers get in touch, explain we can't have the money before then. Now put Laura on again."

Laura talked to him again—rather, she listened to him again. Finally she came back from the phone. "He cares for Dicky," she said in an odd voice. "I think he really cares for him."

"He's his father."

"I—I think he'd forgotten that," Laura said.

The day wore on, summer hot. There was no word from anyone. The village went about its business, unaware of anything out of the ordinary. Jericho felt his nerves getting frayed. To begin with he'd run out of pipe tobacco. Conversation with Laura Redmond had dried up. There was nothing to talk about except the central situation, and they'd gone round it and round it, discussing it from every angle, unable to move in any way until instructions came from the kidnapers.

Why didn't they call? Or send a message? They'd know, Jericho explained, that the kind of money they were asking for must come from Anthony Redmond. They'd know the actor was in California. They'd know it would take at least 24 hours for him to raise the cash and come East. They wouldn't give instructions too far in advance.

While they waited and worried, Jericho couldn't shake the certainty that they were being watched. Time and again he went to the rear windows that looked out on the woods, convinced that sooner or later he would see some movement— some movement of brush on a windless day, some reflection of the afternoon sun against something bright, something that didn't belong there. But there was nothing.

Shortly after five o'clock on the longest afternoon that Jericho could remember, a car drove into the front yard and an attractive-looking man—in his mid-thirties, Jericho guessed—got out and came running up the path to the front door. He didn't knock or ring, but came straight in.

"Laura!" he called out.

She ran to him and was, for a moment, in his arms.

"Darling, I found your message at the office," the man said. "What's wrong?"

She handed him the crumpled note without speaking.

"My God!" he said. Then he became aware of Jericho in a far corner of the room.

"This is John Jericho, Mark, who's taken the Bentley cottage," Laura said. "I went there looking for Dicky. Mr. Jericho's stayed with me. I couldn't find you. I—I—" She started to crack.

Taylor kept his arm around her protectingly. He had candid gray eyes and a wide generous mouth. "I'm grateful to you for standing by, Jericho," he said.

"What else?" Jericho said.

A startled look changed Taylor's face. "My God, I almost forgot this. It was shoved through the mail chute in my office door. For you, Laura." He took an envelope out of his pocket. "It could be—"

It was—instructions from the kidnapers.

We know your husband can't get money to us before tomorrow. $250,000 in tens and twenties, all unmarked bills. You will deliver *the money at noon tomorrow, you or your husband. No one else. We will know if you have called police or the F.B.I. Leave the money in the office of the old mill. Don't muff it if you want your kid to live. There will be no second chance.*

Mark Taylor muttered a string of profanities under his breath.

"Written by a different person," Jericho said, frowning at the note. "Different writing."

"Will Anthony make it by noon tomorrow?" Taylor asked.

"He should," Laura said. "Just make it."

"Where is this old mill they mention?" Jericho asked.

"About a mile from here through the woods," Taylor said. "It's an old sawmill, long abandoned."

"You realize the F.B.I. could surround the woods, move in," Jericho said.

"Not without being seen," Taylor said. "They'd be watching. They might carry out their threat against Dick."

"Please, Mr. Jericho, let Tony pay the money," Laura said. "Let them take it and go. Surely they'll set Dicky free if we do exactly what they tell us."

Jericho drew a deep breath. "It's your ball game," he said. "Now that you're not alone, Mrs. Redmond, I'll go back to my place if you don't mind. There won't be any action until tomorrow morning."

"I'm so grateful to you," she said. "So very grateful."

"I wish there was some positive help I could give," he said.

Jericho drove out of Laura Redmond's yard convinced that eyes were peering at the back of his head from the woods. The drop-off for the money, the whole operation, was so close by.

He got back to his cottage and like a starving man went to the jar of his specially blended pipe tobacco and filled both his pipe and his pouch. Sitting on the terrace, a cloud of blue smoke around his head, a bourbon in his hand, he stared at the woods.

It was tough for Laura, and for the absent ex-husband flying across the continent, hoping, maybe praying. It was tough for Mark Taylor, the loyal friend, still obviously in love with Laura. But it was ten times tougher for the twelve-year-old boy snatched away from everything that represented safety and security, waiting under the gun for his parents to deliver, wondering if his captors would live up to their end of the bargain and set him free. It must be agony for the boy to know that if he could run only a few hundred yards his mother might be able to hear his screams for help.

Twilight settled over the cottage and the summer night was close. Jericho sat on his terrace, drinking and smoking and battling with himself. Over his second slug of bourbon he had developed a theory about the kidnaping. If he was right Dick Redmond was never going to turn up alive—unless Jericho acted on his theory.

Did he have the right to act? Did he have the right to interfere? Suppose he went back to Laura and Mark Taylor and told them his theory and what he believed should be done, and suppose they said "No!" Dick's one chance might be gone. If he went ahead with his plan in spite of the "No" and botched it, they and the whole world would blame him for Dick's death. Stay out of it, he told himself. Mind your own business.

He remembered Dick's young face, the bright inquisitive eyes, the warm eager smile. Just as sure as the coming day the boy would be dead shortly after noon tomorrow if Jericho was right about the situation. Still, he had no business to assume the responsibility, to act on his own.

Darkness closed down over the cottage as clouds blotted out the moon and the stars. Only the red glow from Jericho's pipe and the occasional flicker of a firefly punctuated the black stillness. Down the road a woman waited and prayed. Somewhere in the woods a small boy fought with terror. Or did he? Had the time not yet come for him to be afraid?

Sometime later Jericho got up from his chair, went into the cottage, and switched on lights. He had made his decision. He was going to take it on himself, without consultation, without permission. It was the boy's only chance. He'd finally convinced himself of that.

He changed out of the clothes he was wearing into a black knit turtleneck shirt, charcoal-gray slacks, and a navy-blue cardigan. He stuffed his pipe, pouch, and lighter into the pockets of the sweater; he filled a silver pint flask with bourbon and slid it into his hip pocket. In the kitchen he made himself two thick ham and cheese sandwiches which he wrapped in foil. Ten minutes later he was walking down the main highway, his cottage and his car left behind him.

An old sawmill about a mile up in the woods, Taylor had said. If sometime in the past they had carted or trucked lumber out of the woods there must be the remnants of a trail or road somewhere. It was a long time before he found it. He had walked by it several times, the roadside brush having completely overgrown the mouth of it.

He swore softly as he moved up the trail. The clouds were beginning to drift away. Not too long from now the whole countryside would be bathed in moonlight.

Just ahead the old buildings of the mill loomed up. Jericho was an experienced woodsman and he walked as noiselessly as an Indian. He was looking up at the ancient trees that surrounded the mill. He selected one, waited for a moment, listening, and then he climbed—up to the third sprouting of branches, thirty feet above the ground. He wedged himself into a crotch, his back against the trunk of the tree. He waited. Suddenly the woods were bathed in the bright light of the moon, but Jericho was now out of sight, high in the tree.

Hour after hour went by and finally morning came. Jericho had eaten his sandwiches, the foil was stuffed in the pocket of his sweater. His flask was half empty. From time to time, almost automatically, his hand reached for his pipe and pouch. Each time he checked himself. Every bone and muscle in his body ached. He moved, an inch or two at a time, to change his position slightly.

With daylight he looked down on the dilapidated buildings that had been the old mill. The roof had caved in in places; moss grew on the weather-stained walls still standing. Out of view but within hearing was a stream racing down a rocky bed—water that had once turned the mill wheel that had worked the power saws.

The sun rose. Jericho glanced at his watch. Anthony Redmond, in New York, would have collected the money by now and be racing up the Thruway, sweating with anxiety. He'd probably phoned Laura and got from her the details of the kidnapers' demand—$250,000 in unmarked tens and twenties. He knew he had to make it by noon. Time would be going by for him with terrifying speed. For the man in the tree it dragged painfully.

At last the sun was high in the sky. Jericho, looking at his watch, saw that it was ten minutes to noon. Then he heard the noise of someone coming, making no effort to hide his arrival.

Jericho peered down through the leaves at the old logging road and saw Anthony Redmond hurrying toward the mill, carrying a small black suitcase. There was something dramatic about the man, even alone here in the woods.

Redmond made straight for the crumbling building and went inside. He evidently knew where the office was in the old mill. Moments later he came out, stood looking almost desperately around, then started down the trail without once looking back.

Jericho moved, ever so slightly, and then saw the boy coming. He was coming from higher up on the wooded hill, almost running toward the crumbling mill. Jericho fought the sudden impulse to cry out to Dick, to jump down from his perch in the tree, to take the boy in his arms. He was helped by something he saw, something he'd looked for all yesterday afternoon—the glint of sunlight on a rifle barrel about forty yards up the hill behind the boy.

Dick went into the mill and came out with the suitcase that his father had left. He looked happy! He went up the hill with the bag and a man rose up out of the brush to join him, a rifle tucked under his arm. The two disappeared beyond a rise in the ground.

Jericho came down from the tree, groaning slightly. He was so stiff he could scarcely move at first. But he started after the boy and the man, moving, presently, swift and quiet. Not far over the rise of ground he saw a small cabin, and Dick and the man were just going into it.

Jericho moved down the slope toward the cabin. Eventually, almost on his hands and knees, he reached a window at the back of the cabin and slowly raised himself.

There were three young men in the cabin with Dick Redmond.

"I told you it would work," the man with the rifle said. He was standing with his back to Jericho.

"Let's have a look at it, man," one of the others said. "I never see so much money all in one place at the same time."

Dick had put the suitcase on the table and now he opened it, revealing the money stacked in neat packages.

"It's all there," the third one said. "Brother!"

"Papa came all by himself," the man with the gun said. "So let's not drag our feet."

"He did come, didn't he!" Dick said, beaming.

"Just like you hoped he would, Dick," the man with the gun said. He moved slightly. "I'm sorry to have to do this to you, Dick, but, man, you could draw pictures of all of us, you know."

The boy's face was screwed up in total bewilderment. "I told you I don't care about the money, Frank. I—I don't understand."

"It won't hurt, Dick," Frank said. "You won't ever know what hit you. I'm sorry but we can't let you go free."

"Get it over with, Frank!"

A black figure hurtled through the window. The rifle went off, but the bullet hit the ceiling as Jericho's arm went around the rifleman's neck and snapped his head back. Jericho scrambled for the gun and swung it around.

One of the other men had tugged a revolver out of his belt and Jericho fired. A gaping hole appeared in the man's shirt front as he jackknifed forward and went down. The third man's hands were up and he was screaming for mercy.

"All right, Dick," Jericho said. "Get out of here—fast. Your mother and father are waiting for you. Tell them what happened here and have them send the State Police."

The boy, white as a sheet, stared at the two fallen men. "They—they were going to kill me! I thought they were my friends, but they were going to kill me!"

"They certainly were, Dick. Get moving."

Talking to Anthony Redmond proved to be an odd experience. Jericho had seen him so often in films that he seemed like an old friend—his voice, his mannerisms, his tight little one-cornered smile, all so familiar. And yet the man was a stranger, his nerves tense, Jericho unknown to him. He had come directly to the State Police Barracks where Jericho had finished dictating a statement for the Lieutenant in command.

The three men the police had found in the cabin with Jericho, one of them critical from a gunshot wound in his chest, were wanted for the wanton murder of an entire family in the next state. There had been a ten-state alarm out for them. Kidnaping only added to the long list of charges against them.

"I don't quite know how to thank you," Redmond said. "From what Dick told us they were about to—to rub him out when you broke it up." He turned pale.

Jericho smiled. "Seen you do it a dozen times in films," he said.

"But this was for real," Redmond said. "I know you helped Laura in the afternoon, that you were aware of all the facts we had, so you weren't just up in the woods for exercise."

Jericho stuffed a fresh fill of tobacco into his black pipe and held his lighter to it. "It was a risk," he said. "If I was wrong, if I blew it, there'd have been no life left for me. But I was so damned sure!"

"Of what?"

"In the beginning, when I first went to Mrs. Redmond's house with her, I found myself toying with the idea that there'd been no kidnaping," Jericho said.

"But Dick was gone! The note!"

"It was the note that bothered me. 'Prepare to pay one million dollars or the most you can afford. I will know if it is not enough.' It didn't sound like a hardened professional. It sounded like a kid. Dick's sleeping bag was missing from the tent. I tried to visualize a criminal whose success depended on his getting away with the boy quickly stopping to take along a sleeping bag. I thought to myself that this was some kind of prank of the boy's. He'd gone off by himself, taking the bag to make sure he'd be warm at night, leaving that rather absurd note for his mother."

"Of course if you'd known Dick—"

"I did know him." Jericho smiled faintly. "I met him while he was working for the C.I.A., spying on me in my cottage. Unfortunately for the master spy he fell out of a tree. I couldn't risk my first theory, Redmond, but it stayed with me most of yesterday afternoon. It was re-enforced by things your wife told me. You had loved the boy and he loved you, but you'd been out of touch for two years. I could imagine that active little mind asking, 'Does he still love me? Would he help me if I was in trouble?' So, I told myself, he was trying to find out. A kidnaping—'pay one million dollars or the most you can afford.' He desperately needed you to come through for him."

"My God, I can see how you imagined that," Redmond said. "But of course—"

"Of course that's exactly what happened," Jericho said. "There was no kidnaping—in the beginning. It was all Dick's doing. He went off into the woods with his sleeping bag and waited to see if you would come through for him."

"But these men!" Redmond said, his voice unsteady.

"The second note made me certain of them," Jericho said. "Different writing. Specific instructions. A specific amount demanded. Exact instructions as to place and time for the payoff. Another hand, another kind of mind had come into the picture. I could imagine what had happened. Dick had run into strangers in the woods, dangerous strangers. They had demanded to know what he was doing there. Ingenuously he told them. He was letting his family think he'd been kidnaped. He wanted—I can't guess his exact words—to find out if his father still cared for him. And who was his father? The rich famous actor, Anthony Redmond.

"These men were running for their lives; they needed money the way they needed air to breathe. What a godsend this kid was! They played along with him. They'd help him carry out his plan. They let him see you bring the money. They actually let him collect it for them. But then—then he had to die."

"And you were there—but how did you happen to be there at exactly the right moment?"

"They would be watching in the daytime," Jericho said. "There might be a search party; the family might ignore the warning and call in the F.B.I. *But they couldn't watch at night.* So I went up there in the dark and I took a leaf from Dick's spy manual and climbed a tree." He stretched a little painfully. "I may never be the same. Thirteen hours up a tree! But I was there when they showed. I was sure they would come, and they did. I knew I would have to be there at the exact moment or it would be all up with Dick."

"What can I do to express my gratitude?" Redmond asked.

Jericho's pale-blue eyes fastened on the actor's face. "Reassure the boy—if you really do care for him. He needs it—how badly I leave you to judge."

"Will you come back to the house with me? Laura and Dick will want to thank you."

"Not today," Jericho said. "I need to sleep around the clock, and I'm behind in my work." He reached out a huge hand to the actor's shoulder. "I hope it works out for you, friend."

Jericho and the Sea of Faces

Jeff Tanner's cottage was on the lakefront in the New England town of
Winfield, in the foothills of the Berkshires. The lake, which had an
unpronounceable Indian name, was about three miles long, completely encircled
by woodland. If you stood on the bank of the lake it would almost appear to be
a wilderness, until you noticed a score or more of small docks with sailboats,
rowboats, and canoes moored alongside, or overturned and beached on the
shore. No power boats were allowed on the lake.

Actually, there were dozens of cottages built behind the wood line. Tanner's
was one of them. The whole area seemed beautifully relaxed, a haven for people
who liked peace and quiet and loathed thruways and gasoline fumes and vacation
hysteria. There was no history of violence in the area, unless the lake trout and
other fish could be heard. Hunting in the area surrounding the lake was forbidden,
and it had become a paradise for birds and wildlife. Migrators seemed to know
of it, and literally thousands of Canada geese were known to stop there on their
flights north and south.

There had been a few drownings in the lake over the years, which is not
unusual for any water resort. But on a warm, moonlit August night a man missed
being murdered in Jeff Tanner's cottage by a literal matter of inches. The man
was John Jericho, internationally known artist and adventurer.

Jericho had been sitting in the high-backed overstuffed armchair in front of
the screened picture window that opened onto the lake. He was reading—*Jane
Eyre*, of all things—a crooked-neck lamp bent over his left shoulder. His chair
was turned sideways to the screened window, his huge six-foot-six body almost
hidden by the high wings of the chair.

The sound of a gunshot was something he reacted to instantly, at the same
moment that the bullet hit the chair back and buried itself in the horsehair stuffing
just next to his right temple. Violence was not something new to John Jericho.
He was not a man who would mistake a gunshot for the backfiring of an
automobile.

He was out of the chair and down flat on the floor in an instinctive reaction.
The bullet had only missed him by inches, but even as he lay there on the floor,
waiting and listening for someone to make the next move, it didn't occur to him

for a moment that the bullet had been meant for him. This was Jeff Tanner's cottage, and Jericho knew that there were people who might want Jeff Tanner permanently silenced.

Tanner was what used to be called, in the old days, a journalist. He had started out after college as a reporter on the New York *World-Telegram*, and he had become a very good one, earning a byline for most of his stories. After touching a lot of different bases, politics and power had become his "thing." He stepped on a lot of toes and bloodied a lot of noses along the way. Politicians learned to hate him and at the same time respect him. You had to play it straight with Jeff Tanner or get the donkey tail pinned on you in public. Big money groups, seeking power through the judicious distribution of cash, instantly threw up smoke-screens when Jeff Tanner appeared in their neck of the woods.

When the *World-Telegram* died, as so many great newspapers have in the last couple of decades, Tanner decided to become a freelance instead of looking for another job in a desperately overcrowded field. His brilliance kept him eating handsomely.

Somewhere along the way—actually at a Peace demonstration in Washington—Tanner met the giant red-bearded artist, John Jericho. They hit it off at once, each of them dedicated passionately to Truth. They both fought against violence in their own way, and their primary targets were not the Mafia or the Syndicate or organized crime, but the sleek, sunlamp-tanned men who sat behind big flat-topped desks and manipulated the money markets as well as world politics.

Jericho and Tanner met accidentally at the Players Club late in July of that summer. Tanner, slim, dark, with a fire burning behind his dark eyes, was onto something big.

"I can't tell you about it, Johnny," he said that day at the Players, "except that if I can dig up a few more solid facts the whole system may come tumbling down like Humpty Dumpty, never to be put together again."

"Good luck," Jericho said, chewing on the stem of a charred black pipe. "Since you won't tell me what it is, let's change the subject. Now I need a change. Every now and then I have to remind myself that I am a painter and not a bull-fighter. I need a little peace and solitude."

Tanner glanced at him with affection. "I'm not going to be in this part of the world for a while. I have a cottage on the lake up in Winfield—the Berkshires. It's about as isolated as you could ask for in this date and age when the whole world is becoming one mass suburban. You want it for a month it's yours."

Which explains how Jericho came to be lying on the floor of Tanner's living room on a moonlit August night, waiting for a sniper to make another move.

Jericho thought quite calmly about his own next move. He could reach up and turn off the light. Darkness would be safer, and yet if he turned off the light the sniper would know that he had missed, or missed a fatal wounding. If the light stayed on he might come into the cottage to make sure.

Jericho, staying flat to the floor, inched his way toward the dark kitchen. Very slowly he pulled himself up to a standing position and waited, listening. There were no sounds that didn't belong there—a chorus of bullfrogs down at the lake's edge, the shrill cry of a night bird. He listened for the sound of a car. The sniper might have been convinced and would take off the way he had come.

But there was no car sound. He strained for a cautious footstep outside the cottage—a snapping twig, the click of the front-door catch, or the one that opened out onto the deck beyond the picture window. An owl hooted—that was all.

There was, he remembered, a wall phone in the kitchen. Tanner's cottage was isolated, but with all the comforts of home. Suburbia was creeping in, even here. In a low voice he asked the operator to connect him with the State Trooper barracks. He was answered by a flat impersonal voice. He explained who he was, where he was, and what had happened.

"You're sure you're not just imagining things?" the flat voice asked.

"The bullet is buried in the chair," Jericho said. "I haven't touched it."

"Sit tight," the flat voice said. "Stay out of sight."

In the glove compartment of the red Mercedes parked at the rear of Tanner's cottage Jericho had a handgun. He would, he knew, feel a great deal more comfortable if he had it on him. He moved to the kitchen door and looked out through the screen. Trees cut out the moonlight here and the car was just a dark shadow, a few yards away.

He reached up, disengaged the spring on the door, and pushed it open. The operation was noiseless. He stepped out into the clear and moved quickly to the car. There he hesitated. When he opened the car a little light would go on inside. If the sniper was watching—

Then, suddenly, Jericho laughed. Damned idiot! The sniper wasn't after *him*. He should turn on every bloody light in the place so that the sniper could see Jericho was the wrong man.

He went back into the kitchen and switched on the lights, then to the living room and switched on more lights. He stood framed in the picture window. He could see the hole in the screen made by the sniper's bullet. It must be perfectly clear to the sniper now, if the sniper was still around, that he'd taken a pot shot at the wrong man.

After a moment Jericho went, openly, out to the Mercedes and got his gun from the glove compartment. The danger for him was over, but he still felt better with the gun in the pocket of his corduroy jacket.

The State Police were prompt. Jericho saw the car with the blinking red light on its roof approaching. Two troopers walked into the cottage—Sergeant Maddux and Trooper Brennan. They examined the screen. Brennan dug the bullet out of the chair and dropped it in an envelope.

"All these lights," Maddux said. "You made yourself a perfect target, Mr. Jericho."

Jericho explained. "I suddenly realized the bullet wasn't meant for me," he said. "I don't know anyone in Winfield. I don't know anyone who'd be gunning for me. Best thing seemed to be to let him see he was shooting at the wrong guy."

"Risky," Maddux said. Brennan had gone outside.

"Well, anyway, he didn't shoot again," Jericho said.

Brennan came back. He had found the shell casing from a high-powered rifle. "He fired from two or three feet this side of Tanner's dock," he said. "Not more than twenty yards away."

"He must have seen you were the wrong guy from that close," Maddux said.

Jericho turned and sat down in the big wing chair, just as he had been sitting when the shot came. "The wings of this chair had my face hidden," he said. "About all he could have seen was the top of my head and my hands holding the book I was reading."

"Where is Tanner?" Maddux asked. "He should be warned somebody's out to get him."

"God knows where he is. He didn't tell me where he was going. He just told me I could use the cottage for a month. Maybe your post office has a forwarding address for him."

"We'll need a statement from you, Mr. Jericho. Don't tramp around outside. We'll have to wait till daylight to make any kind of search for a trail," Maddux said.

And so Jericho went to bed. He slept like a baby.

When Jericho woke the next morning, with the sun streaming through his bedroom window, Maddux and company were already outside on the grounds, trying to pick up the sniper's trail. They came to the conclusion he had escaped in a canoe, or a small boat of some kind, drifted around a bend in the lake some fifty yards from Tanner's dock while Jericho was lying on the floor waiting for something more to happen.

The county prosecutor, a man named Cleghorn, asked a few questions. They were about Jeff Tanner mostly. Did Jericho know if Tanner had any enemies?

"I just know he was working with a big story with political overtones," Jericho said. "He told me he was looking for facts that might 'bring the whole system tumbling down like Humpty Dumpty'."

"But you haven't any notion what facts or who he was after?" Cleghorn asked.

"Not the foggiest."

Cleghorn was in his mid-forties, Jericho guessed; sandy hair thinning at the temples, bright and inquisitive blue eyes. He was tanned and fit-looking. He seemed quite relaxed, hands in his pockets jiggling coins or keys.

"No forwarding address at the post office," Cleghorn said. He smiled faintly. "He didn't tell you where he could be reached—I mean, in case the plumbing broke down or someone stole his boat?"

"I'm supposed to be a big boy, able to handle such things. I'm not even sure Tanner knew where he was going. He was on a trail that could lead him anywhere."

"Well, thanks for your help, Mr. Jericho. I don't think we'll need you any more. Watch yourself after dark. He might come back, not realizing he missed the wrong man."

"I wouldn't mind if you spread the word around town so that he would hear it," Jericho said. "That I'm the wrong man, I mean."

He took his painting gear out into the woods and onto a high point of land overlooking the lake. His eye was caught by a small white sailboat with a bright red sail. He set up his easel and prepared his palette—blue-green for the water, white for the sailboat and clouds, another blue for the sky, dark greens, light greens, browns for the woods, and a dab of scarlet for the sail. He began to work, completely absorbed in what he was starting.

The gunshot came from behind him, burned his cheek, and went straight through the center of his canvas.

For the second time in a space of hours Jericho hit the deck. He crawled through the underbrush to a spot surrounded by thick evergreen trees. He could still see the red sail tacking slowly back and forth across the lake. There was no sound of anyone coming or going; no sound of anything except his own breathing and the thumping of his heart against his ribs.

This time there could be no doubt the shot had been meant for him. Broad daylight, out in the open, no possibility of mistaking his two-hundred-and-forty pounds, his massive shoulders, his red Viking beard; Tanner was slim, dark, one-hundred-and-sixty pounds. He touched his cheek and his fingers came away stained with blood. It had been that close.

Jericho stayed crouching in the protection of the evergreens. He reached into his jacket pocket and was reassured by the feel of his handgun. Who in God's name was so intent on killing him? He didn't know anybody in Winfield, though it was possible there was someone he had no reason to think lived here.

But who, if he were standing in the middle of Times Square, would want to kill him? He sat with his back against a tree, gun in his hand, trying to think, and at the same time trying to listen for someone taking off through the woods.

He began to recall a sea of faces from his past—the faces of people who might hate him enough to want to kill him. He had been involved with crime, with violence, in the past. He had helped send men to prison. He had stripped the gears in a score of criminal conspiracies.

The faces floated past him, none of them coming really clear. Not one of the faces stood out so that he could say there is a man who hates me enough to track me down, to risk capture, enough to want to kill me. Dark faces, pale faces, frightened faces, faces red with anger and frustration. They blurred together. But not one of them came downstage and center.

His breathing was normal again, his heartbeat steady. It was a miracle, he thought, that he was still alive. A high-powered rifle fired at close range by a man clever enough to make a noiseless escape might have missed him last night in the chair. But just now he had been standing out in the open, with nothing to interfere with a steady careful aim. Why not a second shot when Jericho moved?

He suddenly knew the answer, as though the marksman had confessed. Killing had not been intended. The sniper had *not* been inefficient, he had been superskillful. He had missed by inches last night; he had missed by the distance of too-close shave this morning. He had missed on purpose.

Why?

To frighten Jericho off, to drive him away from Winfield. There was someone here he did know; someone who, if he was seen by Jericho, would be in deep trouble. Winfield was a hiding place for someone, a hiding place that would be disclosed if Jericho saw a face out of the past.

It could not, Jericho thought, be someone who knew him well. Someone who really knew him would not have considered trying to frighten him away. Jericho had enough imagination to recognize danger, and to feel fear, but nothing in God's world would make him run away, run for safety.

Again the sea of faces paraded in front of his mind's eye. But none of them came clear.

Mr. Samuel Cleghorn, the county prosecutor, stood looking out of his office window at Winfield's village green, his back to Jericho. The artist noticed again the man's nervous habit of jiggling keys or coins in his pocket.

Jericho had done a little simple detective work out there in the woods. He had stood in front of his easel, exactly as he had been standing when the shot was fired. He had figured from that and the hole in his canvas the trajectory of the bullet, which had gone straight through the canvas and out into the lake.

After about half an hour of searching he had found the cartridge case. The sniper had stood about thirty yards away, almost directly behind his target. The case matched the one Trooper Brennan had found at the cottage. Same gun, almost certainly. The pine needles on the floor of the woods, springy and resilient, had retained no footprints.

"I think your theory makes sense," Cleghorn said. "What to do is the question. We can't take in everyone within a twenty-five-mile radius and let you have a look at them—until you see a face you remember."

"I propose to leave town," Jericho said.

"Perhaps that is best," Cleghorn said.

"Leave town ostentatiously—and come back not so ostentatiously," Jericho said.

Cleghorn turned back from the window. His smile was thin. "Somehow I can't imagine your coming back without being seen and without your man knowing," he said. "You're not a man who can disguise himself, Jericho. Your size, your coloring, your beard."

"There is, I understand, a Firemen's Carnival starting tonight."

Cleghorn nodded. "At the town athletic field."

"Almost everyone in the community—natives, summer people, transients—will go to it, won't they?" Jericho asked.

"It's the big event of the summer," Cleghorn said.

"So I'll leave this morning, making sure my departure is noted," Jericho said. "I will slip back tonight, find a place on the carnival grounds where I can look at the hundreds of faces."

"So you don't recognize a face, but he sees you," Cleghorn said. "He knows you haven't taken his warning seriously. This time he aims for the bull's-eye."

"With hundreds of people around him?"

"The carnival is a noisy place, friend," Cleghorn said. "Band music, music from the merry-go-round, a shooting gallery where you aim at moving ducks for a prize, fireworks. A rifle could be fired from a safe place without a single soul paying the slightest attention."

"A chance I'll have to take," Jericho said. "When I leave this office I'm heading out of town. You pass the word that I've been scared away by someone taking pot shots at me."

"My best advice is for you to go and stay gone," Cleghorn said. "But if you insist—"

"I'll see you tonight after the carnival closes," Jericho said, "unless I see you before—with a hammerlock on the sniper if I spot him."

There were noises and smells out of his childhood—the calliope music from the merry-go-round, the clanging of bells at the shooting gallery as people fired at the moving ducks and hit, the endless chatter of the barkers at the various games and rides, the aroma of hot dogs, hamburgers, popcorn, and cotton candy.

Jericho had come through the regular admission gate. There was no other way except to run the risk of attracting even more attention. He could hope his man was not there to spot him right at the beginning.

He studied faces and saw none he recognized. There were armies of kids, bright-eyed, excited. The smaller ones were getting rides on a local fire engine and the larger, bolder ones were sampling the rides, the Ferris wheel, the Whiplash, the airplanes that whirled around a tall mast, almost upside-down when they reached top speed. Little girls screamed with a kind of terrified delight. The little boys looked self-consciously brave.

Jericho found a place between two tents not far from the entrance gate. People left the same way. His man would have to pass this way—if he came at all.

Jericho felt himself smiling. Somehow he had been reminded of Groucho Marx's famous crack: "I never forget a face, but I'll try to make an exception in your case." Jericho hoped to see a face that would instantly bring back a violent memory of some sort. He too never forgot a face and he was not going to make an exception in this case.

It was quite dark now and at the far end of the grounds they were beginning to send up Roman candles and rockets that burst in the air and sent showers of color cascading toward the ground. The guns in the shooting gallery cracked and the bells rang. Directly opposite him little girls screamed as the airplane ride spun them dizzily.

The computer that is the human mind operates a little more erratically than an IBM machine. You can't press a button and ask for the face of someone who hates you. What comes out of that human computer is the result of uncontrolled impulses—a sight, a sound, a smell, a word. Listening to the little girls scream and watching the toy planes swirl, Jericho's computer brought up the image of a face that was not a face.

A couple of years ago he had been on a flight from New York to Atlanta where some of his paintings were being exhibited in a one-man show. Forty-five minutes out of New York the plane was taken over by a skyjacker, a bank robber escaping with his loot. The man had an automatic rifle and he kept two stewardesses in front of him as a shield. The pilot was ordered to alter his course for Cuba. You don't play the hero in such a situation, not with seventy innocent passengers aboard.

Jericho remembered studying the skyjacker carefully in the hope of remembering him if he ever saw him again. He couldn't remember him by his face because he had no visible face. He was wearing a stocking mask pulled over his head. But there *was* a way he would remember the skyjacker if he ever saw him again.

Jericho moistened his lips. His mouth felt dry.

He watched the swinging toy planes circle lower and lower. He watched the deliriously happy kids climbing out, shouting at each other. There was only one face before him now, a masked face.

And he remembered words he had spoken to the skyjacker as the man left the plane in Havana, still keeping the two stewardesses as a shield. It had been reasonably foolhardy because the man could have shot Jericho dead then and there. He had told the man how he would recognize him if he ever saw him again.

The crowd was slowly drifting toward home. The fireworks display was over. The town band had packed up its instruments. Exhausted kids, some of them looking a little green around the gills from too many hot dogs and too much candy, were being shepherded home by parents.

Jericho came out from between the tents where he had stationed himself. He felt in the pocket of his coat for the handgun, and closed his hand over the butt. Near the ticket window he saw Samuel Cleghorn, the county prosecutor, watching some of the local firemen counting the gate receipts.

Cleghorn saw him coming and he smiled a greeting, his hands in his pockets, again nervously jiggling his coins or keys.

"Any luck?" Cleghorn asked.

"I didn't see a face I knew," Jericho said.

"He may have seen you," Cleghorn said.

"I'm sure he did," Jericho said. A muscle rippled along the line of his jaw, under his bright red beard. He reached in his pants pocket with his left hand and produced a dollar bill. "Can you change this dollar for me, Cleghorn? I'd like to make a phone call from that outdoor booth over there."

"I'm afraid I don't have any change," Cleghorn said. He stopped the nervous jingling in his pocket.

"Maybe we should quit playing games," Jericho said, and his voice was unnaturally calm.

"Games?" Cleghorn said. His eyes had narrowed.

"I told you once long ago that I'd recognize you if I ever saw you again," Jericho said.

"Long ago?"

"Eastern flight from New York to Atlanta," Jericho said.

"I've never been to Atlanta," Cleghorn said.

"I'm prepared to believe that," Jericho said. "We didn't get to Atlanta. Havana. Remember?"

"I don't have any idea what you're—"

"Every time I've seen you today, Cleghorn, you've had your hands in your pocket. I'd like to look at your hands."

Cleghorn drew a deep shuddering breath. "I should have shot you that day in Havana," he said. "You told me you'd know me by my hands—by the scars. My hands were damn near burned off when I was a kid." He looked toward the parking lot where he probably had a car. "Why did you have to turn up here? I've gotten turned around. I've become a part of this community, elected to a good job, playing it on the level. You were the one man in the whole world who could uncover my past. Why don't you go away and let me alone?"

"Sorry," Jericho said.

Cleghorn sighed. "I have you covered from my pocket, Jericho. Walk over with me to my car. I'm sorry too, but—"

"And I have you covered from my pocket," Jericho said. "I'm aiming right at your stomach. We can shoot it out here or you can throw in the towel. I suggest you have a better chance with the courts than you have with me."

Very slowly Cleghorn took his scarred hands out of his pocket. There was no gun. "I'm not a killer," he said. "I've had three chances to kill you and I never really tried. I only wanted you to go away!"

"That's every criminal's dream," Jericho said, "that trouble won't close in, that it will just go away."

They walked together, like old friends in a friendly conversation, slowly, toward a State Trooper who was standing outside his car parked on the street.

"Why didn't you wear gloves on that plane?" Jericho asked. "Your hands were so noticeable."

"I found at the last moment I couldn't handle that submachine gun with gloves on," Cleghorn said.

"Why not wear gloves here, when you saw me coming?"

"Or stay out of sight?" Cleghorn's laugh was bitter. "I had been delegated to go to Tanner's cottage to ask you to donate a painting to be auctioned for the benefit of the local hospital. I couldn't duck it. Wouldn't gloves on a hot August day make you wonder, perhaps even ask? Maybe, I thought, you'd have some kind of sixth sense about me. Better to frighten you off if I could. But knowing your reputation, I should have known better."

Jericho and the Frightened Woman

The call had come about ten o'clock in the evening. Jericho was not often to be found at his studio in Jefferson Mews at that time of night. Natural painting light was long gone, and the dark hours were usually a time for friends, for prowling, for watching the night people who were so much a part of the life of a great city like New York.

On this particular evening Jericho was at home, working at his easel under a bright fluorescent light. He was in the planning stages of a painting, working with charcoal on canvas in broad, almost angry strokes. He hadn't found the right balances, the right contrasts for what he wanted to say in paint.

The phone rang and the voice that responded to his sharp hello shook him. He'd not expected ever to hear it again; it was low, husky, and it stirred many memories.

"Johnny—it's Laura," the voice said.

"I know," he said, trying to sound casual.

"Johnny, I need your help. Could you possibly come now, to our apartment?"

"Is your husband there?"

"No."

"Laura, I don't think I should—"

"It's very urgent, Johnny. I wouldn't ask unless it was."

"Twenty minutes," Jericho said.

There had been a time a few years back when she wouldn't have had to call him. He would have been there. It had been an unforgettable time in his life. People turned to look at them when they walked down the city streets, or in the country, or anywhere they might be. He was six-feet-four-inches tall, two-hundred-and-forty pounds of solid bone and muscle, with flaming red hair and a beard like a Viking warrior; she was raven-dark, tall for a girl, striding along beside him, proud to be his. And he was so proud of her. They had lived together and laughed together and loved together and she had joined in his causes which were endless fights against man's injustice to man.

Jericho had thought of himself as gentle, unselfish, endlessly concerned with Laura Walton's happiness. Surely she was all any man could ask for in a woman. But Jericho's fierce need to be where the action was—in the Far East, in Algiers, in the Congo, in Israel, always on the trail of today's terrorists—took him away from Laura for long stretches of time. She couldn't always go with him. She had a very good job with one of the top industrial designers. She didn't mention it often, but she wanted children. That was not for him, not yet. Not till his perpetual restlessness subsided and he could settle down somewhere.

After a three months' absence in the Middle East, Jericho came home to find that he had asked too much of this very special woman. Someone else had recognized her needs—for permanence, for a home, for everyday living, for children. She knew these weren't going to come from Jericho in the foreseeable future, and he knew it too.

So they had parted, sad over what might have been. Jericho found, in the next few years, that a part of every day was devoted to missing her. He never saw her, but he kept track. Her husband, David Power, was an attractive young man doing very well, ironically, as half owner of a highly successful travel agency. Travel had separated Jericho and Laura. But David Power didn't travel much— he only made arrangements for other people. Another fact about the Powers that gave Jericho an occasional bitter twinge was that there were no children. If that hadn't been a key issue he and Laura could have gone on together.

Now, after four years, she was calling for help.

Why me, Jericho asked himself. If her marriage was on the rocks she would never have called on him. She would never have asked him back. What special talent did he have that she could need so urgently? He knew people all over the world. Did she or her husband need a contact somewhere? She could have asked him that on the phone.

He began to feel a curious anxiety as he took a taxi uptown to the East Sixties where the Powers lived. Laura would not, in terms of their past, have asked him for anything at all unless she was desperate, in very real and deep trouble.

The Powers' apartment was in a remodeled brownstone on a very good residential block. Jericho knew it well. It had been Laura's apartment before she'd married and brought her husband there to live. There had been a time when Jericho had a key to the front door.

In the vestibule he glanced at the brass nameplate holder. Familiar names except one, and that was a new name for an old tenant. He pressed the button under *Power*. There was an instant clicking that released the door catch. He went in and started up the stairway, rather slowly, to the second-floor rear apartment. He could remember having bounded eagerly up those stairs.

She was standing in the open doorway at the end of the hall. She was the same beautifully built, dark, slender girl with, Jericho thought, the hell scared out of her. Her eyes were wide and her lips were parted as though breathing was an effort.

"Johnny!"

That husky voice! He kept his hands jammed in his pockets. To reach out and touch her would break the dam. She stepped back into the apartment he knew so well, the books, the drawings, the few very good paintings he had selected for her. Only one thing was missing—a vivid portrait of Laura he'd painted and that had hung over the mantel.

On the coffee table in front of the couch was an ice bucket, a single glass, and a bottle of bourbon whiskey—a brand he'd given up when their time together had ended. Evidently she didn't intend to join him. He stayed away from the bottle and glass, and stood with his back to the mantel. It kept him from looking at the empty space above it.

"I wouldn't have called you, Johnny, unless—"

"I know," Jericho said.

"It isn't fair to ask you—"

"Ask," he said.

She rarely smoked, but she took a cigarette from a box on the coffee table and her hands shook as she lit it.

"I have to tell you things that may hurt," she said. "My marriage to David has been almost everything I dreamed of."

"Almost?"

"We haven't had any children—yet."

He felt suddenly and unaccountably angry. "I don't propose to help you out with that," he said.

"Johnny!"

"Sorry. Look, love, tell me what it is without the background."

"David is paralyzed with fright," she said.

"It seems to be catching."

"It is catching, because he won't tell me what it is. Not knowing what is driving him off the deep end has become unbearable. I do know it's connected with his business."

"The travel agency?"

"Yes. Transocean Travel. He's half owner—one of two partners. The other is Elliot James, an old friend. Two weeks ago David asked me to go away, to leave town, to drop out of sight. He was afraid for me but he wouldn't tell me why. He won't let me go out at night. He's carrying a gun. I went to Elliot to ask him what was wrong, getting him to promise he wouldn't mention it to David. Elliot had no idea what could be wrong—and he told David I'd been there."

"Good friend."

"I think I must have scared him about David. And David—he was furious.

That's the wrong way to say it. He seemed totally panicked. He urged me, he ordered me to go away somewhere—to Mexico or Europe. I told him I wouldn't leave him, that he must tell me what is wrong. Whatever it is, Johnny, he's very close to a total crackup."

"And you want me to find out what it is?"

"I can't go to Elliot again. I can't hire some professional investigator for fear it would get back to David. I couldn't think of anyone who might help but—but you."

Jericho felt his jaw muscles knot. "A woman?"

"Never, Johnny. Not David. Not without telling me, openly and honestly."

"You said you thought it was connected with his business."

"From the way he reacted to my going to Elliot."

"Is the business a success?"

"Fabulous. We've bought a little house in Connecticut where we go for weekends and holidays. The business is fine, at least on the surface."

"And below the surface?"

"I don't know, Johnny. But David is sick with fear about something."

There was the sound of a key in the front door. It opened and David Power came into the room. Jericho was shocked at the way he looked. He had lost weight. There were deep dark circles under his eyes. He looked like a man being tormented. He seemed to freeze for a moment when he saw Jericho.

"What the hell are you doing here?" he asked.

"I called him and asked him to come here, David. I—"

"I know why you called him. You thought I wouldn't be home till much later."

"Don't be a complete idiot," Jericho said. He looked at Laura. She could tell David why. They could discuss the problem, whatever it was.

"I ask you to leave," Power said.

"Please, David," Laura said. "Johnny might be able to—"

"Now!" Power said. His right hand moved toward his left shoulder. "If you don't—"

Laura had said he was carrying a gun.

"I'm sorry, Johnny," Laura said. "I'm sorry I got you into this."

"So now you're out of it," Power said. "So stay out!"

There was nothing to do but go. People who care for each other but can't talk ought to be spanked like children. One thing Jericho was sure of: David Power had not believed for a moment that Jericho's presence spelled the revival of a romance. He had been afraid Laura would do exactly what she had done—ask for help.

Jericho stood aside to let a girl pass him on the stairway, and then he went out into the night and headed back for the studio in Jefferson Mews, walking to try to wear off the things that had stirred in him. Laura was still Laura—she would always be something special for him.

He sat up for a long time when he got home, staring at his canvas, trying to re-establish his concentration, failing, thinking of Laura. Finally he went to bed and slept.

The next morning, while he was getting his breakfast with the radio turned on for the news, he heard that Laura and David Power were dead, brutally butchered by someone with a knife who had ransacked the Power's apartment. The police did not know yet what might have been stolen. Possibly it was some drug-driven creep trying to find money to buy a fix. They were looking for a large red-bearded man who had been seen leaving the apartment a little before midnight.

Lieutenant Andrew Christie, Homicide, was an old friend of Jericho's. A squarely built, somber, gray man with pale blue eyes that had seen too much violence, Christie had worked beside Jericho during some hot summer nights in the city, nights hot with hatred and anger.

"I expected you'd be in," Christie said. He was at his desk at headquarters, working with a metal tool on the stem of a pipe that resisted unclogging.

"The girl I passed on the stairs," Jericho said.

Christie nodded. "And the Powers. You remember that I knew Laura when you and she were a thing. I wish to God I hadn't. It's not easy to stay impersonal when you know the victim."

"Did she—?"

"She fought like a tiger," Christie said. "Perhaps we can be thankful for that. She died in action, Johnny. No time for torture, or hope."

"Knife, the radio said."

"Forget it. Don't try to imagine it."

"Leads?"

"Nothing yet—no weapon, no fingerprints. No way to guess what the killers were searching for."

"You say killers—plural."

"No one man could have handled her the way she fought, and her husband armed with a gun. He got off two shots, both into the ceiling. Someone was struggling with him, while someone else fought with her. Only lead is the girl who saw a big red-bearded man leaving. I knew it had to be you, Johnny. Too much of a coincidence for it to be anyone else. I knew they must have been alive when you left or you'd have been in touch." Christie's eyes asked a question.

"She called me, asked me to come there," Jericho said. "It was the first time I'd seen her in four years. I loved her, Andrew."

"I know. And I know she wouldn't have sent for you unless she was in trouble."

"There was trouble, but God knows what," Jericho said. He gave Christie a blow-by-blow account. "She didn't know what it was, Andrew, but you only had to take one look at David to know it was very bad. She thought it was connected with the business."

"We've talked to Elliot James, the partner," Christie said. "He told us Laura and her husband were upset about something, that Laura had come to see him. He told us, and I quote, he 'hadn't the remotest idea' what was bothering them. Business is flourishing. No problems."

"Laura was certain it had something to do with the business."

Christie shrugged. "How do we find out? James is perfectly willing to give us access to books and records. If there's something there it isn't on paper, Johnny."

"Do you think the killers were searching for something in the apartment?" Jericho asked.

"It was torn apart," Christie said.

"That doesn't answer my question," Jericho said.

Christie raised tired eyes to his friend. He saw fierce anger there. "It may have been made to *look* like a robbery," he said. "But it occurs to me, Johnny, now that I've heard your story, the purpose could have been to silence David Power—and Laura, in case David had told her whatever it is."

"I'll buy that," Jericho said.

"There is something else you might consider buying," Christie said. "If David was being watched, someone else besides the lady you passed on the stair may have known you were there. What may be missing from the apartment is some kind of bugging device—which means they heard Laura's conversation with you. Which means—"

"They may want to silence me too?"

"Could be."

Jericho stood up. His muscles felt stiff from the acid of anger. "I would welcome that, Andrew," he said. "In fact, I think I will invite it."

"Watch your step," Christie said. "And I'd appreciate it if you'd dictate a statement for me before you go—just in case you get your ears pinned back playing hero."

The offices of Transocean Travel, Inc. were located in one of those towering glass fingers pointing to the sky in the midtown Park Avenue area. It was very modern, the office, decorated with colorful travel posters from all over the world. The receptionist wore a simple little $400 Rudy Gernreich creation. She could have cleaned up the beauty contest sweepstakes. The name plate on her desk read *Nan Martin*. She gave Jericho the appraising look of a woman who has no objection whatever to being considered a sex-object.

"Can I help you?" she asked, her smile dazzling.

"I'd like to see Mr. James," Jericho said.

"May I have your name, please?"

"John Jericho."

Her eyes widened. "The artist?"

Score one for a receptionist who knows her job.

"I claim to be," Jericho said.

Elliot James was anything but sinister. He was a healthy-looking, suntanned man in his mid-thirties; his clothes were expensive—mod but not extreme. He got up from his desk as the receptionist ushered Jericho in and came forward, his hand held out.

"This is a real pleasure, Mr. Jericho," he said. "Ever since I saw your Middle East paintings at the McClellan Gallery I've wanted to meet you. I don't think anyone else has ever caught the feeling of that part of the world as you have."

His handshake was firm, but not a crusher. Under any other circumstances Jericho's instinct would have been to like him. James waved him to a chair and went back behind his desk.

"I would never have expected you to come here, Mr. Jericho," he said. "You're the last person I'd have thought needed help with travel arrangements. You must know every trick to the trade."

Jericho took a black shell-briar pipe from his pocket and began to fill it from an oilskin pouch. "I haven't come to talk travel business with you, Mr. James," he said.

"Oh?"

"I was with David and Laura Power last night just a short time before they were—butchered," Jericho said. His pipe was filled but he didn't light it.

James' face twisted with pain. "Oh, God," he said. "The kind of world we're living in today is unbelievable. Those were two of the nicest people I ever knew." His eyes widened. "You're the man that girl saw leaving the apartment?"

"Yes."

"Was there anything wrong with David and Laura when you left them?"

"I think you know there was," Jericho said. "David was your partner. You know there was something wrong."

"I know that David was upset about something but I haven't the least idea what it was," James said.

"That's what you told the police," Jericho said. He held a lighter to his pipe and blew a cloud of smoke toward the ceiling. "But David told me what it was."

"He told you?" James said, and his voice wavered a little.

"He told me, and I've thought about it, and I've decided to cut myself in," Jericho said.

"I don't know what you're talking about!" James said.

Jericho thought he knew then, that James knew what he was talking about even though Jericho himself didn't. "I have decided to cut myself in for fifty percent," he said.

"So help me, Jericho, you're not making any sense. Cut yourself in for fifty percent of what?"

"I suppose you may have to talk to other people about it," Jericho said. "I'm willing to give you time. A little time. Say, till midnight tonight?" He stood up. "If you're not willing to make a deal by then I'll blow the lid off the whole operation. David told me enough to make that easy. And of course there will be a murder charge to ice the cake. I'll be waiting in my studio in Jefferson Mews for your answer."

"You have to be out of your mind!" James said. But he didn't move from his chair as Jericho walked out of the office and past Miss Martin, the hopefully smiling receptionist.

It was a warm, beautiful, summer evening, as though it was the most pleasant of all imaginable worlds. The people on the streets, bathed in late sunshine, seemed less tense and driven than usual. The girls in their summer dresses were provocative. But to Jericho, walking out onto Park Avenue, it was a dark world, full of pain. It was a world of instant emotional replay.

Moments, unrelated to tragedy, kept playing across the screen of his memory. Laura, her face bright with the excitement of living, sitting across the table from him in a little French restaurant they loved, arguing passionately about the right wine to go with a veal dish; Laura, her dark hair blowing around her face, standing with him high above the ocean on a cliff in Maine; Laura, lying beside him on clover-scented grass, staring happily up at a harvest moon. Laura, Laura, Laura. Laura, sick with fear, asking for help—*and not getting it*!

People turned to look at a giant red-bearded man pounding a huge fist against the stone front of a building. Asking for help—from him, Jericho—*and not getting it*!

Jericho had found himself in situations in the past when he wanted revenge, but it had always been revenge for someone else—to square accounts for someone else or some group of people. In those circumstances he operated coolly, his skills, his competences, his strength always in control. But for a long time, as he walked the streets, curdled by a bitter rage, he wanted revenge for himself. This thing had happened to him. He forgot, in his grief, that this thing had happened to Laura and David, not to him.

He had walked, criss-crossing the city for an hour or more, his body damp with sweat from the heat, internal and external, when he slowly began to be aware that anger and pain had deprived him of his professional senses. He had set something in motion back at Transocean. He must have frightened Elliot James out of his shoes, but that wasn't what it was all about. James would strike back and Jericho had already given him a lot of time in which to plan a move.

Jericho turned into a little bar on Eighth Avenue and ordered a beer. He was very thirsty. And while he sipped the beer he saw a familiar face at the far end of the room. It belonged to a thin pinch-faced man wearing dark glasses and studying a racing form. He tried to remember where he'd seen the face before, and suddenly realized it was not something out of the distant past. Half an hour ago he had jaywalked across a crowded avenue and come face to face with this pinch-faced man with the dark glasses as he reached the other side of the street. Half an hour of aimless walking later the same man was on the scene again.

It was like a splash of ice water in a dazed fighter's face. So, little man, you're on my tail! So we'll see how good you are.

Outdoors Jericho began to play a game with the pinch-faced man, making sudden turns into buildings, then waiting calmly for the little man to show. The man had completely blown his cover and he must know it. If he was any good at all he knew what Jericho was doing to him.

After an elaborate maneuver into a building and out through a fire exit Jericho lost him—or thought he'd lost him. But Jericho's instincts and perceptions were very sharp now. Just as he was feeling something like disappointment at having won, he noticed a large fat man constantly wiping his perspiring face with a handkerchief, a man wandering just as aimlessly as Jericho. So there were two men on him, and they were no longer being secretive about it. As he hurried round a corner, taking a mildly sadistic pleasure in making the fat man scurry, he almost barged into the little pinch-faced man who was studying the contents of a bookstore window.

Jericho began to put it together. He had told James to come to Jefferson Mews with an answer to his demand for a cut—of whatever. These men were watching him, waiting for him to head for home, making certain he wasn't setting a trap for Elliot James when he came with an answer or a counter-offer.

It wasn't until the twilight had passed and the street lights were on that Jericho headed directly for his home base. He took a taxi from midtown, aware that another taxi followed close on his heels. There was no way to hide the location of his studio even if he wanted to. It was listed in the phone book. There was no way for a six-foot-four-inch man with a flaming red beard to play hide-and-seek with people who know how to seek. He had invited James to his place and now it was time for him to be on hand to receive him.

The fat man with the handkerchief was half a block behind Jericho when he walked down Jefferson Mews to his apartment building. His studio window opened on the mews, and as he approached the building he saw that lights were on behind that window. Knowing the fat man was behind him, Jericho did not break stride. He walked to the building and straight through the vestibule into the ground-floor hall. Then he moved like lightning, straight to the back of the hall and under the stairway.

He waited, motionless, scarcely breathing. The fat man came in from the vestibule and stood at the foot of the stairway, looking up. He seemed to be listening for the sound of Jericho's footsteps, or perhaps the opening and closing of the studio door. He hesitated for a few moments, then lit a cigarette and walked out into the vestibule, possibly out onto the street again. He was apparently satisfied that Jericho had walked into whatever trap was waiting for him upstairs.

So Jericho walked right into it.

He came out from under the stairs and went up to the second floor. He stood outside the studio door, listening. There was no sound. He took out his key and unlocked the door as quietly as he could. He waited again for some sound, then he took a step back and charged the door, taking a rolling fall into the middle of the room.

Someone laughed.

He turned his head, already on the rise and ready. Leaning back in the corner of his couch was Miss Nan Martin, the glamorous receptionist from Transocean Travel.

"Do you always make your entrances so physical?" she asked. "Not that I didn't hope you were physical."

"What the hell are you doing here and how did you get in?" Jericho asked, getting to his feet.

"What I'm doing here must be fairly obvious," she said. "I'm afraid I told a fib in order to get in. Your janitor, or superintendent, or whatever you call him. Sicilian, isn't he? He has an eye for women. I was afraid if you didn't come soon he might insist on taking care of my spare time. He might be fun at that."

"Giovanni?"

"Nice name," Miss Martin said. "I told him I was a model and that I had an appointment to pose for you. He felt I shouldn't have to wait in the drafty hall, so he let me in. He even showed me where you kept some negligees for your models. I thought it might be coming on a little too strong to change into one of them. You have very good taste in women's things, by the way."

Jericho stood very still. He could feel the small hairs rising on the back of his neck. Every nerve in his body was screaming some kind of warning at him. But he smiled, a broad white smile.

"You came here because you were attracted to me?" he asked.

"Not many men with your kind of electricity walk into Transocean," the girl said.

Jericho reached out and turned off the light switch. The room went dark except for a faint reflection in the skylight from the street lamps outside. He took two steps forward to the couch. The girl laughed.

"No preliminaries?" she asked.

One big hand went over her mouth, and a knee pinned her to the couch.

"You came here to set me up," he whispered. "I've never slugged a woman in my life, but, baby, you're about to make history."

He hit her on the point of her lovely chin and her body went limp. He moved quickly away and into the corner shadows. He was watching the side window. Something darkened it, and then he saw a figure come quietly through it from the fire escape.

Jericho charged, hurling himself on the intruder with all his enormous strength. He felt a sharp pain at his shoulder and then he was slugging a helpless hulk into unconsciousness.

Someone was pounding on the front door.

"Jericho! Are you in there?"

Jericho recognized Lieutenant Christie's voice. He stepped across the body he was straddling and switched on the light. He touched his shoulder and his fingers came away red with his own blood. A few feet away from the man who was sprawled on the floor was a switchblade knife. It flashed across his mind that it could be the same knife that had killed Laura.

"Come in," he called out. "It's open."

Lieutenant Christie came into the room. Behind him were two uniformed cops and Mr. Elliot James, looking gray as parchment.

"The girl set me up, Andrew," Jericho said. "While I was supposed to be making love to her I was to get a knife in the back. That scum on the floor is probably one of the boys who did for Laura and David. Was Elliot-baby the other one? How did you get here?"

"Dull routine," Christie said. "Checking and double checking. And help from Mr. James."

"What kind of help? How did his foot slip?"

"So help me, Jericho, I had nothing to do with any of this," James said.

Jericho clutched his shoulder. It hurt.

"I checked the personnel files of Transocean," Christie said. "We believed something was wrong there, Johnny, didn't we? Miss Martin didn't quite check out. You haven't killed her, have you, man?"

"She was here to set me up for that creep on the fire escape. She'll come around." He looked at his bloodied fingers. "How didn't she check out, Andrew?"

"Her real name is Annette Martine. She is the daughter of Mike Martine. Mean anything to you?"

"Syndicate boss. Drugs. Smuggling. You name it," Jericho said.

"Two and two," Christie said. "A travel agency with all its foreign connections could be a valuable asset to an importer of drugs and other contraband. Your lady friend was the queen of the operation. It will take a while to put it together, but I think David Power caught on somehow. They told him what would happen if he didn't keep his mouth shut and play along."

"Laura?"

Christie nodded. "That's why David was trying to get her to leave the country. He was afraid to tell her why. They were being watched. We picked up a couple of Martine's boys outside who must have been following you. They saw you go to the Power apartment and decided he'd spilled the beans to you. You helped convince them by offering to make a deal with Mr. James, who didn't know what the hell you were talking about. But Miss Martin knew. Office communicator always kept open. She knew everything that went on in the partners' offices." Christie smiled. "If you'd been more interested in her charms *she* might have offered to make a deal with you. You have a thing with women, Johnny.

"Get them out of here!" Jericho roared. He turned away, thinking of Laura. She had been worth a thousand, a hundred thousand creeps like these. There was no way to get even for her.

Jericho and the Unknown Lover

S he had said it to him twice, once long ago during the 1967 Arab-Israeli war and once last night. He had regretted the necessity for it both times.

She had said in effect, both times, "We're just not lucky, dear Johnny. It would be wonderful fun to make love to you, but unhappily I am a one-man-at-a-time woman."

He would never forget the first time they had met. An Egyptian plane had been flying low over the desert, spraying everything in sight with its machine guns. Jericho had taken a dive into a trench dug by the Israeli troops and before he could right himself someone landed on top of him. To his amazement it turned out to be a girl, her face, her turned-up nose smudged with dirt.

"Sorry, but I couldn't wait to be invited," she said, and blew an errant strand of hair out of her eyes.

"What the hell are you doing out here?" Jericho asked.

"I'm Toby Nelson," she said, as though that explained everything. She was wearing slacks and an Israeli uniform jacket that was too large for her. Chestnut-red hair billowed down over her shoulders. She must have been wearing a cap, but she'd lost it in the dive for safety.

The plane had passed over, but it was making a turn for another run over the area. As it approached, Jericho, who was six-feet-four-inches tall and two-hundred-and-forty pounds of bone and muscle, covered one-hundred-and-ten pounds of girl with his body. Bullets ripped into the sandbags at the top of the trench and the plane flew away.

"Your beard is tickling my neck," the girl said in a casual voice. He had a flaming red beard that made him look like an ancient Viking warrior.

He disentangled himself. "You all right?" he asked.

"I'm fine," she said, and again blew the hair out of her eyes. "Do you happen to have a cigarette? I left mine in the jeep." She gestured toward the jeep which was burning merrily a few yards away, a score for the plane.

So it began that way. Someone gave them a ride back to a nearby town. He learned, in bits and pieces, that she was covering the war for a newspaper syndicate. She pretended to be hurt that "Toby Nelson" didn't mean anything to him. After all, she knew who John Jericho was—an artist whose paintings of

191

the horrors of war spoke, perhaps even more vividly than words, about man's inhumanity to man.

For a few days at the front they worked together. In the evenings they drank and talked and admired each other. It was perfectly reasonable that two such vital people should have thought of something more intimate. That was when she first said it.

"I almost wish I wasn't a one-man-at-a-time girl, Johnny," she said. They were sitting together in a little café, drinking a special Greek brandy—Metaxa 5 Star—which she professed to be mad for.

"Who is he?" Jericho asked, feeling sorry for himself.

"A Lieutenant in the Israeli Air Force," Toby said. "Joseph Freed. You'd like him, Johnny."

Her assignment took her away a couple of days later and he didn't see her again. He made an effort to find her the day he saw Joseph Freed's name on the casualty lists, but she seemed to have disappeared. They were like ships that have passed in the night.

And so it was that seven years later he was driving along a highway in Connecticut when he came to a stop light. He pulled up parallel to another car and turned his head casually to look at the driver. Toby Nelson!

He let out a great bellowing noise and she waved excitedly, and when the light permitted they moved on and pulled up at the side of the road. They embraced and he whirled her around and they both talked at once. It seemed she had rented a cottage for the summer not a mile from where they were. If he wasn't hurrying to get somewhere—?

"I've been hurrying to get to you for seven years," Jericho said.

She gave him an odd little smile and even then he thought he got the message. He was too late again.

Her cottage looked out over a lake, and they sat on the terrace and watched a little white boat with a red sail zigzagging in the bright sun. They talked about Israel and the new war and the incredible state of the world in general. She had come to this little town of Winfield to write a book about the Middle East. And then she told him.

"We're just not lucky, dear Johnny. I'm still a one-man-at-a-time girl." She frowned. "This time I've gotten into something I always swore would never happen. The man is married. That's why I chose Winfield as a place to work for the summer. He lives here."

That was all she said about it. He could have gone on, of course. But she was fun to be with, and somehow he sensed that she needed someone who wasn't involved in a complicated triangle. They swam and lay in the sun together and talked and laughed. There was only one more mention of the married man. He would not be visiting today or tonight. And so Jericho stayed for a charcoal-broiled steak and afterward they drank some of that Greek brandy.

"It's hard to find in this country," Toby said, "but I got the local liquor-store man to stock some for me."

He felt, suddenly, uncontrollably sleepy. It was time to go.

"If you'd like to stay in the guest room—knowing the conditions, Johnny dear—you're welcome."

He stayed, and slept as he'd been pole-axed. When he woke the sun was pouring in the windows of his room. He had, perhaps, the most terrible hangover he could ever remember. It didn't make sense Two bourbons before dinner two brandies after. He glanced at his wrist watch. It was nine o'clock. He never slept beyond 6:30 in the morning.

He got up, feeling heavy headed, showered and dressed. He went out into the main part of the cottage. No sign of Toby. No coffee in the pot in the kitchen. He went to the door of her room and knocked. When she didn't answer he opened the door.

"Dear God!" he whispered.

She was there on the bed, naked, a mass of blood and torn flesh. He didn't have to go to her to know that she had been brutally murdered.

Jericho had faced violence in a dozen different shapes and forms in his life. He had covered wars and the holocausts of Nature and assassinations and murders. His inevitable reaction was a kind of fierce anger against the utter senselessness of it all. But as he stood in the doorway of Toby Nelson's bedroom he felt a cold sick horror, not because he had been especially fond of her but because he had been in the next room while someone had hacked her to death and he had heard nothing, had done nothing to save her.

He remembered when he had gone to bed, unexpectedly drowsy, that he had been able to hear her moving around in the next room. The wall separating the two rooms was thin. It was inconceivable that this kind of violence could have happened and he had heard nothing. Yet that was the way it was—he had heard not a sound.

He took a step into the room.

The weapon, which must have been some kind of knife, was not visible anywhere. His brain, coming out of shock, began to tick with logical precision. There was no way, drunk or sober, he could have slept through what had happened here. He couldn't have been drunk on two bourbons and two brandies taken over a period of about three hours. That was normal consumption or less for a social evening.

That damned Greek brandy! He had loathed the taste of it but he hadn't wanted to tell Toby because she thought it was so special. He turned to walk out of the room and stopped. On the headboard of her bed, etched in blood, was a large clear thumbprint. The murderer had left his signature behind.

He was on his way to the phone in the living room when he glanced at the couch where he and Toby had been sitting just before they had decided to turn in. They had left the bottle of Metaxa 5 Star and the two brandy glasses on the low coffee table in front of the couch. Neither the bottle nor the glasses were there now.

Frowning, Jericho walked into the kitchen. Toby could have come out of her room later to put the glasses away. The plates and the silverware they'd used at dinner were still on the drainboard, unwashed, along with the highball glasses they'd used before dinner. But no brandy glasses.

He remembered he'd got them out of a corner cupboard for her. There had been six of the bell-shaped glasses on a shelf, and there were six of them there now. Toby—or someone—had washed the two glasses they'd used and put them back.

He opened the door to the liquor cabinet. There were bourbon and gin and vodka and Scotch and a square bottle of Cointreau, but no brandy. No Metaxa 5 Star or any other brandy. He remembered that the Metaxa bottle was nearly full when they'd poured their first round the night before. It should be somewhere now, about three-quarters full. But he couldn't find it anywhere.

He went to the telephone to call the State Police, knowing for certain what had happened to him, knowing why his mouth tasted dry and bitter, why his head ached. The brandy he had drunk had been drugged. That was why he had slept through a murder.

It wasn't sensible to suppose that Toby Nelson had drugged him so that she could be killed without his interference.

An impersonal voice on the phone told Jericho to stay where he was.

He put down the phone and found himself looking down at the top of Toby's desk. The telephone numbers of the State Police and the Fire Department were written on a small card in Toby's neat script and the card was stuck in the corner of her blotter pad. Somewhere not too far away there was a man who would be shocked, almost beyond endurance, by what had happened here. He was a married man whom Toby had loved. Somewhere in the cottage there might be letters from him, his name in an address book, a telephone number that could be identified by the troopers. Toby would want him protected. She had loved him enough to orient her life around him.

He stood very still, turning a page in his mind. Suppose this man might not be shocked at all when the news reached him? Suppose he had been fed up? Suppose Toby had threatened some sort of security his marriage supplied? Suppose she had made demands of him that he couldn't or wouldn't meet? It could be that this nameless man needed prosecution, not protection.

A police siren sounded not far off. The State Police had been prompt. Jericho's muscles tensed. He knew that the Number One Suspect in the first phase of this investigation was going to be John Jericho.

The two troopers who walked in the front door were quite different and yet quite alike. They both had that cool, impersonal, professional look to them. Trooper Allen was young, playing a role, Jericho thought. Lieutenant Busick was older, a big man tanned a mahogany brown, with a touch of gray at his temples, with cold blue eyes partly hidden behind slightly tinted gold-rimmed glasses.

Jericho took them to the door of Toby's bedroom. Young Allen muttered something under his breath. Busick looked at the dead woman coldly, dispassionately.

"Your name?" Busick asked Jericho.

"John Jericho."

"Address?"

"Jefferson Mews in New York City—Manhattan."

Young Allen took down the answers in a notebook, happy to turn away from the body on the bed.

"You found her?" Busick asked.

"Yes."

"When?"

"When I got up," Jericho said.

Busick's eyes flickered behind the glasses. "Got up?"

"I spent the night in that bedroom next door." Jericho drew a deep breath. "The first thing you will find it hard to believe is that I slept through what happened in here."

"You have to be kidding," Busick said.

"It may not be accurate to say I slept. I think I was drugged."

"How?"

"We drank some brandy after dinner. We'd spent the afternoon on the lake and out in the sun. We both felt, suddenly, very sleepy. I woke up with a splitting headache and a mouth that tasted like the bottom of a birdcage. That was at nine o'clock. I came out here when I was dressed to find Miss Nelson and some coffee. I knocked on her door and when she didn't answer I opened it. It was the way you see it. I haven't touched anything."

"You think the brandy was drugged?"

"Yes."

"So let's check it out."

"Impossible," Jericho said. "Someone washed the snifters we used and the brandy is gone. It was a bottle of a Greek brandy called Metaxa 5 Star, three-quarters full when we went to bed."

"In separate rooms?"

"Yes."

Busick's mouth was a thin straight slit. "I think I'd better advise you of your rights, Mr. Jericho."

"I know my rights," Jericho said. "When you've had a chance to do a rundown on me you may be more inclined to believe what I'm telling you. That will take time, however, and there may be a quick way to make what I say a little more credible. There is a bloody thumbprint there on the headboard of her bed. Lift it. Take my prints. Take Miss Nelson's prints. You'll find there was a third person here last night."

The two troopers looked at the bloody thumbprint. Young Allen went out to the car to get the equipment to deal with it.

"How do you suggest I start a rundown on you, Jericho?" Busick asked.

"Call Lieutenant Pascal of the Homicide Squad in Manhattan. He's an old friend."

"So while we check these prints," Busick said, "suppose you begin at the beginning."

"It began seven years ago in Israel," Jericho said. He began with the trench in the desert and carried on to the traffic light on the Connecticut road. He told about an afternoon and evening, old friends glad to see each other. Then he hesitated for a moment. "There is something I think I have to tell you, Lieutenant. It's rather personal, but it may be very important. Miss Nelson and I are—were—good healthy normal people. I spent my nights when I knew her in Israel in other bedrooms than hers because she was involved with an Israeli pilot. She was what she called a 'one-man-at-a-time' woman. I spent last night in that other bedroom because she was still a one-man-at-a-time woman. There is a man here in Winfield."

"Who?" Busick asked.

"I have no idea. I do know that he's married."

"How do you know that?"

"Toby told me."

"She told you that, but not his name?"

"That fingerprint may reveal it to you."

"It could have been a tramp, a hopped-up creep who just stumbled in on you," Busick said.

"Who drugged the brandy in advance, washed the glasses afterwards, and went off with the brandy bottle?"

"Could be."

"If he drank what was in that bottle he's either asleep or dead somewhere," Jericho said.

Busick was methodical and efficient. Young Allen knew his job with the fingerprints. Jericho pressed his thumbs on an ink pad and Allen also took Toby's prints. While this was going on an ambulance arrived with the local medical officer. Two other troopers appeared. The medical man guessed that Toby had been stabbed to death with something like a carving or butcher knife. There was no such knife in the cottage. Troopers began making a methodical search of the grounds outside.

"I suggest you have them keep an eye out for a bottle of Metaxa 5 Star," Jericho said.

Busick gave him a cold look. He wasn't a man who relished suggestions, but he passed on the order. He involved himself in a search for an address book or a list of telephone numbers. If there was a man in Winfield there should be some record of him.

"He didn't keep any personal things here," Busick said at one point. "No razor or clothes or even a bathrobe or dressing gown. Maybe she invented him, Jericho, to keep from shacking up with you."

"She was much too straight-forward to play games," Jericho said.

Trooper Allen reported. The bloody fingerprint was not Jericho's or Toby Nelson's. There had been a third person in the murder room and from the size of the print it must have been a man.

Busick seemed to relax a little. He gave Jericho a tight smile. "That makes it possible to begin to believe you a little," he said.

"Thanks."

"We'll match the print against our State Police records," Busick said. "Send it on to the F.B.I. That will take some time."

"Meanwhile the guy is somewhere within whistling distance," Jericho said.

The eyes behind Busick's tinted glasses narrowed. "Assuming there *is* a boy friend here in Winfield," he said, "does it necessarily follow that he's the killer? It could have been someone else who resented the relationship."

"The wife?"

"That fingerprint is a man's," Busick said. He turned his head, his face stony. The ambulance people were carrying out Toby's body on a stretcher. "Some other boy friend? A jealous one? Can you suggest someone who fits that, Jericho?"

"I don't know anything about Toby's private life for the last seven years. The man she was in love with when I first met her was killed in the Middle East war. Seven years later, yesterday, she told me she was having an affair with a married man who lives here in Winfield. Period."

"We'll find him," Busick said. "I'd appreciate it if you'd come down to the barracks and make a full statement. Then you're free to go."

"I'm not going anywhere," Jericho said, his voice angry, "until we run the man who did this through the nearest meat chopper."

In the bleak State Police barracks Jericho dictated a statement on tape and then waited restlessly for the police stenographer to transcribe it so that he could sign it. How could he, a stranger in town, go about locating Toby's lover? There could be gossip in a small town like this, but how would a stranger get to hear it? That was an avenue open to Busick.

Facing a whitewashed hallway, Jericho put together a theory. The truth was he hadn't known Toby very well or how she would behave in an emotional situation. Perhaps she had put unbearable pressure on her man to break up his marriage. Perhaps she had threatened to go to the man's wife and for some reason the man couldn't face that. He had to be rid of her, in spite of the fact that he loved her. But he couldn't face her in cold blood and do away with her.

Knowing Toby's habits and that she drank some of the Metaxa every night after dinner, the killer had poisoned the bottle in her liquor cabinet. Later in the evening she would be unconscious from the drug and he could kill her, without reproaches from her, making it look like the senseless violence of—what had Busick suggested?—a hopped-up creep. What a shock it must have been to him to arrive at the cottage and find another person, Jericho, passed out in the next room! But he had known Jericho wouldn't wake up.

But why wash the glasses and take away the bottle? The drugged brandy would, of course, do away with the hopped-up creep theory. It would show advance planning. He had had to get rid of the bottle, hoping Jericho wouldn't guess why he had slept through it all. As it stood now there was no proof the brandy had been drugged. There was only Jericho's headache and his conviction about it. By now, even if the bottle was found, the killer would surely have washed away all evidence of a drug before he discarded the bottle. The killer was safe in spite of the unexpected presence of Jericho.

Busick appeared in the hallway. The statement was ready to sign.

"The computer turns up nothing on that fingerprint in our local records," he told Jericho. "It will take a while to hear from the F.B.I."

"We've got plenty of time," Jericho said.

After Jericho signed the statement he drove his red Mercedes into town. It was early afternoon when he stopped in the local sandwich shop for some coffee and a hamburger. The word about the murder was out, and while he was finishing his second coffee a breathless young man from the local weekly newspaper caught up with him. Jericho, it seemed, was already a local celebrity—the man who had slept through a murder.

Jericho had his own questions to ask. Who in town had got to know Toby Nelson? What friends had she made? Someone, somewhere must have made a connection between the foreign correspondent who had rented the cottage on the lake and a married couple in town.

But as the afternoon dragged on and he asked questions in a dozen places no one had an answer. Toby had kept strictly to herself. She had given no parties and gone to no parties. Jericho remembered that Toby had told him she'd come to Winfield because her man was here, which implied that she had met him somewhere else. In any case, there seemed to be no trail to pick up in Winfield.

Twilight was closing in when he found himself opposite the local liquor store. An idea struck him and he parked his car and went into the store.

It was a small one-man operation, the proprietor professionally cheerful. Jericho saw the sign on the window that said "Paul Johnston, Permitee." He ordered a fifth of Jack Daniels, then proceeded to look around the shelves behind the counter.

"I'm looking for a specially nice brandy to give someone as a gift," he said.

Mr. Johnson grinned. "Price no object?"

"No object."

"Because I have an unusual Greek brandy here that I can recommend," Johnston said. He reached down under the counter and came up with a fifth of Metaxa 5 Star.

"I'll be damned," Jericho said. "I haven't seen any of that for years. Used to drink it when I was doing a job in Egypt some time back."

"I ordered it for a special customer who won't be needing it any more," Johnston said. "You just passing through, Mister?"

"You could say that."

"This customer was a lady," Johnston said. "Somebody murdered her last night. She won't be wanting this Metaxa any more."

"I know about Miss Nelson," Jericho said. "I'm the man who was sleeping in the next room."

Johnston's eyes almost popped out of his head. "Holy cow!" he said.

"Look, Mr. Johnston, Miss Nelson was an old friend of mine. So far Lieutenant Busick has drawn a blank. I'm interested in finding out who her friends were here in Winfield and if there was any gossip about her and some man."

"Never heard a thing about her, good or bad," Johnston said. "She was a writer, the way I heard it. Kept pretty much to herself. If she had friends in town I never heard who they were. They say you never heard what happened last night at the cottage. Passed out, they say. Mind you, I don't criticize a good drinking bout now and then. How could I in this business?" His laughter was about as feeble as the joke.

"I'll tell you about it sometime," Jericho said. "Right now I'm interested in her friends, if any. I thought someone might have given her a present. A friend would know how fond she was of this Metaxa and bought her a bottle."

Johnston shook his head. "I had it out on the shelf for a while but I guess the price scared people off," he said. "Would you believe I only sold one bottle except what Miss Nelson bought each week?"

Jericho fought to sound casual. "Who did you sell it to?"

Johnston laughed. "Won't do you much good, I guess. I sold it to Dan Busick a couple of days ago."

Jericho felt his jaw muscles stiffen. "Lieutenant Busick?"

"Yeah, Dan Busick."

"He asked for it or did he just happen to see it on the shelf?"

"Neither one," Johnston said. "You see, yesterday was Sally's birthday."

"Who is Sally?"

"Dan's wife," Johnston said. "Sally's old family here in Winfield—the Hadleys. I grew up with her. Old man Hadley owned half the town. So Dan wanted to buy her something special—an expensive liqueur or brandy."

"And he asked for the Metaxa?"

"No." Johnston laughed. "I guess you could say I conned him into buying it. You see Miss Nelson rented the Larkin cottage for three months. She asked me to get some Metaxa for her. I bought two cases from my wholesaler, but at the rate she was buying I figured I might be overstocked. So when Dan asked for something special I decided I'd try to unload a fifth on him."

"And he went for it?"

"Yeah, on my recommendation he bought it. That's the only one I ever sold. I guess that won't help you very much."

"I guess not," Jericho said very quietly. "By the way, where do the Busicks live?"

"Take your right at the traffic light down the street. About a mile beyond you'll see a big stone house set back from the road. That's the place Sally inherited from her old man."

"Thanks for passing the time of day, Mr. Johnston."

"My pleasure. I hope you and Dan find the one who did it. She was a nice lady."

Jericho went out and climbed into his car. He felt a cold finger run down his spine. He was asking himself a question. If Mr. Johnston hadn't come up with the bottle of Metaxa would Busick eventually have asked for it?

The stone house beyond the traffic light was impressive. His tires made a luxurious sound on the bluestone semicircular driveway. As he approached the front of the house he saw a high-priced foreign sports car parked by the door. A tall, rather handsome blonde woman in her late forties, wearing garden gloves, was pruning a rosebush by the side of the house.

Jericho pulled up beside her and turned off his motor.

"Mrs. Busick?" he asked.

"Yes, I'm Mrs. Busick." It was a pleasant, husky, cultivated voice.

"My name is Jericho, Mrs. Busick. I'm looking for your husband."

Little crow's-feet contracted at the corners of her bright blue eyes. "You're the man who—who was in the Nelson woman's cottage," she said.

"Unfortunately."

"Dan's still on duty," she said. "Have you tried the barracks?"

"He's evidently out on the road somewhere," Jericho said vaguely. He smiled. "It's a little late to wish you a happy birthday."

"How—how did you know that I—"

"Small-town gossip," Jericho said. He sounded almost too cheerful. "I was looking for a special brandy in the liquor store. Your Mr. Johnston told me your husband had bought you a bottle of Metaxa 5 Star for your birthday."

She smiled a very thin smile. "I'm afraid you've let the cat out of the bag, Mr. Jericho. Because Dan was on duty last night we're celebrating my birthday tonight—if this Nelson case doesn't interfere. The brandy must be a surprise he intends for dinner tonight."

"Sorry I let it slip," Jericho said. "If the Lieutenant checks in here will you tell him I'm anxious to see him? I'm going back to the Nelson cottage to have a look around. I have the feeling we must have missed something."

"I'll tell him, Mr. Jericho."

Jericho watched her in his rear-view mirror as he drove down the bluestone. She was staring after him, standing straight and still. He wondered how much she knew. Could she possibly guess that last night her husband had killed his mistress because he couldn't give up this beautiful home, the expensive car, his status in the community? Because that was what Jericho believed as he turned out of the big stone gates.

Busick had never meant the brandy as a gift to her. He had drugged that bottle, switched it with the one in Toby's liquor cabinet when Toby was away from the cottage, waited for her to follow her after-dinner custom of drinking it, and come in the middle of the night to kill her. He had found Jericho sleeping there and risked it anyway, knowing how potent the drug was.

He had made only one slip, Jericho thought. The thumbprint on the headboard was almost certainly his. But how much of a slip was it? Busick was in charge of the investigation. His fingerprints were certainly on file, but he could cover that.

There was one other hope. An autopsy would show traces of the drug in Toby's system. Was there a way Busick could cover that, too?

Jericho reached Toby's cottage and parked his car. The woods around the cottage were dark and still, the last faint reflection of the lost day showing only on the lake. Jericho was certain that if Sally Busick gave her husband an account of his visit, the Lieutenant would come, wondering just how close to the truth Jericho was.

At last the darkness was total and Jericho felt his tension mounting. Busick must always have come here after dark. Everyone in town knew him. He couldn't have risked coming here openly. So he would come now, the night his ally.

Jericho turned on a couple of lamps in the living room. Then he wandered out onto the terrace overlooking the lake which was streaked with silver from the new moon.

"Come on! Let's get it over with, buster!" he said aloud.

The shot rang loud and clear and a bullet split the cottage paneling not inches from Jericho's head. He started an instinctive dive away and at the same moment was knocked violently off his feet by someone who literally climbed on his back. He found himself struggling to get free from a bear-hug embrace.

"For God's sake stay down!"

It was Busick who was wrestling with him.

For a moment they held each other, faces close together in the moonlight.

"I didn't shoot at you," Busick said. "I wasn't ten feet away! I don't miss at ten feet. Now stay down while I take a look."

Somehow it was believable. The trooper's gun was in its holster. Jericho loosened his grip on Busick's powerful arms and the trooper rose slowly to a crouching position. He moved, still crouching, to the terrace wall. Then slowly he stood up.

The rifle cracked from not too far away and the bullet hit Busick squarely in the chest. From off toward the lake Jericho heard something that sounded like a cry of pain, and then the sound of someone hurrying off through the brush. He started to follow but when he reached Busick he changed his mind. It was a terrible wound in the trooper's chest and he was coughing blood.

Jericho had had experience with wounds. One look told him this needed more skills and equipment than he had.

"Lie still. I'll get help," he said.

Busick reached out and his hand closed over Jericho's wrist like a steel vise. "Forget it," he said in a choked voice. A little river of blood ran out of the corner of his mouth. "It—it's better this way. I—I drove her to it."

"Your wife?"

Busick laughed, a strange gurgling sound. "I taught her to shoot," he said.

"She was after me," Jericho said.

"She missed, so she wasn't after you," Busick said. "I had betrayed her. She wanted me to come out in the open and I guess I knew it. I had to pay for it all. You see, she killed Toby last night. I bought the bottle of Metaxa, not for Sally's birthday but for Toby. Sally found it and it was a kind of—a kind of clincher. She drugged it—switched bottles—and waited. Then she came here and—and had her revenge. When you talked to her today she must have known the game was up."

"The fingerprint?" Jericho asked. "It was a man's print."

"Mine," Busick said. "When I found Sally missing last night I guessed what was happening. I thought she'd come here to—to confront Toby—to scream and yell and threaten. I—I didn't dream—"

He twisted with pain as choking stopped him.

"Take it easy," Jericho said gently.

"I—I came here and found Toby—and you. I tried to see if there was some way to help Toby. I touched her and saw that there was nothing I could do. That accounts for the bloody print. I was sure Sally had done it, but I—I felt guilty myself. I couldn't give up all that went with Sally, but I loved Toby. Now—now I've killed them both."

"Your wife will have to be arrested and charged," Jericho said.

"I tell you I killed them both!" Busick said. "Because Sally will be dead when you find her. The rest of the poison, or a gun barrel in her mouth. Full—full circle."

The grip on Jericho's wrist relaxed and Busick turned his head away with a last struggling gasp for breath.

A faint breeze blew in off the lake and to Jericho it felt like the first chill of winter.

Jericho and the Studio Murders

It was said of J. C. Cordell that he owned half of the world—oil, electronics, airlines, shipping, hotels, you name it. In an article about him Cordell was quoted as saying that he had the only three things in the world that could matter to any man. "I have my son, my health, and the wealth and power to live and do exactly as I please," he told his interviewer.

On a warm lovely summer day J. C. Cordell was deprived of one of those assets. His son lay dead in a small studio-apartment in New York's Greenwich Village, with three bullet holes in his head. "The police suspect gangland revenge," an early radio report informed the world.

It revived an old waterfront story—old by at least two years. Special guards in the employ of J. C. Cordell had trapped some men trying to steal a cargo of expensive watch mechanisms from the hold of one of Cordell's ships. The guards had opened fire and one of the thieves was killed. The dead man turned out to be Mike Roberts, son of the reputed czar of the waterfront underworld, Reno Roberts. The word was out at the time that Reno Roberts would even that score with J. C. Cordell, but two years had gone by without reprisals, and Roberts' threats were forgotten.

Now J. C.'s only child, Paul Cordell, was dead, and the waterfront and the Village were alive with police trying to pin a Murder One rap on Reno Roberts and his men.

It was almost overlooked in the heat of that climate that a second man had died in the Village studio, also of gunshot wounds. He was the artist who lived there. Richard Sheridan was considered to have been an innocent and unfortunate bystander. It turned out that J. C. Cordell indulged himself in the buying of paintings and sculpture. He had come across the work of Richard Sheridan in a Madison Avenue gallery, been impressed, and had commissioned Sheridan to paint a portrait of his son.

Paul Cordell had gone to Sheridan's studio in the Village for a series of sittings. Ever since the shooting of Reno Roberts' son on the waterfront and Roberts' threats, Paul Cordell had been accompanied everywhere by a bodyguard.

One had to assume that the tensions had relaxed after two years. The bodyguard, a private eye named Jake Martin, had grown fat and careless on his assignment. He had waited outside dozens of places where Paul was gambling or involved in one kind of party or another. Jake Martin's life was almost entirely made up of waiting for Paul Cordell to satisfy his various appetites.

On that particular summer day Paul had told Martin that his sitting for Sheridan would last a couple of hours. Certain that no one had followed them to Sheridan's studio, Martin had gone across the street to a bar to have himself a few beers. It was a hot day. While Martin was away from his post a killer had struck, wasting Paul Cordell and Richard Sheridan, the innocent bystander.

Telephone lines were busy with the story. J. C. Cordell was in touch with the Mayor, the Waterfront Commission, the F.B.I. Reno Roberts was going to have to pay for this. The Mayor, in turn, was in touch with the Police Commissioner. Unless a cap was put on this case, fast, bloody waterfront violence was facing them. A girl who had been with Paul Cordell only the night before called her friends. My God, did you hear what happened to Paul Cordell? And the news had spread like wildfire…

John Jericho was not in the habit of listening to the radio. He didn't own a television set. He had been working with a kind of burning concentration on a painting in his studio in Jefferson Mews at the exact moment when Paul Cordell and Richard Sheridan had been wiped out only a few houses down the block. When Jericho, six-feet-four-inches of solid muscle, his red hair and red beard giving him the look of an old Viking warrior, got absorbed in a painting, the sky could have fallen in on Chicken Little and he wouldn't have been remotely aware of it.

Exhausted after the last brilliant strokes on his canvas, Jericho had thrown himself down on his bed and slept. An unfamiliar creak in a floorboard would have awakened him instantly. He heard the telephone ring, but it was a nuisance, so he ignored it. But the caller was persistent, dialing the number every five minutes over a long stretch of time. Finally, outraged, Jericho reached for the instrument on his bedside table and shouted an angry hello.

"Mr. Jericho?" It was an unsteady female voice. "This is Amanda Kent."

"Oh, for God's sake, Amanda." Jericho glanced at his wrist watch. "It's after one o'clock in the morning!"

"Did you hear what happened to Rick Sheridan?" the girl asked.

It was, perhaps, a notable question because all the people who had made all the phone calls during the evening had always asked: "What happened to Paul Cordell?"

Amanda Kent, Jericho had heard, had been desperately in love with Rick Sheridan. To her Paul Cordell was a nobody, a zero.

To Jericho, Greenwich Village was a small town in which he lived, not a geographical segment of a huge metropolis. He knew the shopkeepers, the bartenders and restaurant people, the artists and writers. He knew the cops. He knew the waterfront people who lived on the fringes of his "village." The ships and the men who worked on the docks had been the subject matter of many of his paintings. He ignored the new drug culture. He walked the streets at any time of day or night without any fear of muggers. He was too formidable a figure to invite violence.

A little before two o'clock on the morning of Amanda Kent's phone call Jericho walked into the neighborhood police station and into the office of Lieutenant Pat Carmody. Carmody, a ruddy Irishman with a bawdy wit when he wasn't troubled, was an old friend. On this morning he was troubled. He was frowning at a sheaf of reports, a patrolman at his elbow. He waved at Jericho, gave the patrolman some orders, and leaned back in his chair.

"I expected you'd be showing up sooner or later, Johnny," he said. "Young Sheridan was a friend of yours, I know."

"More than a friend," Jericho said. "A protégé, you might say. He mattered to me, Pat. What exactly happened?"

"He was painting a portrait of Paul Cordell, J. C. Cordell's son," Carmody said. "Damn good from what's there left to see. You remember the rumble between J. C. Cordell and Reno Roberts?"

Jericho nodded.

"Ever since Roberts' son was shot by Cordell's watchmen, Paul Cordell has had a bodyguard—followed him everywhere, like Mary's little lamb. He was a lamb this afternoon, all right, while Paul sat for his portrait. Wandered off to pour a couple. Hell, there hadn't been any trouble for two years. Anyway, someone persuaded Sheridan to open his studio door and whoever it was blasted Paul Cordell and him. No witnesses, nobody saw anyone. No one admits hearing the shots. Lot of neighbors at work that time of day. Clean hit and run."

"And you think it was Roberts' man?"

"Who else?" Carmody shrugged. "Roberts bided his time, then ordered a kill. Like always, when there's trouble on the waterfront, Reno was at his house on the Jersey coast with a dozen people to alibi him. Not that he would pull the trigger himself. He probably imported a hit-man from someplace out of the city, somebody who's long gone by now."

"No solid leads?"

"You mean something like fingerprints?" Carmody made a wry face. "Nothing. No gun. Meanwhile the town is starting to boil. J. C. Cordell isn't going to wait for us to solve the case. There's going to be a war, Cordell versus Roberts.

There's going to be a lot of blood spilled unless we can come up with the killer in the next few hours."

Jericho pounded on the door of Amanda Kent's apartment on Jane Street. He could see a little streak of light under the door. Amanda, he told himself, would not be sleeping this night.

She opened the door for him eventually and stood facing him, wearing some sort of flimsy negligee that revealed her magnificent body. Amanda was a model, and stacked away in Jericho's studio were dozens of sketches of her body, drawn when she had posed for him professionally.

Amanda's physical perfection was marred now by the fact that she was sporting a magnificent black eye.

"Mr. Jericho!" she cried, her voice muffled, and hurled herself into his arms.

He eased her back into the apartment, her blonde head buried against his chest. The small living room was something of a shambles—liquor glasses and bottles upturned on a small coffee table, ashtrays overflowing with cigarette butts, sketch-pad drawings scattered everywhere. Looking down over the girl's shoulder Jericho recognized Rick Sheridan's distinctive technique. Rick had evidently made dozens of drawings of Amanda's perfections.

Jericho settled Amanda on the couch and passed her the box of tissues on the coffee table.

"What happened to your eye?" he asked.

She gave him a twisted little-girl smile. "I bumped into a door," she said. Her face crinkled into grief again. "Oh, God, Mr. Jericho, he was so young, so great, he was going so far!"

"I haven't come here to join you in a wake," Jericho said. He was remembering that after you had savored Amanda's physical perfection you were confronted with a very dull girl who delighted in cliché and hyperbole. "Why did you call me, Amanda?"

"Because I thought Rick's friends ought to know what happened to him," she said. "The radio and television are only talking about this gangster who was killed—as if Rick hadn't even been there. I thought his friends—"

"You've got it wrong," Jericho said. "It wasn't a gangster who was killed, it was a gangster they think did the killing."

"Only Rick matters to me," Amanda said. "Oh, God!" She looked up at him through one good eye and one badly swollen one. "There's no reason any more for it to be a secret, Mr. Jericho. You see, Rick and I were having a—a—thing."

"Lucky Rick," Jericho said. "But spare me the details, Amanda. If you were that intimate with Rick you might be able to supply some information. Who would have wanted to kill Rick?"

Her good eye widened. "Nobody! It was this Cordell man they were after, wasn't it? Rick was shot because he could identify the killer. Isn't that the way it was?"

"Maybe," Jericho said. He appeared to be looking away into the distance somewhere. "But there's a chance it may have been some other way, doll. Did Rick have a row with anyone? Was there some girl who was jealous of the—the 'thing' you and Rick were having?"

"I was everything to Rick," Amanda said. "There hadn't been any other girl for a long, long time. Rick didn't have rows with people, either. He was the kindest, gentlest, sweetest—"

"He had the makings of a great painter," Jericho said. "*That's* the tragedy of it."

There was the sound of a key in the front-door lock. Jericho turned and saw a huge young man carrying a small glass jar in a hamlike hand.

"Oh, gee, you got company," the young man said. "How are you, Mr. Jericho?"

Jericho searched for the young man's name in his memory and came up with it. Val Kramer. He had grown up in the Village and was close to being retarded. There had been moves to exploit his size and extraordinary strength. Someone had tried to make a fighter out of him, but he proved hopeless. Much smaller but faster and brighter men had cut him to ribbons.

He'd been tried as a wrestler, but he was no actor, the key to success in the wrestling game, and his only thought was to crush and possibly kill his opponents. He couldn't get matches. He was now, Jericho remembered, a kind of handyman and bouncer for a rather disreputable saloon on Seventh Avenue.

"I couldn't find a meat market open noplace, love," the giant said to Amanda. He grinned shyly at Jericho. "For her eye, you know." He advanced on the girl, holding out the glass jar. "Friend of mine runs a drug store on Hudson Street. I got him up and he gave me this."

"What is it?" Amanda asked.

Jericho saw what it was. There was a wormlike creature in the jar. Long ago leeches had been used to bleed people—the medical fashion of the time—and particularly to suck the black blood out of bruised eyes.

"You must put this little guy on your eye," Val explained to Amanda, "and he sucks out all the blues and purples." He was unscrewing the lid of the glass jar, fumbling with his clumsy fingers for the slimy slug.

Jericho felt a faint shudder of revulsion run over him. He remembered hacking his way through a Korean swamp with those dreadful bloodsuckers fastened to his chest, his arms, his legs.

Somehow the giant boy-man had Amanda helpless on the couch, pinioned by the weight of his body while he held her head still with his left hand and aimed the loathsome leech at her black eye with his right. Amanda screamed at him.

"No, Val! Please! No, *no!*"

"It's for your own good, Manda," the giant crooned at her.

"No!"

Then Val Kramer did an extraordinary thing. He lowered his head and fastened his mouth on Amanda's, smothering her scream. For a moment she resisted him, kicking and pounding at him with her fists. And then, suddenly, she was just as eagerly accepting him as she had been resisting, her arms locked around his neck. Gently Val managed to release himself and without any further outcry from Amanda placed the repulsive leech on her swollen eye.

"Have you fixed up in no time," Val said.

He stood up. Amanda lay still, her eyes closed, the leech swelling and growing larger as it sucked her blood.

Val Kramer gave Jericho a sheepish grin. "It's hard to convince anyone what's good for them," he said. "I gave Manda that black eye, so I'm responsible for fixing it up."

"She said she bumped into something," Jericho said.

"This," Kramer said, grinning down at his huge fist. "She was acting crazy about this artist fellow that got shot. She was going to run over there, get mixed up with the cops and all. I had to try to stop her, and somehow, in trying, I kind of backhanded her alongside the eye. I didn't mean to, of course."

"Of course," Jericho said. "But it was natural for her to want to go to Rick, wasn't it? She tells me they were pretty close."

Val Kramer looked up and the smile was gone from his face. "She belongs to me, Jericho," he said. "I can turn her on or off. You saw that just now, didn't you? She belongs to me."

Jericho took a deep breath and let it out in a long sigh. "Well, I'm sorry to have interfered with your blood-letting, Val," he said. He looked at Amanda, lying so still on the couch, her eyes closed, the leech swelling like an obscene infection. "I came because she called me."

"That was before I told her she could only get in trouble with Roberts' people if she stuck her nose in," Kramer said. "We appreciate your coming, though."

"My pleasure," Jericho said. "When Amanda comes to, tell her that."

Jericho walked west from Jane Street toward the waterfront. The scene in Amanda's apartment was something out of Grand Guignol, he thought. The girl, grief-stricken for a lost love, suddenly turned on by that giant child, submitting to his kiss, and to the disgusting creature held fixed on her eye. Jericho supposed that reactions to the physical were Amanda's whole life.

There was a house near the abandoned West Side Highway which Jericho had visited before. During a longshoremen's strike some years ago Jericho had done drawings and paintings of the violence, and he had met Reno Roberts and been invited to an incredible Italian dinner given by the crime boss. Reno Roberts had admired Jericho's size, his bawdy humor, and in particular his ability to draw extraordinary caricatures of the dinner guests. Jericho had earned a pass to the gangster's presence that night and he decided to use it now.

The security was unexpectedly tight. More than a block from the house Jericho was picked up by two of Roberts' men who recognized him.

"Better not try to see Reno this morning," they told him. "You heard what happened?"

"That's why I'm here," Jericho said. "I might be able to help him."

"He don't need no help," one of the men said.

"Everybody can always use help," Jericho said. "Ask Reno to let me see him for five minutes."

Reno Roberts was a short squat man, bald, with burning black eyes that were hot with anger when Jericho was ushered into his presence. A large diamond ring on a stubby finger glittered in the light from a desk lamp.

"Not a time for fun and games, Johnny boy," he said. "Pasquale says you want to help. What help? Can you turn off the cops?"

"Maybe," Jericho said.

"Can you turn off J. C. Cordell? Because he has his own army which won't wait for the police. A lot of us are going to die on both sides in the next forty-eight hours. I am supposed to have killed Paul Cordell."

"But you didn't," Jericho said.

"What makes you think I didn't?" Reno asked, his eyes narrowed. "J. C.'s people killed my boy Michael. We don't let such things pass in my world."

"But you did," Jericho said. "You let two years pass. You didn't strike when your anger was hot. Why? I'm guessing it was because your boy was involved in an unauthorized theft. The guards on Cordell's pier only did their duty. They didn't know whom they were shooting. You were filled with grief and sorrow, but there was no cause for revenge. Your boy pulled a stupid stunt and paid the price for it."

"Not a bad guess," Reno said.

"So why strike back now, after two years?" Jericho asked. "And why do it so stupidly? That's not your style."

"Why stupidly?" Reno asked, his eyes bright.

"It would have been easy to finger Paul Cordell without having a witness present," Jericho said. "Why do it when it was also necessary to kill a completely innocent man? Why do it in broad daylight in a building where there might be other witnesses? Why choose a moment when Paul Cordell's bodyguard might walk in on you before the job was done? All those risks, Reno, when it could have been done with no risks. Not your style. Not professional."

"Can you convince the cops and J. C. Cordell of that?" Reno asked.

"By producing the killer," Jericho said.

Reno leaned forward in his chair. "You know who it was?"

"A hunch, Reno. But I need your help."

"What kind of help?"

"I need you to persuade someone to talk to me without any holding back."

"Name him," Reno said. "And why are you doing this for me, Johnny boy? You don't owe me anything."

"Rick Sheridan was my friend. I owe him," Jericho said.

"I don't talk about my customers," Florio, proprietor of Florio's Bar & Grill, said to Jericho. He was a tall, thin, dark man who looked older than his 50 years. "You come into my place with some guy's wife and I don't talk about it. It's none of my business."

"But Reno has made it clear to you that you must talk," Jericho said.

"I would rather cut out my tongue than betray my friends," Florio said. "You are a friend of the cops."

"Didn't Reno tell you that I am also his friend?"

"The heat is on Reno. He would do anything to take it off."

"Maybe the people I want to talk about are not friends you would cut out your tongue to keep from betraying," Jericho said. "One of them works for you now and then. Val Kramer."

Florio's face relaxed. "Poor dumb kid," he said. "Yeah, he fills in behind the bar when I'm shorthanded."

"Yesterday?"

"From five in the afternoon till midnight. My regular bartender was home with the flu."

"My friend Rick Sheridan was murdered at about four in the afternoon. Did you know Rick?"

"Sure, I knew him. He came in here three, four times a week. A great guy. Very bad luck for him he was there when they hit Paul Cordell."

"If that's what happened," Jericho said. "Did you know Rick's girl, Amanda Kent?"

Florio laughed. "Rick's girl? He couldn't stand the sight of her. He used her as a model, I guess. She fell for him. She's a crazy kid, but he wanted no part of her. Only a couple of nights ago he told her off, right here in my place. He told her to get lost, to leave him alone."

"What do you know about Amanda Kent and Val Kramer? Is Val one of her lovers?"

"Oh, he was gone on her. Over his head gone. He followed her around like some faithful collie dog. But she had no time for him." Florio's face clouded. "Funny thing. She came in here with Val yesterday—at five o'clock—when he came on the job. She stayed here all night, till he went off at midnight. She left here with him then. When they came in at five we hadn't heard anything about the shooting. The news came over the radio a little before seven. Amanda went into a kind of hysterics, but she didn't leave. Some of the customers sat with her, tried to console her. You want to know who they were?"

Jericho shook his head slowly. "I don't think so," he said. "She had hysterics, but she waited for Val Kramer to finish his tour, some five hours after she heard the news on the radio?"

"Yeah. I suppose—well, I don't know exactly what I suppose. Maybe she was afraid to go home. Maybe she thought Reno's boys might be after anyone who might have been around Sheridan's place at the time of the shooting."

"Are you saying Amanda was around Rick's studio at four o'clock?"

Florio shrugged. "I don't know for sure, Mr. Jericho. When the news came on the radio she had, like I told you, hysterics. She kept saying, over and over, 'I just saw him a little while ago!' "

"Did she get potted while she waited for Kramer?"

"Funny you should ask," Florio said, "because I remember being surprised that she didn't. She usually drank a lot. I figured she'd really go overboard when she heard about Rick Sheridan. But she didn't. She stayed cold-sober."

"And waited for Kramer?"

"Val would make her a perfect bodyguard," Florio said. "He's too stupid to be afraid of anybody or anything."

The gray light of dawn was sifting through the city's canyons when Jericho again knocked on the door of Amanda Kent's Jane Street apartment. It was Val Kramer who opened the door.

"Gee, Mr. Jericho, you got some news for us?" he asked.

"Perhaps," Jericho said. "May I come in?"

"Sure. Come in," the childlike giant said. "Have some coffee? I just made a fresh pot of coffee."

"I'd like that," Jericho said, moving into the apartment. "How's Amanda?"

"She's fine," Kramer said, his smile almost jubilant. "That bloodsucker really did his thing."

"Would you believe it?" Amanda asked from the bedroom doorway. She was still wearing the see-through negligee, but the swollen and discolored eye had vanished. "That little sucker really sucked. You found out something, Mr. Jericho?"

Jericho took the mug of hot coffee Kramer brought him. "I found out who killed Rick and Paul Cordell," he said quietly.

"Who?" they asked simultaneously.

"One of you," Jericho said, very quietly. He took a cautious sip of the scalding-hot coffee.

The childlike giant giggled. "You gotta be kidding," he said.

"I was never more serious in my life, Val," Jericho said.

The room was deathly still. Kramer looked at Amanda who had suddenly braced herself against the doorframe.

"I don't think you should say things like that, Mr. Jericho," the girl said, her voice shaken. "Because it's crazy!"

"Oh, it's crazy enough," Jericho said. "Rick had turned you down, Amanda, and he had to be killed for that. How crazy can you get? I came here to get you to turn over the gun to me, whichever one of you had it. I can't put it off, friends. There is about to be a war on the streets in which dozens of innocent people will die. So hand it over."

Val Kramer made a slow hesitant move toward the pocket of his canvas jacket. He produced a small pearl-handled gun that was almost hidden in his massive hand. He pointed it at Jericho, clumsily, like a man unaccustomed to handling such a weapon.

"It's too bad you couldn't mind your own business, Mr. Jericho," he said.

"Amanda called me, asked me for help," Jericho said, not moving a muscle.

"No such thing!" Amanda protested. "You were Rick's friend. I thought you should know what happened to him."

"Six hours after you'd heard the news? Why didn't you call me from Florio's bar? You were there for five hours after you heard the news."

"I—I was hysterical. I didn't have my head together," Amanda said. "After I got home I began to think of friends of Rick's who ought to be told."

"You wanted me to nail Val, didn't you, Amanda? Because you were afraid of him. When he found out you'd called me he hit you. You didn't bump into any door, did you, Amanda?"

"So I killed him," Val said, in a strange little boy's voice. "He couldn't get away with what he did to Manda. I went to his studio and I told him he had to pay for what he'd done to Manda, so I killed him. And I killed the guy who was there, because he could tell on me. I didn't know it was Paul Cordell and that it would make a lot of trouble. And now I'm going to kill you, Mr. Jericho, because you can tell on me."

He lifted the gun a little so that it was aimed at Jericho's heart. Jericho threw the hot coffee full in the childlike giant's face. There was a roar of pain and Kramer dropped the gun as he lifted his hands to his scalded face. Then he lunged at Jericho.

It was a matter of strength against strength and skill. Jericho sidestepped the rush, and a savage chopping blow to Kramer's neck sent the giant crashing to the floor like a poled ox. He lay still, frighteningly still. Jericho bent down and picked up the little pearl-handled gun.

Then Amanda was clinging to him, weeping. "Oh, thank God, thank God!" she said. "I was so terrified of him!"

Jericho's fingers bit into her arms and held her away from him. "You scum," he said. It was more like a statement of fact than an angry expletive. "That poor guy would do anything on earth for you, including taking the rap for a murder you committed. Followed you around like a faithful collie dog, I was told. Followed you to Rick's studio yesterday afternoon. It was a habit with him—the faithful collie dog.

"He was too late to stop your killing a man who simply wasn't interested in what your body had to offer. 'Hell hath no fury—' He couldn't stop your killing, but he helped you get away. He took you to Florio's where he had to work. You stayed there for seven long hours. Why? Because you needed a bodyguard? Because you were grateful? No, because he had you cold and you knew you were going to have to do whatever he told you to do."

"No! No!" It was only a whisper.

"But you knew how to handle him, and you had to wait till it was possible. You knew that if you gave yourself to him he was yours forever, to handle as you pleased. You knew he would take the blame for you if the going got tough, no matter what. You waited for him, all those hours in Florio's, because until you could pretend that you cared for him he had you trapped. You took him home here and you offered him something he'd never really dreamed of having."

"I—I had no choice," Amanda said. "He killed Rick just like he said. I—"

"He hit you in the eye in some kind of struggle with you," Jericho said. "And because he really loves you, in his simple-minded and faithful way, he went out to find a piece of beef to put on your eye and when he saw there was no butcher shop open he found you that leech. While he was gone, you called me. You were already thinking of a way out. You would have fed me bits and pieces if I hadn't discovered them for myself. Unfortunately for you I found the right pieces and not the phony ones you'd have fed me."

"I swear to you—"

"It won't do, Amanda," Jericho said. "You're going out of here with me now, and just pray to God that your confession comes in time to stop blood from running in the gutters." He looked down at the unconscious giant. "And just pray that I can make that poor jerk believe that your body wasn't worth the price he was willing to pay. Get moving, Amanda."

Jericho on Campus

Jericho had learned long ago that you don't go back to old loves with any real chance of success. It's best to remember them for all the things you imagined they were, but couldn't have been, or there wouldn't have been an ending. But on that beautiful fall day, the trees ablaze with color, he found himself tooling his red Mercedes along the thruway toward an upstate town and to a lost love, a lost magic.

Liz Bowen's letter had been so gay, so warm, so full of her special kind of life, that he had decided to do the favor she asked of him, mostly because he was curious to see what she had become over the years. Was it five years—six years?

"Dear Johnny," she had written. She was one of the few people who had ever called the six-foot-four-inch John Jericho, two-hundred-and-forty pounds of bone and muscle, with his blazing red Viking beard and mustache, by the diminutive "Johnny."

"Dear Johnny:"

"A favor, please. One that you can easily refuse on the grounds that you are too busy. Would you believe I am teaching art at the Walton School for Boys? To talk about teaching art to the maestro himself is absurd to start with. But everything I knew about painting I learned from you, Johnny. I quote you shamelessly, declaring your wisdom to be my own.

"But I have a problem. I am the first woman teacher at the Walton School for Boys, and the school is over a hundred years old, having educated—it says here—the sons of the rich and socially prominent for all that time. But times have changed, sadly, I think, for the powers that be. Like most of the other fine New England prep schools, Walton now enrolls girls—the daughters, of course, of the rich and socially prominent.

"They wander around our elegant campus, their hair hanging long, their trim bodies encased in tight blue jeans. They look as though they expected to be attacked from any direction at any time."

"So I teach them art, boys and girls together, and I have mentioned the fact that the great John Jericho is my friend and I realize they think I am name-dropping. It reduces my effectiveness no end and I know only one thing that would restore my standing. I can't tell them that I once shared your life, and that

216

we were in love for one whole marvelous summer. They would think I'd flipped my wig for sure.

"So surely you are going to want to take one of these fall days to paint the foliage. And surely the foliage here is as perfect as you could find. And if you time it so that you could drop by here at Walton and walk into my class—! My prestige would be intact again."

Liz, Jericho knew, would not play games with him. It was as if she knew he might be thinking just that. She had concluded her letter by saying:

"I loved you, Johnny, but don't draw the conclusion that I am asking for your love again. You see, I think I am really in love at last, and I'm saving whatever I have to give to my guy. But if you could help out a chick whose boasting has got her in trouble I'd be everlastingly in your debt—as if I wasn't already."

They had spent a whole summer together five years ago—or was it six? It had been at a little village by the sea in southern France. It had involved no self-analysis, no discussion of motives. In the end, when Jericho had to go—he always had to go where the helpless were being bullied by the arrogant and the powerful—Liz had wept no tears. He knew that she had wanted permanence, and she knew that he couldn't give it. The day he left, having given her no more than a comment at breakfast—their last night together had had no overtones of a "last time"—she had taken it quite calmly.

"You have given me something, Johnny, I never dreamed existed," she had said. "I will owe you for that always and always."

Quite a girl! It was little enough to drop by her art class and let her adolescent pupils know that she hadn't been name-dropping. Would she have changed? Would being "really in love" have made her even more attractive?

He had called her on the phone at the school. She sounded just like her old self. Her class was at two in the afternoon. He promised he would be there.

"And dinner at the end of the day?" he asked.

"I'd love it, Johnny."

"Bring your true love along with you. I'd like to meet him."

There was a moment's hesitation. "If it wouldn't bore you I'd like it to be just us, Johnny," she said. "I need your advice about something."

He laughed. "I'm no good at advising people about their love lives," he said. "Too much self-interest."

"It isn't about my love life, but it's important."

"Count on me," he said.

The campus at Walton was complicated, and it was agreed that Jericho would ask directions at the Administration Building. He would be directed to Liz's "apartment" and she would take him on to the class.

When he drove through the main gates Jericho saw what Liz had meant by complicated. There were dozens of big buildings—dormitories in red brick, classrooms, an observatory pointing like a glass finger to the sky, a gymnasium with a huge glass dome; there were soccer fields, football fields, baseball diamonds, an outdoor hockey rink, and a golf course that wound its way around the perimeter of the campus. The headmaster's mansion was on top of a hill.

At the Administration Building a pleasant girl directed Jericho to Liz's apartment. It was in what must have been one of the original buildings, a beautiful old Colonial house.

"First door on your right as you go in the front door, Mr. Jericho," the girl said. "Miss Bowen said you were just to walk in if she didn't answer. She has some kind of special consultation she thought might not be finished when you got here."

Outside, boys and girls hurried from one building to another, books and briefcases clutched under arms. Jericho was used to having people turn to look at him. The girls, "encased in tight blue jeans," stared at him and then put their heads together. There was a man!

Jericho parked the Mercedes outside the Colonial house and knocked on the first door to the right inside the main entrance. There was no answer, so he walked in, calling out Liz's name as he closed the door behind him.

She didn't answer.

She couldn't answer. She was lying on the floor beside an easel on which there was an unfinished canvas. She was wearing a blue smock, paint-stained. She was staring up at the ceiling. Someone had given her a brutal blow high up on her forehead over her left eye. It had stained her golden blonde hair red.

The blow might not have been enough to kill her, but someone had made sure. Her throat had been cut from ear to ear.

Jericho turned away, fighting the urge to be violently ill.

Jericho had devoted most of his adult life to confronting violence. His paintings with their brilliant and vivid colors were a crusade against man's brutality to man all over the world. But he was like most of us who assume "it can't happen to me, or to people I care for." It can only happen to "others."

But it had happened to Liz Bowen, a girl with whom he had been in love, with whom he had laughed and shared his ideas and spent his nights, and, perhaps more binding than anything, had shared his working time, painting the sea and the mountains and the people, and arguing over techniques and concepts. She had been his woman for three wonderful months. She had almost made him believe in a permanent relationship.

Now he had come back, too late. He knew, as he regained his objectivity, that he had only been just a little too late. She had been dead only a very short time. The blood on the floor under her had still not dried. For a moment he told himself there might still be a chance. He knelt beside her, reaching for a pulse he knew could not be there.

You don't touch anything, not even the telephone. He went out into the hall and knocked on the door across the way. He could hear a record player and complex rock music with vague undertones of Bach. The door was promptly opened by a young man with a trim blond beard and very bright blue eyes.

"Miss Bowen—" Jericho began.

"Just across the hall there," the young man said.

"She's been murdered," Jericho said, in a flat unemotional voice. "Please call the local police, or the State Troopers, or whoever handles that kind of thing at Walton. And someone in authority here at the school."

"Lord almighty!" the young man said.

Jericho turned and went back into Liz's apartment. He steeled himself to look around. He gathered there was this studio-living room, a bedroom off to the right, a small kitchenette to the left. He could see a coffee percolator with a little red light showing that the coffee was still hot.

There was no sign of any struggle. Liz had been struck down by someone she knew and hadn't feared. From the wound on her forehead she must have been facing the killer when he struck.

He saw a brass candlestick lying on the floor a few feet from the body. That must have been the bludgeon, tossed aside by the killer. It had a smooth, polished surface, perfect to retain fingerprints. But the weapon used to slash Liz's throat was nowhere.

He fought the impulse to tear the place apart, looking for it. But he knew he should leave things exactly as they were, for the trained investigators to examine. To avoid looking at Liz, staring blankly into eternity, he turned away toward the telephone on the table at the end of the couch. A little appointment book was lying open beside it. She had written in it, on the page for this date.

12.30—H.M.

1.00—J.J.

J.J. had to be John Jericho. He had said he would arrive about one. They'd have a little time to chat before he went to her class at two. He had been prompt. His wrist watch told him it was now just twenty minutes past one. If "H.M." had been as prompt, he was either the killer, or he had left the killer almost no time between the 12:30 appointment and Jericho's arrival.

Then Jericho remembered the girl in the office. Liz had had "some kind of special consultation" and might not be in her apartment. Was the 12:30 appointment with H.M. to have been before or after that special consultation, or was the special consultation with H.M. to be held away from the apartment?

The door opened behind Jericho and the young man with the blond beard and the bright blue eyes came in. His face was the color of ashes as he stared down at Liz.

"Are you John Jericho?" he asked finally.

"Yes."

"Liz said you were coming. I was to keep an eye out for you in case she wasn't here. There was coffee prepared and—oh, my God." He turned away from Liz. "I teach history here at Walton, Mr. Jericho. My name is Howard Marsten."

They came then, in little swirling groups. First, some sort of security guard in a gray uniform, accompanied by a couple of young faculty members; then Dr. Cramer, the school doctor; then a gathering crowd of students and teachers in the outer hall; through them bustled the headmaster, a gray-haired, hearty-looking man in his late fifties. Eric Baldwin was the third generation of Baldwins to be headmaster at Walton.

Then there were sirens and two carloads of State Troopers. Just as Captain Johnson, the trooper in charge, was trying to create some order in the place there was a late arrival. He came charging into the room, brushing aside the people in the doorway, pulled the pudgy little doctor away from the body, and with a great cry of anguish took what was left of Liz Bowen in his arms, while Captain Johnson shouted at him.

"I must ask you not to touch anything, Mr. McNiel!"

Angus McNiel looked up at the trooper, obviously considering the possibility of killing him for using the word "anything." "Anything" was Liz Bowen! McNiel was almost as big a man as Jericho. He was wearing an athletic sweat-suit and sneakers, a silver whistle hung around his neck on a black cord, and a baseball cap was pulled down on his crew-cut head.

"You really must not touch her, Coach," the doctor said.

Jericho didn't need to be told that this was Liz Bowen's love, the man she had found "at last." Angus McNiel ignored the doctor, and held the bloodied face of his woman against his own cheek. Then, very gently, almost reverently, he lowered the body to the floor again. He stood up, his face stained with her blood, his eyes blazing.

"You're Jericho?" he demanded, facing Jericho.

"Yes."

"You just couldn't let her go? Is that it? You didn't want her but you couldn't let anyone else have her? Is that it?"

He moved so quickly and unexpectedly that Jericho, whose reflexes were normally lightning-fast, was caught flatfooted. A right cross to the jaw staggered Jericho. He felt his knees buckle. He managed to block the left that followed, and then the troopers were all over McNiel, dragging him away. Jericho tasted blood in his mouth.

"You damned idiot!" he heard himself say.

Some sort of order was restored. The troopers herded everyone out of the room except Dr. Cramer and Eric Baldwin, the headmaster. Jericho told his story. It checked out in more ways than one. Baldwin had known he was coming to appear at Liz's art class. Several people had seen the red Mercedes arrive about one o'clock. The girl in the office had directed him to Liz's apartment at one o'clock. Howard Marsten reported that Jericho had knocked on his door only a few minutes after one, had reported the murder, and asked Marsten to call for help.

Captain Johnson appreciated a man who had known enough to touch nothing, not even the body. Jericho pointed out the appointment pad with his initials on it and Marsten's.

"I didn't exactly have an appointment with her," Marsten said. "She told me Mr. Jericho was due to arrive about one. She had an appointment somewhere— she didn't say where or with whom—and was afraid she might not be here when he arrived. If she wasn't here about a quarter to one I was to come in and plug in the coffee percolator."

"And did you plug in the pot?" Johnson asked.

"No," Marsten said, "because I heard her come in just as I was about to."

"You saw her?"

"No, but I heard her. She called out a greeting to someone and I heard her door open and close."

"Do you know whom she greeted?"

"No idea. She just said, 'Hi, there!' Something like that. Then I heard the door open and close."

Johnson ordered one of his men to find out who Liz had spoken to in the hall. Then he turned to Jericho. "What was McNiel talking about?" he asked.

Jericho's anger had diminished. "I think he was in love with Liz," he said.

"That's no secret," Eric Baldwin said. "They were talking of getting married during the Christmas vacation."

"Liz must have told him that five or six years ago she and I were close," Jericho said. "Your Mr. McNiel is a jealous adolescent. I'd like to put him straight."

"You'd better wait till he cools down," Baldwin said.

"I don't care whether he's cooled down or not," Jericho said. His smile was tight. "The next time he tries something like that I'll take him apart, piece by piece."

Angus McNiel was in no frame of mind to try anything again. Jericho found him sitting alone on a bench outside the old Colonial house. There is something unusually pathetic about a big strong man who comes apart at the seams. Angus McNiel, hands covering his face, was weeping quietly.

Jericho sat down on the bench beside him.

"You were off your rocker about me, you know," Jericho said.

McNiel lifted swollen eyes. "I know. I'm sorry. But at that moment I had to—to strike out at something, someone."

"I think I understand," Jericho said. "She loved you, you know. She told me so in the letter she wrote, asking me to come here to speak to her class."

"She mentioned me?"

"Not by name. But she said she was really in love at last. Who else?"

"Oh, God!" McNiel said.

"I talked to her on the phone, telling her I'd come," Jericho said. "I invited her to dinner and suggested she bring you. She said she'd rather come alone. She needed advice about some problem. Do you have any idea what it was?"

"Something about me?"

"Don't be so damned self-centered," Jericho said. "Some other kind of problem in which you weren't included."

McNiel was silent for a moment. "We've all got problems here at Walton since the change," McNiel said.

"What change?"

"Going co-ed, the admission of girls," McNiel said. "It adds another dimension. I mean, everybody becomes girl watchers instead of students. I mean, even the faculty."

"The faculty?"

"Some of these sixteen-year-olds are pretty luscious dishes," McNiel said. "I think Liz was concerned about one of the girl's being involved with a teacher."

"Howard Marsten?"

"Howard's gay, for Pete's sake," McNiel said. "She didn't tell me who. She said it was her problem to solve, that I shouldn't have it on my conscience. I think—well, she knew I was something of a bull in a china shop. She wanted to be more diplomatic than I knew how to be."

"A teacher who got involved with one of the girls would be kicked out, wouldn't he?"

"In spades! And a tough time getting another job anywhere else," McNiel said.

Jericho nodded slowly. "That would be a motive, wouldn't it?"

As Jericho turned back toward the house, Captain Johnson came down the path.

"Nothing," he said. "No prints on the candlestick. Wiped clean. No sign of the weapon used to cut her throat. Not a lead of any kind."

"You come up with the person she spoke to in the hall?" Jericho asked.

Johnson shook his head. "And it's odd, don't you think? You'd think whoever it was would come forward."

"Not if he was the killer," Jericho said.

There was nothing more he could do in the house. He walked down the path with the trooper captain toward his red Mercedes. To solve this he would have to settle into the community, he thought, get to know dozens of people, listen to endless gossip. It was for the locals to handle. And yet he knew he couldn't walk away and leave Liz lying on a slab in the morgue without doing something to square accounts for her.

The captain headed for his blue-and-white trooper car and Jericho turned toward the Mercedes. A girl with long blonde hair, hanging straight and shining down her back, was standing by the car, looking in at the leather upholstery and the fancy instrument board. She was wearing the tight blue jeans that were evidently a kind of uniform at Walton, and a navy-blue pullover sweater with long sleeves. She turned as he came up to her.

"Mr. Jericho?"

"Yes."

"I'm April Powers," she said. She had bright, inquisitive gray-blue eyes, a pert, upturned nose, and a shiny no-makeup face. "It's terrible about Miss Bowen."

"Very terrible," he said.

"I was supposed to come over here to escort you to her class," April said. "I heard about it just before I got here. Who could have done such a thing?"

"Someone who hated her or was afraid of her," Jericho said.

"But everybody loved her," April said.

Some instinct created a tightening of Jericho's muscles. The girl had said that as if it were something she had memorized; there was no emotion, no real feeling.

"You were in her class?"

"Yes. And she is—was—a marvelous teacher."

"Painting?"

"My gig is sculpture," April said. "Right now I'm involved with wood carving."

"Figures?"

"Right now I'm doing a bust of Mr. Baldwin, the headmaster."

"He sits for you?"

"I go to his house three afternoons a week. Mostly I go at it while he works at his desk."

"I'd like to see it sometime," Jericho said. "The bust, I mean."

"I'd be terribly flattered," the girl said. "The whole class is in shock right now. They were so looking forward to your coming."

"I promised Liz," Jericho said. "Maybe I will some time, when this is over."

"Over?" she asked, her eyes very bright.

"When they've caught the murderer," Jericho said.

He could see her in his rear-view mirror as he drove away. The campus was busy now. Kids threw frisbies and played touch football on the wide lawns between buildings. As he turned a corner he caught a glimpse of bright-jerseyed soccer players on a distant field. Liz was dead; Liz who had been so full of life and love and concern for others. The people around her said "Wow! How awful!"—and went on with their fun and games.

He had been driving slowly, but his tires screamed as he suddenly jammed his foot down on the power-brake pedal. The Mercedes stopped dead, and he sat behind the wheel, staring straight ahead of him. He felt like an old-fashioned safecracker, trying to guess the combination, turning the dial, listening for the tumblers to drop. One of the tumblers that would crack this case had dropped in his mind, actually while he'd been thinking of something else.

He had thought at first that the initials H.M. had stood for Howard Marsten. But Marsten's story didn't fit. If Marsten was lying he still didn't fit as someone involved in a scandal with a girl student—that is, if Angus McNiel was right about Marsten. But talking with April Powers about her wood carving had, inadvertently, given him another explanation of the initials.

He leaned forward so that he could look up at the hill to his right. The Headmaster's house was there, another graceful old Colonial. He put the Mercedes in gear, turned off to his right, and headed up the hill.

There was a casual elegance about Eric Baldwin in his own setting. The house was tastefully furnished with early American antiques, but it appeared to be a home, not a museum. The study, where Baldwin received his caller, was a place where a man worked—it was not a showplace. Yet it had been put together with perfect taste. The mirror over the mantle above the fieldstone fireplace reflected the floor-to-ceiling walls of books. Jericho commented on the charm of the place.

"I am in my twenty-first year as headmaster," Baldwin said. He leaned back in his desk chair, making a steeple out of his fingers. He was a man who had kept in shape, slim, graceful, weather-tanned. His tweed jacket was expensive, expertly tailored to appear casual. "My late wife and I put this house together, bit by bit. Unfortunately she didn't live long enough to really enjoy it when it was done. But it is really all her taste."

Baldwin pulled himself away from the past. "What can I do for you, Mr. Jericho?"

"I happen to know that Liz Bowen has no family," Jericho said. "I wanted you to know that, unless she has a will with proper instructions, I'll take care of whatever has to be done for her. She was a valued friend."

Baldwin nodded. "A very special girl," he said. "She was a fine teacher with unusual gifts. I can't tell you how shocked I am."

Jericho took a black shell briar from his pocket and began to fill it from an oilskin pouch. "Concerned for the school and for the school community," he said. "It was that concern that brought her here to see you today at twelve thirty, wasn't it?"

Suddenly fear stared out of Baldwin's eyes.

"I don't know what makes you think—"

"The initials on her appointment pad," Jericho said. "I thought they stood for Howard Marsten. Now I think they stood for Head Master. Why didn't you mention to Captain Johnson that you had seen her at twelve thirty?"

Baldwin's tongue edged out of his mouth and moistened his lips. "I just didn't think of it," he said. "It had no connection with that horror down there."

"Oh, I think it did, Mr. Baldwin. I think she came here to get your decision on how to handle a scandal in the school. You satisfied her, and she left you to go back to her rooms to wait for me. What did you tell her, Baldwin? That you would get rid of that girl and then quietly resign as headmaster?"

"My dear sir, I simply don't understand—"

Jericho thought he could smell fear when it was intense enough. "I have sympathy for the hungers that possess a man, particularly when he has suffered your kind of loss," he said.

"Hungers?"

"I've seen April Powers, talked to her," Jericho said. "What is she? Sixteen would you say? But I knew from the way she looked at me, the way she assessed me as a man, how she must have looked at you when she came here to carve a bust of you. I could see a little schemer in that child. Seduce you and she could run the school. She could blackmail you. After all, it was more than simply conduct unbecoming a headmaster, Baldwin. At sixteen she is jail bait. There is no such thing as consent at the age of sixteen."

"Oh, God!" Baldwin's words were a soft moan.

"You were really in a tough spot, weren't you?" Jericho said. "You couldn't expel the girl, or she would talk. You couldn't simply walk away, or she would talk. You had to somehow stall Liz Bowen while you thought of a way out."

"But I had nothing to do with—!"

"Oh, I know you didn't kill her, Baldwin. But I think when you had stalled Liz with phony assurances at that twelve-thirty meeting, you called your little companion and warned her that the fire was getting very hot. I think Miss April went quickly to Liz's rooms. I think it was she whom Liz spoke to in the hall. 'Hi, there!' Marsten heard Liz say. April had been due there later to escort me to the class. She was early, but Liz waved her into the rooms. It would be a chance for Liz to talk to her."

Baldwin was looking past Jericho at some kind of nightmare. Jericho glanced at the mirror over the fireplace and his muscles tightened. He saw April coming up behind him, a bright evil smile on her lips. She was carrying a poker she had taken from the fire irons in the next room.

"She killed Liz," Jericho said quietly, not moving. "She knocked her out with the candlestick—Liz was totally unprepared for an attack. And then she cut her throat with the wood carving knife which will be found in her school briefcase. So you are not only a morals offender, Baldwin, but an accessory to murder and attempted murder."

"Attempted murder?"

"You miserable coward, you see her coming at me, don't you? And not a word from you!"

The girl moved quickly, but not quickly enough. Jericho kicked out behind him. The poker clattered to the floor and there was a sound from April like air being let out of a punctured balloon.

Jericho turned and looked down at the girl who lay gasping for breath.

"Why is it," Jericho asked, in a voice that trembled with anger, "that the decent and kind people of this earth are always being destroyed by the indecent and the vicious?" He drew a deep breath. "I think you'd better get Captain Johnson here fast, Mr. Baldwin, or I might decide to become the judge and the executioner myself."

Sources

"Jericho and the Skiing Clue," *Ellery Queen's Magazine* [hereafter, *EQMM*],
    November 1964
"Jericho and the Painting Clue," *EQMM*, July 1965
"Jericho and the Dying Clue," *EQMM*, October 1965
"Jericho and the Silent Witnesses," *EQMM*, November 1965
"Jericho and the Nuisance Clue," *EQMM*, August 1966
"Jericho and the Dead Clue," *EQMM*, December 1971
"Jericho and the Two Ways to Die," *EQMM*, September 1972
"Jericho and the Deadly Errand," *EQMM*, January 1973
"Jericho Plays It Cool," *EQMM*, July 1973
"Jericho and the Missing Boy," *EQMM*, October 1973
"Jericho and the Sea of Faces," *EQMM*, June 1974
"Jericho and the Frightened Woman," *EQMM*, November 1974
"Jericho and the Unknown Lover," *EQMM*, February 1975
"Jericho and the Studio Murders," *EQMM*, November 1975
"Jericho on Campus," *EQMM*, October 1976

Afterword

by Daniel Philips

When I was born, the local newspaper ran an announcement with a small headline that read, "A Star is Born." This was a reference to my marvelously gifted actress mother and my award-winning mystery writer father. Surely from such talented genes would spring a star! I am convinced, however, that the real star of our family finally flickered out on the morning of March 7, 1989. He was Judson Pentecost Philips—my dad—known also to thousands of avid mystery readers by his pen name, Hugh Pentecost. It's been more than fifteen years since his death, and I must confess that I still haven't completely accepted the fact that he is gone. Somehow I thought that when I was bouncing my grandchildren on my knee, I'd be able to dial the phone and hear the unmistakable note of loving pleasure in his gravelly voice as he answered, "Daniel!"

I know that I'm not really grieving for Dad, but for myself. I miss him. He fought for so long against the emphysema that finally killed him; he deserves to enjoy the rest. I like to think that there is a beautifully manicured golf course where he is now, and my father (who was a 3-handicap golfer even into his sixties) is striding down the fairway, no longer struggling for breath, getting ready to line up a short chip shot onto the green. Perhaps there is a summer theatre there to run, and Dad, who so passionately loved the arts that he founded The Sharon Playhouse in 1951, is once again engrossed with the day-to-day crises of summer stock, surrounded by dozens of energetic young people with bright dreams of stardom to nurture and encourage. And surely there will be time to sit on a breezy screened porch with a couple of his favorite dogs curled at his feet, his beloved wife Norma nearby, and a Yankees game on the radio. They'll be playing the Red Sox: "It's the bottom of the ninth, Yanks are down 5–2, two out, bases loaded ... and the payoff pitch is on the way to Ruth...!"

How he loved baseball. Radio broadcasts were the best medium because they allowed his marvelous mind to roam. Summer Sunday afternoons would find my father sitting on the porch in our Connecticut farmhouse, sipping iced coffee and listening to the Yankees' game. Perhaps the Yanks would be playing the Mariners. Dad would give no sign that he was even listening as he gazed out at the swaying pine trees and puffed contentedly at his briarwood pipe; no doubt he was working out the intricacies of plot for his latest book or short story.

The Yankees get a couple of men on base and the Seattle manager heads to the mound. My father would glance over at me. "He's going to bring in Jones, the left-hander, to pitch to Mattingly," he'd say. The broadcasters had said no more than to tell us that the Mariners had pitchers warming up in the bullpen.

"C'mon, Dad, you can't know who's coming in to pitch!" I would say skeptically—only to be interrupted by the announcement that Jones, a left-handed middle reliever, is entering the game.

I would glance sheepishly over at Judson Philips, who was still gazing out at the sparkling New England vista. Was that a smile tugging at the corner of his mouth? "Dad," I would exclaim, "how did you even know they had a pitcher named Jones? You don't read the box scores, you read the editorial page; it's the Seattle *Mariners*, for heaven's sake, they're clear across the country, how often do you hear them on the radio, maybe four times a year?"

He'd just shrug. "Oh, I must have heard the name somewhere," he'd say blandly. No mistaking that smile now.

Dad loved a good story or a joke. Have you ever heard a great joke, and you can't wait to tell it to your family, but on the way home the story just disappears? Dad used his marvelous memory to remember, and even improve on a joke by wringing a concise twist of language here, or an ironic description there.

His favorite jokes were true comedy—they related to the foibles and pitfalls that beset us all. If a joke was vicious or bigoted, it really wasn't funny. If someone was to be the butt of one of his jokes, it was often Dad himself.

One story I heard him tell several times concerned his baseball career at Columbia University. Dad played second base for Columbia, but on one occasion a sudden illness suffered by the team's catcher forced my father to fill in behind the plate on a day when Columbia's ace was pitching. The pitcher's name was Lou Gehrig, who went on to a Hall of Fame career with the Yankees. Gehrig threw a one-hitter that day, striking out seventeen batters. Think of that: my father caught the great "Iron Man" of baseball! You might imagine that this was one of Dad's most cherished memories.

"We lost the game, 6–1," my father recalled. "The problem," he would explain, his blue eyes twinkling, "was that sixteen of the seventeen strikeouts reached base on passed balls. The batters couldn't hit the ball, but I couldn't catch it, either!" Then Dad would laugh and shake his head. "Gehrig didn't speak to me for a week after that."

One thing that was no laughing matter was his writing. Writing was not what Judson Philips did to make money; writing was what he *was*. He wrote three or four books a year, along with a number of short stories. Oh yes, and there was a regular newspaper column, "Artfully Speaking," which covered current events in the social and political scene. Dad loved to write, and the more passionately he believed in something, the more biting his commentary became.

I remember, as a boy, being outraged by a letter to the editor suggesting that my father was a fool.

"Dad, what are you going to *do* about this?" I demanded.

"Well, it's nice to know someone is reading the column," he replied placidly, that mischievous light dancing in his eyes. I wouldn't let it go. I guess I wanted my dad to go beat up his critic … at least in print if not in the middle of Madison Square Garden!

When he saw that it was important to me, Dad instantly grew serious. "You see, Daniel," he explained gently, "it isn't really all that important whether that man likes me or not, or even if he agrees with me or not. What *does* matter is that he reads about the issues and he *cares* what's cooking in this country. If he feels strongly enough about what I wrote to send a letter to the editor, so much the better. If I can just get people to *think*, that's what's important." He stayed there at the kitchen table for a few more moments, asking questions to be sure that I understood. Then he smiled again, this time with tender affection, touched my arm, and headed back to the typewriter to fire off another salvo.

More than anything else, he loved my mother, Norma Burton Philips. Dad had married and divorced four times before he met Mom. They were together for 37 years until his death in 1987. I never thought about all the love and loss that must have been a part of his life before I was born. I just knew him as a man who loved people and who loved to make his friends laugh. When my first marriage ended in divorce, he was no longer there to ask about how one dealt with that particular pain.

Whenever the subject of divorce and remarriage came up in the Philips' home, Dad would tell our guests a joke about an opera singer who came to the front of the stage during a performance to sing the *aria*. At the end of his rendition, the audience erupted in thunderous applause. Cheers and whistles and cries of "Encore!" filled the auditorium. Beaming with pleasure, the soloist bowed to the crowd and sang the song a second time. Again there was an enormous burst of applause at the end of his rendition, and more calls for an encore. The soloist, no doubt struggling to contain his swelling pride, bowed and sang the solo for a third time.

After the third straight rendition, Dad would say, the audience burst forth again, clapping, whistling, stamping their feet, and calling for him to sing the *aria* once again. The soloist moved to the front of the stage and raised his hands for silence. "My friends," he intoned, "I thank you, but the show must go on."

Suddenly the room was completely still. A man in the back of the hall leapt to his feet and pointed an accusing finger at the singer's chest. The man's voice rang clear into the icy silence: "You'll sing it till you get it *right!*" he demanded.

Dad would wait for the laughter to subside, and then look affectionately at my mother. "I'm like the opera singer," he would say softly. "I had to keep trying till I got it right. And I finally did!"

I miss his stories, and I miss the laughter.

I hope you, dear reader, have enjoyed this collection of stories, into which he poured his love and laughter and skill.

The Battles of Jericho

The Battles of Jericho by Hugh Pentecost, with an introduction by S.T. Karnick and an afterword by Daniel Philips, is set in Times New Roman (the text) and Century Schoolbook (the chapter titles and running titles) by Mudra Typesetters. It is printed on 60 pound Natural, recycled, acid-free paper. The cover illustration is by Gail Cross, and the Lost Classics series design is by Deborah Miller. *The Battles of Jericho* was printed and bound by Thomson-Shore, Dexter, Michigan, and published in August 2008 by Crippen & Landru Publishers, Norfolk, Virginia.

CRIPPEN & LANDRU, PUBLISHERS

P. O. Box 9315, Norfolk, VA 23505
E-mail: info@crippenlandru.com; toll-free 877 622-6656
Web: www.crippenlandru.com

LOST CLASSICS

Crippen & Landru is proud to publish a series of *new* short-story collections by great authors of the past who specialized in traditional mysteries. Each book collects stories from crumbling pages of old pulp, digest, and slick magazines, and most of the stories have been "lost" since their first publication. The following books are in print:

Peter Godfrey, *The Newtonian Egg and Other Cases of Rolf le Roux*, introduction by Ronald Godfrey. 2002.

Craig Rice, *Murder, Mystery and Malone*, edited by Jeffrey A. Marks. 2002.

Charles B. Child, *The Sleuth of Baghdad: The Inspector Chafik Stories*. 2002.

Stuart Palmer, *Hildegarde Withers: Uncollected Riddles*, introduction by Mrs. Stuart Palmer. 2002.

Christianna Brand, *The Spotted Cat and Other Mysteries from Inspector Cockrill's Casebook*, edited by Tony Medawar. 2002.

William Campbell Gault, *Marksman and Other Stories*, edited by Bill Pronzini; afterword by Shelley Gault. 2003.

Gerald Kersh, *Karmesin: The World's Greatest Criminal — Or Most Outrageous Liar*, edited by Paul Duncan. 2003.

C. Daly King, *The Complete Curious Mr. Tarrant*, introduction by Edward D. Hoch. 2003.

Helen McCloy, *The Pleasant Assassin and Other Cases of Dr. Basil Willing*, introduction by B.A. Pike. 2003.

William L. DeAndrea, *Murder – All Kinds*, introduction by Jane Haddam. 2003.

Anthony Berkeley, *The Avenging Chance and Other Mysteries from Roger Sheringham's Casebook*, edited by Tony Medawar and Arthur Robinson. 2004.

Joseph Commings, *Banner Deadlines: The Impossible Files of Senator Brooks U. Banner*, edited by Robert Adey; memoir by Edward D. Hoch. 2004.

Erle Stanley Gardner, *The Danger Zone and Other Stories*, edited by Bill Pronzini. 2004.

T.S. Stribling, *Dr. Poggioli: Criminologist*, edited by Arthur Vidro. 2004.

Margaret Miller, *The Couple Next Door: Collected Short Mysteries*, edited by Tom Nolan. 2004.

Gladys Mitchell, *Sleuth's Alchemy: Cases of Mrs. Bradley and Others*, edited by Nicholas Fuller. 2005.

Philip S. Warne/Howard W. Macy, *Who Was Guilty? Two Dime Novels*, edited by Marlena E. Bremseth. 2005.

Dennis Lynds writing as Michael Collins, *Slot-Machine Kelly: The Collected Private Eye Cases of the One-Armed Bandit*, introduction by Robert J. Randisi. 2005.

Julian Symons, *The Detections of Francis Quarles*, edited by John Cooper; afterword by Kathleen Symons. 2006.

Rafael Sabatini, *The Evidence of the Sword and Other Mysteries*, edited by Jesse F. Knight. 2006.

Erle Stanley Gardner, *The Casebook of Sidney Zoom*, edited by Bill Pronzini. 2006.

Ellis Peters (Edith Pargeter), *The Trinity Cat and Other Mysteries*, edited by Martin Edwards and Sue Feder. 2006.

Lloyd Biggle, Jr., *The Grandfather Rastin Mysteries*, edited by Kenneth Lloyd Biggle and Donna Biggle Emerson. 2007.

Max Brand, *Masquerade: Ten Crime Stories*, edited by William F. Nolan. 2007.

Mignon G. Eberhart, *Dead Yesterday and Other Mysteries*, edited by Rick Cypert and Kirby McCauley. 2007.

Hugh Pentecost, *The Battles of Jericho*, introduction by S.T. Karnick; afterword by Daniel Phillips. 2008.

FORTHCOMING LOST CLASSICS

Victor Canning, *The Minerva Club, The Department of Patterns and Other Stories*, edited by John Higgins.

Anthony Boucher and Denis Green, *The Casebook of Gregory Hood*, edited by Joe R. Christopher.

Elizabeth Ferrars, *The Casebook of Jonas P. Jonas and Others*, edited by John Cooper.

Philip Wylie, *Ten Thousand Blunt Instruments*, edited by Bill Pronzini.

Erle Stanley Gardner, *The Exploits of the Patent Leather Kid*, edited by Bill Pronzini.

Vincent Cornier, *Duel of Shadows*, edited by Mike Ashley.

Phyllis Bentley, *Author in Search of a Character: The Detections of Miss Phipps*, edited by Marvin Lachman.

Vera Caspary, *Murder at the Stork Club and Other Stories* by, edited by Barbara Emrys.

Balduin Groller, *Detective Dagobert: Master Sleuth of Old Vienna*, translated by Thomas Riediker.

SUBSCRIPTIONS

Crippen & Landru offers discounts to individuals and institutions who place Standing Order Subscriptions for its forthcoming publications, either all the Regular Series or all the Lost Classics or (preferably) both. Collectors can thereby guarantee receiving limited editions, and readers won't miss any favorite stories. Standing Order Subscribers receive a specially commissioned story in a deluxe edition as a gift at the end of the year. Please write or e-mail for more details.

Lost Classics